PENGUIN BOOKS

Nicole Alexander has a Master of Letters in creative writing and her novels, poetry, travel and creative writing, and genealogy articles have been published in Australia, New Zealand, Canada, Ukraine, Germany, the United States and Singapore.

She is the author of ten other historical novels. Nicole lives in north-west New South Wales.

Also by Nicole Alexander

The Bark Cutters
A Changing Land
Absolution Creek
Sunset Ridge
The Great Plains
Wild Lands
River Run
An Uncommon Woman
Stone Country
The Cedar Tree

Divertissements: Love, War, Society – Selected Poems

NICOLE ALEXANDER

The Last Station

PENGUIN BOOKS

PENGUIN BOOKS

UK | USA | Canada | Ireland | Australia
India | New Zealand | South Africa | China

Penguin Books is part of the Penguin Random House group of companies
whose addresses can be found at global.penguinrandomhouse.com

First published by Bantam in 2022
This edition published by Penguin Books in 2023

Cover images by Ian Crocker/Shutterstock
Cover design by Louisa Maggio © Penguin Random House Australia Pty Ltd
Typeset in Fairfield by Midland Typesetters, Australia
Printed and bound in Australia by Griffin Press, an accredited
ISO AS/NZS 14001 Environmental Management Systems printer

 A catalogue record for this
book is available from the
National Library of Australia

ISBN 978 1 76089 823 6

penguin.com.au

The author acknowledges the Aboriginal and Torres Strait Islander people as the traditional owners of the land on which this story takes place. She pays her respects to all Elders, past and present.

⊰ Prologue ⊱

1889

Benjamin Dalhunty twitched the curtain in the study. Outside on the veranda, the wool broker from Goldsbrough Mort & Co. awaited an audience, his filthy hands making a sorry mess of the hat he held. He was stocky. Spade-headed. The type of rugged fellow Ben's father admired. The sort of man Ben knew he could never be, though he suspected his father still believed in the possibility of miraculous transformation. As if it were conceivable for Ben at some future point to become the man expected of him and suddenly find the wherewithal to manage hundreds of thousands of acres.

Beyond the white paling fence of the homestead fifteen stockmen rode past, followed by the overseer. The Goldsbrough wool broker turned to watch as one flat-topped wool wagon and then another and another trundled by, the towering bales momentarily blocking the agapanthus sky. This was fortuitous timing, for it allowed the broker to understand the enormity of the business he hoped to vie for. And yet even as Ben stared at the man's broad back, a vision arose of sandstone buildings. There he was. Benjamin Dalhunty. Striding along a city street toward his office. Black umbrella

1

swinging jauntily. Ink-stained fingers eagerly awaiting blank paper. His copperplate was second to none.

The slide and thud of a drawer drew Ben reluctantly back into the present: the cedar-lined study with its thick Aubusson rug. His father, Alfred, remained ensconced behind the mahogany desk, squaring up different denominations of pound notes, the growing stacks perfectly aligned. Once satisfied with his counting he marked down the amount in a green ledger and packed the money into a metal box, keeping a portion of it aside. That afternoon, before he left on the paddle-steamer for Bourke, from where the Sydney-bound train was due to depart the next day, Alfred would slip out to the grove of palm trees located a half-mile from the rear of the homestead and bury the cash for safekeeping. The palms had been a passion of Ben's late mother, who had spent time in Ceylon, and it was beneath them that Alfred stashed his hoard. This miserly attribute amused Ben. It was hard to leave behind humble beginnings forged on the outskirts of London.

Alfred Dalhunty was wary of banks, his main complaint being the expectation that money borrowed should be repaid, and invariably sooner than was convenient. These infernal institutions, he declared, never made anyone's fortune, which was why he'd mastered the art of prevarication. Drip-feeding the Commercial Banking Company of Sydney and the London Chartered Bank of Australia kept them marginally content – and besides, neither bank wished to lose any Dalhunty business.

Alfred locked the box and patted the lid affectionately before pocketing the remaining notes and sitting the container on the floor. He straightened curved shoulders and swivelled his office chair, displaying the profile that drew comparisons with Napoleon, along with the sweep of hair that fell across his brow. Ben waited for the usual speech about the importance of the station running smoothly in his father's absence. The unstated message was clear. Ben was to heed the station's manager, Mr Todd, in all things. Mr Todd was, after all, the finest manager west of the divide.

And didn't the man know it. Riding about with his superior air.

It was not unusual for Mr Todd to ignore Ben, as if he were merely another worker, and a barely useful one at that.

'And keep that young wife of yours out of mischief. It's one thing for her to have visitors, but I'm not partial to her gallivanting about the countryside and leaving my grandson alone in the care of the Aboriginal domestics. People come to us. It's what's expected. Rachael isn't in the city anymore. We have a hierarchy out here for good reason.' Alfred squinted at Ben's necktie. 'Purple? Dalhuntys don't wear purple.'

Ben considered the colour rather chirpy. It lifted the drab cloth of the suits he wore and Rachael agreed it complemented his tanned skin. 'I thought—'

'Well, don't think, son. It doesn't suit you. We have a valet for that,' decreed his father.

At last count, the homestead staff consisted of four house-maids, a cook and her assistant, the valet, two washerwomen, a boy to chop wood and Mrs Wilson, head of the household and all matters domestic, who also doubled as a lady's maid for Ben's wife. A man was likely to trip over one of the many people running about the place, and that was before he took a step beyond the gate, where the business of making money supplanted everything else.

To keep the cogs of pastoralism oiled, it was necessary to employ a village of eighty, comprised of stockmen, blacksmiths, farm-workers, carpenters, contractors and general labourers. There were so many people Ben was at a loss as to why his father felt it neces-sary to spend three months in Sydney every year when station life could be just as noisy as the city. At times, with numerous men riding about the place and steamboat whistles continually screech-ing when the river ran, it was all Ben could do not to retreat to his bedroom and place a pillow over his head.

Ben was reluctant to interrupt his father, who was now collat-ing papers for planned business meetings in Sydney, but quietly he reminded him that the wool broker was still outside, here to tout for their business, and the heat was punishing.

3

Alfred clacked his dentures in irritation. He was fond of the teeth left him by his father. 'Waterloo teeth' he called them, a grisly reminder of their battlefield provenance, although to Ben the inclusion of hippopotamus ivory was far more reminiscent of fashionable Piccadilly than the Waterloo killing field. Alfred liked to believe that the scavenged teeth belonged to one of Wellington's ex-Hanoverian sabre-wielding soldiers. The essence of a dead warrior was deemed an advantage when their pastoral existence was hard-won. There was a certain combative element to their lives.

Mrs Wilson entered, following a single knock on the door. She greeted her long-time employer with a curt hello and with the briefest acknowledgement to Ben, sat a silver tea tray on the desk. She straightened her five-foot-five frame, deftly avoiding the low-hanging candelabrum and poured a single cup. Once the task was completed she ensured the solid silver teapot, sugar bowl and creamer were perfectly positioned to display the $\mathscr{D}$ insignia etched on each piece.

Alfred proceeded to give the housekeeper final instructions. The Aboriginal women and girls working in the house were to be treated firmly but not harshly. Managing them appropriately was a civic duty if they were to assimilate into society and the use of any language other than English was not to be tolerated. The head gardener was to pay careful attention to the watering of the orchard (marmalade and homemade cordial being particular favourites of Alfred's). And the bird netting protecting the orange koi in the pond, purchased at great cost from Victoria, was to be checked thrice daily. Mrs Wilson was dismissed and, with three neat steps backwards as if departing royalty, she eventually left the room.

Were it not for Mrs Wilson, Ben would have dispensed with the household domestics entirely during his father's absence and spent languorous hours with his wife and baby son dozing on a blanket next to the manmade pond. Being 'left in charge', as Alfred termed it, meant little. His power was restricted to riding about the run and tipping his hat in greeting to Mr Todd. Not that Ben had the slightest idea what he might order the staff to do, even if they were willing to listen to him. Frankly, he preferred watching his wife embroider grub roses on Julian's baby socks than pretend interest in the differing qualities of clean and greasy wool. But pretend he must.

The Dalhuntys' land spread south-west, near the confluence of the Culgoa and Barwon Rivers, where the mighty Darling began, and it was a day's ride to their closest neighbour and the fence that separated their sheep. Between here and there a man could cross river flats dense with black soil, meander through redgums and cross rusted ridges, doing his best to spot nobs of merinos among clusters of saltbush. In a good season the land was plump and fertile, the trees full leafed, the grasses greener than green and the animals bulging. In a bad one, settlers bowed their heads and tried hard not to stare. At times, the savagery of the place could make a man weep. It still astounded Ben how his father loved it so.

Outside, the wool broker was speaking to their manager. Mr Todd, bespectacled and heavily bearded, gave his usual animated response, a single scratch of the forehead. Of more interest to Ben was the stranger who had joined them. The third man was tall and spare with a peaked cap. Undoubtedly Captain Augustus Ashby. The riverboat captain had, during a chance meeting in Bourke eighteen months prior, managed to convince Alfred to assign him the highly coveted transportation of Dalhunty Station's wool clip after the previous riverboat tasked with the contract had hit a snag in the river and sunk, resulting in a shambolic attempt to save the beer on board, and taking a crewman to his muddy end. Ashby's unapologetic approach had been novel, brash and timely, and had impressed Alfred. That feat alone was worthy of admiration and Ben could not begrudge the justified pride that radiated from the man who was soon to float nearly two thousand bales of Dalhunty wool to South Australia.

Ashby was granted immediate entry to the study. Alfred put aside the tea just served. Stout glasses of brandy were offered all round and Ben was introduced to the Captain, who reciprocated with a firm handshake and a jovial manner. He cut a fine figure in a tailored coat, polished boots and close-clipped beard and yet still retained the aura of a can-do individual. Capable and presentable. Already the robust wool broker, still suffering ignominy outdoors in the heat, had fallen a notch in Ben's estimation.

'A pleasure to meet you, Benjamin. I look forward to a long association.' Captain Ashby didn't stand on ceremony. He drained the brandy and sat the glass on the desk. 'I see Goldsbrough Mort are here to offer their services.'

'It would be churlish to decline a meeting. They are taking on more clients now the railway is opening up the west. The direct route from Bourke to Sydney is proving popular,' replied Alfred.

Ben stayed by the window and sipped at the brandy as his father and the captain took up seats opposite each other. The captain was yet to fully gain the measure of Alfred. If that were possible. A wariness overtook his sociable charms.

'So you're in agreement with this trade minimisation strategy the government has in play, using railways to stop the transport of wool to South Australia?'

Alfred peered about the study as if formulating the correct tone in which to convey unwelcome news. This was one of a series of tactical traits that included sitting a guest on the veranda facing the brutal afternoon sun. Railways were foremost in Alfred's mind. He was nothing if not progressive, as long as advancements were in his best interests. The politicians would rather build roads and railways than locks, especially if it meant the profitable wool trade was delivered to Sydney rather than down the Murray-Darling to the southern states. The fact Ashby was unwilling to grasp the significance of the railway's importance boded ill for the man's business, but that was not Alfred's concern.

Subsidised rail freight was being offered to entice growers away from the waterway, however Alfred was holding out for a better deal and championing a new mode of transport when the current most economical method sat across the desk was not conducive to business. Alfred enjoyed a moment more of power posturing, however if Captain Ashby experienced any discomfort it was short-lived.

'They've been barking about trade minimisation since '77, Ashby. Until I have a complaint, Dalhunty Station will be shipping its wool to the railhead at Murray Bridge. I'd not fix what is yet to prove troublesome.'

Immediately, the budding tension vanished. More brandy was offered and the cargo manifest for goods currently en route to the storehouse was checked by his father. Alfred ran a manicured finger down the extensive list. Tobacco, flour and sugar was awaited by the Aboriginals as eagerly as the Dalhuntys and their labourers anticipated their stores. Next came the confirmation of insurance, the bill of lading not being completed until the wool was stacked on Ashby's barges, his flotilla of vessels numbering three. Money was not mentioned, the shipping rate having already been haggled over at Bourke's Central Australian Hotel. Their South Australian broker would sell the wool on their behalf less commission and expenses, ensure Ashby was paid for his services and then arrange the timely deposit of wool proceeds into the Dalhunty bank account. A perfectly succinct arrangement.

'The waters will hold?' Alfred folded the manifest, which would eventually be delivered to the overseer and then the storekeeper.

Captain Ashby toyed with the rim of his now empty glass. The slightest movement of his head suggested a third brandy would not be refused if offered. 'It's a fair flow. I've heard word there's near eighty steamers running between here and Wentworth as we speak. The customs officials on the border have their work cut out. They're reckoning on twelve thousand bales of wool being shipped from the Darling River woolsheds this year.'

Alfred sat back in his chair. There was nothing he liked better than having the value of the wool industry underlined. There was a great importance to their business, one that literally guaranteed the Australian economy's seamless transition into the next century with the wealth wool produced.

'There will be opportunity to continue our discussion en route to Bourke. Idling down our great water highway with my wool holds great appeal, however it is the Sydney train for me. Tiresome journey though it is.' Alfred rose, ending the meeting.

With business concluded and the captain departed, his father refused to waste further time. It was Alfred's prerogative to be magnanimous one moment and then renege on an arrangement the next, and on this occasion it fell to Ben to placate the wool broker who'd spent the better part of two hours languishing on the veranda.

In the hallway lined with portraits of Dalhuntys now risen to prominence through slightly revised life stories and the benefit of a commissioned painter adept at creating likenesses based on Alfred's memory, Ben was met by his wife.

Rachael Dalhunty was twisting the double rope of pearls at her neck and humming absently, the mushroom pink of her gown grey in the half-light. She was waiting for the cargo to be delivered and never failed to be delighted when a new selection of muslins and silks arrived. Ben dare not ruin her happiness by mentioning the arduous journey the Bourke dressmaker would be undertaking by dray in a fortnight. Instead he admired the glint of auburn in her braided and curled hair and the whittled waist encased in whalebone. He so enjoyed plucking away at those laces at night.

'Frank was looking for you,' she said.

'He's always looking for someone.' Frank the Englishman, no one knew his last name, had arrived from the west nine years prior with a camel in tow and a sorry story of deprivation endured in the desert country. Alfred had been keen to throw the man off their land, however Ben was rather taken with the thought of having their own camel on the property, and a one-year stay of execution was granted. In hindsight, persuading Alfred to let Frank remain for a little longer proved to be one of Ben's sillier requests. Frank had taken to calling him 'Honoured Brother', an audacity, was rude to every man on the property and was generally a nuisance.

His constant presence grated at Ben, while Alfred grew to admire Frank's careful tending of the palm grove. The mad Englishman, Ben knew, was best ignored.

Rachael backed into the drawing room and beckoned. Ben was tempted to follow, and she pouted at his hesitation. He pointed to the front door and his shoulders sagged. She laughed. In a couple of hours his father would be gone.

Outside, the wool broker was crossing the scythed grass and opening the freshly painted front gate. He turned on seeing Ben, his Scottish accent thick and curt.

'Captain Ashby was more than pleased to explain to me that your South Australian broker had Dalhunty Station's business. Sewn up tight were the exact words he used.'

He closed the gate, effectively barring Ben. The man was annoyed, and rightly so. It was rude of his father to ignore a meeting that had been agreed to, but this was not the first time superiority outranked politeness.

'I'm terribly sorry for the wait, Mr . . .?'

The wool broker was clearly keen to depart. 'Fraser. Glen Fraser. And who are you? Another lackey? I've met a manager and an overseer and sundry other men of different rank. You assume I'll be impressed, no doubt, but frankly I did not expect such treatment.'

Ben instantly liked Fraser. He was all too aware of his father's rudeness, but never had he been so forcefully reminded of it. Most people didn't dare risk Alfred's ire, for fear a daughter's well-planned engagement failed, a son's managerial position on a far-flung property was withdrawn, or a business transaction cancelled.

'I'm, I'm sorry, Mr Fraser. I'm Benjamin Dalhunty.'

Fraser was drawn to the purple necktie. Reluctantly he took Ben's offered hand, although the gate remained between them.

'I say, do come inside and have some lemon cordial. Are you a breeder of chickens? Father has some very fine Double-combed Hamburgs. We've been raising them for some years now and they really are superior layers.' Ben opened the gate. Mr Fraser gave the impression that he was somewhat confused, although Ben wasn't sure if it was due to the offer of a refreshing drink or the opportunity to view their prized Hamburgs.

'Ben! Ben! Julian is crawling.' Rachael was on the veranda, excitement streaming from her. 'Oh, I'm sorry to interrupt.'

'My first child. A boy. Julian.' Ben leant confidentially towards Mr Fraser as Rachael dallied briefly before heading indoors. 'Father is awfully pleased, but what if the lad doesn't like sheep?' The thought tickled Ben no end and he burst out laughing. When he stopped he noticed Mr Fraser wore a similar expression to that of his dearly departed mother, as if he were trying to ascertain whether Ben were quite all there, up top.

'Yes. Well, I too have a son. Ian.' Mr Fraser made no effort to walk through the gate.

'To our boys then,' said Ben, privately pleased the Hamburgs were not to be disturbed. They didn't always take to strangers.

'Yes,' agreed Mr Fraser, a glint of amusement softening a hard-edged face. 'To our sons.'

⫷ Part 1 ⫸

The Station

⋘ Chapter I ⋙

Mid-January, 1909

Julian Dalhunty grew up in a place his father called God's country. As a young boy it was impossible for him to gauge how much land God owned, but somehow his family had won a chunk from the fringes of it. When Julian asked his father where the Lord's best paddocks were, he would wave vaguely to the east, so Julian knew God was pretty darn smart. Eastwards, unseen mountains straddled the plains, wreathed by bloated clouds that gave up their filling regularly. If the Dalhuntys were lucky, sometimes their pasture would get a taste of that providence, once God's run was saturated and those westward-flowing rivers converged and streamed towards them. But God sure did seem to need a lot of water, while their land grew dryer every year.

Julian was born the eldest of four children to Benjamin and Rachael Dalhunty in 1888, two years before the big flood came down the Darling River. Day by day, the waters had crept across the vast flats and plains, filling cracks, gilgais and dry creek beds, until the land was soggy and could hold no more. Although Ben manhandled gunny sacks filled with sand in an effort to lessen the torrent, his parents had spent a week on the homestead

13

roof during the worst of the deluge, cradling him until their arms cramped. They lived on raw sheep meat and a pot of cold tea, surrounded by their waterlogged belongings, staring at the partially submerged station buildings. Grandfather Alfred was in Sydney enjoying his yearly jaunt and most of their workers were either miles away mustering or had headed to Bourke on his father's suggestion to help construct a levee around the town. To fill in the time, his parents read the Bible, tried to catch fish and prayed that some of their sheep had survived.

In the end, they were saved from starvation by a riverboat, which had left the channel and struck out towards them. A dense patch of scrub ripped the wheel casings from the steamer and the trapped branches churned the brown water, spraying it outwards in twin arcs. Julian's father told him later he was sure Noah himself was coming to their rescue that day. So it was with a fleeting degree of disappointment and then unbridled gratefulness that Ben had recognised Captain Augustus Ashby as he steamed towards them. Julian, being only two at the time, recalled nothing of this, however he was left with the legacy of that great inundation. The sheep that had sustained their family for generations had melted into the earth.

Who the Dalhuntys were, where they had been and, crucially, the direction in which they were heading, were weighing on Julian this particular morning. If one family was to be given a pile of average-to-ruination luck, it was them. Any sane person would leave, strike out on their own. This was Australia after all. There were tin, gold and opal mines, and sheep properties aplenty, more opportunity than a man could imagine.

And yet he was still here, like the three generations of Dalhuntys before him. Digging in like a soldier. Ready to defend, no matter the cost. And the enemies were plentiful. Drought. Flood. Fire. Although his father reckoned a person couldn't blame the land. Hell, Julian supposed he was right. The soil held on to any drop of moisture thrown its way, gobbling it down like a scrub turkey come in from the caked silt of the plains. Now it was mid-summer, a season that lasted longer than man or beast cared for, and the rain was still sitting out east, too far away to see or smell.

Dawn announced itself with the sound of the wind swishing through palm fronds, lagging footsteps in the hallway and the sight of Bony ambling past Julian's window. The dog had arrived one winter, unasked for and unwanted. A bullet was the most likely reward for stray dogs on sheep land, and, were it not for one of Julian's younger sisters, Meg, Bony would have ended in the dead ditch next to the rubbish tip. He was a complaining mutt, likely to piddle on a person if they stayed put in one spot for too long. That detail only helped to further endear the animal to Meg and at her insistence their father allowed Bony to stay. He saw the benefit of a dog that left its calling card were a person idle. Ben Dalhunty was not one to fritter away time, and he expected the same of others. An extraordinary characteristic, considering his ability to immerse himself in a task and then spend an inordinate length of time accomplishing it.

Through the window Julian observed Bony as he lifted a leg on the copper, whining with pleasure. A stream of pee ran down the side of the pot. The dog scratched at the ground, sniffed a bit and then, crouching low, raced from sight. Julian counted to three then, sure enough, the familiar sounds of chickens screeching were followed by Meg screaming abuse. His father bellowed – insofar as he was capable of bellowing – for peace to return.

Sighing, Julian located the hole in his mattress, pulling free a yellowing train schedule cut from the newspaper. *Bourke to Sydney*. He ran a finger across the print. He only needed the fare.

He had never thought of his decision to leave in terms of running away. It was far easier to reframe it as a yearning for a different life – a fair wish for a boy anchored to the sameness of the land. The desire to quit the bush had not come without consternation. He knew what his family expected of him as the only son. Except that Julian didn't want it. Not the debt nor the struggle nor the endless round of pretending their lives would improve. There was every possibility they would end up impoverished, and he wasn't staying around for that. By chance, it was an article written in an old copy of the *Sydney Morning Herald* that stirred his interest. Listed on the same page as the regular shipping news, which occasionally noted the departures, destinations and wool cargo of the largest paddle-steamers plying the Murray-Darling, was an editorial about the SS *Osterley*. She was to be launched in London and with luck was expected to arrive in Sydney in September of this year on her maiden voyage. Maiden voyage. It had a ring to it. A voyage that would take a person along the Suez Canal through Egypt. Julian imagined running across the scrubbed decks as they passed Africa on one side and Asia on the other. It was as far removed from this life as he could possibly get. And so, for want of another idea, the sea beckoned.

A flash of red bobbed towards the window. Julian quickly slid the timetable under the pillow and covered his nakedness with a shirt as Meg scrambled through the opening, falling on top of him. A mess of dirt, crumpled dress and curly carrot hair righted itself.

'Goddamn dog. It's the same every morning. Why aren't youse dressed, Julian? Morning's half gone.'

'Jeez, Meg, can't a man get up when he's good and ready?' Julian pulled his feet out from under his sister. Her invasion of his privacy was becoming downright bothersome. There were parts of a man's body that weren't controllable in the morning and even if the flag was only at half-mast he didn't need Meg catching sight of it. He kicked out at her and she scrambled to the end of the bed. 'And where did you hear that word? Don't be saying goddamn in front of Mother or Father.'

'Goddamn preacher says goddamn. Frank said so. "Praise the Lord, goddamn," he says, sitting on the steps out the back of the hall. Then he crosses himself and belches on account of the rum he drinks to wash away Lucifer.' Meg gave him an innocent look. 'I'm just saying what Frank says. Anyways, youse still not sleeping with yer pants on. I'm telling youse, Julian, one of these days something's gonna happen and youse'll be striding out in your glory afore youse remember youse're starkers.'

Meg rolled out of his reach, snatching up a dropped slingshot.

'And one of these days Mother is going to find out you go wandering over to Frank's place when you're meant to be doing lessons and she'll tan your hide for it. Now turn around.'

Julian waited until she obeyed then pulled on his moleskin trousers.

'Don't see why I can't spend time with Frank.' Meg spoke to the bedroom door, drawing a shape on the timber, her backside wiggling left and right. 'Everybody else has gone and left us. Frank's cooking pickled vegetables and rice today. Wese could sneak over to his place later.'

Being reminded of the wizened Englishman's cooking was an unwelcome detail. Julian had spent more time with his pants down than up after the last meal he'd shared with Frank. The food tasted good, but the after-effects – of feeling your innards being drained from your body – were compounded by Bony, who followed him about ready to lick up any offerings.

'The fox came back,' Meg said. 'I can smell him something fierce. I reckon I could find his hidey place. I've got the sense of a tracker.'

'All right, all right. You can turn around now. Don't forget Mother expects you to talk properly and act properly. And if you miss another reading and writing lesson with me, I'll be the one to get the blame. Talking to Frank and hunting with a mongrel dog doesn't fit in with Mother's idea of educating a thirteen-year-old. You better get cleaned up.'

'Fine.' Meg stuffed the slingshot in the pocket of her dress. 'I'll be *proper.*' She drew the word out as if she were a haughty society matron and bobbed a flounce of a curtsy. 'I'm always proper at breakfast.'

Julian knew from experience that was a straight-out lie.

∝≪ Chapter 2 ≫∝

Every morning their father would finish his breakfast and hold his stomach as he eyed each of his children around the kitchen table, his gratefulness for food and family causing all to return his smile. Today was no different. Ben Dalhunty cleared his throat, causing his wife Rachael to glance up from her needlework and meet her husband's gaze. Ben winked at his wife and she gave him a special look that spoke of secret things. Julian dreaded this intimate reaction for it meant his father was about to hold forth on the story of how he met his wife. It was a convoluted account that began with their traipsing about the Sydney streets in the company of Rachael's mother and ended with a proposal of marriage and a sweaty kiss in a drawing room. Much to the delight of Laura, who at fifteen should have known better, Ben always added some fancy to round out the tale. Laura waited, fist under chin in dreamy silence, while Meg began kicking the table leg, wordlessly imploring Julian to save them.

Julian did what any twenty-one-year-old man would do in the circumstances, even if it meant breakage of their very best breakfast set: he knocked the porcelain bread and butter plate, which clattered against cup and saucer. His mother scolded him for his clumsiness, then Laura chastised him as she cleaned the spill, scrunching the folds of her dress between her legs as she knelt on the knobbly boards. Meg placed her elbows on the table and grinned. Julian found his mother watching him.

Their father nodded at his wife's sewing. 'Are you finished?'

'Not quite.' She held up the stencilled outline of a calico geranium filled with rows of stitched fish scales. Her painstaking efforts would complete a vase of flowers artfully attached to wire stamens.

'Well, that's mighty fine, Rachael,' said their father proudly.

Meg edged a toe across the floor, which was partially covered by baskets of fish-scale ornamental flowers. 'Fish scales. Wese're surrounded by fish scales.' Her attention drifted to the $\mathcal{D}$ engraved breakfast set and she played chess with the empty silver sugar bowl, creamer and hot-water pot, receiving a wrist slap from her mother.

'But we don't use 'em anymore,' she complained.

'One day in the future we might, and what will happen then when you two girls don't know how to set a table, or your brother hesitates over the correct cutlery?' said her mother.

'I like stuffed birds.' Meg sat back in her chair. 'Wese could have stuffed that last parrot if that mongrel dog hadn't chewed it. Maybe you could stuff another bird, Mother, and I could help with the taxidermy. Wese could buy one of them glass domes and put a stuffed parrot inside. Then when anyone came to visit, they'd *ooh* and *ahh* and think us fancy.'

'But no one ever comes.' Laura carefully wrapped an embroidery in calico.

'Oh, they used to,' said their father. Ben launched into his favourite diversion: the past. Soon they were being entertained with stories of visitors who came on horseback and in their carriages. Of the grand dinners held by candlelight and the flitch of bacon and the fresh milk available when Josephine the cow was alive, for those guests who stayed on until dawn.

Julian could barely recall any of it. Not the visiting politicians nor the jewel-bedecked women, nor the avenue of orange and lemon trees, now reduced to a single, gnarled specimen, nor even the afternoons spent by the pond feeding the fish while his parents drank lemon cordial. The fish were long gone – the original inhabitants washed away by the Great Flood and their replacements snatched by hawks when the protective netting rotted.

Their mother brought the floppy geranium closer to the kerosene lamp and, pressing down on an obstinate scale, stabbed at it with a needle.

'You should be sewing, Meg.' Laura delved into one of the baskets and extracted an oblong piece of material ornamented with orange-and-red flowers and green-and-yellow birds. 'At your age I was already well past samplers.'

Julian knew nothing about women's pastimes. The closest he got to understanding them was when he tripped over a basket in the house. Or when carelessness led him to the water tank, where he spent a great deal of time brushing out manure or mud or whatever else he'd deposited on the needlework. But there was no doubting Laura's sewing was top rate, soon to equal their mother's, and everyone in the family was hopeful money would also flow from her talent.

'Meg, your sister is right. Laura, I want you to start teaching Meg the basics of good needlework again,' replied their mother.

'Really?' complained Laura.

'Really?' Meg implored their father, who was instantly attracted to trailing ants on the floor.

Julian felt sorry for the older of his sisters. There had been an incident of pin-sticking last year after Laura had told Meg that she had the domestic aptitude of a goldfish.

Laura gathered her long blonde hair and twisted it over one shoulder and then the other, playing with the ends. 'Meg should read Mrs Wicken's *Australian Home*. Then she might realise the importance of behaving like a lady instead of catching tadpoles and keeping lizards.'

'And maybe youse could stop brushing youse hair a hundred times every day and practise riding, so youse were better at that, then youse wouldn't fall off so much,' countered Meg with satisfaction as the remark hit home. 'Riding side-saddle is for sissies,' she added for good measure.

'You're plain nappy-headed!' shouted Laura.

'And youse is an ijit!' shrieked Meg, the colour of her skin flaring to match her hair.

'The word is *you*, my dear. Not *youse*,' their mother reprimanded. 'There is no such word as youse. Where do you get this pronunciation from? Julian, are you working on elocution with Meg?'

Meg managed a sneaky glance in Julian's direction.

'Sort of,' said Julian. The word Meg had taken to recently was 'shit', which she could pronounce perfectly. 'Turd-chewer' and 'hay-eater' were also favourites, having been allocated respectively to the bitser Bony and horses in general. But 'shit', which his sister was capable of stringing out for a long four seconds, was on Frank's lips as well. It was going to be hard to eradicate, especially since competition had edged into its use. Meg and the old Englishman spent long afternoons repeating the word to each other while sitting cross-legged in the roofless overseer's house (the iron roof had landed in the Darling a decade ago thanks to a whirly-wind, and was most likely sunk at sea by now). Julian figured his kid sister and Frank weren't doing that much harm. The problem was once Meg got a fixation it was hard to shift.

'Listen to your mother, Meg,' said their father. 'Speaking the King's English correctly is the only thing that separates us from savages.'

'But there ain't any savages here. Only the Afghans, Aboriginals, Chinese and us. If you were going to call anyone a savage it would be us whites, the people that killed Ned Kelly. And they're meant to be the law. Frank says the law should go to buggery,' said Meg with conviction.

'Meg!' shouted their mother.

'I might finish my tea outside.' Ben poured the remains of his drink from the delicate cup into a pannikin as their mother scolded Meg. 'I'm *sure* Captain Ashby will grace us with his presence today. Still, what's another week when we've been waiting two years.'

'It's not like I said *s-h-i-t*,' Meg said with conviction.

Their mother grew white. She lay the geranium and needle on the table.

'Paddock language, Meg,' admonished their father.

'That's it? That is all you're going to say?' Rachael snapped.

'You should know better, Meg,' he added. 'You're a Dalhunty after all.'

Ben went to the glass jar on the shelf that sat between the toilet vinegar and Woods Great Peppermint Cure and tilted the bottle. Two pennies slid back and forth. He studied the contents as if thunderstruck and then returned the jar to its place.

'Julian,' he said above his squabbling womenfolk, then he walked along the open passageway joining the kitchen to the rest of the house. In the flood-warped hallway he stopped briefly at the locked doorway that led to the remainder of the homestead that was no longer used, took his hat from the bamboo hallstand, a battered bowler, and covered his grey woolly hair with it. He called to Julian again.

'Ben, you must speak to Frank this instant,' shouted his wife above the din. 'I'll not have that old man leading my youngest astray. And don't you take that walking cane to the river. It's an affectation.'

'Yes, dear.'

Julian entered the hallway just in time to see his father's hand hovering above the silver-topped cane near the front door. Ben left the homestead empty-handed, then moments later ducked back into the house and grabbed the cane.

⤜ Chapter 3 ⤛

Julian caught up with his father as Ben rested his cup of black tea on the gatepost and hitched his pants over reedy hips. The trousers were black, large in the waist and three inches short in the leg. Ben enjoyed the use of three trunks of various shirts, trousers, neckties and suit coats, a legacy of previous Dalhunty men, consummate hoarders all. Unlike the Dalhunty ladies' fine silk gowns, which were ruined by the Great Flood, the Dalhunty men's clothes had been stored in the poky attic and escaped the worst of the devastation. According to mood Ben could dress for work in a starch-collared white shirt, bowtie, tall hat and the elk horn walking cane, or don long black leather boots, flannel shirt and waistcoat. Toffee-coloured worsted wool trousers often accompanied his selection. Today the bowler hat and ankle-cooler trousers were in fashion. A chicken feather poked daintily from his suit-coat pocket.

'Your mother was the youngest of five, you know, son. Now there's only her and Aunt Nancy left. With five there are plenty of children to take the burden from the parents. Imagine the babble with five. If we had five children I would have carved a canoe from one of the trees and disappeared downstream long ago. Still, a man can stand a bit of noise.' His father squatted and scraped at the soil, squeezing it long and hard. He looked happily at Julian.

'Well,' he said, standing. 'I best have a yarn with Frank.' He stabbed at the ground with the cane and waited at the gate.

A born and bred Englishman, Frank had been at the station since Julian's grandfather's time. Legend had it that before he'd appeared out of nowhere in the 1880s, he'd been lost in the desert for many years. The ordeal had apparently started shortly after Frank joined Scottish explorer John McDouall Stuart's expedition team in 1861. Midway through traversing the continent, Stuart and Frank had argued. Frank held no trust in Stuart's sextants, compasses or binoculars. He had been convinced they were heading in the wrong direction. Stuart had called him ignorant, and Frank replied that the Scot was uppity. They parted ways, Stuart and his men veering right and Frank to the left. Frank believed in his innate ability to navigate by the stars. Alas, history showed him incapable of the task for, by his own account, he'd wandered the desert for nineteen years. When Julian pointed out that Frank was not mentioned in any of Stuart's exploration records, Frank insisted that only proved his version of events, as Stuart and he were far from bosom pals.

Despite Frank's clearly fabricated story, the one thing Julian was convinced of was that the man's brain was fried. Frank often skipped words when speaking or ran them all together and when he wasn't digging holes, searching in vain for Grandfather Alfred's moneybox, or inciting Meg to mischief, he was in the overseer's house with his camel, Henrietta, drinking a concoction made from distilled rice manufactured using empty kerosene tins. He swore the kerosene gave the drink an added zest.

Ben checked his pocket watch as pink tipped the horizon. 'Here he is. Right on time.'

The old man walked by in lace-less brown canvas tennis shoes, a sack coat and an ancient cabbage-tree hat minus the crown, Henrietta a few paces behind, saddled as if about to embark on a desert crossing.

'By jove this camel is a very fine camel,' Frank said, by way of greeting. 'This camel walked from Bourke to Maree in South Australia, never once faltering or letting me, Frank Dalhunty, perish of thirst. This very fine camel needs a proper home.' Henrietta stopped abruptly. 'Hooshta, hooshta,' ordered Frank, tugging on the reins. The camel spat in response and then started moving again.

'Frank, no more teaching Meg naughty words,' called Ben. 'No swear words, all right? Mrs Dalhunty won't stand for it, and neither will I. And you are *not* a Dalhunty.'

Frank and Henrietta embarked on their customary three-loop circuit of the homestead, which Frank maintained was for lumbago, a sometimes debilitating condition from which both he and the camel suffered.

'Well, hopefully the swearing problem's solved,' Ben declared optimistically. Overhead, light cloud skittered. 'I do believe it will remain dry today.' He spun towards their house and stared appreciatively at the mudbrick and cypress construction, white-washed with lime. The front wall was covered with more than one hundred tarnished stirrup irons glinting in the morning light. 'Beautiful. All those men. All those years. It's something. Really something.'

Julian stared at the crumbling mudbrick and the once shadowy veranda wings, which drooped forlornly on subsided veranda posts. Each year when the spring storms arrived he prayed the homestead would stay upright.

Frank returned from his first circuit sooner than expected. The camel, straggling behind, carried a bucket and coils of rope.

'This is a jolly good day.' Frank's grey tufted eyebrows lifted. He gestured animatedly in the direction of the palm grove and addressed Ben. 'Your father would call this a red-letter day. We will have a good harvest this year. If you are very nice, I shall share the spoils.'

'Share the spoils? They are *my* dates, Frank,' Ben argued. 'Besides which your past harvests have been less than bountiful.'

'My dear boy, it would be far more magnanimous for you to simply say thank you. Without me there would be no dates at all.'

Frank and the camel threw up puffs of silt as they resumed their circuit.

Ben angrily stuck the walking cane into the ground and glared after the Englishman.

Julian left his father and walked to the shed where the dray was parked. He hitched the horses and then untied the tarp protecting the bagged lettuce, onions and tomatoes. Then he dragged the canvas free and rested a palm on the lettuce. Heat rose through the hessian. If Captain Ashby didn't arrive today everything would have to be unpacked, and the lettuce and tomatoes cooled with water before they spoilt. Julian drove the dray back to the homestead and climbed down.

Ben was standing near the front gate talking to a magpie foraging about on the ground. On seeing Julian he nodded his approval and clapped him on the shoulder.

Despite stringent rationing they were running short of everything: flour, golden syrup, currants, tea, nails, rice and dates. They had used up all their credit with the storekeeper in Bourke. Deciding to wait on a riverboat, even one helmed by the estimable Captain Ashby, when their last remaining flat-topped wool wagon could easily transport their meagre clip to the railway at Bourke, was considered lunacy by Julian, and his mother and sisters agreed. However once the riverboat arrived, their goods – their wool, the women's craft and the hessian bags stuffed full with vegetables – would be collected and find a ready market, and the money jar would fill again.

The enormity of this being Dalhunty Station's last ever wool clip was softened somewhat by the length of time they'd waited to get their wool to market, but the heaviness of the milestone weighed on Julian. Two years ago, his father had made an extraordinary choice. He had sold nearly all their sheep, leaving them with a piddly number for rations and the gaping problem of how to make a living. Despite the many arguments Julian offered when this impulsive decision was announced, his father was convinced that a sheep station that didn't produce wool was undoubtedly a superlative idea.

A moment later, Rachael walked out onto the veranda, her auburn hair swept back from what Julian had heard his father call aristocratic features, although to Julian's knowledge there was not a fragment of upper-class in his mother's veins. She looked across the yard at her husband, and Julian sensed in that singular stare the bottomless grief that had usurped their matrimonial bonds.

Julian's little brother would have been nearing eight years of age by now, but he'd drowned in the well the previous year. At times he still imagined the boy playing on the veranda with his toy wagon – a piece of wood with cotton reels for wheels – an infectious grin spreading across his small round face. Julian wiped at his nose with a grimy shirt cuff, then stared at the ground. It held no consolation.

Julian's sisters came to their mother's side. Laura was swishing freshly braided hair, Meg immediately distracted by Bony, who was nosing a withered orange from the lone struggling tree across remnants of couch grass. The girls were wearing their best going-out clothes – dresses of lilac, cut down from one of their mother's. Laura, neat and shiny clean; Meg, dishevelled and peevish, as if she had recently lost a great battle. Twice a week they visited Davey. Julian and his father were relegated to Sunday afternoons, which Ben declared suited him fine, although Julian could not understand why they never went as a family.

The grave was barely a half mile from the house on a slight ridge. Julian's brother lay alone in a fenced off portion of land, beneath his favourite tree, which Rachael had declared was a far lovelier place than the original Dalhunty cemetery, which was filled with cantankerous old men, stubborn women, Grandfather Alfred's much-loved horse and the odd child who, like Davey, glimpsed something better and left to follow it.

With the morning's tasks established – Rachael was to drive the dray to the river after the women finished packing their handicrafts in it – without warning Ben left the garden gate and began striding in the direction of the two-acre vegetable plot. It was a five-minute walk away, located just west of the homestead near the now disused quarters that once housed the workers employed to chip weeds from rows of wheat. Julian hurried to keep up as Ben slid through the top wires of the rabbit-proof fence and, walking to where a stand of vine tomatoes grew, lay down on his stomach.

'Now, I'm aware you've got no company,' began Ben, squeezing the ripening fruit, 'but rest assured we'll be planting tomorrow. It's our first attempt at cucumbers, and while this isn't the prime growing season for them, they must adhere to the program. They are an ungainly creeping vine, but one the great Tiberius ate in Roman times. If it's good enough for kings and emperors . . .'

'Father—' said Julian.

'. . . I believe they are best consumed with a little salt and are quite stimulating to the body, being full of water,' his father prattled on. 'And, as we know, there are numerous times when a little water is a wondrous affair.'

'Father,' repeated Julian, trying his best not to become annoyed. Counting to ten sometimes helped when Ben was having one of his moments, such as the time they had found him asleep among sprouting potatoes. However Julian was discovering that with childhood behind him, he was less willing to indulge his father in these eccentricities. In the past, he'd tried not to apportion blame for the sorry state of the family business, however following Ben's decision to sell their sheep, Julian was faced with the awful reality that the Dalhuntys' lost fortune was not solely due to floods, rabbit plagues, depression, shearers' strikes and droughts – although Ben believed otherwise.

'*Father!*' he yelled.

Ben patted a bulbous tomato. 'Right then. Well, Julian, why are you dallying? Lead the way.'

They headed towards the river, Ben keeping a brisk pace, trousers flapping about skinny ankles, arms swinging, the bowler hat perched thoughtlessly to one side. 'Beautiful sight, isn't it?'

Julian looked about, trying to see what his father was refer-ring to. A rotary-disc plough and steam-driven chaff-cutter were rusting away in the middle of the flat. A wagon was missing the sturdy planks that had once carried wool bales. Every tree, root and stump in a half-mile radius had been grubbed up for firewood or building material.

'Sure is,' said Julian, defeated.

'Impossible not to love this place,' replied Ben.

⋘ Chapter 4 ⋙

Ben and Julian walked towards the river. Not far behind them trailed a brown gelding of immeasurable faults, one any other man may well have sold to a knackery. Ben whistled and stretched his arms wide, and in response Goliath came towards them at a gallop. Yet Ben remained in the middle of the track. In his dark coat and hat, with his shirt buttoned to the neck, he might well have been a minister intent on welcoming a member of his congregation. Julian dived towards a tree as the wily animal skidded in the dried silt, finally coming to a halt mere inches from his father. The horse bared his teeth and whinnied, and Ben repaid the greeting with a fair imitation, his own teeth displayed in a fierce grimace. Satisfied, Goliath allowed his mane to be ruffled, then he backed off and headed home.

Julian picked himself up and rejoined his father. 'You can't trust that horse.'

'He's only fractious because I didn't tell him what was happening today. Everyone likes to be informed,' Ben replied, before setting off once more.

Julian took a deep breath, held it for a second, then caught up with his father. They jumped the irrigation channel that curved from the bore head, repositioned the timber planks so the dray could cross later, and passed the abandoned storehouse, the halfway mark to the river. There, a small, weathered flat-bottomed boat, tarred, pitched and caulked by Frank, sat wedged in the branches of a tree, where the Great Flood had deposited it.

Julian crumbled bark from the base of one cream-and-brown-patched river red gum as they neared the waterway. A red-tailed black cockatoo was nesting in a tree hollow and it backed away shyly at their approach.

The stacked wool was waiting for them on the riverbank. Eighty bales of middling quality, carted here by dray two years earlier and off-loaded next to the wooden decking. Ben slapped one of the bales and dust rose from the sturdy jute hessian that had weathered the dry storms and the few brief showers. He stamped across the platform, checking the soundness of the timber. The deck was six feet long and four feet wide and was re-built after every flood in honour of Julian's great-grandfather Lance Dalhunty, the London butcher, who purchased the first Dalhunty run for a quantity of tobacco and a gallon of rum. Lance had been fond of cogitation by the water and reciting Tennyson's 'The Charge of the Light Brigade'. The poem formed a part of the Dalhunty school syllabus.

Ben ran a loving palm across the huge D axed into the trunk of a massive eucalyptus that signposted the property's location on the river and then leant on a bale, crossed his ankles and began a survey of the waterway.

'I have nothing against the teamsters, bullocks or horses, or, for that matter, the cameleers,' he began as if already partway through conversation. 'The men are reliable and the animals long-suffering beasts. But there's something appealing about seeing the fruits of our endeavours being rolled onto Captain Ashby's freshly scrubbed deck. Although a man should give consideration to the perils of water transport. There are plenty of fine riverboats that have burned to the waterline taking their cargo with them.

But I don't believe such a catastrophe would ever befall Captain Ashby. A finer individual never steered the Murray-Darling.'

'Do you really think the *Lady Matilda* will come today?' asked Julian.

If it didn't, they would have to deliver the vegetables to Bourke themselves.

His father glanced at the sky, hesitated. 'Yes, yes I do believe she will.'

Julian stared heavenward too, speculating not for the first time on whether his father conversed with a higher power. Thanks to recent rain in Queensland the great rivers and anabranches to the north were flowing through and across a network of channels, gilgais and floodplains, and God himself had let a little water pass into the east. A fresh announced its imminent arrival a few days ago, first with the gathering of leaves, twigs and frothy bubbles on the water's brown surface and then the gradual disappearance of the wooden peg that marked the river's height in their part of the Darling. There was now enough depth for the 44-tonne *Lady Matilda* to waltz downstream from the sandy hole she had been marooned in for months thanks to the dried river, run the Brewarrina falls and finally collect the last of their wool.

A crackle of leaves announced the arrival of Frank and Henrietta. Frank, sitting cross-legged in the saddle, gave the camel a nudge with a long stick and Henrietta slowly eased down onto her front legs and then her rear. He opened a hessian bag and carefully lifted a very small bunch of ripening red date fruit. 'See, I told you, Benjamin Dalhunty. Look. It is the best year yet. Where is the boat?' he asked, as he replaced the fruit in the bag.

'It will come,' said Ben.

'Are you to receive many supplies?' asked Frank.

'No not much. Only kerosene. We haven't sold the wool yet,' replied Ben.

'Will there be dates? One can never have too many dates,' said Frank.

'I thought you were expecting a bountiful harvest.'

'My dear boy, are there dates arriving?'

'Not today. We have to sell the wool first.'

'If you had used the wagon, the wool would already be in Sydney, the children would have food and I would have dates. For a Dalhunty, you are a very stupid individual.'

'And for a mad Englishman who's living here gratis you've got a strange way of showing your thanks.' Julian's father stabbed the air with the cane.

'Mad? *I'm* mad? And what is this "gratis"? I thanked your father. Alfred said to me, "Frank, you are a loyal member of this family. You may stay here for the rest of your life and I will treat you like an honoured son." Therefore, I request a new roof on the overseer's cottage. And dates to tide me over until the harvest is in.'

'Not that anyone else was privy to that particular conversation,' Ben informed him. 'And may I remind you that you already have a very nice cottage. It has a roof and its own long drop. Which you don't have to share with anyone.' He emphasised this last point.

As the head of the household Julian knew it troubled his father that he was invariably relegated to a tree in times of dire need. More than once, Bony had snuck up and taken advantage when he squatted.

'I request a roof. This is only proper,' said Frank.

'Darnation. I'm not putting up a new roof for a camel,' said Julian's father loudly. 'I don't recall you saving me, Julian or Mrs Dalhunty during the Great Flood. You high-tailed it away on Henrietta.'

Frank made a series of clucking noises and Henrietta rose partially on her front legs, then her back legs and then completely on her front, until she was standing. All the while Frank swayed back and forth as gently as a blown dandelion petal. 'You have an appalling memory. Henrietta does not like water.'

'You could always leave. No need to stay here on my account,' suggested Ben.

'They throw cameleers off the bridge in Bourke. Hooshta. Hooshta.' Frank retreated into the timber. 'As a member of the camel and carters' union, I strike,' he yelled.

'Well that about covers roofing and dates.' Julian's father moved to the edge of the ramp, the river rushing below. 'Not much point reminding the old coot that he's not a cameleer.'

'Now what?' asked Julian, though he knew the answer.

His father pushed the bowler hat onto the back of his head. 'Now we wait.'

⋘ Chapter 5 ⋙

Three hours later the hum of an engine and the whipping of water gradually broke the stillness. A whistle sounded, harsh and shrill. Grazing kangaroos scattered on the opposite bank and birds fluttered from the trees. The toe of Ben's boot edged over the water as he strained to see the vessel appear around the curve of the river. He was perfectly still, as if the world depended on what happened next.

The slosh of water and the hiss of steam grew louder as the gleaming white paddle-steamer showed itself around the river bend. With its appearance came the sound of music. A tinkling, fluttering melody that could only come from the gramophone in the saloon.

'There she is!' announced his father triumphantly. 'All painted up and ready for the season!' He danced about the wooden platform, jumped and tapped his heels together and then spun Julian about in a brief waltz.

Although he didn't share his father's excitement, Julian tried to drum up some enthusiasm. They needed the money from the sale of the wool, and it was comforting to see Captain Ashby's riverboat working the Darling again. Even before the dry of the last few years, the river trade had been dwindling as trains became the preferred mode of transport for many. His family had missed the comings and goings of river life.

Two all-seeing lamps hung at the *Lady Matilda*'s bow. Overhead, dark woodsmoke billowed from her chimney. On the deck at the bow of the vessel sat what Julian assumed was a piano. He could see nothing but a tall oblong of dark timber, the music that poured forth like a strengthening undercurrent against the vessel's steam-chugging wheels. As the port side neared, Julian made out a dark-haired woman at the piano; one minute her head bowed, the next lifted to the sun-bright sky. Occasionally the pianist struck a wrong chord, yet the music held their attention until the whistle sounded a second time, signalling to the engineer that the vessel was drawing closer to land. The woman closed the lid on the piano and edged her way through chaff bags to the front of the steamer, her skirt fluttering in the breeze. She reminded Julian of the figure-heads on ocean-going vessels, standing guard to appease the water gods and to point a safe way home to port.

In the wheelhouse Captain Augustus Ashby gave a salute as the paddles slowed. The deck was crowded with wooden crates filled with condiments, vegetables, bags of sugar, tins of kerosene and bric-a-brac that appealed to ladies. On the foredeck a wrought-iron bedhead was positioned near the piano. A row of wind chimes tinkled from the railings. A large bull stood on the rear deck, along with a single goat, her two offspring and half a dozen free-ranging chickens, their heads bobbing right and left at the sight of land closing in. Ben rubbed his hands in anticipation, excitement fizzing through his body. It was a veritable menagerie of wares and animals.

Two deckhands moved at a shouted command and the shallow-draft vessel eased alongside the bank, one of the men throwing ropes to Julian, who knotted them around tree stumps. The barge upon which the Dalhuntys' wool was to be transported was being towed fifty feet behind the steamer and was similarly manoeu-vred to shore with the aid of a pole by the barge master Rick the

Dane. The barge already held a large quantity of wool belonging to another grower and Rick was perched on a wooden platform on the topmost bale. He flung a meaty fist upwards upon seeing Julian, as the deckhands ran to assist with its mooring.

'Julian, you wool-wrangler. Have you not found yourself a long-haired one born of man?' He helped secure the barge to another stump and leapt ashore, yellow hair flying.

'Not yet,' called Julian, pumping his own fist skyward in greeting.

'The sky candle will not wait forever. One day it will sink and you will be old.' The big man took Julian by the shoulders, lifting him a good foot from the ground. 'You must pray to Freya for a pretty one. But choose carefully. Better to poke a honey pot, ja? Not too big and not too hollow-cheeked. She must be strong to bring forth your cubs.'

He dropped Julian to the ground, squeezed his cheeks with meaty paws and then hurdled the gap to land heavily on the steamer's deck.

Captain Ashby stepped nimbly to earth. Once tall and spare with a close-cropped beard, now the captain's beard was full, his eyes clouding with advancing age, his pot belly suggesting an enjoyable enforced rest.

'Benjamin Dalhunty, my dear friend.' The two men met with a handshake. 'Apologies for Sabbath breaking. Well, we're here at last. Held up for some time in the shallows, but nonetheless ready to transport your cargo.'

'Augustus. Good to see you. It's a fair run in the river.' Ben hitched his trousers.

'Not quite as big as in 1890.' He patted the letter D carved into the eucalyptus tree. 'I feel a few words are necessary to mark the occasion, this being your last wool clip. Dalhunty Station without sheep. There are many who will find the news difficult to believe. It is the end of an era.'

'We've still forty ewes and six rams. Enough ration sheep to complement what the land provides. Vegetables are the future now,' said Ben.

Captain Ashby scratched his full white beard. Maybe Julian was mistaken, however it seemed the Captain took this news gravely. They read in the months-old newspapers that came their way that people hungered in various places all over the world. And Julian recognised on the Captain's face the same troubled expression that crossed his father's countenance when he worried about the fate of the poor. Here they were, not far from the largest inland port for wool in the world, and the Dalhuntys were growing lettuce and sending handsewn curios south to city ladies. But unlike Julian, Ben hadn't noticed any change in the Captain's demeanour. Ben was distracted by the piano.

'Yes. A fine piece,' replied Captain Ashby, following Ben's gaze. 'And the marvel of it is having an accomplished woman aboard to play. It's been quite the musical interlude. And there's nothing like music for soothing the inner man. Culture is the soul of a country.'

The bull on the boat began snorting. The animal was red in colour, fat and muscular, clearly raised in the east. As the deck-hands positioned loading planks, the reckless goat skittered across the timber decking. The haughty bull observed the smaller animal approaching and bided his time. He lowered his head, waited until the goat drew closer and, straining the leg rope, butted the animal into the water. The steamer tilted with this movement of weight and the crew scrambled to keep upright as the goat disappeared into the brown depths and the vessel levelled out. The animal reappeared, splashing and bleating, and tried vainly to make for the bank. The Captain gave orders to his startled crew to retrieve the poor creature before the current took hold.

The young woman holding tight to the railings was joined by the engineer, Mr Cummins, who appeared from the boiler room complaining about the ruckus. Mr Quaine, the cook, was close behind.

After a brief argument between the two deckhands, the string-ier fellow set about reluctantly tying a rope around his waist and, with a tentative glance at the goat, jumped fully clothed into the river. He thrashed about in the water as if he too might drown and when he eventually reached the animal, both went under.

Captain Ashby shook his head in dismay. 'Only the Dane can swim, but he hates getting wet. As for the new chum, Awang' – he pointed to the water – 'he grew up on the Sarawak River, but frankly I don't like his chances.'

'Can you swim, Captain Ashby?' asked Julian.

'Not necessary, Julian. A captain always goes down with his ship.'

The man and goat bobbed back into view.

'Success!' the Captain cheered.

Rick pulled the goat and Awang to the side of the boat and with difficulty the animal and then the rescuer were dragged aboard. Both shook themselves like shaggy dogs before the lard-waisted cook grabbed the goat, hugging it possessively.

Julian turned to his father, but it seemed partially drowned goats were not of interest, for Ben was walking up the gang plank onto the steamer. He examined the piano in detail and, lifting the lid, played a number of keys. Within a few seconds he was asking the Captain about the possibility of purchasing it. Julian listened to the request in amazement and heard the same disbelief in the Captain's reply.

'Why would you want to go and lumber yourself with the expense, especially in the early stages of a new venture?'

Ben swished imaginary air as if lifting coattails, and positioned himself on the piano stool. He hit a key with gusto. Then another.

'We can't afford a piano.' Julian knew he was being too bold.

Ben leapt up and jumped from the steamer to the bank. He ignored Julian and appealed directly to the captain. 'There were the losses,' he began, 'after the Great Flood, then the Federation drought struck, then young Davey passed. It's a lot for a city-bred woman to endure and women need culture and refinement.'

'I'm only in charge of the piano's delivery to Bourke. It's not mine to sell.'

'Come, Augustus. How long have we been friends? Long enough for me to appreciate your acumen when it comes to wheeling and dealing. Did you not once own three fine paddle-steamers? A man doesn't have that sort of success without looking outside the square.'

'They were heady days, all right. We'll never see their likes again,' replied the Captain.

'The money I wire you once our wool is sold can be used to replace this fine instrument. So the delivery of a piano to Bourke would simply be . . . delayed,' said Ben.

'Is it valuable, do you think?'

Ben struck on this smidgeon of interest, lowering his voice and whispering a sum to the Captain, who in turn whistled through his teeth, marvelling at the price Ben had named.

Julian listened to their conversation with increasing disbelief. How was it possible his father could even contemplate buying a piano? Especially one that already belonged to someone else. He was used to Ben acting on a whim, had learned to recognise his father's impulsive behaviour from an early age, however the selling of their sheep had marked a new level – and now this. They needed that wool money to survive, at least until the vegetable business became profitable. *If* it became profitable. What did a son do with a father who refused to see reason?

'Father, we can't use the proceeds from our last ever clip on a *piano*.'

Ben appeared to ignore his son, appealing to the Captain once more. 'Augustus. It's for Rachael.'

It was as if Julian could sense the crows gathering in the nearby trees and the ominous feeling refused to budge. He knew trying to change his father's mind was useless. Once Ben Dalhunty got an idea in his brain it grew roots that splayed out in myriad directions. Julian summoned all his strength to will his father away from such a scheme. He would not plead in the Captain's presence. It was beneath him. And nor did he want to undermine his father in front of his closest friend. If anything, he was relying on the Captain to dissuade Ben. Captain Ashby was a businessman. He knew their situation. And he was in charge of freighting the instrument to Bourke, so why was he remaining silent?

'Father—'

'This is for your mother. She is still mourning Davey.'

'We all are,' replied Julian.

'One day when you marry, Julian, you will understand the importance of having a good woman by your side,' said his father.

Did a woman need to be pacified with toys like a child to stay at a man's side? And when had his mother ever expressed a desire for a piano? Never, that Julian could recall.

Captain Ashby clasped the lapels of his jacket. 'Aren't the wool proceeds from this last clip crucial, particularly as you've yet to establish this vegetable venture?'

'I'm in regular contact with a number of merchants who are keen to invest in Dalhunty Station's new produce business.'

'Father!' It was a blatant lie.

Ben gave Julian a smooth smile and then turned that same believable, convivial persona back to the Captain.

Captain Ashby seemed to accept Ben's word and mulled on the possibility of selling the piano, matching his deliberations with a frequent narrowing of his eyes. Ben seized the opportunity.

'That's the spirit, Augustus. And never fear – a lack of sheep does not mean the end of our trade. Your services will still be required in the future,' replied Ben.

Julian reckoned on his father having given more thought to Captain Ashby's visits than he had the demise of the merino on Dalhunty Station, such was his admiration for the man who had steamed to their rescue across the flooded paddock all those years prior.

The two men shook hands as if they had concluded some trade of great importance, and they had, of sorts, having just agreed on the sale of the piano.

Julian walked away and sat on one of the wool bales. The morning had become a disaster. Wait until his mother learnt of her husband's purchase.

The Captain passed Ben a parcel and his father carefully untied the string, excited at the sight of the periodicals and newspapers. Julian knew it was not a fair trade for the cut timber they were providing to keep the *Lady Matilda*'s boiler stoked. Five shillings for a tonne of wood was far more valuable to them than swapping the wood for reading matter. Money could buy boiled lollies for Meg and thread for Laura. And his mother could do with new dress material. Instead they now owned out-of-date newspapers and a piano.

'You might offer your services to the amiable Mr Cummins, Julian, while I have a private chat with your father,' said the Captain.

Julian nodded bleakly, and walked towards Mr Cummins, now on dry ground, who had the disgruntled look of a man kept in the sweaty bowels of a steamer.

'How's the *Lady Matilda*, Mr Cummins?' asked Julian, watching a deckhand use an iron hook to lift a lumpy wool bale. It rolled down the sloping bank, across creaking planks and into place on the barge, which listed briefly with the shifting weight.

'She's fair, Julian. Very fair. We took her as far as Mungindi before being beached. A narrower snagged stream I've never seen. Still we've started our homeward run.'

The engineer surveyed the stack of cut timber and gave a grunt that passed for approval. They piled the two-foot lengths in their arms and carried the loads aboard and down into the bowels of the steamer before returning for more.

The dray carrying the Dalhunty womenfolk arrived as Julian heaped more wood in his arms. Meg jumped from the slowing dray with unladylike speed and ran towards the activity.

Rachael shouted at her youngest and, with a longing glance at the riverboat, Meg made a slow zig-zag back towards the dray where she was immediately set the task of helping Laura carry the carefully packed crates and bags of craft creations to the decking on the riverbank.

Once they reached the deck, greetings were exchanged, permission was given to Laura and Meg to board the steamer and then

42

Rachael began a detailed description of her wares. There were stencilled ferns to be displayed beneath glass on dressers; three dozen decorative sprays of fuchsia, rose and jessamine, perfect for glass domes. And some embroidery pieces large enough for armchairs or framing. Rachael praised Laura's work and went into detail regarding the fish-scale embroidery, having overseen the curing herself, knowing what a curiosity the use of scales were in the south.

Captain Ashby was pleased and in reply described his current stock. It was some time since the *Sarah Francis* steamer had floated around these parts, taking care of the ladies on the river so the Captain thoughtfully offered a variety of dress fabrics to avoid neighbours selecting the same material. There were Sicilian lustres, Chinese silks, white calicoes, belts and clasps, ruchings, braids and gimp trimmings. Lace remained popular, especially guipure, Chantilly and edelweiss.

'I still recall the fine silks and muslins I used to deliver here. It was often commented by my other clients that you set the bar for elegance in the west, Mrs Dalhunty. And it is only seven months until the second running of the Darling River Picnic Races. The milliners will be booking their seats on the train from Sydney, readying to dress all you fine ladies.'

'I thank you, Captain. However that time now seems long ago and we won't be attending the races,' Rachael replied stiffly. She readjusted the contents of a crate, tending to a fish-scale geranium come loose of its swaddling and sparkling in the sun.

Julian felt his mother's embarrassment. He hurriedly lifted more timber as Ben took Rachael's arm, steering her towards the vessel. It was best he not watch what happened next, however morbid curiosity kept him motionless as Ben announced to his wife that he had purchased a gift for her.

'Your very own piano!' said Ben with delight. 'You once said to me you missed playing and if we had a piano you would teach the girls, ensure they developed the refinements expected of a Dalhunty woman.'

'I never said that, Ben.'

43

'Well, we have one now.'

Julian was sure his mother gave a little shudder. 'You spent our wool money on a piano?'

'Exceptional, isn't it? The timber is superb, and the tone . . . it's not my area of expertise, however it sounds very fine to me.'

'Is it one of them ones that has a roll of paper in its innards that plays itself?' asked Meg, swinging on a railing, her cheek swollen with the cake Quaine had shared with her.

The cook shook his head adamantly. 'It's a real one.'

'Oh,' said Meg, quickly losing interest.

'It's a Steinway. Quite a good brand if I'm not mistaken,' said their father.

Rachael appeared as if she might faint.

'Didn't you tell me President Theodore Roosevelt has one in the White House? Yes, I'm sure you did. The little I've read of the man suggests a certain quality of nature. Impeccable taste. And impeccable taste only comes from impeccable breeding. That's what my mother used to say.' Their father turned to the Captain. 'Augustus, what happened to its crate? Surely it didn't travel all the way from Sydney like that.'

'It was faulty. I couldn't risk winching it aboard for fear the packing would give way. Now, enough of pianos, I believe there's a telegram,' the Captain said, his voice becoming subdued as he turned back to Rachael. 'It was redirected from Bourke to Brewarrina when news reached the telegraph office of *Lady Matilda* catching the rise. And it's addressed to you, Mrs Dalhunty.'

Mr Cummins gave Julian a nod of solidarity as his mother took the telegram and retreated to the dray, ashen-faced. Their wool broker was the only person who sent telegrams, and they were always addressed to Ben. What business could anyone have with his mother?

Meg sped down the gangway, and straight to the Captain, where she extracted the blade from the leather belt around her dress and held it out for him to examine. 'Sometimes I use it to gut fish and sometimes for skinning rabbits and when Mother does her taxidermy I help with that too. When she stuffed the parrot to prettify the fire-screen I used it to chop the innards up.'

'You are clever. Here's something to keep you warm over winter.' The Captain pulled a red knitted scarf from a travelling bag, draping it over Meg's head, and twisting the lengths so each end rested over a shoulder. 'And give this ribbon to your sister.'

Meg tucked the ribbon in a pocket. Laura was on the steamer, engrossed in bolts of dress material. She unrolled a pale pink satin and draped it across her body.

Mr Cummins mumbled to Julian as they stacked the last of the wood on deck. 'The Cap spent near eighteen hours playing cards with an opal prospector from Lightning Ridge. If I'd not dragged him away it's likely the *Lady* herself would have ended up on the table. Boredom and a dwindling trade doesn't suit him.'

The sacks of lettuce and onions from Dalhunty Station were carried aboard, while tins of kerosene were placed on the bank and then the piano was strapped for lifting. A thick chain was attached to the knotted ropes and the steamer's winch lifted the instrument, swinging the cargo from the deck to land with the utmost care. The piano settled on the wooden platform. Once the ropes were untied Julian walked about it, trying to equate years of sheep work with the glossy musical instrument sitting among sacks and tins.

'Blast,' he said.

'Ladies present, Julian,' the engineer warned. 'That's Miss Carlisle.'

The female passenger alighted and without so much as a hello to anyone walked idly along the riverbank.

'She offered her services as cook, but the position is already taken by our resident poisoner. Before we were marooned, she spent time with us on the Murray. Captain Ashby lets her come and go as she likes.'

The young woman floated a stick on the water, the hem of her skirt dipping in the river. The branch travelled downstream, gliding on the current, traversing the narrow gap between the steamer and bank. With the light behind her, Miss Carlisle was a sun-blurred figure made more dazzling by a lemon-coloured gown. She sought a shady tree and looked confidently at him. Julian felt his throat dry as he abruptly turned away.

Women Julian's age were in short supply. The only ones he knew were the three daughters of Mr Fraser, their nearest neighbour and an old acquaintance of Ben's, who, along with one son, made up the entire complement of young people he knew by name. Julian had met the girls when his father sought permission from Mr Fraser to show Julian one of their original boundary huts that sat on a portion of Dalhunty Station that had been purchased by the company Mr Fraser was employed by. Strangely, Julian wasn't the slightest bit lost for conversation that day. He talked on and on about bridles, reins and girth straps and the promised land in the east, all the while, wondering what it would be like to get one of those slim-thighed girls alone. The more he thought about the prospect, the more he talked. And the more he spoke, the more he blathered. Two months of daydreaming followed. Every lesson about men and women – whether from his father, from Frank, from watching animals or marvelling at naked Italian statues in books – failed to explain how talk led to a prod. But as Frank had deemed talking an important precursor to prodding, it seemed crucial information had been omitted by both men.

Meg sidled up beside him. 'Is she prettier than Mr Fraser's girls?'

'Who? Miss Carlisle? Maybe.' Julian tried his best at disinterest.

'Them Fraser girls is too big for their britches. Father said they barely spoke to youse that time youse visited. He said they was uppity. Imagine being uppity. Their father's only a manager, ain't he?' asked Meg.

It was true that Fraser was only a manager, however the company he worked for was buying land. Some pastoralists were willing to sell to these organisations. Others, like the Dalhuntys, pressured by their bank, were obliged to sell off portions of land through necessity.

'He works for Goldsbrough Mort & Co.,' explained Julian.

"Zactly. A manager,' said Meg.

That made Julian feel a little better.

Captain Ashby removed his jacket and set about rolling the last bale onto the barge himself, as the deckhands scuttled out of the way. When the bale was securely aboard he returned to Julian and Meg. 'You've no staff left?'

'The last of them went after shearing. Ain't been no one here nearly two years, excepting for the Aboriginal folks, and there ain't many of them left either,' Meg explained. 'It's been quieter, than quiet. Why, I took to talking to my tadpoles until Julian told me to stop.'

'But surely you need labourers, fencers, boundary riders, blacksmiths?'

'The Aboriginal people do some repairs in exchange for hunting and fishing and the odd sheep,' said Julian. 'We haven't got much else to offer them. We've only the homestead lease left.'

Captain Ashby flicked sweat from his brow. 'You'll be needing to grow *a lot* of vegetables and they'll have to be quality. The Chinese have much of the trade,' he replied.

An uncomfortable silence grew between them.

'It's been hard for many,' the Captain ran on. 'I know what your father said about having investors lined up but you could sell out. I hear your neighbour Mr Fraser, while still ensconced with Goldsbrough Mort & Co., is on the lookout to buy his own land now. He's as tight-fisted as some of our most moneyed pastoralists, so you can be assured he'll have the wherewithal to buy the rest of the station.'

Meg scowled at him.

'All I'm saying is a person can't stay in a place for sentiment alone,' replied the Captain.

Julian yearned to tell the Captain that even if they were faced with ruin their father was perfectly capable of staying put for that reason. Although why he would want to was yet another of the unfathomables that made up Benjamin Dalhunty.

'We ain't staying for no sentiment. This is our home. And we ain't selling out to no manager, are we, Julian?' said Meg.

His sister waited for an answer Julian was incapable of giving. Meg nudged him and he hacked up spittle as if a cough prevented speech, picturing the Chinese with their flourishing gardens, and the sheepless Dalhuntys now with a new piano to be paid for out of their last wool proceeds. Pride was a god-awful thing. Next to him, Meg muttered a string of swear words that concluded with *pe-anna*.

The wind gusted along the Darling. Captain Ashby was drawn to the rippling water. At the dray Ben and Rachael embraced. His mother dropped the telegram she clutched and Julian watched the piece of paper blow across the ground, tossing and turning over and over until it caught in clumpy grass.

⊰ Chapter 6 ⊱

Their mother's only surviving sibling, Aunt Nancy, was dying. They sat at the kitchen table as Rachael recalled the sombre contents of the wind-snatched telegram sent by Nancy's husband, their Uncle Carter. Ben nodded supportively as his wife remembered the words used to describe the dire situation, phrases such as 'it is with regret', 'she has taken ill', 'it is severe this time', and 'little chance of recovery' were spoken softly, painfully. Aunt Nancy had specifically asked to see Rachael before she died, and as their mother uttered this final request, she bit the sodden handkerchief she held.

Julian and his sisters tried to appear suitably upset by the news, however the little they knew of their Sydney-based aunt came from letters; they'd never met her.

'Will we have to wear black again?' asked Laura. 'Meg ruined her dress, but there's still some bombazine left over from when Davey—' She stopped mid-sentence, perhaps shocked by her thoughtlessness.

Rachael gave a little gasp and wept. Everyone bowed their heads.

'Your mother will be travelling to Sydney. You really must get ready, dear,' said Ben.

Rachael rose unsteadily from her chair.

'Sydney?' repeated Julian.

'Yes, Sydney,' said Ben.

Meg shook her head. 'But—'

'Can I come too? As your companion?' asked Laura.

'No, Laura, dear.' Their mother left the room.

Ben looked at each of his children. 'Everything will be fine.'

The battered travelling trunk was carried from the drawing room to the bedroom, where the musty blankets it usually held were placed on a chair. Within an hour it was packed with their mother's belongings. The burden of moving her possessions from one room to another struck Julian as he dragged the trunk from his parents' bedroom to the front hallway. How would their lives function in her absence? Rachael had never left them before. In the open breezeway connecting kitchen and house he foresaw the next few weeks in the flimsy blue of the sky.

Laura sat huddled on an upturned bucket near the front door, cradling a basket of scabby oranges. Julian knew she kept watch, as he did. When the trunk was ready to go, so too would their mother and it seemed vital they now spend every last minute in her presence. On seeing Julian, Laura whinged about Rachael's leaving and then whined again at the cooking and cleaning that would fall to her. She swept at the droplets pearling above her lip, gathered there from the exertion of bucketing hot water from the copper so their mother could bathe, a task originally allocated to Meg, who had disappeared.

'I should be going with her,' sniffed Laura. 'She should have a travelling companion and . . . I never get to go anywhere.'

Their father arrived with a brush and cloth. He rubbed at the trunk's tarnished brass buckles then examined his efforts. Laura gave a little pout, a trait reserved for manipulating her way out of any task not involving sewing, foraging for wildflowers or drying herbs. She played with a braid of hair she wore pinned across her head, the rest of her blonde locks falling free to the middle of her back. Once in receipt of her father's approving smile she demanded that Meg do more in the house to help her. Naturally, Ben agreed, however Laura's contribution to the ongoing upkeep of home and hearth must also broaden. Laura's extra responsibilities would now include assisting Julian to scrape the hide after the sheep was killed in the morning. It was time she learnt, Ben said.

This declaration was met with more whining, Laura never before having been called upon to be involved in such a nasty, messy act.

'It's not fair. Father, why is Mother leaving? Especially when you bought her the piano. Surely you can *tell* her to stay. Aren't wives meant to stay with their husbands? Till death. And anyway I heard her tell you that you shouldn't have bought it. That we'll starve.'

'Rachael, we must be going,' their father called brightly, although the skin on his face was tight.

It had only been two hours since their return from the river, but the woman walking down the hallway looked nothing like the mother who'd waved at Julian from the veranda earlier. This one was wearing a navy-blue skirt and close-fitting jacket with a crisp white blouse, which accentuated a remarkably small waist. Her hair was piled atop her head and her wide straw hat was festooned with a swirl of grey-blue gauzy material and bunches of flowers in shades from the palest of pinks to a deep rose. The hat appeared to need the mass of hair to support it.

The gown was the same one that spent its life on a dressmaker's dummy in his parents' bedroom. Rachael altered it every year after studying the latest advice in the *Town and Country Journal*.

'Is it all right, Ben? I would simply die of shame if I appeared out of fashion when I arrive in Sydney. I know, it is quite ridiculous for a grown woman to be bowing to the maestros in Paris and Vienna when she lives in a place unknown to most of the world. But you understand how first impressions count.'

'We know where we live, Rachael, that is what matters. And you look very fine,' said their father, taking the Gladstone bag from her grasp. He was dressed for the momentous occasion, swapping the bowler for a tall hat, embroidered waistcoat and swallow-tail coat.

Rachael remained unconvinced. She fussed a little with the worn edging of her high collar and twiddled with a small wreath brooch on her lapel. 'What I wouldn't give for new patent leather boots and grey suede uppers. They are quite the mode.'

'Your hyacinth is drooping,' said Laura flatly.

'Really?' Rachael went to the mirror on the hallstand, teasing the flower on her hat into obeisance. 'I knew the rose-coloured velvet ribbon would be best. Fetch a needle and thread, Laura, I can't leave the house looking like the wreck of the *Hesperus*.'

'There's no time,' said Ben. 'Captain Ashby won't wait another hour while you debate the merits of a travelling outfit, Rachael.'

'Careful it doesn't fall off,' said Laura, with more than a little enthusiasm.

Their mother looked askance. 'What do you really think, Laura?' She gave a slow spin.

'I wouldn't be leaving,' her elder daughter replied.

Rachael's mouth turned up slightly. 'Not to worry. I have needle and thread with me. I can stitch the flower on board.'

Meg bustled indoors. Her lilac dress had been discarded for a tatty pinafore, the new red scarf draped about her head. She poured sand into her mother's palm and pressed Rachael's fingers closed on the mass. 'A bit of home. For when youse're sad at night.'

Rachael thanked her youngest and then she glanced at each of her children assembled guard-like at the front door.

'Well then,' she said, as if that was all that needed to be uttered, and then they were carrying her luggage outside while her skirts swayed ever so prettily across dying couch grass.

Frank and Henrietta were waiting near the dray. The camel was sitting, saddled and ready for work. The Englishman was lying on top of his charge, his back supported by the hump, his ankles crossed at the animal's neck and his arms dangling either side of Henrietta's body. On hearing noise he sat upright, glanced left to right and then slid to the ground. Rolls of twine were spooled about his arm, ready to tie the heavy bunches of date fruit to palm fronds. Netting protruded from a saddle pack. He touched a hand to his heart and bowed.

'You are leaving, Mrs Dalhunty?'

'Yes, Frank. My sister is ill and I must go to Sydney,' she explained.

Frank glanced at the heavens and then back at his audience. 'My dear lady. God says amen, God bless, good luck. It is a peculiarity of man that we can never actually say what must be said at this time. And so I will say bon voyage.' He gestured to the hitched dray. 'These are very poor horses. If I were the owner I would sell them. It is better that you place your belongings in the care of me.' He thumbed his chest. 'I have a very fine camel.'

'Mrs Dalhunty prefers the trunk to go in the dray, Frank,' said their father.

Frank offered up a waif-like expression, which was extraordinarily effective considering his seventy years. 'I am thinking of changing my name to Ukulele. Ukulele is a very fine name. Better than Dalhunty, I daresay.'

'You can't call yourself Ukulele, it's a musical instrument,' said their father.

'You have a musical instrument. A piano. You call yourself Benjamin. That's a stupid name,' countered Frank.

'Please, let's not argue. Frank, your offer is very kind,' said their mother. 'I would be grateful if Henrietta carried the trunk to the river and I'm sorry to have interrupted your work in the palm grove.'

Frank gave a mournful nod. The protection of the date fruit from marauding birds required extra vigilance. 'It is but one small crinkle in a rumpled blanket.' He waited patiently until Rachael passed by, before homing in on Ben. 'Maybe I shall keep my new name and place an advertisement about it in the *Western Herald*. Then everyone will know you're related to me, Frank Ukulele Dalhunty.'

Their father frowned – a tight, annoyed frown. 'You wouldn't dare.'

'Ben, don't,' pleaded Rachael.

'Come on.' Julian pulled on his father's arm. It took muscle to drag Ben through the dirt to the waiting trunk. The two of them carried it to Frank, where he secured it expertly to the camel, making a show of checking the ropes twice.

'Jolly good. This morning is a very fine morning.' Frank flung a leg across the camel's back. 'Hooshta.' Henrietta rose with a complaining grunt. 'New roof. Yes?'

'*No*,' said their father.

Julian rode at the rear on Legless, the grey mare named for her shaky start to life. Ahead, the dray trundled, Meg's and Laura's legs dangling over the back. Their parents sat up front, shoulder to shoulder, so that not a scrap of light showed between them. The slight hump at the top of their father's spine almost flat as he flicked the reins less than needed.

'We're like a travelling circus,' said Laura bitterly.

His sister was right. Goliath trotted at a respectful distance behind them. Bony scurried about like a ferreting rat. In the lead, Henrietta's rolling gait led them onwards, like a prow pushing the bush aside.

The belah woodlands slanted protectively inwards as the procession journeyed back to the river. It seemed to Julian he could hear every rustle of grass, every beetle that crawled, every cockatoo and magpie that scratched and squawked for a living. He reasoned on the fairness of their mother abandoning them. If his sister were dying and he had no remaining family, Julian knew he would want to be by her side. Yet he could not fathom why his mother's departure bothered him so. She was a calming influence on their father, a tether of sorts to the reality of their lives, but there was something more. Other than her sadness at Aunt Nancy's illness, Rachael did not seem very perturbed at leaving them.

Sydney was hundreds of miles away. It would take time for her to travel there and to return. And the length of her stay was as unknowable as the duration of the rise that flowed past their lands. How long did it take for someone to die? Was it as quick as a bird falling from a tree during a drought hot spell? Julian remembered that it had taken a favoured dog less than two days to die after being bitten by a snake, although they cut his ear and bled him to try to save him. And an unrideable stallion none could control was stabbed in the neck and allowed to run until he dropped. A quick end by any measure. As for Davey, by the time they had found his little body, he was long gone. Julian's Aunt Nancy was forty-seven years young. Her illness, having come like a black frost last winter, had progressed. The telegram spoke of little time remaining. What was the use of his mother going?

They broke free of stunted red gums and reached the cleared portion of the riverbank. A group of Aboriginal men, having elected to remain on their homelands, instead of leaving for employment and better rations, were standing off to one side, drawn by the steamer's whistle. They were strong individuals, dressed for work on a station that no longer offered steady employment. Their shirt-sleeves were rolled to their elbows, revealing sinewy arms and they watched the proceedings with closed expressions, smoking and talking amongst themselves.

Opposite the steamer on the riverbank Captain Ashby was sitting with his men – Mr Cummins, Rick, Quaine the cook and the two deckhands, Awang and Joe – around a small fire. Awang and Joe were fighting over the last scone, a blackened edifice that spoke to Quaine's culinary ability.

'Mutton. Roasted. Boiled. Salted. Stewed. Broiled. Fried. That's your calling, Quaine,' announced the Captain.

Their laughter quietened at the procession's arrival. The deck-hands tossed the unfinished tea on the fire. Joe quickly grabbed the scone.

Quaine snatched the tin cups from the men and rested them on the ledge of his roly-poly stomach. 'Anyone would think you ain't never seen a parade.'

'Fire up the boiler, Mr Cummins,' directed the Captain.

'Aye, aye, Cap,' replied the engineer.

Julian tied his horse to the now stationary dray and looked across the top of the saddle directly at Miss Carlisle. She must have been exploring the bush skirting the river for she was walking from the timber back towards the riverboat and had to bypass Julian and his family to reach her destination. As she grew closer he saw she was pretty, her skin dewy and plum plump. Not as pretty as the Fraser girls. A different kind of pretty.

'Julian, stop gawping.' Meg sneaked a wink.

Embarrassed Julian spun about and headed straight to Henrietta. Once the trunk was untied, he went to lift it. One of the Aboriginal men came forward to take Julian's place and, together with Frank, carried it across to the landing, where the piano waited.

Julian's father offered the former stockman a pouch of tobacco and asked if he and his men were willing to lift the piano onto the rear of the dray. The man agreed, then accepted the tobacco and went back to the group, tipping his hat at Rachael as he passed her. The men sat, waiting until they were needed.

The Captain remained by the campfire sewing a cross onto the river map spread across his lap. 'Snags. Every trip. More snags.' Biting the thread he rolled the two ends of the diagram together.

'If youse take all the snags out of the river where are the fishes going to live?' asked Meg.

'There's plenty of river for everyone,' he replied. 'Here is the inventory for your vegetables, Ben.' The captain would deliver the produce to Webster's store at Bourke, and the storekeeper would mail Ben a receipt and credit note. Rachael's fancywork was accepted on consignment, until it was sold, less the captain's commission and the cost of the kerosene. As usual, all monies were to be deposited into the Dalhuntys' bank account.

Julian's father read through the listed items and numbers as if the Captain's writing was a model of exemplary penmanship, not cramped and indecipherable. The sale of the wool was to take place in a couple of months and it fell to the Sydney wool broker to pay Ashby's shipping fee to Bourke. Once that transaction was concluded, Ben was to wire the funds for the piano to the captain's account.

'I remember when we shipped Dalhunty wool all the way to the railhead at Murray Bridge. The railway has certainly changed our lives.' The Captain grew subdued and then gave an all-encompassing goodbye. 'We must keep abreast with the rise.'

Rachael touched each of her children on the cheek. 'I expect you all to do your best while I'm away. Look after each other and help your father.' She stepped lightly towards the steamer and at the decking was confronted with the piano in all its newness.

'My, my.'

She spoke quietly, tentatively, placing her palm on the lid before withdrawing it and offering her children a stoic smile.

As the deckhands carried the trunk aboard and Mr Cummins descended to stoke the boiler, Julian's parents walked a distance away. His father kissed their mother long enough for Julian to feel a flush of embarrassment in Miss Carlisle's presence. Then Ben escorted his wife aboard, passed her the Gladstone bag, their fingers lingering until Captain Ashby suggested Mrs Dalhunty might prefer to stand at the blackened railings, and their father was forced to return to land.

Miss Carlisle nodded briefly at Julian before reboarding the steamer. It was the same tragic look of understanding that dismantled the two usually serene Sisters of Mercy from the Catholic Church who came to visit following Davey's passing.

'Everything will be all right, ja?' called Rick from the barge. 'And wool-wrangler, don't forget about the long hair. Ja?'

The Captain entered the wheelhouse, the ropes were untied, the whistle screeched, and the steamer slowly drew away. Ben walked along the riverbank, waving, continually waving, as if their goodbye hinged on his pivoting wrist. Julian shoved his hands in his pockets as the last Dalhunty wool clip floated away. He still couldn't shake the sense of doom as the paddle-steamer gathered speed and a once-golden era came to an inglorious end.

It struck Julian how quickly his mother had focused on where she was heading. She had left their home, her family, with the minimum of fuss and little to say, except for the concern at her appearance. Even now all her attention was given to the river and nothing at all for what was left behind. She never once looked back.

≪ Chapter 7 ≫

Late January

Laura and Meg arrived at the breakfast table in scabby moods. There were mumblings about kicks to legs and jabs with elbows, interspersed with yawns, suggesting a torrid night. Julian concentrated on drinking the black tea with its leaf floaters, the cup tipping precariously as he tried his best to hold the delicate porcelain handle. He rose, intending to swap the cup for a pannikin and found his father sympathetic. Ben had held his pinkie aloft as he sipped from the fine bone china but he cleared the very best breakfast crockery and *D*-etched silverware to one side. Julian went to the pantry and bustled about, re-emerging with pannikins and the plain cream-coloured plates Rachael detested. Laura was only mollified upon realising that the tin pannikins were easier to rinse and the cream plates unlikely to be missed by their mother if they broke. Less worry and less work cleaning. As if in reply, a dry gutter wind blew grit through the window. It had taken nearly two full weeks before their father elected not to keep up their mother's high standards.

Julian flicked through the selected school readers for the afternoon's lessons, doubting his ability to instruct Meg in the benefits of arithmetic. Education held as much appeal to his sister as being bitten by a green ant.

'I'd like to see some rain,' said Ben.

'Wese should get the rainmakers to come visit. Youse know. There's them Muruwari men up on the Culgoa. They sing the rain down,' Meg explained. 'If we had some bone fertiliser, we could dig that into the soil first. Nothing like bits of a human to make plants grow.'

Half-raised pannikins and pieces of bread were slowly lowered.

'What? Everyone knows the story. Great-grandfather told it to Grandfather and then he told Father and then Father told us. Actually, he told you, Julian, but I overheard.' Meg turned to Laura. 'After the Battle of Waterloo and all them brave soldiers were buried, some peoples went back and dug the bones up, crushed them, shovelled them into sacks and then shipped the bits and pieces back to London. Prime fertiliser.'

Laura put a hand to her mouth and her body lurched as if she might be sick. 'That's a terrible lie.'

Meg looked to their father. With infinite slowness he took a sip of tea and cradled the pannikin. 'It happens to be true.'

'How awful,' said Laura.

'They took their teeth out first, didn't they, Father. Grandfather owned a fine set of chompers that were Great-grandfather's first. Thought to have belonged to one of Wellington's men, an ex-Hanoverian. But the teeth floated away in the Great Flood, along with most other things. Frank reckons every bit of us can be put to good use after the Reaper takes us. Reckon I'd grow a few big fat tomatoes.'

Accepting the policy that any response might stir Meg to greater disclosures, the family went back to finishing breakfast, although Laura only poked at hers.

Meg selected an egg from the basket on the table, squeezed her eyebrows together and concentrated as she held it in front of a candle. 'Reckon this one's buggered. And that rooster. Doesn't know how to roost. How's wese gonna get more chickens?

There's good money in chickens. Good eating too. Reckon we got a mighty problem.'

Laura sat a bowl in front of her sister, took the egg from her and placed it in the salt water where it floated. 'We want eggs, Meg, not chickens. Stop wasting candles and start searching more carefully. This egg's five days old.'

'It ain't my fault they lay all over the place.' Meg wiped the egg carefully with a towel, putting it back in the basket with the others. 'Seven eggs. Seven whole eggs from fifteen hens. Wese be better off eating the darn rooster. Ain't had no chicken for a while, excepting the boiler hen and the stone was cooked before she was. I thought the rock was meant to make the meat soft, Father?'

'Our rooster is a descendant of your grandfather's Double-combed Hamburg. He kept Dorkings, being partial to their extra toe, however the Hamburg was his favourite. Now people only want Leghorns or Rhode Island Reds or black Orpingtons. But in my mind there's no superior layer than the Hamburg,' he declared.

'So can wese eat him?' asked Meg.

'No. We'd hardly eat Reginald. He's the top chook. Beaky is next, being of Rhode Island pedigree, and the rest, they're Leghorns, they don't rate in the pecking order.' Their father licked at the rendered fat on the bread. 'As of tomorrow we must do with a half-loaf of bread each day and let's save the currants and rice for Sundays until the wool is sold and we receive word from the broker the funds have been deposited into our bank account. Then we can order a good lot of supplies.'

It fell to Julian to remind his father of the payment due to Captain Ashby for the piano, and added, 'I hope there's money left over for us.' He slurped his tea as his sisters stopped eating and waited for their father to respond.

'Everything will be fine, fine, fine. But we'll save the money we receive from the sale of the vegetables at Mr Webster's for a rainy day, so we're still on short rations until the wool is sold.'

'But we'll starve,' said Laura.

'There's potatoes, turnips and meat,' stated their father.

'What about the investors Captain Ashby talked about? Are they gonna put money into the vegetable business?' asked Meg.

Ben's attention shifted about the room, avoiding Julian.

'Yes, what about the investors?' asked Julian.

'There's no need for you children to worry about anything,' replied Ben.

'Don't kick me, Meg,' said Laura.

'I never. God damn.' Meg scratched viciously at her scalp.

'You're potty-mouthed and a liar!' shouted Laura.

Julian had hoped the sweetness of the golden syrup lacing the tea would lessen the squabbling, but his sisters' bickering started up with vigour. He reached for the bread baked by their father before dawn and chewed with determination. There was weeding to be done in the vegetable garden, a wheel on the dray needed repairing and more wood was to be cut for the next steamer that passed, although he was secretly hoping one of the Aboriginal stockmen might take the job on in exchange for a quantity of swede turnips.

Their father sat steadfastly through the breakfast ordeal as Laura and Meg sniped at each other. At the far end of the table Rachael's unfinished geranium petal still sat undisturbed, the fish scales catching the growing light.

Meg squealed and scratched at her head again. Almost simultaneously, Laura was taken by a similar fit. Together they rubbed their hair and wailed like flea-bitten dogs. Julian expected his father to tell his sisters to quieten. Instead, he observed their hysterics patiently and then, with a sigh, abruptly took hold of Meg and perched her on the table. He plucked at her scalp, quickly and diligently, and then with the same considered motion searched Laura's beautiful, shining hair.

'Lice,' he announced.

He left the kitchen and entered their bedroom, returning a short time later with the woollen scarf gifted to Meg by Captain Ashby. He promptly threw it on the fire. Meg let out a howl of protest.

'Not a soul has visited us since the *Lady Matilda* was here. The lice must have been in the scarf.' Their father scrubbed his hands in the water bucket.

'You've given me lice!' yelled Laura. 'How disgusting.'

'It's not my fault. I told Mother Laura should have her own room. Why can't wese open up the other half of the house? There are four other bedrooms. And a dining room. And a study. Laura could have one of those,' announced Meg.

'I'm not moving in there. It's full of ghosts. I can hear them at night,' said Laura.

'That's just mice,' Meg insisted. 'Ghosts don't rustle about too much unless they're trying to get youse attention. Sometimes they talk and sometimes they sit, mostly they just walk about the homestead. Grandfather Alfred groans a bit on account of the barbed wire that ripped his stomach, which is why he smokes his pipe so much to get his mind off the accident. He blames the horse, youse know. Great-grandfather Lance, he mainly stays put on the porch. He likes it there. 'Specially at dusk. That's his favourite part of the day. Sometimes he's at the river reciting Tennyson, but he don't go there much on account of the spear in his side. It makes a dragging noise. That's how I know he's about,' she ended matter-of-factly.

Laura turned the colour of weevilly flour.

'Now, Meg, I thought we'd got over these daydreams,' replied their father.

'They ain't daydreams. I've seen youse in the drawing room, putting down your book and glancing about as if someone's there. I heard you talking to your father once, too, about the state of the wool industry. By the way, he says you never should have sold the sheep but youse never listen to his advice.'

Their father blinked and cleared his throat, took a gulp of tea. 'That part of the homestead hasn't been used since your grandfather died and we don't need the space. Julian, set the timber under the copper and fill it with water.'

'But it's not washing day,' protested Laura.

'You should have told me about this before, Laura. Meg has welts on her scalp. You'll have to wash your clothes, bedding and brushes. And as for your hair . . .'

Laura's eyes expanded to twice the size. 'What about our hair?'

Without answering, their father left the kitchen in a hurry and, for the first time in years, there was no half-drunk tea sitting on the post when Julian met him at the yard gate.

'Get the fire started, Julian. It will take the girls' minds off things if they have something to do, and Meg loves putting the washed clothes through the mangle.' He reached for the gatepost, holding firm to the extra support. 'I wish your mother were here.'

His seriousness made Julian consider what it meant for a father to take on a mother's role. The past weeks had been reasonably happy. There was freedom in not being bound to chores at a specific time, and Ben was unconcerned if they stayed up a little later, the Milky Way being crystal clear.

'We *could* open up the rest of the house,' Julian suggested. 'Give Laura her own room.'

His father shook his head. 'The Mathews remodelled their original home, even rebuilt some parts with cedar. Once the house was repaired, Mrs Wilson declared new furniture was needed and then staff, enough to cook and clean. Then they started hosting monthly balls. They were fine gatherings. Your mother and I would set off at the first sign of a swelling moon, all smart and gleaming like new pennies, and your mother gussied up like the fine woman she is. This monthly cavorting went on for two straight years. Then the balls became more infrequent. For months, your mother searched the mail for invitations that eventually stopped coming. It devastated her for a bit, made her maudlin something terrible. But it ruined the Wilsons in the end. All that posturing, and for what? To relive the glory of another century. So, no, son. I'm not opening up the house.'

'What's that got to do with everyone having a bit more space?' Julian could feel his frustration building; he knew he should start counting to ten.

'Because, son, one thing leads to another and before we know it your mother will be home and she'll start having delusions about being another Mrs Mathews.'

'Fat chance of that happening when we've no money.'

One, two, three, four . . .

'What about this ghost business Meg talks about?' asked his father.

'You've been here longer than me. If there are ghosts, wouldn't you have seen them?'

Julian went around back near the chicken coop, recalling the pipe smoke he smelt on occasion and the way the hairs on his forearm rose one late afternoon alone on the porch. He passed Laura's potted herbs, grouped for protection along the outside wall of the coop, and stacked wood for a fire. Then he started carting water from the tank at the side of the house to the copper, crossing the slight depression where his grandfather's pond was once located. When the weather had been pleasant his parents had spent long afternoons sitting outdoors while he had toddled about the edge feeding the fish.

On the other side of the fence, two hundred yards away at the edge of the palm grove, Frank shimmied down the trunk of a fruit-heavy palm, expertly moving the rope wrapped about the tree and his spine. Old fronds needed to be removed and new fronds de-thorned to enable access to the fruit, and the bird netting used to protect the ripening dates was checked daily. At the bottom he removed the bag slung crossways over his body and then, walking a few paces, resumed digging a hole begun a few days earlier.

'Hey, Frank!' called Julian. 'Found any treasure yet? The way you're chomping into the earth you're either digging to China or Afghani land.'

Frank rested on the shovel. 'I know your father bought that piano because I couldn't carry it on Henrietta. Henrietta is very upset.'

'It took us two days to move it from the river to the house, Frank. It's not going anywhere,' replied Julian.

'Never make a present to a woman and let her leave. No good can come of it. No good at all.' Frank dropped the shovel into the hole and lowered his body into it.

When the copper was filled and the fire was burning smartly, Julian returned to the kitchen to find his father holding Laura's thick braid in one hand. In the other he lifted the shears from the table and, with a protracted wince, cut clean through her beautiful hair. He lay the glossy tresses on the table with the reverence of a holy man with a religious relic.

Laura stroked the locks laid before her, tears rolling down her cheeks, while their father chopped at her remaining hair until it was reduced to short tufts sticking out from her skull, blowing at the ends gathered about her neck. Then he dipped a shaving brush in a bowl and lathered her skull. He took the cut-throat razor and, walking to the leather strap hanging from a nail, ran it back and forth. Slowly at first, gathering momentum, a metallic zing echoing in the room each time the razor left the leather.

Laura stared at Julian and then dropped her gaze to her younger sister, a deadly anger in her teary eyes.

'One hundred strokes every morning,' said Meg. 'Mother said Laura had to brush her hair one hundred times to keep it nice.' Meg's head was already shaved. She was completely bald.

It had been nearly two weeks since Rachael had left and they had heard not a word.

≪ Chapter 8 ≫

Mid-February

The sun was dangling in a grimy sky as Julian rode along the river on his way home. What was his mother doing? Did her thoughts linger on their house near the bend in the river? Aunt Nancy lived in his mother's family home in a place called Paddington. It was a sandstone building with a staircase and there was a lemon tree in the garden. They lived on a street where meat, milk and mail were delivered to their door. In the early hours of the morning a man would trundle along in a cart and empty their outhouse, as if it were nothing special to be moving other people's shit from one place to another. This was civilisation, according to Laura, although Julian often wondered if the man doing the shit-shovelling would be so quick to agree.

'There isn't much difference between them and us,' Julian tried telling her the previous day, avoiding her swollen eyes and bald pate. 'Me shovelling the manure out of the stables and Meg being lickety-quick in case a snake snatches the eggs before she collects them. Civilisation isn't always what people imagine.'

Laura called him a stupid idiot, which barely made a dent. Julian was regularly called an idiot by Meg, and when she said it,

66

plonking her hands on her skinny hips and rolling out the letters so that the 'd' became a 'j' and the 'o' was omitted completely . . . well, you pretty much felt like one.

The trouble was after that conversation Julian wasn't quite sure who he was trying to convince, Laura or himself. The timetable was still concealed in his mattress, which had been its hiding place for the past year. And he'd not been able to suppress the jealousy that accompanied the sight of the crew scuttling about the decks on the *Lady Matilda*'s departure. In retrospect, some of his concern at their mother's leaving was tainted with envy. Why her, not him?

Julian pulled on the length of rope he was using for reins, and pricked his thumb. He sucked on the welt and prised the fibre free by pinching it between thumb and nail. Then he twisted the reins and walked through the timber. A half-dozen lean-tos were scattered among the trees. The huts were a mixture of corrugated iron, bark and cane grass. Older people, mainly women, were sitting in the shade weaving baskets, cooking, talking. One woman was pounding a plant on a flat stone. The men were away. Hunting, probably. Or maybe they'd taken up mustering jobs for Fraser.

Ben appeared, trotting through the scrub on Goliath, straining backwards in the saddle, reins taut, trying to compel his mount to keep a steady pace. He called out, bright with happiness. Marcus Wendell had rode past not an hour ago en route to Fraser's run. He had met the coach by chance and kindly detoured to make a special delivery. Rachael had finally written. Ben waved the folded piece of paper as he delivered the news.

'Dearest family. I have arrived safely.' His father raised his voice, trying to restrain the horse. Goliath broke into a trot.

Julian lifted a leg and crossed it over his other thigh, twisting in the saddle to watch as his father was carried away.

'Aunt Nancy remains on the outer limits of life,' his father called over a shoulder. 'What is the matter with you, Goliath?' He smacked Goliath across the skull. With the horse controlled he trotted back to Julian, and uncrumpled the telegram. 'With loving thoughts.'

'That's it?' queried Julian. 'It doesn't say much.'

'It's enough. She's safe.' His father whistled a patchy tune as he tucked the telegram in a pocket and straightened the derby on his head. 'I know. I know. Terribly middle class, the derby, but needs must. Your mother will be home soon and by then the wool proceeds will have been wired to the bank. Until then, we must live off the land. Like the old days.'

Julian was drawn back to another time when funds were short. They'd plucked wool from rotting skeletons, boiling the fleece pieces in the copper and then spreading the sodden bits on wire racks to dry so they were clean for sale. The stink of the process had stayed with him for weeks.

Was it not time, he asked his father, to spend the vegetable money that waited as a credit at Mr Webster's store? Ben stopped whistling. Rachael's telegram was not the only correspondence received that morning. Mr Webster had written to advise them that the vegetables had fetched a disappointing price.

'If Mr Webster knew that our wool was on its way to market surely he'd advance us credit,' said Julian.

'He only extended us credit once and he said he wouldn't do it again. Besides we aren't desperate,' said his father.

But they were short on staples, the majority of the wool proceeds were allocated to a useless piano and their future income was reliant on vegetables. It sounded a lot like desperation to Julian.

'I bet Mr Fraser gets as much credit as he wants. Especially now he owns most of our sheep,' said Julian testily.

Slowly they walked the horses back to where the riverboats moored on their infrequent visits. His father's placid state barely altered while Julian felt as if he were standing at the edge of a massive chasm.

Squeals of laughter carried through the timber and they found Meg at the river. She had climbed a tree and was hanging from the ten-gallon bucket on the flying fox, riding it down to the water.

She shrieked as the bucket flew down the line, her weight raising a water-filled bucket from the river and sending it back in the opposite direction as she landed with a splash in the clear water. She drank from the river and then waded towards dry land.

'What are you doing here by yourself, Meg?' their father said sternly.

Meg's nose wrinkled as she stopped in the shallows among the weeds. She was barefoot, dressed in a pair of Julian's childhood short pants with a well-mended dress, which had been roughly cut off at the waist.

'Getting mussels.' She scooped up water and sand, throwing it between her legs. 'See?' She held up a mussel. A pile of wood was ready to be lit and, scattered among the twigs and leaves, were shells. 'I was hungry and Laura isn't about. This morning she said she didn't want to see anyone or speak to anyone. I haven't seen her for the longest time.'

'Leave the mussels and hop up with me, Meg,' said their father.

'No. I'm staying here. Laura's in an awful mood. She loved her hair more than anything. Mother used to say it was her best feature. Now Laura reckons she looks like a boy. Do I look like a boy, Julian? I thought if I were a boy, I could come with you and Father instead of staying with Laura. It'd be better to be a boy.'

Their father pulled a clay pipe from his coat and chewed on the stem. There was a case of pipes in the storehouse dating back to the 1880s, left over from the days when boundary riders, stockmen and other labourers expected pipes and tobacco as part of their rations.

'We best go look for your sister,' said their father, his teeth rattling against the stem. 'You'll ride with me, Meg, and don't go roving again.'

Just then a steamer rounded the bend in the river, towing a barge heavily laden with wool bales. *The Wandering Jew* thrashed towards them, Captain White at the helm. Julian's father raised the derby and the vessel's whistle replied, the wake hitting the bank in a series of waves as it steamed towards Bourke.

'Never get too close to *The Wandering Jew*,' said their father. 'It's already burned twice. And most things come in threes. Come, Meg, let's find your sister.'

Meg gave an exasperated sigh and then tossed all the mussels back into the water. 'It'll sure be something when I'm grown.'

'Lord save us,' said their father.

Meg placed a bare foot on her father's boot in the stirrup and scrambled up to sit before him. 'Mother promised to come home soon and that didn't happen, so why should I not come to the river if I want to?'

'You know why,' he replied, urging Goliath to a trot. 'We don't go walkabout.'

'No law against it,' said Meg quickly.

'There is if I say so,' he replied.

⪻ Chapter 9 ⪼

In their search for Laura, they rode towards the old well located a quarter mile from the house. Stopping a distance from the water source, their father handed Goliath's reins to Julian. The cunning gelding was reasonably obedient, as if aware he carried special cargo.

Meg took her hat off and chewed at the brim nervously as their father walked on alone. Julian tried his best to calm her, although his own thoughts were swinging violently, as if preparing for the worst. Meg's knuckles tightened on Goliath's mane.

The well, dug by Julian's great grandfather, had been brackish from the beginning. There was a fence around it now and he watched as his father hurdled it easily, then waited a long minute, his shoulders rising slightly. The older man slowly moved forwards.

The mudbrick structure had once included an A-frame with a rope for lowering a bucket. Now there was only the circular wall and the new timber boarding secured across the opening, though their mother had asked Ben for the repairs to be done before the tragedy. The original cover had rotted through. That was how they had lost Davey. Their little brother had fallen inside while playing and become entangled in rope.

Their father called out that all was fine, pounding the cover with a fist to confirm its soundness. He came bounding towards them, his stride lighter, surer. It was decided they would head east and do a circle. When they were moving again, he turned to Julian, as if wanting to apologise for putting his children through such stress. He ran a sun-darkened hand across the inch-long hair on Meg's head. Then he sat her hat back on and tapped her chin playfully.

Julian spat bile in the grass. It glistened as they rode on.

They travelled eastwards, riding two hundred yards apart, avoiding low branches and skirting the thick girths of widow-maker gums. The horses stepped through clumps of coolabah that had germinated at the edge of previous floodwater. Sweat gathered in the space between Julian's hat and eyebrows despite the cooling breeze. The first hour edged into the second and then a third. They headed south and then west, weaving back and forth through the scrub, *cooee*ing. At the river the horses pushed through lignum and nosed along the sandy bank. Then they rode back to check the homestead and, with still no sign of Laura, headed north. Julian flexed his fingers, loosening his hold on the reins. They were losing the day and hope began to slink away with it.

The ground and the sky had a habit of settling into each other and the trees, shrubs and grasses all looked the same unless a person knew better. He tried not to think the worst; tried not to contemplate what might have happened. What would become of their family if they lost Laura, when Davey's loss was still so raw?

Ben's concern showed in the tautness of his arms, in the way he shushed Meg to quiet, the way he drew on the reins every so often and stood tall in the stirrups as if capable of seeing further than a mortal man. Julian prayed that with a father's vision he could find his daughter and bring them all home safely, but age and Davey's loss had shaken loose Julian's belief in the rightness of the world and he now knew one man could not always be expected to save another.

And then she was in front of them, barely three miles from the house. A slight figure sitting under a shade-lean tree, a basket at her side. It should have been a sight to undo any father, especially one who had already lost a child, but there was only one major rule in Julian's family – and going walkabout alone was not tolerated without word of your intention. His father drew on the reins and simply waited. Laura hung a waterbag over a shoulder and gathered up the basket. She brushed down her skirt, her bald head shining pink in the afternoon light and then shoved on a straw hat. Her gaze was direct and unforgiving. Julian glimpsed the woman she was becoming.

'Thank heavens you're all right, girl,' their father called, his anger drifting away at the sight of her.

'Laura!' cried Meg, struggling to be released. 'Youse come home this instant. Wese been riding around all these long hours and youse not meant to go walkabout. Youse know nothing about what to do if youse find youseself in a stitch.'

Their father patted Meg's head. 'Well, that about covers walkabouts. Laura, get up on the horse with your brother.'

'But you were really angry, Father. Tell her how angry you were.' Meg waited for a reply and in response received another pat to the head. She shook away her father's hand.

'She knows we were worried. Isn't that right, Laura?' asked their father.

Laura walked silently towards them. Julian held out his arm. Laura hooked hers through his and he pulled her up onto the back of Legless. She had been gathering grasses, the type their mother used to weave baskets. As if there wasn't enough to do with their mother away.

'You all right?' Julian steered the mare to follow Goliath.

'He shouldn't have cut my hair. Mother wouldn't have,' she said. 'Frank told Meg we could have washed our hair with kerosene. If we were clear of any fire, we would have been all right.'

'What does it matter? It'll grow back,' replied Julian.

She smacked him hard across the shoulder.

The problem was it wasn't growing back as quickly as Meg's. Laura's hair was like a thin stubble, and there were patches on her skull where there was no growth at all. Was it due to the shock of being shaved? It reminded Julian of when a clump of their mother's hair had fallen out after Davey's death.

'You remember Whiskey Joe,' Julian said. 'The fella who idles about the Port-O-Bourke wharf. We saw him once. He was born bald. A shinier pate you never saw. People talk about him all the time. The tourists point and say, "Hey, it's Whiskey Joe." Guess what I'm saying is, if your hair wasn't to come back, you'd be the girl who was bald. Might even make some money out of it. That'd be something.'

'What woman wants to be *bald*? You're an idiot,' Laura hissed and slapped him again for good measure.

Julian guessed it wasn't the time to tell his sister that their mother wasn't coming home just yet. Not if he wanted to eat any time soon.

⪻ Chapter 10 ⪼

April

Autumn cleared out many of the pestering flies, mosquitos and gnats, and with the insects' departure, one by one the horses were being liberated of their fly-swishing glory. Four geldings and seven mares were as carefully snipped as Ben Dalhunty's two youngest children.

Julian straightened each length of coarse hair across a hay bale in the stables as his father smoothed the stumpy remnants of Goliath's tail and came to sit beside him. Ben smelt of saddle grease and the damp soil that he'd tilled earlier, scents ingrained as much in the stables as his skin.

'Are you sure about this, Father?'

Ben's decision to refurbish Julian's saddle blanket was sure to make Laura furious. She had been promised the next one.

Ben selected three of the cut lengths, matching them against each other. He and Laura were barely speaking. Their relationship had grown steadily worse since the day of the shaving, and if Laura could not forgive Ben's actions, nor could he forgive his daughter's wandering from the homestead. It was as if a stubborn anger were taking root inside them both. His sister's

75

previously amenable nature now barely cloaked a temper grown fiery.

His father examined the cut tails. 'If a horse is going to give something of itself for a human then the human concerned needs to be worthy of it. And the maker has to receive some satisfaction in the process. And I have to tell you, Julian, I'm right disappointed with Laura's attitude.'

'Have you told her that?' Julian knew it unlikely. Ben Dalhunty wasn't one for confrontation, unless it was directed towards Frank. The two men needled each other simply by sharing the same land. 'It's because of her hair.'

'It'll grow back in no time. Look at Meg's. It's short, but growing. Laura's overreacting. Women tend to live that way. You tell them something, they counter back like you're haggling over the purchase of a horse. Darndest thing. Takes a bit to learn to live with them. And we've got three to contend with. Mostly I head to the paddocks. But doing chores around the home is appreciated,' added his father, bringing his concentration back to the bristly tails.

It took time to plait a horse-hair blanket, to get the weave right. Saddle blankets made of horse's tails were a leftover from the old Dalhunty people, who were keen to use and make whatever they could in the days before Grandfather Alfred became obsessed with buying things new. The plaiting took skill and, to be fair to the animal, the cutting could only be done in the cooler months. However the benefit of a horse that never got saddle-sore with their own hair on their backs no matter how hard or far you rode them was not to be underrated.

Julian's stomach gurgled. Laura was cooking mutton. It was the last of the sheep-meat until their diminished flock reproduced. Ducks, parrots, fish and mussels substituted their diet year-round, but now they were to form the bulk of their meals and kangaroo was likely to be back on the menu. Although the wool was now sold and the proceeds deposited in the bank, their father had put off mailing their orders to Webster's General Store and the farming supply outlet. It was as if he were unwilling to spend any money

76

now they finally had some. Julian worried that the dust-gathering piano may have dwindled their precious funds far more than any of them realised. His worst suspicions grew real when his father let it slip that he was only paying Captain Ashby one half of what was owed for the piano. Ben sent the cheque promising a further payment when the vegetable business came good. Julian thought it a poor guarantee.

When their father finally mailed the orders for the station supplies, it was a number of weeks before the invoices arrived from the stores and then another span of time until he once again sat reluctantly at the kitchen table to write out their cheques. Only once the store-holders were paid in advance would the orders be filled and the goods released. That was what it meant to be a debtor. The river was sluggish again, with few steamers having navigated the muddy depths since January. A land trip to Bourke was the only alternative to collect their long-awaited supplies, however Ben wouldn't leave the property in case Rachael unexpectedly returned in their absence. Julian's repeated offer to travel to Bourke was also refused. Ben wanted his family to stay together. Julian could have pushed his case further. Making do was becoming harder. More importantly, the excitement of the arrival of the stores would brighten them all, especially his sisters. The reason he didn't set off in the dray was due to the neediness in his father's voice. A slight quaver that suggested uncertainty, of being afraid, of wanting what remained of his family around him. It worried Julian that the loss of Davey might always haunt them.

They walked the short distance from the stables to the house in failing light. Reginald the rooster was waiting on their return. Perched on the yard fence, he gave a single flap of his wings and then flopped to the ground as if a sentry being relieved. The white walls of the building darkened as the sun lowered. They scraped off their boots, took turns to wash in a barrel of water and shared a piece of towelling to dry off. The pungent aroma of chicken manure barrowed to the vegetable plot hung in the air, replacing the once pervasive smell of sheep.

Inside, Ben stopped at the drawing-room door. The room had once been the original selector's hut built by Julian's great-grandfather. When the Dalhuntys' increasing prosperity had called for a finer residence, the hut had been incorporated into the larger house at the insistence of the station's first Mrs Dalhunty, who had been known for her sentimentality. The daub and wattle hut with its single window was allocated as a storage space during Grandfather Alfred's life. Now it was crammed with furniture and books and partially wall-papered with images from illustrated magazines. Carriages, street scenes, landscapes and distinguished personalities fitted neatly across boards and were smoothed over grooves. As a boy, Julian received a history lesson on the members of the Royal family by perusing the pictures.

Julian's father went to the piano. 'Your great-grandmother was a fine pianist. She brought one with her when she came here. Refused to leave its side for fear the crew of the steamer would damage it. She sat next to it on the barge in a large carved chair for five days while she was towed along the Darling. Your great-grandfather was at the river when the steamer arrived. He said it was the most extraordinary sight. A beautiful woman in white silk and lace, strands of pearls strung about her neck, a maid holding a parasol. His new wife sitting there like a queen arriving to take possession of her throne.'

'What happened to the piano?' asked Julian.

'The mice ate the silk panels, the white ants invaded, then the flood came. Your mother and I watched it float out the door. Saw it bobble about like a buoy on the ocean until it was marooned on an anthill. Eventually we used it to fire the copper. Still, we have one again now.' He ran a hand across the polished lid. 'When your mother comes home you'll hear what a first-rate pianist she is. It's something that strikes me, Julian. How is it a person cannot be here and yet all the objects they used and loved remain, as if nothing's happened. It takes some getting used to.'

'I guess,' said Julian.

'What? No adamant opinion?' replied his father.

'Did you buy the piano for Mother or yourself?' asked Julian angrily. After hearing this story, he now suspected the latter.

Ben smoothed his shirt. A long-dead insect had left a residue of yellow-edged holes across the once cream material. He tucked the shirttail firmly into too-tight trousers, fighting with the waistband, and then tugged free the detachable collar hanging loosely about his lined neck. 'I'm so hungry I could eat a duck through the base of a cane-bottomed chair.'

Julian stared at the useless piano and then followed his father from the room.

The scent of roasted meat led them towards the kitchen, their hunger becoming concern as they realised they could also smell smoke. Julian and his father increased their pace. The air grew thicker. They entered the hazy kitchen where Meg sat blinking watery eyes. Laura lifted the roasting tray from the oven and sat it on the table with a thud next to bunches of drying lavender and bush mint. She shone with sweat and was the colour of the beets they sometimes grew in the spring. The joint was burned black, the swedes and potatoes shrivelled. Shrunken dates sizzled in the fat – Frank's harvest, infested by grubs and eaten by birds, had been poor. Laura fetched a bowl of warrigal greens blanched to destruction.

Ben peered at the meat and then removed Rachael's needlework and the months-old telegram from her setting. He glanced about for somewhere to place the items and finally propped them on the windowsill. Then he moved to the head of the table.

'God bless this family and this food so lovingly cooked by Laura in her mother's absence. Amen.'

Julian poked at the dried-up swedes as Laura removed the herbs from the table. Their father stabbed at the roast with a fork and sliced deep into the meat with a carving knife, his biceps stretching the material of his shirt as he sawed through the mutton. 'God's own country,' he praised.

≪ Chapter 11 ≫

Early June

Nearly five months after Rachael's departure, supplies reached Dalhunty Station, courtesy of the Sisters of Mercy, who steamed up and down the river between Bourke and Brewarrina, administering as much to the people along the water as the schools they travelled between. With the arrival of the steamer, Julian quickly left off trying to salvage the windmill that lay collapsed further along the riverbank and rode towards the boat. He remained convinced that the Sisters' shallow draught vessel was kept afloat by the twin efforts of their pilot, Mr Peters, and their Catholic faith. They navigated the snagging timbers that could quickly bring a boat to ruin, delivering what little mail the Dalhuntys received and the occasional well-read newspaper. A link to the rest of the world. The tightness in Julian's stomach eased as he trotted towards Mr Peters, who was unloading their supplies.

'Julian.' Mr Peters gave a bow and tipped his hat. 'It's a perfectly glorious day, is it not? And we bring long-awaited goods, thanks to the slight run in the river.'

'Thank you so much. We really appreciate this. I'll go straight home and fetch the dray.'

'Not at all. The Sisters were in Webster's store and heard you were yet to collect your order, and so here we are.'

Sister Rosalee stepped ashore, the black cloth of her order fluttering. 'Are you quite well, Julian?'

'Yes, Sister Rosalee, and thank you for delivering our stores.'

'They were ordered some time ago, I believe. Is everything all right? You are all coping with your mother's absence?'

'Yes, we've just been busy. That's all.'

Sister Rosalee gave a beatific smile. 'It takes time to recover from the loss of a loved one, especially a child. Be gentle to others and yourself.' Her hand disappeared into the folds of her habit and reappeared with a letter. 'I hope this brings comfort.'

Julian recognised his mother's handwriting.

'God has a plan for all of us,' said Sister Rosalee.

So far Julian considered the one mapped out for the Dalhuntys to be pretty poor.

On Julian's return to the homestead he spied his father at the stables near the dray and called out the good news of the sisters' arrival with their stores.

'Damn and blast Frank.' Ben hitched up his toffee-coloured trousers until the waistband was cocked up on one hip and dangling about his rump on the opposite side. One of the wheels on the dray had been removed and was leaning against the stable wall. Ben stared at it as if planning revenge. 'The stores are here, you say? Well then, he did take the wheel off the blasted dray. Actually removed it. Now we're forced to use Henrietta to transport our stores. Unbelievable.' Ben walked around the dray. 'How did he know there was a fresh coming?'

'Maybe there were signs.' Julian was impressed by Frank's skulduggery.

'What signs?' demanded his father. 'Were the birds flying backwards? Did the frogs lose their croak?'

Frank loped past on Henrietta, following the serpentine track to the river, beaten to powder by the camel's hooves. 'This is a very fine camel and she is underutilised. We will transport the goods for you. No need for thanks.'

Ben gave chase. 'How advantageous to find you ready for the task,' he puffed, jogging alongside Henrietta, holding up the dangling trousers.

'Hooshta!' The camel increased its pace at Frank's command.

'Come back here!' His father shook a fist in the air. 'And stop digging holes in my land, Frank. There is no treasure.'

'Frank Ukulele Dalhunty to you, good sir!' shouted Frank.

'Father, let him go,' called Julian.

'He's mad as a hatter. I should tie him to that camel of his and point him north.' His father started moving towards the homestead. 'Go with him, Julian. Make sure everything gets back here in one piece.'

'Wait. There's something else. From Mother.' Julian delivered the mail.

'A letter?' Ben pushed the green-and-gold cricketer's cap to the back of his head and lit up like a candle. Then, just as quickly, the brightness was snuffed out. 'A letter. Not a telegram?' He pored over the writing as if a lengthy correspondence was written on the envelope, and then marched stiffly towards the homestead. 'Don't mention it to the girls. I'll tell them tonight. It's hard enough your sisters mope about for days after rotten news. I need them to at least finish their work for today.'

'How do you know it's bad news?'

'Because it's not a telegram.' Julian could tell his father was disappointed.

'Oh.' Julian understood. A telegram meant the death of Aunt Nancy, and the swift return of their mother, a letter suggested the woman held on. What a sorry place he found himself in, wishing the worst for a woman he had never met.

The whole family waited impatiently for Frank and Henrietta at the back gate, the Englishman making a spectacle on his return from the river by embarking on celebratory loops around the homestead, which Henrietta submitted to with her customary loping stride. Their cargo was tied on either side of the hump. Crates and bags bulged from her flanks. A rattle suggesting breakage.

'We'll be here until dark at this rate,' complained Laura as Frank passed by for a second time.

Meg tilted her head to one side. 'Or until Henrietta falls over.'

'He's certainly making the most of his win,' said their father impatiently.

'Frank says sometimes the desert sand still gets in his eyes. Maybe that's why he hasn't stopped.' Meg leant her chin on the fence rail and dangled her arms over the side.

'You shouldn't listen to the rubbish Frank tells you, Meg. For all we know he's never seen the desert,' Ben said. Then he yelled out, 'You get back here, Frank! Right now.' Angry veins stuck out in his neck.

'Well, Frank still reckons he's Grandfather's honoured son, which does make you Frank's brother, and he wants to move into the overseer's house, but it needs a roof,' said Meg.

'*Et tu, Brute?*' Their father looked at the sky. 'I've had enough. You do realise, Meg, there is no proof Frank and my father ever had a conversation about him living here permanently. In fact, my father only let him stay because I fancied having a camel on the property on the condition that when I grew tired of the novelty Frank would be asked to leave. And I have asked him to leave. On numerous occasions.'

'He is a little hard of hearing at times. That's probably due to his family leaving Somerset and living in India when his father was in the British Army. All the gunfire and canons,' said Meg.

'I've never heard such codswallop,' replied their father.

Meg crossed her arms. 'I'm just saying.'

On completion of the fourth turn about the house Frank and the camel stopped, and with a show of expertly placed strikes of the crop and a guttural complaint from Henrietta, he eased the animal slowly to the ground. There was a gaseous explosion that caused all to take a step backwards and the distinct cracking of bone. Julian could not be sure if it was the camel's knees or the ageing Frank's.

They eagerly unpacked their supplies as a family, carrying each precious parcel into the homestead, along the hall and through the breezeway to the kitchen, checking the items against the invoice, while taking turns to alternately stick their fingers into the new tin of golden syrup and the sugar bag. Meg and Laura talked excitedly about the weevilly bags of flour as they dragged them into the pantry, bread having been non-existent for some weeks. There was a large quantity of stores, including currants, tea, rice, salt, copious bottles of Worcestershire sauce and a single large hessian bag of potatoes, which would see them out until their own vegetables were grown. And, among the other foodstuffs, dates. All the while, Julian worried at the contents of their mother's letter.

Frank, having finished unpacking, sat cross-legged next to Henrietta as Julian carried nails, tins of kerosene, axle grease and a bundle of fencing wire to the stables. He returned to see Meg walking from the house, holding the tin of dates as if it were a crown. Julian leant against the garden fence in amusement as Frank rose, accepting the fruit with the same ceremony in which they were offered. He placed a hand over his heart and then seized the date tin.

'Frank, Father doesn't believe you were in the desert or India,' said Meg.

'What would he know.' Frank shook the tin.

'But you were born in Somerset?' she persisted.

Frank stared at the tin of dates. 'I am a British Imperial subject. One quarter English, one quarter Irish.'

'And the other half?' asked Meg. 'That's English too?'

'Do I need another half?' Frank thought on this as if it were a troublesome problem. 'I have been to Timbuktu,' he replied as if this was the answer Meg sought, 'a place far away, at the end of the world. The most distant place imaginable. I am like Lady Duff-Gordon, the English writer your Grandfather Alfred told me about. "I didn't like Cairo anymore," she said, "it was growing more Cockney by the day." She was a very clever lady. So, Henrietta and I went to *Timbuktu*, like she did.'

Meg narrowed her eyes. 'You've never mentioned you'd been to Egypt before, and you told me you found Henrietta wandering in the desert. Here in Australia.'

'Did I? All deserts look the same, little one. Sand everywhere. Plays havoc with one's sight. Henrietta came with me to Australia in a boat. We shared a cabin.' He patted Henrietta's big-lipped mouth and she hissed in annoyance.

'Are you talking codswallop to me?' queried Meg, wiggling her backside.

Julian left the fence and walked towards them. 'Sounds like it.'

Frank opened the tin and offered Meg a date before popping one in his mouth, a dreamy expression forming as he chewed. Then he carefully replaced the lid, ignoring Julian.

'I'm not sure we should be giving you dates after what you did to the dray. Father is pretty cranky with you,' said Julian.

'My dear fellow, he's always cranky. Always believes he knows best. Never listens. He's always yelling, yelling, yelling.' Frank stepped closer to Julian and Meg and glanced about. 'I'm sorry to tell you this, however my Honoured Brother is slightly unhinged. A gentleman never wears a swallow-tail coat *and* a derby, it's quite infra dig.'

'Please save us,' droned Julian. 'Honestly, Frank, I think you're both slightly off kilter. Can't you try and get on with each other?'

Frank snorted haughtily.

'Father does behave strangely at times,' Meg conceded, 'but he never shared a cabin with a camel.'

'I suggest that Benjamin goes to Sydney to see Mrs Dalhunty. That will help his crankiness. Your mother's sister is not so sick, I think,' said Frank thoughtfully.

'Don't listen to him, Meg,' answered Julian.

'Every few years this sister writes she is ill. Every few years she asks your mother go to Sydney. Every few years,' said Frank.

'That's ridiculous. How could you know that?' asked Julian.

'This Honorary Brother has not always disagreed with your father. Now you are grown he talks to you.' He pointed at Julian. 'Hooshta.' He struck Henrietta lightly on the leg with a crop and she spat in response before struggling to standing. 'Yes. I feel the same way.' He led his charge towards the roofless cottage, the dates held tightly under an arm.

'What does he mean about Mother?' asked Meg.

'Pay no attention.' Julian was also trying to make sense of what the older man had said.

Their father walked from the house onto the veranda and called to them. He waved them over and then retreated to the squatter's chair. One leg was slung across an extended armrest, his posterior sunk into the sagging length of canvas, the white-washed walls of the homestead luminous in the dwindling light. A chill wind had risen during the afternoon. It pelted bits of the country at their bodies, as if trying to start a fight, and moaned around the corners of the house.

Laura moved along the wall, keeping her body square to the building. Her hair was a scant two inches long and a length of material concealed a burn on her arm no amount of lard would heal.

'Is there a reason we're all shivering out here?' she asked.

'We're still on rations,' said Ben. 'At least until the vegetable business picks up.'

With this information digested, their father waved an envelope, drowning out the complaints. The letter, he told them, was from their mother, as if the square of folded paper would solve the world's problems.

As Julian predicted, Laura and Meg were instantly annoyed not to have been told sooner. He looked past his family to the paddock beyond, where a darting magpie reached a kookaburra, pecking at his back mid-flight. Laura pressed her shoulder blades to the pitted wall.

'Is Mama coming home?' asked Meg. "Cause she's been away long enough.'

Julian was astounded when his father tore open the envelope. The letter had sat through the afternoon unread. Ben's eyes flitted to each of his children as he pulled the letter free, unfolded it and held it close to silently read. Laura was clutching at her shawl, hope as vivid as a green shoot. Julian wished he'd told her about the letter's arrival, wished he had forewarned her. He wasn't convinced the mail was good news, having come at the start of winter.

Their father leant back in the squatter's chair. A quietness gathered. 'She's not coming back. Not yet.'

'It's ridiculous. You must write her immediately and tell her to return!' Laura adjusted the shawl, waiting for their father to respond. 'She can't stay away forever.'

'*She* is your mother, Laura,' Ben snapped. 'And we'd all be grateful if our meal wasn't ruined again tonight. Stop spouting forth from Mrs Wicken's domestic bible and wasting daylight with those herbs of yours, they neither feed us or get your chores done.'

Laura looked to Julian. He was as stunned as she was by their father's outburst. Benjamin Dalhunty was not one for rousing, as their mother called it. She had complained about his lack of parental discipline for years. And now here was their father, showing a side none of his children had ever witnessed before.

'Don't speak to me like that. Why don't you contact the mission? There are girls there being trained to clean and cook,' Laura stated. 'The Dalhuntys had staff in the past. It's ridiculous I have to work like a slave.'

'No,' their father said quietly.

'Why not? If you don't care for my cooking then maybe someone else should do it.'

'Mind your manners, girl!' Ben's words were sharp enough to force Laura back inside the house. The front door slammed.

Julian concentrated on the line creasing his skin in a sweep from his wrist almost to the base of his index finger. Their family was falling apart. How had he not seen it coming sooner? Life was difficult for Laura in their mother's absence. From dawn to dusk she swept and scrubbed floors, dusted furniture, bucketed water and prepared their food, although her dedication was beginning to wane. More than once he'd picked up a broom and swept boot-deposited manure from the hallway. In contrast, his father's suffering had crept up on Julian. He saw now how Ben's loneliness was burrowing into him, making his shoulders stooped, his movements lethargic. His joy for everyday living had been replaced with a deepening sorrow.

Ben scanned the note. Even in the diminishing light Julian could tell there were few lines. Only a single page's worth, barely enough to warrant the distance travelled. When Ben began to read aloud, the words caught a little, as if they couldn't quite escape, and Julian felt his father's hurt, as hard and as tight as his own.

Aunt Nancy had rallied since their mother's arrival and they had started going on brief walks to the Sydney Harbour foreshore, where the land met the sea. A whole paragraph was devoted to the bracing air and exhilarating salt spray before the core of the letter was revealed. The doctor had concluded Aunt Nancy's improving health was a brief respite before the inevitable, and with that prognosis Rachael's decision to remain in Sydney and see out the dire situation until the end was made.

'How long will that be?' asked Meg, who'd been sitting quietly. 'Until summer? Cause if Laura keeps on being the cook there ain't no telling what will happen. We might all get a fit of gripe, or worse, like when we ate that crook fish a year back. Why we were all so sick we filled our p—'

'That's enough, Meg. Only God knows when your mother will return.' Ben folded the letter in half, then in half again, flattening the paper on the arm of the chair. 'We must bear up under the strain of it all, eh?'

'I'm just saying.' Meg ran her feet back and forth across the floorboards where she sat and then reached for the letter and, holding it tightly, ran inside the house.

About them the outbuildings grew shadowy. It seemed to Julian in the summer they waited a lifetime for night to come. They would sprawl outside while the light plodded towards the horizon, sometimes dragging the worst of the heat with it, other times leaving a good portion behind. Now winter was before them and they would suck in their bellies against the cold, begging for the heat to come again.

Ben stepped from the veranda into the twilight. Julian followed to where he leant on the fence surrounding the vegetable plot. Along the bottom were a series of small burrows where rabbits were trying to invade.

'Three months. I reckoned on her being away for three months. It could be six. Perhaps more. I shouldn't have let her go.' He tugged on the top wire and it sprung back when released, the tinny noise vibrating. 'It's the lack of feminine comforts they most miss. My father's first wife passed away from melancholy. The second, my mother, loved it here. Loved the sky and the Darling. Even loved the dry spells. On a Sunday after Bible reading, she would take her easel to the river. Always changing, she would say. But she was lonely. Maybe if she'd borne more children.' He rested his forehead on the top wire. 'It is good land. Well, it was in the past. We just need a break in the season. A long break. Ten years or more.' He laughed and caught sight of Julian's hand tentatively reaching out. 'I'm all right, lad.'

'Has Aunt Nancy been sick before?' asked Julian, unable to shake what Frank had said about previous letters from her.

'There's been the odd telegram over the years. Nothing serious enough to warrant a visit, in your mother's opinion. We will have to get on as best we can. In a place like Sydney, every time a person takes a step out their front door, their pockets are soon empty and we only had one wool clip to sell. I wrote and told her to be careful with our money.'

'She's spending our wool money?' Julian thought of his father's procrastination when ordering their stores. He'd assumed it was due to the piano. Here was another reason. Between their mother and the purchase of the piano their bank account was undoubtedly suffering. 'We shouldn't have bought the piano,' challenged Julian. It was the first time he had said it outright and he felt better for voicing his concerns, but it was also too late. The piano was theirs. And their mother was still down south. Spending.

'When I'm dead and buried, you can make the decisions,' his father said bluntly.

'It'll be too late by then.'

'Are you finished? Are you *quite finished*?'

Spittle sprayed towards Julian and he took a step backwards. Night was drawing in, and suddenly the air felt thicker and colder. This wasn't the man who stepped outside every morning with a jaunty hat, hitching his trousers and singing the blessings of their home. Julian pictured a worsening spiral, one where his father, known for his unconventionality, was replaced by a stranger and a bitter one at that.

'Maybe Mother is tired of being here.' Laura wound the shawl tightly about her body. Neither man had heard her arrive.

'Now, now. That's not true, Laura,' said their father gently, although his answer came with a querying tone as if he wasn't quite sure himself. 'I'm sorry for what I said earlier. You're doing a fine job.'

'The ibis has been stewing for a good two hours, so don't complain when you finally sit down to eat it,' she replied.

Julian wasn't in any rush. He had shot one of the Ibis's legs off by accident and a further two bullets were needed to bring the bird down. His once excellent marksmanship was as directionless as their lives, and the wildlife was bearing the pain.

Ben walked into the dark. He wasn't yet hungry. Once they were alone Laura asked flippantly after Julian's new saddle blanket. He waited for the bite of her tongue but her sarcasm was eroded by tiredness and pragmatism. She was far too busy to go out riding, but she could be of help if his saddle-blanket ever needed mending. Laura had saved her shorn hair from the fire. It was clean and dry, lying in a drawer.

'Your hair is growing back,' said Julian for the umpteenth time. 'It's already a few inches long.'

Laura ignored this. 'It's been nearly five months since Mother left. Sometimes I doubt Aunt Nancy *is* dying. People have been known to stretch things to get their own way. And now Mother's walking at the beach and living in a grand house, making the most of her holiday. She may not have gone to Sydney with that intention but it would be hard to up and leave once you got a taste for it. And Mother misses her old life, you know. She talks about it. Usually when we're sewing. The houses and parties and nice clothes. The food and domestics. The ease of that life.'

'I understand that she must miss it. She married Father when he was wealthy, and now we're not, but she did take wedding vows.'

'Yes, but she can't forget what it means to have money. To have a cook and a lady's maid. People to clean. Most people have Aboriginal help in the homesteads. We had them in the past. I can't understand why Father's so stubborn, or why I was born into this generation. Our grandparents used to take Father to the seaside for holidays. Mother spent summers in the Blue Mountains before she married.'

Listening to Laura got Julian riled. What she said made sense. Either a person was dying, or they were not. There wasn't any middle ground.

Laura touched Julian's arm, so slightly he barely noticed. 'Father loves Mother more than any of us. That's going to be our biggest problem. If she doesn't come home.'

The uncertainties Laura raised stayed with Julian while he ate the stewed wading bird. Across the table his father's plate remained untouched, the food congealing in the cold air. Julian could not recall the last time the four of them had eaten together. Laura washed plates in the bucket and Meg wiped a dripping cloth across the kitchen table, lifting Julian's elbows to clean around him. Every bite Julian took chafed his stomach as he thought of their mother in her new life and their father outside in the chilly night. If a man was to spend all his life with one woman, raise a family, run a business, keep everyone fed, then there had to be an immensity of feeling at the very core to choose her. Which made the possibility of their mother's desertion even worse, and his thoughts of leaving impossible.

⊰ Chapter 12 ⊱

Early July

On the morning they would be shearing their few remaining
sheep, Julian sat in the kitchen as his sisters prepared breakfast in the pre-dawn. With the possibility of Rachael returning
home unexpectedly no longer likely, Ben was recently back from
Bourke, having delivered the latest crop of vegetables, for which
he received a paltry price. Laura, her slow-growing hair covered by
a scarf, turned a freshly baked loaf from the tin. She cut the loaf,
saving half for the next day, and then sat the bread on the table
along with the pot of tea. Meg yawned and struck the surface of
the water in the bucket, cracking the ice. She dunked a pannikin
in and slurped. The kerosene lamp flickered.

'Don't them Bourke women know the Chinese fertilise their
vegetables. And it ain't chook poop I'm talking about either.' Meg
reached for a slice of bread, splashing water from the pannikin as
she sat. 'That's what wese should do. Don't let Bony go skulking
about. We should bucket up our own doings and spread them
around the vegetables. Bet youse the price for our vegetables would
go sky-high.'

'Meg, that is revolting,' said Laura.

93

Julian leant over and tickled his sister, feeling Meg's ribs through the sleeveless kangaroo-hide jacket she'd belted tightly about her lean frame.

'I'm just saying it as it is,' Meg broke the bread into pieces. 'If it's good enough for the Chinese—'

Laura clattered a teaspoon against the side of her pannikin. 'That's enough.'

'Wese use to talk about everything when I was little. I dreamt last night wese were a family again. When we'd sit in the drawing room and Father would read to us. Then after Davey died Father stopped reading and he and Mother went for walks instead.'

Julian was unsure how to respond. 'They were sad, Meg.'

'Everyone was sad. What made their sadness more special than ours?'

Laura rested the beginnings of a quilt on the table and measured a man's tie alongside the pinned squares. She lifted the scissors and, with a flourish, cut the tie in half. 'Yes, it's from the not-to-be-touched Dalhunty ancestral trunks. Father won't even notice. The front gate's been broken for a month and the tap on the water tank's leaking. If Mother was here, they would have been repaired immediately.'

'I was waiting for Father to notice before I fixed them.' Julian opened the kitchen door. The breezeway was empty. The house quiet. Frost layered the grass. He returned to the table.

'He left real early. I checked. His boots were gone.' Meg pulled her knife from its sheath and picked at the edge of the table with the blade. Her hair was a mass of short curls bobbing about her ears.

Laura got up and cleared their father's unused place setting. Julian slowly interlaced his fingers. Most mornings there was barely time for a gulp of black tea at dawn before his father was out the door. With Goliath quickly saddled he would spur the flighty horse beneath a waking sky and Julian would have to tail him through the scrub at breakneck speed, their few sheep scattering from their path. Although he would urge Legless to keep pace, it was often difficult to reach his father's side. He feared Ben was trying to outrun the new life they found themselves in. And he worried for them all.

Julian swallowed the last of his tea and offered to read to Meg that evening. She lit up, bright and grateful. Laura gave Julian a small nod. With their father's increasing detachment, the truth of how things were blistered up between them. They were forming a new family, and there was only the three of them.

As Julian left in search of his father, Frank and Henrietta arrived on their usual loop. It occurred to Julian the issue of the roofless house had not been mentioned for some weeks. Although on last count there were three newly dug holes of varying depths scattered among the palm trees. It was highly probable that Frank's treasure hunt for Alfred's strongbox would last for his entire life.

The camel slowed at Frank's urging. 'Not even the sight of this very fine camel can make this brother of mine glad. He is in a very damaging mood. Actually, it could be stated that Dalhunty men are always in awful moods before a calamity, and Henrietta does not like a calamity. She usually has an attack of nervousness.' Even as he spoke the camel deposited a mass of turds on the ground. 'This is not a good place. It is better suited to crows and dingos, not sheep and fine living.'

It would have been better not to prolong the conversation, however the question in Julian's mind would not shake free. 'When do you think my mother will return, Frank?'

'My dear boy, your mother is a very fine woman. But this very fine woman is like a very fine camel. She should not be allowed to stray.' Frank tugged on Henrietta's lead and they walked away.

At the stables Julian saddled Legless and rode to the woolshed as the sun rose. The sixty-stand construction was in semi-darkness. Goliath shivered in the bitter air. He tied the reins of the mare to a broken post and patted Goliath's rump, then walked inside, past the wool bins and skirting tables. Ben was shearing by the light of a slush lamp, the ruffle of white wool spilling onto the board as the blade-shears cut the fleece free. His arm moved slowly with precision, veins swelling, the pale blue of his singlet rippling across his pot belly and gaunt frame.

He rested the shears on the boards, shoved the blade-nicked ewe down the chute and stretched his back. 'Good. You're here.'

Julian counted the sheep in the pen. The woollies were bunched together at the rear. He moved close to his father until they were inches apart. 'Have you been up half the night?'

Ben squeezed the shears shut and let them spring open. Repeated the action.

'Father, talk to me. It's ages since you sat at the table with the girls.'

The sheep's hooves drummed the timber slats in the pen. In the deep brown of his father's eyes, Julian saw a grown man desperately trying to form a response.

'I know you're upset Mother's staying away for so long, but you can't keep ignoring Meg.' Julian might well have been speaking to a statue. He turned away, intending to leave, but then found himself blurting out, 'And you can't expect Laura and me to take your place. You have to behave like a father. At least try and get one of the Aboriginal girls from the mission to help Laura.'

'Your mother won't have them in the homestead. She says the pretty ones are too pretty.'

'That's ridiculous.'

'You heard me. There was a girl here, eight years ago. Maryanne. She was smart. You remember her. I talked to her a lot, tried to help locate her family. Her sisters were also domestics, but she had no idea where they were. They were all given new names, you see. English names. Untraceable names. It was wrong, and still is. All a person has is family.'

Julian recalled the cakes Maryanne made, the way she hummed in the kitchen and made him clean his face with a wet cloth. He'd never considered the possibility of her having a different name. Yet his father had, deeply.

'Maryanne and I were friendly, and she liked clothes. I gave her a fuchsia shawl that your mother never wore and Rachael took umbrage. She said nice people weren't in the habit of befriending the help or offering them gifts. Soon after, I was out riding one afternoon and I saw the Aboriginal women, including Maryanne, walking back to their camp. Your mother had told them all to leave. Said she was prepared to cook and clean if it meant decorum was restored to the household. After that we spent three years advertising for a city girl, with no result. That was the last of the domestics at Dalhunty Station.'

Here was an insight into his parents' marriage. One that measured Ben's compassion against what Rachael considered accepted norms. Worse, it showed his mother as mulish, and all for the sake of an unwanted shawl.

'*That's* the reason? I've never heard of anything so stupid.'

'Tell your mother that.'

A dreary light showed in the skylight overhead. 'We need to be the family we were before Mother left,' implored Julian. 'You need to be there for Meg and Laura.'

'You don't understand.'

'Then tell me,' said Julian, 'because I'm having a hard time putting up with all of this.'

'*You're* having a hard time?' His father opened and closed the shears. 'I shouldn't have let your mother go. It was within my rights as a husband to stop her.' He spat on a stone and gave the shears a brief sharpening, three quick strokes on either side.

'Then why didn't you?' asked Julian.

'Because she's never asked for anything since the Great Flood. Ever. And then there's Davey. It was an accident that shouldn't have happened. The bloody boards. I intended to replace them.'

'It wasn't your fault.'

'Tell your mother that. Get me another, will you, son.'

Julian dragged a wool-heavy sheep from the pen to his father, and Ben started shearing, the blades moving deftly across skin. Once Ben finished, Julian dabbed tar on the odd bloody nick, and then pushed the bedraggled animal down the chute to freedom. He gathered the fleece, throwing it high and wide across the table.

He dragged another sheep from the pen for his father and then returned to the fleece on the table, where he pulled burr and dung from the edges and rolled it up, the soft underside showing.

With every shorn sheep his father straightened his back and wiped his trousers to staunch his bleeding calluses.

Before even reconciling himself to the asking, the question was there. 'Will she come back?' Rather than fetching another ewe, Julian waited. A reply was too long in coming. 'You could send her a telegram. Ask her to come home.'

Slanted light streamed down to rest on the coarse grey hairs poking up from the singlet his father wore.

'You don't think she's coming home, do you?' said Julian. 'If you did you'd ask her straight out to leave Aunt Nancy. Tell her that she's got responsibilities here and they're sure as heck more important than flouncing around Sydney.'

'Fine. I'll send a telegram. I'll tell your mother we're useless without her. That her husband is the most useless of all. Incapable of managing a property or growing a decent vegetable or saving their youngest boy.'

Julian immediately thought back to the days following Davey's death. To Rachael wailing in the drawing room, Ben's attempts at comfort beaten into submission, until finally his father stopped trying to offer solace, and the rest of the family was left to stumble through their grief alone, without the support of their mother and wife. Rachael was not accusatory in nature and to Julian's knowledge never once blamed Ben for the rotting boards that cost Davey's life, though Ben's litany of excuses for not attending to the repairs persisted for some months before Rachael told her husband to stop.

Ben threw the shears, the pointy ends stuck in the timber board wobbling fiercely. 'Nothing's changed. I'll tell Rachael that, and I'm sure she'll get the first train home. You want to add anything? Do you?'

He'd turned dark, but Julian wasn't scared. In some ways it was a relief to know that the man who waded through debt and decay and played fancy-dress most of his life did recognise their problems. And now Julian did as well.

⋘ Chapter 13 ⋙

Mid-August

Where once the homestead had lain tranquil through the long nights, cradled by the land, now Julian listened to his father's footfall in the hallway at midnight. The boards creaked as he left his room and again as he walked the breezeway to the kitchen. Back and forth his father traipsed, as if the action might solve the angst within, before he headed outside to the woodpile.

Julian lay awake as Bony howled and the crack of axe met timber, the rustle of mice and the flap of a night bird filling the void between. Ben's worst nights always followed the arrival of a letter from Rachael. Although the family gathered like the seagulls Rachael wrote of, ready for any crumb she cared to throw their way, they already knew how the letter would end. Afterwards, their father would sit Meg and Laura at the kitchen table and ensure they wrote a reply, including his own message in the envelope before it was sealed. Julian rejected all attempts to put pen to paper. How could he explain to his family that he had nothing to say to a mother who had drifted into a better life?

It was at such a time, following the receipt of a letter, that Julian sat hunched on the bed in his room, clasping the stitched rabbit pelts to his body in the seeping cold. Their mother had visited Katoomba in the Blue Mountains. There, she had eaten scones and clotted cream, drank tea with a friend and had taken in the sights of her childhood. Julian rubbed at the glass, creating a smeared hole. Outside, his father was pacing back and forth, his steps accompanied by the wind through the palm fronds.

When the splintering of timber rang out and their chained half-breed mutt began to yowl, Julian smacked at the wall with a fist. Next month it was September. The SS *Osterley* was due in Sydney. He smacked the wall again and cursed his mother. Was she even aware of what she was putting her family through? Did she even care? He thought of his plans. Catch the train to Sydney. Find employment on the docks. Perhaps gain working passage on the steamer. He must find another opportunity. Another steamer. There was little choice. In the meantime, pray he must for his mother's return. For normality to be restored.

Yet still his mother's behaviour irked him. Was there really a need to write of her new life with such enjoyment? Better to describe their aunt's slow decline than draw attention to her pleasure, but there was barely a mention of the ailing woman except in terms of *prolongness* – was there even such a word? Julian rested his brow on the cold glass. The vegetables were frost-bitten. The potatoes nearly eaten. And there were still a few weeks of winter left.

Winter made him think of summer, and the chance of rain, and a young woman playing the piano. Miss Carlisle. Her penetrating gaze. The way she kept apart from them when she alighted from the steamer. Not particularly friendly – unsure perhaps, for she had offered unspoken sympathy on leaving. It was a singular kindness that ensured Julian would not forget Miss Carlisle. He could fill a whole afternoon riding around their empty paddocks selecting first names that might be hers. And she was with Julian quite regularly on the days when his father woke closed and sour, and often in bed when he made busy beneath the covers. It was something to have the memory of her. He held it close.

A shape moved in the distance. It travelled quickly beyond the homestead yard, an outline magnified by the chill clarity of the air. It might well have been a kangaroo except Julian knew better. He slid out the window, holding tight to the pelt, and ran across the icy ground, avoiding his father's nocturnal activities around the wood heap. The harshness of August hit his lungs with force as he straddled the fence and struck out after Meg. His sister was now moving at a steadier pace, avoiding Frank's burrows as she cut through the grove of palms towards the dried soak that in a rare season could overflow into a narrow chain of watering holes.

They were over a mile from the homestead when he finally lost sight of her. Julian stopped and listened. Though he called Meg's name, there was no answer. He moved slowly and came across a lean-to constructed in the middle of three close-growing trees. He crawled into the rough bark dwelling and found Meg lighting a kerosene lamp. The area was cramped, he could barely sit upright. A waterbag hung from a nail in the tree trunk next to her head and the place stank of mice. 'What are you doing out here in the middle of the night?'

'Youse make more noise than a galloping horse.' She rubbed her bare feet and then tucked them under a stack of blankets. 'Don't be telling me I shouldn't be out here, Julian. I like it better than Laura snoring and complaining and Father stomping and chopping all the long night.'

'But aren't you cold?' He blew on his fingers.

'I found these blankets. There's a broken board on the western side of the house that we're not allowed to use anymore. I crawled right in and no one saw. There's a room with a long table in it and more bedrooms. There's one with a big four-poster bed, and a fancy light with glass baubles and little lanterns hangs from the ceiling. Is that the place where Great-grandfather and Grandfather died? I heard you talking to Father about it when I was little.'

'That's the room,' he replied.

'So youse seen it? Thought so. It sure is big. Them high ceilings and that shiny wood. Don't reckon I'd be doing my dying there, though, if I was Father. It's just too much dying in one place.

Probably too much dying for you too, if youse was to die there,' said Meg.

'I'm not planning on dying there, Meg. Besides, Father doesn't want us using that part of the house. It was closed up when Grandfather Alfred died. And I guess we don't really need the space.'

'Well good, but I reckon that's why Father boarded it up. To stop Dalhunty men from dying in there.' Satisfied, Meg settled against the tree trunk. 'Do you want to see something?' She lifted a piece of hessian and a pair of yellow eyes shone back.

Julian peered at the animal in the roughly made cage.

'It's the fox I was telling youse about before Mama left. I caught him in a snare. Now I sleep next to him and feed him. Been walking him around in the dark for the last month. Pretty soon he'll be like a regular dog.' She took a piece of cooked meat from her pocket and poked it into the cage. The fox gobbled it up.

'You can't train a fox,' argued Julian.

'Who says? Bony's a half-breed. He ain't much of a dog, but there ain't no reason a fox can't get used to people too.' She foraged about in a bag and started chewing on what came out of the sack. 'You want some? It's wheat. Frank says a person never gets real hungry if they have a bit of wheat to chew on.'

'You shouldn't be out here in the cold, and you shouldn't be training a fox either. Mother will have a conniption.'

'Mother ain't here, Julian. Not anymore. You want me to go back to a scratchy sister and a father . . . a father . . . it don't matter.' The fox pushed its head against the struts of the cage, its nose gradually moving nearer until it met Meg's skin. 'I've been thinking, Julian. One day, when you're running things, everything will be better. We just have to wait and hope Laura doesn't poison us first. You'd reckon she'd be better at cooking seeing she spent so much time with Mother, but she's always fussing about doing sewing and such-like.' Meg patted the fox. 'It's not that I don't love Laura or Father, I just don't like them a whole lot. Laura will forever blame me for losing her hair and Father doesn't care nothing about no one since Mother left. I don't think she's coming back either. I've been thinking about the day she left, Julian. She never looked back. Not once. Laura reckoned it was because the going was hard for her as well, but I'm not so sure. Even a dog looks back. Don't matter if a person's following or not, the dog always looks if they're friendly and you've been kind to them. Maybe we weren't kind. Maybe Mother believed she'd been treated badly and she didn't want to stay anymore.' Meg turned the wick low on the lantern.

'I don't reckon she meant anything by it,' said Julian.

They bunched together, pulling the rabbit pelts over their bodies and stuck their heads out the lean-to to look up through the branches at a sky bubbling with stars. Julian wished he could tell Meg their mother would soon return, but it wasn't a certainty. Certainty was seeing rain pooling on the ground, not wishing for it.

'I've forgotten what she looks like.' Meg nestled into his shoulder.

'No you haven't. Why, if you close your eyes, I bet you can see her as clear as day. She's nearly as tall as me. Tall for a woman. With auburn hair, a bit like yours, except yours is more reddish gold. Can you see her? Light brown eyes. Warm smile,' explained Julian.

'Maybe for you. I ain't seen much happiness from her on account of me being a disappointment.'

'You're not a disappointment,' replied Julian.

'Thanks, Julian. But I know what I know.'

Meg saw the world straight and true. It was a gift of sorts but also a burden. He wrapped an arm about her and closed his eyes.

≪ Chapter 14 ≫

Mid-October

The sun struck the tops of the red gums at such an angle the brown river glistened like silk. Although the water was low and the bank steep, the reflection of the trees on either side stretched across the surface so it appeared as if numerous fingers were interlinked in prayer. Julian considered imploring God to return their mother, if only for their father's sake, but in previous years He had not delivered rain when needed or saved his brother. It was one thing to try to see the good in all matters, even those that crippled, quite another to live with the reality. Perhaps that was the reason his father no longer visited Davey's grave or bothered to pretend that their lives were fine. It was hard to go on as if nothing had changed.

It was Sunday. Nine months and some days since their mother had boarded the steamer.

Julian threw the line into the river and sat on the edge of the ramp, his legs dangling in the eight-foot gap above the water. Three cod lay beside him. Another, and there would be enough to feed the family. Out of habit, a reed basket sat next to him. His mother had bartered it from one of the Aboriginal women who lived in the nearby camp, and had carefully lined it with canvas so it could be used to keep the fish scales Julian saved for her. He picked it up and angrily threw it into the water, where it bobbed righteously.

Twenty-three months had passed since Julian had last left the property. Twenty-three months since that family trip to Bourke. They had eaten madeira cake and driven past the town blocks purchased by their grandfather for £2500 pounds apiece in 1882. There was money to be made from savvy land investments at that time. Bourke was thriving. The trainline from Sydney was under construction. The Cobb & Co. coaches and paddle-steamers all enjoyed robust trade. *Hold tight,* Grandfather Alfred advised Ben on his deathbed, *hold on to those blocks. Bourke will boom. You'll see.*

The boom, like the water in the Darling, came and went. Those same blocks had been sold for £20 in 1907. Still, it was a grand trip. Everyone travelled in the dray. His parents up front with Davey seated between them; Laura and Meg making rude gestures at Julian as he rode behind singing 'The Song of Australia' at the top of his lungs.

The sound of a riverboat carried towards him. Julian recognised the shallow-draught vessel and rolled up the fishing line as Mr Peters steered the narrow boat towards the bank. Sister Rosalee was waving, her black-clothed arm stroking the air. The helmet and breastplate of her garments were starkly white beneath a billowing black veil. Next to her was a woman in a cream-and-green gown, her wide matching hat festooned with flowers and ribbons as edible as one of the confections that had sat temptingly behind the plate glass at the Bourke bakery. For a fleeting moment Julian had visions of Miss Carlisle alighting from the vessel. Mr Peters tossed the rope ashore and Sister Rosalee leapt after it, skirts flying, tying it off on an axed tree trunk.

Mr Peters gave a flourish of his hat and finished with a deep bow. 'Julian. It's a phenomenally splendiferous day. What a canvas you have at your disposal. At one glance whimsical and the next profound. Should we be closer settled I would take to your decking

105

and make it my stage, and the audience would punt along the river to enjoy the spectacle. Alas I must content myself with nature and the infrequent but very welcome travellers that come my way.' Mr Peters gestured with an exaggerated sweep at the muddy river and then to the waiting passengers.

The woman opened a parasol and with Mr Peters' assistance alighted with a younger man Julian hadn't noticed before. The two strangers struggled up the bank. It was rare for visitors to stop at Dalhunty Station, although occasionally a traveller might briefly stretch their legs there.

'A wonderful surprise!' called Sister Rosalee from the steamer.

Julian shoved his hands into torn pockets, readying for the arrival of a letter and the round of pleasantries expected by the travellers. He'd once heard a story downstream of a Melbourne man who'd complained about not receiving coffee and hot buns at a station stop, as if he'd been expecting a kiosk awaiting his arrival.

Mr Peters tipped his hat. 'Greetings to your father, Julian. I'll unload the baggage and then we must be away if we're to reach Brewarrina. The river will be a chain of puddles in a matter of days if this hot weather keeps up.'

'Baggage?' queried Julian.

'Julian, my dear,' the woman announced with a breathy air. She held out an arm and the young man at her side steered her gently up the steep bank to the ramp, where she stamped her shoes as if she had trod in manure, before tilting her parasol.

Before these finely dressed people, Julian felt an unexpected awkwardness. He had not bothered with shoes that morning, and his clothes were well past the need for washing. When the parasol closed, Julian finally saw the woman before him. He gasped. She was full-cheeked and pretty. Too pretty to be standing on a platform warped by age and weather, next to a listless river in the growing heat. He took in the finery of her clothes, the pleats, full skirt and puffy sleeves. The extent of the transformation went beyond clothing. His mother was almost brand new.

She saw his hesitation and in response frowned at her scrappily dressed son. She went to him and kissed him on the cheek, the warmth of her body emitting a flowery scent. How was he meant to react? He should have been pleased, but instead he thought of his father's ghostlike figure chopping wood in the night while his mother ate scones with clotted cream, dressed up in fine clothes. He wanted to ask her, was it worth it? Was it worth deserting her family? It pained him to realise that the answer was yes.

'What, no happy greeting? You are a sourpuss, Julian,' said his mother. She pressed the stranger forwards. 'Ethan, this is Julian. Julian, meet your new brother Ethan.'

'B-brother?' replied Julian, confused. 'Aunt Nancy doesn't have any children.'

The boy, although a half-foot shorter than Julian, was broad in the shoulders and probably only a year younger. He was nothing like any of them. The Dalhuntys were all bronze and gold and russet, like the country they inhabited. The boy-man before him was stockily built with black hair and dark eyes, and a nose that could be considered beaky.

'Good to meet you.' Ethan extended a hand. His face bore the type of expression seen on a stray dog when he dodged from your path and ran off a short distance to sum you up, to see if you were friend or foe. He was dressed better than any boy Julian had ever seen, with a stiff-collared shirt, tie and jacket and smoothed-down hair, the type pictured in advertisements.

Normally Julian would have accepted the greeting, politeness having been instilled in him. Instead he was fixed on his mother's abrupt return with this boy, another son. Maybe he had heard wrong. Who was this Ethan anyway? A replacement for Davey?

'Why were you away so long?' he asked Rachael, ignoring Ethan's outstretched hand.

Ethan was seemingly unaffected by the rebuff.

'You know why I've been away. It has been a very difficult time for me. However, my dear Nancy, your beloved aunt, is at peace now.' His mother tugged off the gloves she wore and tucked them into a bag, which hung from her arm by a thin silver chain. Then she looked to Mr Peters who was off-loading the baggage. Three new travelling trunks. The buckles glinted in the sunlight. 'Where's the dray?'

Was this what their precious wool proceeds had been spent on? Julian took in her finery and tried to calm down. Surely she wouldn't have used their hard-earned income on such frippery.

'We . . . we didn't know you were coming home.'

'No, of course not. The unpredicted is so much more exciting. I'm not sure if these shoes are up to the challenge of the walk, though.' She squeezed Ethan's shoulder. 'Still, it will be nice to stretch our legs.'

Ethan was staring at Julian's bare feet. In comparison, the leather lace-ups he wore were black and shiny. It was many years since Julian had seen new shoes. 'You're a size eleven.'

'What?' replied Julian, looking down at his mud-crusted toes.

'Ethan is a shoe expert. His specialty was women's and children's footwear, wasn't it, Ethan? But Ethan will tell everyone about his life once we're at home. We enjoyed a lovely week in Bourke, waiting for Mr Peters, but naturally a provincial town is no equal to a good walk in the country. Good, clean air. Breathe it in, Ethan. This is your home now. Well, come now, Julian, lead the way,' Rachael commanded cheerily.

It was nearing noon and the birds and animals were already settling before the afternoon's coming heat. Julian walked slightly ahead of his mother and the stranger, unsure of what to do or say, still absorbing Rachael's return and trying to fathom the change in her and the possibility of having a brother. He concentrated on the rutted wheel tracks, sensed the watchful trees. He wanted to walk away, to acquire the clarity only solitude brought, however he could not leave them alone to meet Ben. Julian needed to fully witness their mother's homecoming, to see his father's reaction when the boy was introduced.

'Is everyone well?' asked his mother.

'Well enough.'

'How are your sisters?'

'Fine.'

'And your father?'

'Good.'

Not once had she asked how they had coped during her absence or apologised for the length of time away.

'How many sheep do you run?' asked Ethan, as if he were speaking as one seasoned grazier to another.

Julian was caught off guard by the question. 'Sheep? Not many. Those days are gone.'

'I'm afraid I was probably a little light on details.' Rachael's laugh sounded like a twittering bird. 'You might have to slow down a little, Julian,' she protested.

Julian increased his pace. 'When did Aunt Nancy die?' he called over his shoulder.

'Seven weeks ago,' replied his mother.

'Seven weeks!' Julian turned abruptly, and his mother and Ethan stopped walking.

Rachael considered him for a moment. 'Don't look at me that way, Julian. Aunt Nancy's estate required time to organise and Ethan had to see out his position at Bon Marche. The department store. Had I telegraphed sooner you would have expected me home immediately, which was simply impossible.'

'Because you were eating scones in the mountains?' said Julian.

Rachael's mouth tightened and he could tell it was an effort for her not to speak harshly. 'You are a funny boy, Julian.'

It took longer to reach the house than Julian would have liked. As they neared the homestead it wasn't the glare of sunlight striking the stirrup irons on the walls that announced their destination but rather a commotion of noise and dust coming from the yard. Meg was doubling Laura bareback on Legless. They galloped around the interior of the yard, Meg yelling at the horse to go faster, Laura screaming for Meg to stop. Bony was chasing them and barking dementedly. Soil was flying; chickens were squawking. Reginald the rooster was crowing from the veranda railing. It was more noise and general yahooing than their quiet lives were used to.

Julian stopped at the broken-hinged front gate and on the next circuit the girls spun their necks to see who was with him. Meg tugged on the reins and the mare drew up short. Laura slipped straight off and onto the ground, hitting the loamy soil hard with her backside and she cried out in pain. Meg was by her side in seconds, the mare snuffling Laura's raggedy head as Meg, in her grubby cut-off trousers and two-sizes-too-big shirt, tugged her older sister to standing and began picking bindi-eyes from the rear of her dress.

Rachael pushed past Julian and walked towards them, all green and cream in a mottled-brown world. His sisters were stock-still, mesmerised by the apparition filling the yard with colour and grace. Then Laura was gazing this way and that, at Julian and Ethan, to their mother and back towards the house, although only the heavens knew where their father was. A streak of dirt smeared her cheek and perspiration patched the dress she wore. What did their mother, in her perfect clothes with a brand-new boy she called her son, think of the straggly children she had returned to?

Meg allowed herself to be folded into their mother's arms. Not one word escaped his sister, and Julian reckoned on that meaning something, although he was not sure what.

Laura hung back, staring from Julian to Ethan to Julian again. Julian shrugged.

Rachael released Meg and walked towards Laura. 'My darling girls, what happened to your hair?'

'Lice.' Laura submitted to her mother's kiss, her arms hanging straight.

'Oh. Heavens.' Rachael touched her hair and glanced uncomfortably at Ethan. 'And Meg, why are you wearing those clothes? You look quite ridiculous. I am glad we're not expecting any callers.' The sound of their mother's voice danced across the yard. 'We must devise a tonic for you, Laura. You really can't be seen looking so . . . so . . . Ethan, come here.'

Ethan pushed past Julian, just as his mother had done, and walked straight up to the women. The boy kept his hand outstretched until Laura's was slowly offered and then he gazed about the yard and homestead like the outsider he was. Julian saw their home through the stranger's eyes. The tumbled pile of empty kerosene tins on the end of the veranda, the roughly boarded-up windows on the abandoned part of the house, and the ridiculous stirrup irons decorating the wall. Bony came straight up to Ethan and peed on his leg.

'What the?' Ethan kicked out, hitting the dog on its side.

'Don't youse be hitting my dog!' Meg yelled.

'Get that awful animal away, Meg,' said their mother.

Meg gave a tinny whistle and Bony went to her. 'It's not his fault. A person stands in one place long enough, he pees, is all.'

Ethan grunted and shook his leg, then grunted some more.

'Ethan has come to live with us,' declared their mother.

Laura's face crinkled as if she were going to laugh and then just as quickly flattened out when she realised their mother was serious. 'Why?' she asked.

'Because I asked him to.'

'Forever?' asked Meg, as if the concept was ludicrous.

'Yes. Forever. He's your new brother.'

At that moment, their father appeared on the veranda, unshaven and barefoot, wearing a blue singlet and old-fashioned beige breeches held up by braces. The unlit pipe moved in his mouth as he chewed.

'Have you two broken any bones yet? Because the closest doctor is Bourke. And I've no damn inclination to drag my horses and dray through the scrub to tend to your stupidity.'

He gazed about his patch of heaven and, finally noticing the people in his care had grown from three to five, squinted in comprehension. He took the pipe from his lips.

Rachael went to him, dragging the forest-green finery of her gown in the dry earth, stepping onto the splintering boards,

111

handbag still dangling from her arm. She kissed him on one cheek, and then on the other, as if twice made her real.

Julian walked across the yard towards the house, flanked by his sisters. Ethan stayed close by. Julian caught sight of his father's mouth twitching with emotion, then he was hugging his wife closer than Julian imagined a man could ever hug a woman. His head nestled against hers, eyes squeezed shut. The miracle of their mother's homecoming caused the desolation to leave his father so quickly that Julian could see the planes of his face growing young again. He turned away from his father's tears.

⋘ Chapter 15 ⋙

'This is Ethan. Ethan Harris.' Rachael drew the boy to her side as she made the announcement. 'He's come to live with us, Ben.'

They were gathered on the veranda. Laura with a puzzled brow, Meg edging closer to Julian. Together, they watched their father's reaction. He looked at Ethan and then quizzically at his wife, and Julian thought for a moment he may have to drag a chair to their father.

'Ethan was employed in the shoe section at Bon Marche. The department store,' she explained gaily. 'We took to each other, didn't we, Ethan? The floor manager allowed Ethan to escort me around whenever I visited, and I was grateful for his company. After dear Nancy's passing we went on picnics together. Ate oysters and ice cream. Well, not both at the same time—' Rachael spread her fingers across her perfect bodice and gave an affected laugh. 'I asked Ethan if he would like to come home with me and he said yes. I should have sent word, Ben, however it seemed so right.'

From nowhere came the squeak of a board against a rusty nail. Meg elbowed Julian.

Ghost, she mouthed.

He set a hard look upon her and she gave one back.

Their father was clearly flummoxed by their mother's extra-ordinary actions, for he kept on gazing at her and Ethan for so long it was Meg who spoke first.

'You're from away,' was all she said, but it was enough to finally stir Ben.

Julian saw the way every kink was gradually leaving his body, like crumpled iron belted smooth again. The darkness they had lived in over the previous months was already shifting with their mother's return.

Ben ruffled Ethan's oiled hair and rubbed his fingers clean on the grimy blue singlet. He looked again at his wife. One by one he took in the rest of his children with unanticipated warmth, before returning to the boy before him. 'Welcome to the family, young man.'

'Thank you, sir,' replied Ethan, with studied politeness.

Their father hugged his wife again, bewildered joy spilling out from him.

'Where is your family?' Meg asked Ethan.

'I don't have any,' said Ethan.

'Are you an orphan? Like when a ewe dies and we have to feed the lamb until it's grown?' asked Meg.

'I'm nineteen, and I'm not an orphan.' Ethan was clearly annoyed at this suggestion.

'Look, here are Frank and Henrietta,' said Ben with uncustomary enthusiasm.

They all turned to see Frank and his charge plodding from the direction of the palm grove. Meg waved and yelled out that their mother was home, and man and beast came to a standstill at the gate.

Frank gave Rachael a low bow from atop the camel. 'Mrs Dalhunty, warmest greetings on your return. It is very good to see you. I am sure you did not come across a finer camel during your time away.'

114

'Indeed I did not, Frank, and it is good to see you again too,' she said with affection.

'Do you have belongings at the river? Henrietta and I will fetch them.' Frank glanced at Ben, waiting for the usual complaining to begin, but none came.

'Thank you, Frank, and this is Ethan. He's part of the family now.'

Frank bowed. 'I am Frank Ukulele Dalhunty. Chief cameleer and owner of this very fine camel. Adopted son of Alfred Dalhunty. Former desert explorer and world traveller. And I must say, I'm very sorry for you, Ethan. I have a very fine camel if you wish to return to Bourke. Hooshta.' He tugged on the lead and walked on.

'That's my uncle,' said Meg proudly. 'He's half British Imperial subject: one quarter English, one quarter Irish.'

'And the other half?' asked Ethan.

'Australian.'

Ethan glanced about uncertainly. Julian knew the boy was uncomfortable and he couldn't help feel it was deserved. What had possessed him to follow Rachael home?

'He is absolutely no relation, Ethan,' announced their mother. 'Frank was given permission to live here by my husband's father. I hope you haven't been spending too much time with him, Meg?'

'Meg's been doing fine with us.' Julian was pleased by how controlled his reply was.

His mother gave a nervous laugh as they all made their way into the house. Julian pushed his hat back in the interior dimness as Rachael set about giving Ethan a tour.

'Main bedroom next to the drawing room, children's rooms across the hall. Kitchen at the rear, separated by a breezeway.' She lifted her skirts to avoid the unswept floors. 'Laura, you've been tardy with the housework.'

'I've not had your free time,' Laura retaliated.

Rachael ignored her. 'We only live in part of the house, having no need for the extra space.' Outside the original selector's hut she paused for what Mr Peters would call dramatic effect, explaining the first Mrs Dalhunty's decision to include the structure in the bigger home. She laughed at this and called it a woman's romanticism and then stepped inside the drawing room, with everyone following in her wake.

Rachael patted the foxskin footstool, with its beady black eyes, and lifted the vase of spilt fish-scale flowers from the floor, restoring them to their place. A large gecko scurried across one of the papered walls. Ethan started at the movement.

'Oh. The piano.' She ran a finger across its filmy surface.

Ben cleared his throat. 'It's ready for you to tinkle the ivories, my dear.'

Their mother lifted the lid and touched one key, then another. Meg dragged a chair across to the piano, snubbing Ethan's offer to assist.

As if a practised performer, their mother took up position at the keys and straightened the expensive material of her gown. She freed the hat pin securing the pale green straw in place and patiently held it at arm's length for Laura to take. Then she started to play. Her right hand moved towards the centre, striking the keys with precision, gaining momentum as her left added bold new notes. It was a chaotic tune and once or twice she stopped to tap the keys as if testing the sound.

Meg winced. 'Is it meant to be so noisy?'

'It's "The Flight of the Bumble Bee". However it is quite off-key,' their mother replied with a defeatist air before finally stopping.

'Sounds squashed to me,' said Meg.

'Off-key? It's brand new.' Their father strode across the room, struck a number of keys and listened. 'The young lady aboard the *Lady Matilda* played it perfectly. It sounded very fine.'

'Miss Carlisle is an excellent pianist,' said Julian.

'It has nothing to do with my playing,' replied his mother sharply.

'It's broken. Broken,' declared Meg, throwing her hands in the air.

'The soundboard could be cracked. Was it dropped?' Rachael looked accusingly at her husband and then Julian.

'It did get jolted a bit in the dray and wese rolled it on logs to get it inside,' Meg explained.

Ben scratched his head and then embarked on testing every key. As Rachael rose and tucked the chair close to the piano, he grew more frantic, banging the keys in frustration.

'Ben. Stop!' She touched his arm and he finally drew back.

'We didn't break it. We should get our money back from Captain Ashby,' said Julian.

'You're quite right, Julian,' replied his mother.

'It was a present, Rachael.' Their father sat heavily in the horsehair-stuffed chair.

'Pity. It's a Steinway. They cost a few shillings.' Ethan was examining everything. The magazine-plastered walls. The twin painted emu eggs on the mantel above the rough-hewn fireplace. The heat-crazed oil painting of Lance Dalhunty, whose dark suit and scooped eyes gave him the appearance of an undertaker. And attached to the firescreen Rachael's stuffed parrot, the feathers on the floor a sign that the bird had been mauled by mice.

Ethan moved towards the collection of spears, throwing-sticks and grinding-stones in a corner of the room, and felt a spear's point with a finger.

'It's a little different to my sister's house, Ethan,' said their mother. 'No second storey or cook and maid, I'm afraid.'

Next to Julian, Laura's lips formed a circle. It was all too easy to guess what his sister thought. How had this shoe salesman managed to wangle his way into Aunt Nancy's home?

Julian stomped outside and through the yard to the stables, where he sat on a hay bale opposite the empty stalls. After a few minutes, his father came to sit beside him.

'Julian,' he said kindly. Whatever lecture his father planned on giving was replaced with a sigh. 'Be kind to the boy. He will be feeling like an outsider. We have to make him welcome.'

'He *is* an outsider. He's from away. You once told me people from away lived different lives to us. They had no concept of the bush and it was better that way, for it was impossible for them to comprehend what it meant to live out here.'

'Sometimes we have to make exceptions,' replied his father.

'For Mother or for that boy? I don't understand her. You don't walk into a shop and select people to join the family like they're items for sale on a shelf. How can you let him stay? She said he's my brother. He is *not* my brother.' Julian choked up. 'No one can take Davey's place.'

'And no one ever will.' Ben got up and leant against one of the stalls, smoothing a horsetail blanket hanging on a railing. 'Your mother didn't mean to upset us, she's only trying to do good. Give someone less fortunate than us a home.'

'Less fortunate? Have you seen his fancy clothes? He doesn't belong here,' complained Julian.

'I imagine we paid for those clothes.' His father's knobbly fingers pressed down on the hair blanket. 'Your mother could hardly appear in public with him looking like a waif. The Dalhunty name is still well known. Rachael needed to be looked after while she was in Sydney. You knew that. She borrowed money from Aunt Nancy's husband until our wool was sold.'

'So now we owe him as well.'

Julian thought of Meg dressing as a boy and Laura with her shabby clothes and ruined hair. Was it possible his father was actually unaware how much their mother's leaving hurt them, and how his failings as a father worsened in her absence?

'Aunt Nancy died seven weeks ago. Mother should have sent a telegram.'

His father thought on this unexpected news and was slow in replying, as if he were carefully fashioning an answer in his mind. 'It takes time to settle such matters.'

'Mother should have asked your permission about Ethan. She should have asked us,' argued Julian.

'Well now, we're past that. Ethan will have to share with you.

And before you say anything, there is nowhere else for him to sleep. I'm not opening up the other part of the house and there is plenty of space in your room. Be good to Ethan, I'll be expecting you to treat him like a—'

'A what?'

His father scraped the inside of his ear and flicked away the findings. 'Ethan is here now and he's obviously alone in the world. He hasn't had much family life for a long time by the sounds of it.'

'And we haven't had much of one either recently!'

'Don't be too hard on your mother. She won't be going back to Sydney anytime soon. Do you want to come with me to the river? I need to check on Frank.'

'No.'

Julian was left alone to pluck at straw. Ben Dalhunty was no layabout Sunday Christian but nor was he the type of man to turn a boy away, especially a boy brought home by his wife. Their lives would resume as if nothing out of the ordinary had occurred. And tomorrow the broken gate would be mended and his father would rest his tea on the post and look once again at the cloud-skittering sky.

≪ Chapter 16 ≫

Julian stayed up late that night with Bony, where he was chained to the yard fence, sharing a hollow made warm by the dog's body. He stuck a finger under Bony's collar, feeling the tufted remains of the string Davey used to drag the dog about. Julian could have sworn his little brother was at his side, plucking at his shirtsleeve, yabbering on about some great adventure down by the river. About him the air shimmered and stilled. He reached out into the night's heat at an emptiness impossible to fill. A new boy was claiming his little brother's bed, where even his sisters hadn't dared to sleep. The pain of the loss came fresh and raw.

When the kerosene lamp in the drawing room window was finally extinguished, Julian left Bony to his scrabbling. Inside the house he moved along the flood-buckled hallway. His sisters' bedroom door creaked open to reveal Laura. Beyond her, Julian caught a glimpse of Meg, sitting upright in bed fully dressed, playing cat's cradle with a length of twine.

'It was Great-grandfather.' Meg tucked red curls behind an ear. 'The noise on the veranda this afternoon. Well, youse can't expect Mother to bring a new boy here and the old people not to have something to say about it. He's not a Dalhunty. He's not staff. He's not nothing. Still, Great-grandfather didn't get real angry like I thought he might. That's something, although I reckon Ethan won't be sleeping much.'

Laura stepped into the hall, closing the door on Meg. 'She's convinced we're surrounded by ghosts.'

'Maybe we are. He in there?' Julian gestured to the next room.

'Yes,' whispered Laura. 'Where were you?'

'With Bony,' he replied.

'Preferring the company of dogs now?' she said, sympathetically. 'Did you see how slowly he ate the curried parrot? No more oysters and ice cream now.'

Julian thought of the fish he'd left lying on the riverbank; their lives taken for nothing. The morning seemed long ago.

Laura took his arm, shuffling them further along the hall to where their mother's trunks sat open waiting for her to finish unpacking. One whole trunk was filled with Aunt Nancy's clothes. Laura held up a lace adorned blouse.

'She's just like Father now. Selecting dead people's clothes to wear and loving it.'

Laura carefully returned the blouse to the trunk and went on to tell Julian that after dinner Rachael had presented gifts of hair ribbons for Laura and Meg, which had been rejected by Julian's younger sister, along with Rachael's suggestion that Meg change into her nightgown. Rachael's request of Laura to clean the silver was also met with refusal. Laura explained they had not used it while she was away, while Meg told their mother that pannikins were just fine, and playing at being fancy was plain silly.

'Well, the look Mother gave Meg. She stormed from the room. When I went to talk with Meg she was cutting her hair. She keeps the bits in a tin and says she's going to keep cutting it every time it gets longer until she can stuff a mattress and have her own bed, then she'll never give me lice again.'

'You don't blame Meg, do you?' asked Julian.

121

'Only sometimes,' admitted Laura. 'Mostly I blame Captain Ashby. Do you think Mother brought Ethan here to take Davey's place? It just doesn't seem right. She's been away for so long and then she comes back with a complete stranger. We don't know anything about him.'

Julian was pleased his sister felt the same as he did. 'Well, he's here now and for the time being Father isn't going to send him back to Sydney.'

'Then we're stuck with him,' said Laura.

They both fell quiet, hoping that an answer might present itself.

'I didn't think Mother would come home,' admitted Julian. 'Neither did Meg.'

'Truthfully, Julian, neither did I.'

They said goodnight and Julian half-heartedly entered his room.

Ethan was lying in Davey's narrow bed, facing the wall. A jacket hung from a peg, the new shoes were neatly placed on the floor. On a chair were folded shirts and trousers. Julian took off his clothes and dragged the patchwork cover over his nakedness. Come morning he would be sprawled across the bed, the coverlet on the floor, the heat of the night having pushed him from side to side. Julian figured Ethan would have to get used to him, rather than the other way around. He leant across to put out the kerosene lamp.

Before he could do that Ethan propped himself up on an elbow and nodded at the military pictures glued to the wall above Julian's bed. 'What's that?'

'It's the Sudan War. Didn't you learn about it in school?' asked Julian. The boy didn't reply. 'Did you go to school?'

'Sure,' answered Ethan, eyes straight ahead. 'Who taught you?'

'There was a governess for a while. Then my parents. It's difficult to get women to stay out here,' he replied. 'How long were you at the department store?'

'Seven years.'

'Where were you before?'

'Why?' replied Ethan.

'You're in my home sleeping next to me and apparently you're staying.'

'I was in a tannery until Mr Crammer came in one day looking for a leather supplier. He was in charge of shoes at Bon Marche and was considering going into business himself, designing his own and having them made for the trade. I showed him the different types of leather when I should have waited for my supervisor. He offered me a job.' The story rushed out, as if it was not often shared.

'Because you knew about leather?' asked Julian.

'Tell me about the war.'

'Well, General Charles Gordon was killed in North Africa, and Australia sent soldiers to help put down a rebellion,' explained Julian.

'When?'

'In the 1880s, before the Great Flood.'

'What's the Great Flood?'

'Mother didn't tell you much, did she? It was a couple of years after I was born. We lost nearly all our sheep.'

Ethan lay on his back, cradling his head. 'Mr Crammer told me I was very fortunate that your mother took a liking to me. He encouraged me to help her when she came into the store. Not that it was difficult. She's the kindest person I've ever met and Mr Crammer said I was very lucky to have made such a friend. He said your family were great pastoralists, with thousands of acres and thousands of sheep, and your wool clip floated to market on riverboats.'

'Not anymore,' admitted Julian. 'We mainly grow vegetables now.'

'Like the Chinese,' said Ethan dismissively. 'Your mother didn't tell me that either.'

'What did she tell you?'

'Not enough.'

Julian put out the kerosene lamp, listening to the bed springs as Ethan rolled onto his side. Ethan had belittled his family with a few choice words. 'Why did you come here?' he asked. 'You were employed. Had a roof over your head, didn't you?'

'What does it matter now?' replied Ethan. 'After all, your father tells me if I look to the east I can see the Promised Land.'

⚔ Chapter 17 ⚔

On the morning after Rachael's homecoming Julian woke well before dawn and crept to the kitchen without waking Ethan, gathering with the rest of the family for breakfast. There was fresh bread, boiled eggs and preserves to choose from, courtesy of Aunt Nancy's pantry. The table was set with their best plate, the tarnished $\mathscr{D}$-engraved silverware taking centre stage. Their mother served them dressed in a buttercup-yellow skirt and the lace-trimmed blouse, the flaring skirt swishing across the floor as she fussed and cooed and clucked around the table, ensuring everyone was well fed.

Julian observed her attentiveness with reservation. Having grown up with a mother who rarely bustled, this flitting person in her fine morning outfit was not the woman he knew. And yet there was tasty food, and a lot of it, eventually they were all so busy eating and licking jam from their fingers that Julian didn't mind how clumsy he felt using a porcelain teacup.

Then Ethan appeared. He hovered at the doorway, smiling awkwardly, and said good morning.

They all looked at him. It was as if they had forgotten all about the new arrival. Meg pushed out her chair to stare at him.

Their father – scrubbed, shaved and dressed in an overly large white shirt with a cherry silk waistcoat and burgundy necktie – told Julian to move along one seat to make room for Ethan. Julian looked at his plate and then Laura, who was toying with a piece of bread, and did as he was told. Meg stabbed at a boiled egg with her knife and was slapped on the wrist by their mother.

'Did you sleep well, Ethan?' Rachael asked after he was seated, cutting a slice of bread and setting it on his plate.

'Not really, no. I kept waking up.' Ethan looked at Julian, Laura and Meg and then at the kitchen, as if the seeping daylight might improve his new home.

'Told you,' said Meg to Julian. She turned to Ethan. 'Youse see any ghosts last night, Ethan? It's them that probably woke youse. I thought they might come, youse being an outsider. If you hear a strange howling sound, part dog, part human, it's them. Only a few inches separates youse from the rest of the homestead with its brass beds and candle chandeliers. It's all closed up on account of the dying room. You heard about the dying room yet?'

Ethan stopped slathering dripping on the bread. His knife dangled mid-air.

'It's where all the Dalhunty men go to die. Guess you'll be going there too, being adopted and all,' said Meg with a matter-of-factness.

'Stop this nonsense,' said their mother. 'Ethan is not adopted. Who told you that?'

Meg looked at Laura. 'No one. I'm just saying. Wese talked about the ghosts when youse were away. Why can't we talk about them now?'

'I said stop it,' said their mother.

'They don't mind. They knows wese talking about them. And I knows they talk about us.' Meg stuffed bread in her mouth and kept on speaking, oblivious to the ridges and valleys growing on their mother's forehead. 'Great-grandfather came yesterday when youse arrived, Ethan. On the veranda. Youse hear that squeaky board? That was him. Coming to check on youse, I reckon. First thing, youse have to be educated. Learn Tennyson's "Charge of the Light Brigade" by heart. The reason Great-grandfather liked "Charge of the Light Brigade" was because of the cavalry. Bravely carrying out their orders, regardless of the outcome. Like us here. Isn't that right, Father?'

'Enough, please,' said Ben firmly.

Meg, partway through chewing egg, opened her mouth in amazement and stayed that way, until Julian gave her the slightest of nods and she swallowed loudly. 'I just thought Ethan should know. About the ghosts and the cavalry. They was slaughtered.'

'Well, now he knows,' said their father.

A disapproving look had taken root on their mother's face. 'Ben, Meg needs to be disciplined and she should apologise to Ethan. Immediately.'

'Oh, I think Ethan's fine. Aren't you, Ethan?' said their father.

'Yes, sir.' Ethan toyed with the plate before him while Rachael sat back in her chair and folded her arms. He offered Meg a conspiratorial smile. She kept right on staring at him.

Ben cut some more bread, and the preserves were pushed across the table to Ethan along with a boiled egg. Then he leant close to the boy and spoke softly. Ethan relaxed a little and spooned orange preserve on his bread. He said it was his favourite and Rachael replied they would order a case specially for him. Ben laughed loudly, and his mother pattered on about quandongs and oranges and how they'd once had a large orchard and a pond with fish. No matter what his mother said, his father laughed as if it were the funniest thing in the world. Next to Julian, Meg started giggling. Even Laura loosened up a little. Julian felt the mood lighten around the table, aware his father was trying to draw his family inwards towards the new unit they were to become.

After breakfast their mother lined up the goods brought from Sydney. There was an array of tinned food, such as dugong pâté, sheep's tongue and turtle soup, and a trove of silver photo frames and memento boxes belonging to her parents. Julian could only guess at how his uncle truly felt having his pantry raided. In the middle of their mother's animated listing of new belongings, Meg left the table and scooped water from the bucket into her pannikin. 'Meg, why are you wearing those awful trousers?'

Meg went to Julian, standing so close he could feel her hot breath.

'She likes wearing them,' said Julian.

The glow on his mother's face dimmed, however she arranged her features into pleasantness. 'Your Uncle Carter has agreed I can have most of my family's furniture, which is very generous.'

Julian fixed on this point. There was no longer a Sydney house for his mother to live in now her sister was dead. Perhaps that was why she came home. He studied her carefully to see whether her happy disposition masked disappointment, as his father declared that once the furniture was railed to Bourke, Captain Ashby could float it to the station. A far safer alternative than a rough land passage.

'The furniture's already been moved to a warehouse for storage.' Their mother spoke to the entire table, however she singled out Julian. 'As you can imagine it takes quite a few weeks to organise these things.'

No one else probably noticed this gentle rebuke. It stayed with Julian while their father discussed teaching Ethan to ride and their mother talked to Laura of the importance of massaging cod liver oil into her scalp to encourage her hair to grow.

Julian could not recall ever disagreeing with his mother before her trip to Sydney. And combined with the way she had spoken to Meg earlier, he now had no doubt that she had changed.

Outside a dreadful ruckus started up. There was snarling and barking; one high-pitched, the other harsher. The noise drew everyone to the window where two dogs were fighting. Fur twisted and merged and broke apart only to be fused together in a ball of red and yellow-brown. Meg threw herself out the window before anyone could stop her and roused at the animals fiercely while Ben fetched a rifle and aimed it through the window, telling Meg to stand aside.

'Don't youse shoot my fox. He's mine, Father! I trained him.

He and Bony have gotta learn to get on.' Meg stood before the dogs, protecting them as the battle raged behind her, then she picked up a stick and hit both animals. They broke apart, the fox retreating to lick his wounds some yards away, Bony standing firm near Meg.

Despite Rachael demanding that the fox be shot, Ben lowered the rifle.

'If Meg said she trained the fox, well, we'd better give the animal the benefit of the doubt,' offered Ben. 'I'll have a chat to the little fellow later today when he's quietened down.'

'And that will make all the difference in the world.' Rachael angrily spooned jam into a jar at the table. 'How in heaven's name did you not know about this? A child doesn't train a wild animal overnight, Ben.'

'A dog, a fox and a camel?' said Ethan wonderingly, as Frank and Henrietta appeared outside the homestead fence on their way to the palm grove.

Rachael went to Ethan and rested a hand briefly on his shoulder as she apologised for her wild young daughter.

'So can I can keep Mr Fox?' Meg shouted.

'I don't see why not,' Ben replied. 'But no favouring him over Bony. Treat them equally and tie the fox up at night. We don't want him eating the chickens.'

Meg jumped into the air excitedly, waggled her finger at the fox and then ran back to the window. 'Don't go petting him, Ethan. He might bite youse,' she warned.

'Unbelievable.' Their mother left Ethan's side and started to pile the breakfast plates one on top of another, the crockery clanging.

Meg leaned through the window. 'Are wese stackers now? I thought wese was gentry,' she said to her mother.

'Be quiet, Meg. Ethan will think you're a simpleton. And come back to the table this instant.'

'What can I help with?' asked Ethan.

Meg settled her elbows on the windowsill. 'Depends. What can youse do?'

'Tell me what you want done and I'll have a go,' offered Ethan.

There it was. That eagerness again. It was as if the boy's night of tossing and turning had turned him into a different person, for there was none of the bitterness of their bedtime conversation. This new version of Ethan Harris was now willing and affable.

Their father kissed his irritated wife on the cheek and left to finish his tea outside.

Meg climbed back through the window and returned to her chair, where she sat quietly, her legs swinging back and forth. Rachael was emptying her purse, counting out shilling coins, pennies and three one-pound notes, which she dropped into the money jar to join the two pennies.

Julian stared at the jar so hard after it was returned to the shelf that Meg asked what he was doing.

'Nothing.' He looked at his mother. 'Is that Uncle Carter's money? How are we expected to pay him back?'

His mother dunked a plate in a bucket of water and ran a rag over it. 'Your father and I will worry about that.'

Laura gave him a gentle nudge. 'Ethan's gone with Father.'

Julian had been so intently focused on the money jar that he had not noticed Ethan slipping from the room. He left the kitchen in a rush. On the veranda he upended his boots, shaking out the grass and burr, then swiftly pulled them on and looked across the yard to Ethan and Ben.

After months of disregarding his children, their father was happily welcoming a stranger into their midst. A hollow sensation moved through Julian. He heard his father's low, warm voice. He was discussing the blue sky and the fineness of their land until Ethan burst forth, asking how a girl could train a fox, what had happened to their sheep, if they really were related to Frank and whether there was money in vegetables. Ethan's questions were coming so thick and so fast that Ben seemed a touch disorientated. He took off the plain felt hat he wore and, perching it on a finger, twirled it around until it spun like a pinwheel.

Laura came out onto the veranda with a basket in one hand. 'At least Father's happy.'

'The man Ethan worked for at the department store thought we were still the Dalhuntys of old, with sheep and money. Ethan obviously didn't bother Mother with many questions,' Julian told her.

Laura let out a little gulp of disbelief. 'He thought we were wealthy pastoralists?'

'Yes,' replied Julian. 'And I'd lay a trip to Bourke on Ethan reckoning he was cleverer than most. At least until he arrived at Dalhunty Station and saw the truth.'

She nodded to where Ben and Ethan had started to move towards the stables. 'You better go before he gives Father a corn in his ear.'

Julian trailed behind his father and Ethan. The new boy was finally out of questions and now Ben was holding forth on the power and prestige of the pioneering Dalhuntys, as if Ethan had a right to knowing their heritage. Partway to the stables Goliath whinnied from the timber and rushed towards Ben, the animal's dark body elongating and compressing with each powerful stride. As usual, his father met the gelding's charge head on. Ethan stayed firm at Ben's side, watching the horse and watching Julian's father, waiting to see who would surrender first. The horse kept coming and Ethan never moved, never drew back or even flinched. When Goliath finally came to a skating halt, his father rubbed his forehead against the plate of the horse's skull as Ethan patted the gelding's neck. Ben and Ethan beamed at each other.

'Julian. There you are. I'm going to give Ethan a lesson on Legless. She's the quietest.'

'But Legless is my horse,' Julian protested. His grievance went unnoticed. He briefly thought of complaining again, and then recalled Laura's comment. Ben was happy. Happier than he had been in a long while.

In the stables Goliath snuck up to nibble hay and his father slipped a bridle on the gelding, tethering him securely to a rail. Then he saddled the mare with Julian's horsehair blanket and tack, while explaining the rudiments of riding to Ethan, who listened with a concentrated expression as if he were branding the teachings in his brain.

Ben gave Ethan detailed instructions about seat and thighs and muscle control and who was in command, then he covered Ethan's hand where he grasped the reins resting on the mare's neck and turned the stirrup out so Ethan could place his foot more easily. He talked Ethan through the basics of mounting a horse with a calmness Julian had not heard in his voice for months, and then with a few encouraging words held tight to Ethan's ankle in the stirrup until he was seated in the saddle, just as he had done for each of his children.

Ethan adjusted his backside in the saddle and straightened his spine as directed.

Ben's admiration was obvious. 'Tap her flanks with the heels of your shoes.'

Ethan nudged the mare's flanks and flipped the reins and the horse walked out of the stables as if she were the best-trained animal in the world, while Ethan kept square in the saddle.

'Will you look at that,' said Ben. 'A natural.'

Julian was looking. At the pleasure radiating from his father and at the new boy who was riding his horse and sleeping in Davey's bed. Ethan was sliding into the family more quickly than Julian cared for.

⋙ Chapter 18 ⋘

Mid-November

The Natural was walking about the outbuildings with a hammer and nails as if he were an inspector, determined to point out Dalhunty failings. Having recently fashioned a carpenter's belt from a blacksmith's apron, the tools were now always at the ready and Ethan was keeping busy. He had replaced numerous boards in the overseer's cottage and was currently in the stables banging away as if he were the only one capable of restoring the station after years of decline.

Julian, Laura and Meg were leaning on the veranda railing next to the stack of empty kerosene tins. It was a hot afternoon. A time for sprawling flat in the hallway and trying to keep cool until evening and the last of the day's chores. However Rachael had declared that it was no longer acceptable to have the front and back doors wedged open; too much dust blew in with the breeze. Besides, if Ethan was capable of working through the afternoon heat then they were as well. A mother's decree. They collected outside, listening to Ethan trailing from one wrecked building to the next.

'Three o'clock and all's well,' said Meg as the Steinway was subjected to rambunctious pounding in the drawing room.

'She's wrecking it. I sure wish Captain Ashby would hurry back so Father can get rid of it like he said he would.' Meg aimed the slingshot at the pyramid-shaped pile of dried camel manure that she had arranged on the top of the kerosene tin for target practice. She fired, scattering the target. 'What's the point of Ethan fixing them old buildings anyways? We ain't never gonna use them again.'

'He hammered those loose boards on the side of the house back into place yesterday,' Julian told her.

'Nooo!' said Meg.

'You shouldn't be crawling in there anyway. It's all falling down,' replied Laura.

'It's just plain stupid,' said Meg. 'Ethan could have his own room. We all could. Isn't that right, Julian?'

'You said too many Dalhuntys had died in there,' Julian reminded her.

'That was before Mother started taking in orphans.' Meg gathered up the camel turds. 'A person can't sleep nowhere no more.' She pocketed the manure and then picked grit from her knees, which were showing through holes in her trousers.

His little sister was right. During summer, they usually dragged their mattresses out onto the veranda at night. However when Rachael had discovered that Ethan had not been invited to join them, she had banned it entirely. A month had flown by since her return and the same questions were left unanswered. Why had their mother brought Ethan here? And why would an outsider, particularly one who grew up in the city, stay on the station?

Nesting pigeons flew from the stable roof as Ethan's hammering recommenced. Julian and his sisters chewed daily over the possibility of Ethan having nowhere else to go, and that bothered Julian more than he cared to say. The boy barely spoke to him unless to query a job, although yesterday Ethan had been keen to see a paddock map of what they'd once owned. Julian had explained about the flood, the resumptions when the government took some of their land and opened it up for selection, then how the drought cut their sheep numbers by two-thirds at the turn of the century. Ethan couldn't comprehend that the Dalhuntys had once owned 540,000 acres of land, and Julian was glad. He'd wanted to impress the boy. To make him realise how important the Dalhuntys once were.

Laura was beginning to warm to Ethan or feel sorry for him, Julian couldn't tell which. She thought they should all be a bit nicer.

'I can't complain about him,' said Laura. 'He's always very polite, neatly dressed, and he offers to carry the washing in if he's about. He's pretty friendly, actually. And he does whatever is asked of him. There's nothing wrong with manners and speaking correctly.'

'Does he? Well ain't he all gentlemanly,' said Meg. 'Ethan asks me stuff. About how often the riverboats come. If people visit. What Mr Fraser's like. If wese have any friends. I was gonna tell him we used to, before everyone cleared out, but nuh.'

While they were talking, they saw Frank wander into the stables. Meg was the first to move. Nimbly hurdling the veranda railing, she darted across the yard, slipped through the fence and ran to the building, followed closely by Julian and Laura. They stopped outside, flattening their bodies against the stable wall so they could hear what was happening inside. Meg and Laura giggled. Julian held a finger to his lips and they quietened.

'My dear boy. Those boards. They are very fine boards. Thank you for repairing the gaps in the wall of my cottage. Could you speak to my Honoured Brother about a new roof as well? I see he has taken to you like another son,' Frank was saying.

Julian was keen to interrupt their conversation. It disturbed him that even Frank recognised how quickly Ethan had managed to ingratiate himself.

'That's all right and sure, I'll mention it to Mr Dalhunty. If you need anything else repaired let me know. I'm not used to lazing about like the others and there's plenty of work to do. Half this place should have a fire stick put through it,' stated Ethan, with a haughtiness that was missing from his usual interactions with the family.

'In the old days this place was very fine,' said Frank. 'There was a lot of money. The homestead was grand, fringed by a big garden and there were thirty trees in the orchard. That was before the droughts. Everyone knew of the Dalhuntys, and every man wanted to work here. Alfred Dalhunty was a great boss. When a stockman left the property he made a gift of a stirrup iron for the homestead wall. It was a great honour to be employed here.'

'So what happened?' asked Ethan.

'All great empires rise and fall. This one crashed,' explained Frank.

'Yes, but *why* did it fall?'

'It was time,' replied Frank cryptically.

'And why are you still here then?'

'Mr Alfred Dalhunty was like a father to me. He said I was like a son the way I tended his wife's palm grove, and so I stayed,' Frank told him.

'So you don't have anywhere else to go. Well, it doesn't look like much has been done around here for a long time. And what about Mr Dalhunty wearing a different get-up every day? It seems a bit strange to me. I know they're poor but surely Mrs Dalhunty could at least make her husband dress like a normal person.'

'Goddamn orphan,' hissed Meg. 'I'll give him poor. I'll give him normal. Boarding up every goddamn thing.'

She tried to enter the stables but Julian grabbed her by the shoulders, feeling the indentations of bone beneath skin as she squirmed from his grasp.

'Leave it be, Meg,' he said. 'Ethan doesn't know what he's talking about.'

She finally wriggled free, tears filling her eyes. 'He should leave! I don't want no replacement brother!' she screamed.

Any hope of slipping away from the stables undetected disappeared. Ethan and Frank, having heard the commotion, were now standing at the door of the stables watching them.

'Replacement brother? You had another brother?' asked Ethan finally.

'Youse shouldn't be eavesdropping,' said Meg.

'I have plenty of places to go to. Plenty,' muttered Frank, stalking away.

'Yes. We had a little brother. Davey,' said Julian.

'I'm sorry,' answered Ethan. 'Really sorry. Meg, I'm not here to replace Davey.'

'Well, youse are replacing everything else.' She swept her hand through the air.

Ethan undid the carpenter's belt and dropped it on the ground. 'I'm just trying to help. But if you lot aren't bothered by everything falling around you in a heap, then I shouldn't be either.'

'There's just no point to what you're doing,' argued Julian.

'Not to you there isn't.'

Ethan left them standing in the shade of a peppercorn tree and headed for the house. Their mother's piano playing filled the vacuum left with his departure as relentlessly as the heat.

'Maybe he'll leave,' said Laura.

'Nup,' replied Meg. 'He's like Frank. Don't reckon he's got any other place to go either.'

⫸ Chapter 19 ⫷

Mid-January, 1910

Ben was positioned in the centre of the yard as Ethan rode Legless. The horse was on a lead and their father, wearing cricketing whites and a straw boater, kept the rope tight as he taught Ethan the subtleties of riding a horse. That was the exact word he used: subtleties. From where they perched on the top railing, Meg and Julian concentrated on the rider, who sat straight and tall, as if he was a ringer born to their world and not the outsider they knew him to be. Neither Julian nor Meg had ever heard their father using the word 'subtleties' before and his explanation, that it meant refinements, made them lock on to the perfect form of Ethan Harris as if he were a creature from another world.

Riding was something instilled in them from the moment they were able to toddle out of the house, and to Julian there was nothing refined about it. His record of having fallen off more times by age ten than any other Dalhunty man before him, had earnt a citation in the Dalhunty Yearbook of 1898. This was a most uncommon honour following as it did the lauded achievements of the Dalhunty Cricket Champions of 1880, 1882 and 1885 and the sombre recording of a great uncle, twice removed, decapitated by a Zulu's cowhide shield at Rorke's Drift in 1879.

Meg's first dragging had occurred when she was a mite of four years. The horse had been spooked by a snake, and the resultant scars on her legs and arms came close to meriting an entry. His sister had spent the next few years trying to earn a citation, until the novelty of being laid up in bed wore off.

Yet here was their father, clicking his tongue and swishing at the mare with a stick, making her trot on command, telling Ethan to grip with his thighs and lift his backside out of the saddle. As if there was honour in learning to ride like a dandy.

When the mare moved to a canter and then eased to a walk, Ethan's bearing effortlessly matched the changing gait of his mount. Their father's pride swelled. 'Excellent, Ethan. Excellent.'

Legless could have at least given a pig root or thrown a shoe or stopped short without warning. *Traitor*, was the thought that came to Julian's mind.

'Have you really never ridden before coming here?' their father asked as Ethan trotted around the yard.

'Never. It's pretty easy, though. You just have to listen to the horse. My mother taught me a person could pick up most things by listening.' Ethan patted the mare on the neck.

'I suspect you need to ask a few questions occasionally too,' called Julian.

'Don't interrupt, Julian,' said Ben. 'I believe you'd make a fine polo player with practice, Ethan. Have you heard of polo? It's played on horseback. You hit a ball with a mallet into goals at either end of the field. Mr Fraser mounts a team. They were soundly beaten at Coonabarabran last year, however the papers said it was an excellent show. If you were interested, I could approach Mr Fraser when you're ready. It would be quite something to have a player from Dalhunty Station again.'

'I could give it a try,' replied Ethan.

'That's the spirit,' said Ben.

'Just open the gate and let Legless go, Father.' Meg walked along the top railing like a performer on a high wire. 'Ethan doesn't need no babysitting. He rides good enough now.' Meg pivoted on her heel and walked back to where Julian sat. 'Teach him like youse taught us, Father.'

'Be quiet, Meg!' yelled their father.

'Father's awfully scratchy, ain't he? Everything's Ethan this and Ethan that.' Meg pulled her hat low over her head and stretched her mouth wide, showing her two front teeth in imitation of their father, her voice dropping. '"Why Ethan can fix a fence in no time. Ethan can drive a nail straighter than I've ever seen. Why, I do believe the vegetables are growing faster now Ethan's here." *S-h-i-t*. This place has gone to buggery.'

'Nothing you say will make any difference, Meg. Father's got himself a prodigy, someone who's good at everything.'

Julian hadn't expected Ethan to upend their lives so completely as he had in the three months since his arrival. How was it possible for an outsider, especially a shoe salesman from Sydney, to be so capable and take so easily to bush life. It was the last thing any of them expected.

And their father loved him for it.

Julian knew Ben was rash and changeable. However it was plain that the slightly unbalanced man had found in Ethan a new favourite son. Ben sought Ethan's opinion first on any matter concerning the day's work, shushing Julian if he dared to interrupt. More than the seat at his father's right-hand side had been stolen by Ethan on the first morning following his arrival. Julian was being supplanted on every level. He doubted he could feel more injured if he were suffering from a seeping wound.

Yet his parents went blithely on, as if the boy was a gift from the heavens. Ethan persisted in spending his time replacing or repairing broken boards in the house, in the disused cottages and in the woolshed. He even replaced the splintered boards in the long-drop, sanding them smooth. Their mother loved Ethan even more for that.

Meg flopped down next to Julian. 'Youse could do what he does, if youse wanted. Don't reckon youse want to, though. Anyway I bet Ethan can't do this.'

Meg placed two fingers in her mouth and let out a piercing whistle. The noise startled the mare and the horse reared up. Ethan might have kept his seat but for the arrival of the fox and Bony. The mutt snapped at the mare's heels and Legless struck out, high and fast. Ethan landed with a thump on the ground.

'It's harder than it looks,' called Meg, as Ethan pushed himself up and dusted down his clothes.

'For pity's sake, girl!' their father shouted. 'Do you have to behave like that? If you can't keep those mongrels under control, I'll be getting rid of them.'

Meg gasped. She brushed off Julian's attempts to comfort her and climbed down from the rail. 'Come on, youse dogs, it's no good barking at Ethan, he's *special*. The best rider in the *whole darn world*.'

'Meg, don't leave,' said Julian.

'Must be something to be a prodigy,' she mumbled. 'Better than being a nappy-headed girl.'

Ethan walked towards the railings. 'What's the matter with you?'

'Ain't nothing wrong with me, *Ethan*. It's not my fault youse ain't used to bush life. Shit. Anyone would think we was having a catastrophe.' Meg flung her hands in the air in disbelief.

'Apologise to Ethan,' called their father.

'No. Think I'll go yabbying.' Meg turned and ran.

'Come back here!' shouted Ethan angrily as he slipped through the yard rails. 'Come back here right now.' He broke into a run.

'You'll never catch her.' Julian climbed back to the top railing. From that height there was a clear view of the paddock and Meg sprinting towards the grove of palms until her petite figure blurred into the bush.

Ethan gave a good account of himself in following, but just as he reached the palms he abruptly disappeared into thin air. Julian waited, feeling slightly perturbed. The palms were not so closely planted that it was possible to lose sight of someone for long. A moment later Ethan emerged from one of Frank's holes.

Julian climbed down from the railing, trying not to chuckle. Meg was a crafty one.

'Don't be encouraging your sister,' Ben said to Julian. 'She's already running wild. And we can't be having that. You and Laura need to take her under your wings a bit more.'

'She's not just *our* responsibility, Father,' replied Julian. 'Laura's teaching Meg needlework and I'm helping to educate her.'

'Well, her elocution hasn't improved,' replied Ben.

Julian bristled. 'Maybe you and Mother should take a bit more notice of her, instead of centring all your attention on Ethan. Laura and I aren't her parents.'

'No, we're a family. Consider that when you and your sisters are calling Ethan names behind his back. Really, Julian, I expected more of you.' Ben pulled on the lead rope as Legless trotted towards them. 'About your horse. Ethan and Legless have taken to each other. I'd like to lend her to him, if that's all right. You can handle any of the other horses but there's a particular connection between the mare and the boy that I'd like to foster.'

In his mind's eye Julian saw himself as a thirteen-year-old, kneeling beside Legless as a foal, slippery with birth matter, rolling uselessly in the straw as she tried to stand, her mother nudging her as he wiped the filly down. He had been there from the beginning, coaching the mother through the long night, taking hold of those tiny hooves to gently ease the newborn free. After a desperate hour the foal had wobbled to standing, legs splayed, and Julian had almost cried with joy.

'Are you listening?' said his father. 'It's not like you have a really close relationship with the mare. If you had you would have given her a more appropriate name.'

'It *is* an appropriate name,' replied Julian quietly. He knew the arrangement had every possibility of becoming permanent.

Ethan arrived back at the yards limping, perspiration staining his shirt.

Ben placed a hand on Ethan's back. 'It looks like Meg led you on a pretty chase, son.'

Ethan grimaced. 'She can run.'

'You and Legless have to get to know each other and practise every day,' Ben said with mounting enthusiasm. 'It's the only way you'll have a chance of being selected for Fraser's polo team. And that would be something, my boy. A Dalhunty taking to the field again after all these years. And we'll need a new name for Legless, something more appropriate.' He scribbled in the air with a finger. 'Hot Pursuit or Glory Girl or Dalhunty Dame. Yes. That's it. Dalhunty Dame.'

'It's a fine name, sir. Dalhunty Dame it is,' replied Ethan.

'There we are. It's all agreed. Well, I must take up the Steinway tussle anew. Captain Ashby may not come past again for months and it can't be that difficult to understand the mechanics of it.'

Julian observed his retreating father. Why wasn't he enough for him? What important attributes was he missing that allowed Ethan to so easily replace him?

'She's your horse, mate. I'll just be borrowing her,' Ethan told Julian once Ben was out of earshot.

'You're wasting your time,' Julian replied dismissively. 'Fraser's team have been riding together for years. Anyway, do you really think we have money for new polo tack?'

'Maybe this isn't about making the team. Did you see the way your father cheered up when he talked about the possibility? I'm giving him a bit of hope. There doesn't seem to have been much of that around here for a while.'

'So this is all part of your grand plan, eh? Keep the parents happy and repair every derelict building on the property. Weasel your way into the family until you become the golden child. You've got some ego if you believe you can come here and change things,' said Julian spitefully. The anger within him was raw. He couldn't stop it from bubbling up.

'Ego?' Ethan spat. 'Take a long hard look at yourself. It takes a mighty pride to do nothing when your world is falling down around you.'

As unwilling as Julian was to admit it, Ethan was right. His life was disintegrating. While he was still keen to leave the property, the new boy was trying to restore its glory. He hated Ethan for that. For seeing possibility, where he did not. For wanting to be here.

'You're an outsider. You'll never understand what it means to live here, what it's really like. It's just a novelty to you.'

'I'm not blind. I can see it's a struggle.'

'Well, good for you.' Julian was beyond arguing. If Ethan was so keen to restore Dalhunty Station to pre-eminence, let him. He'd soon find out it was an impossible task.

≪ Chapter 20 ≫

Sick to the stomach after his conversation with Ethan, Julian went in search of Meg. He spotted her among the grove of palms sitting cross-legged opposite Frank, Henrietta standing sentinel nearby. He took refuge behind one of the palms, curious to hear what they were discussing. The trunk was like a bony spine where fronds had been pruned and Julian absently touched the knobby protuberances. A few of Frank's holes were nearby, varying in depth depending on the man's enthusiasm. Some of the holes were mere scratchings, burrows that an animal might dig. Others were eight feet deep. The hole closest to Julian had been abandoned after only a few inches. The hard soil and the shallow fibrous roots of the palm made excavations difficult, even for the mad Englishman.

Julian observed his sister. If Meg remained upset by the incident in the yards it didn't show. She was cupping freshly dug soil, the clumps falling to the ground as she repeated the word 'bastard'. Frank urged her on, encouraging her to draw the word out so that it became two. *Baa-staard*, she repeated, her intonation clear and confident. *Baa-staard*. Julian almost felt her concentration. He was loath to interrupt her. He never thought that being close to his little sister could cause such difficulty. For himself and, ultimately, for her.

'I was thinking about the river,' Meg said, clearly satisfied with her mastery of the new word. 'How old it is. Being older than old. And I reckon life flies past like an eagle on the wind. That it's the same for the river. Maybe it flows so fast it can't remember, like Father. He forgets that he's father to three other children. Some days he's just plain old Ben Dalhunty to me.' Meg took a pipe from her pocket. 'Have youse got some tobacco?'

Frank shook a finger at her. 'Why should I give you tobacco?'

''Cause I gave it to you,' replied Meg.

Frank threw her the tin and she rubbed the tobacco in her palms, easing the strands apart before pushing them into the bowl of the pipe.

'My dear young Meg, it does a person no good, anger. Everyone's got their own path. I've told you this.' Frank drew heavily on his own pipe and blew smoke into the air. 'Are you going to light that pipe?'

'Nah. I'll just suck on it some.' Meg threw back the tobacco tin and Frank caught it. 'I want to know about Davey, but no one left here's got the sight.'

'He's gone now. This brother of yours was very fine, but he's gone,' said Frank adamantly.

'Before everyone left I had a friend, Mickey. He said it does no good thinking on a person after they've gone. You say their name too much or think too much about them and they can't rest. They keep coming back to you. But I don't talk about Great-grandfather that much and he's still here. Stalking around with that spear. Making a dragging noise. Sometimes it wakes me up at night. I go outside when the moon's round and Great-grandfather is watching Mickey's people from the veranda porch. And they're watching him. Youse know what I reckon, Frank? The badness of them days is deep in the soil. Ain't enough rain to wash it away. That's why we're heading for ruination.' Meg got up and circled one of the holes. 'Sometimes I hear the river. Like it's telling stories about where

146

it's been. Over rocks and down gullies. Pushing up sand. Coming from country where other folk live. I see swamps and dunes and people from long ago. But mostly the river speaks of where it's going. All the way to the sea. That's when I reckon maybe it would be better to come from away. To be an outsider. To know how to be amenable. That's what my parents want. I heard them. Amenable children. Like Ethan. But I wasn't growed that way.' Meg edged closer to the deep hole. 'Sometimes being here stinks.'

Julian stepped out from behind the palm and made a show of wandering towards them as if out for a stroll. 'What are you two talking about?'

'Nuthin'.' Meg dangled her legs in the hole.

'You've been digging here since I was a child, Frank,' said Julian, joining his sister. 'Why do you keep doing it? You know there's nothing to find.'

'Someone said this was a free country. And your grandfather was a canny man.' Frank peered into the hole and Meg did the same.

'But he spent it all,' Julian explained, not for the first time. 'Every last shilling. Father told you what happened. Grandfather dug up the money when he came back from Sydney after the 1890 flood. The government was resuming a portion of our land and with our sheep losses, he needed the cash. The Dalhunty fortune is long gone.'

Frank rose and walked to Henrietta. His back was slightly crooked as he eased to the ground and lay down next to the camel, occasionally looking back over towards Julian and Meg, as if deliberating on what he had been told.

'He'd rather not believe me,' said Julian.

'*I'd* rather not believe youse, Julian. It gives Frank something to hang on to and everyone needs that. What's a few holes anyway? He fills some of them in,' asked Meg. 'Youse ever wanted to play polo?'

'Never thought about it. And Father's never spoken about it before today.'

'He thinks Ethan is so special. He doesn't see that we're special too.' She patted away tears and shook her head fiercely. 'I think we should send Ethan back to Sydney with the piano and sell the both of 'em.'

'I don't think he'd make much money,' said Julian, trying to lighten the conversation and failing.

'I wish everything was the way it used to be. But it won't ever be the same again, will it, Julian?'

'Probably not.' Julian stared with unfocused eyes at the land about him and thought of the foal that grew to become Legless. He tried to unpick the matted yarn that comprised his father. Every bone and muscle within him itched to escape what the Dalhuntys had become and yet there was always this pull that drew him backwards, as if he were still attached by an umbilical cord to his home. What kept him from leaving? His family and the simple truth that, as the only son, the burden of working the soil fell to him.

And yet he wasn't an only son anymore. There was another young man in the fold. The idea had grown gradually and now it was firm in his mind. Planted and watered by his father's affection for Ethan. It was that reality that gave him courage, though not enough courage to share his plans with Meg. In a few years, when she was older, Meg would forgive him. For now, his decision to leave after the next vegetable watering had to remain a secret.

≼ Chapter 21 ≽

Late January

Julian checked the regulating valve and turned the wheel. The water rumbled up the four-foot pipe, shooting high and fast from deep within the earth. It cascaded down to fill the small muddy dam and then slowly fed into the open trough. He waited until the dam was full and the excess water began trickling into a depression a few hundred yards away where the horses grazed, and then swung into the saddle and walked along the filling trough. Water dripped from numerous places, however the iron held. It took another few minutes or so to reach the point where the trough eventually ran into the earth-dug channel.

Julian heard his father yell, 'Here it comes!' and with that confirmation he trotted through the timber on Calamity. The gelding was named for the damage done to the dray when the animal had bolted a few years prior. Now he was Julian's to ride following Dalhunty Dame's elevation to the dizzying ranks of polo pony.

The three figures in the vegetable plot grew closer. Meg hopped from one strip of dry ground to the next, her trousers rolled up, the fox at her heels. Too little water and the plants would go thirsty and become stunted in growth; too much and the channels would overflow, flooding the beds. Ben was hunkered down, running his palm across vine tomatoes, shading balls of green lettuce – Julian imagined him coaxing the vegetables to drink – as Ethan dragged his hoe along the bottom of one channel, teasing the water to run faster. Then he stopped and Julian saw him wave in Ben's direction. The two men, young and old, jumped across dry and wet land until they met and then his father gestured wildly as Julian approached.

'It's stopped running!' his father hollered.

'Righto.' Julian trotted the gelding back along the channel and trough, checking for the cause of the problem. It was rare for the trough to crack but rust had a way of peeling away at the layers. He rode all the way to the bore head, arriving in time to see a pee-spray of water drop back to a drizzle and then cease running. He dismounted and checked the regulator valve and then twisted the wheel. Gave the pipe a kick, and another. Then he fetched his father.

They gathered at the bore head. Ben bashed at the valve with a hammer and rotated the wheel back and forth.

'Has it run out?' asked Ethan.

'It can't, silly.' Meg clicked her fingers and the fox padded to her side.

'How do you know?' he replied.

'Because it *can't*,' came her adamant reply. 'Father says the water has lain there for a million trillion years. You wouldn't know. You're from away.'

Ethan looked at Julian for validation, a rare occurrence. 'What happens now? Where do we get the water from? The river?'

'It takes a bit to cart enough water from there. Either we fix the windmill or build a trough from the next closest bore. It's fifteen miles away,' said Julian.

'Fifteen miles? The vegetables will be dead by then,' replied Ethan.

Ben began bashing the pipe in frustration, the hammer smashing with precision blows, the veins in his neck distending. The pipe reverberated, the noise echoing so loudly that Julian imagined the few worms in the soil burrowing far away.

Frank arrived on Henrietta. Once the camel was sitting, he walked close to the pond. 'My good people. There is always a drama.'

'Don't tell me you grow vegetables and you have no other way to get water quickly.' Ethan gave a pitiful laugh.

'Shut the hell up,' said Julian.

'Why don't you?' Ethan shoved Julian in the chest.

'Stop it, both of youse! Youse can bicker all you like but no fisticuffs!' shouted Meg.

'Fine,' said Ethan, palms up.

Julian turned to his father, who was still bashing the pipe. He called to him to stop, reaching his side between hammer blows.

Ben tore his arm free and muttered a curse. The profanities were the very worst and Frank cupped Meg's ears. When Ben finally gathered himself, his mouth puckered open and shut like a beached cod. They all stilled and waited. It was Frank who urged Ben to action.

'Use the water in the dam, Benjamin,' instructed Frank. 'Use what you have, my brother.'

Their father dithered, surveying the scene before him, then dropped the hammer and ordered Julian to ride like the wind to the homestead and bring back some buckets. Ethan was directed to close up the excess pipe so no more water was lost. By emptying the pond into the trough, the remaining water could be used on the vegetables.

Ethan skittered past Meg, nearly knocking her over, as Julian rushed for his horse. He leapt onto the gelding and Calamity broke into a reluctant canter.

He was on his way back from the stables when he passed Meg as she legged it home, the fox running at her side. He waved at her with grim desperation, then tugged his hat low over his forehead, and prayed as he rode.

◅ Chapter 22 ►

Ben kicked the gate open and walked across the earth-cracked yard. He stomped up onto the veranda and washed up in the water barrel. Julian waited his turn at the barrel behind Ethan, peeling mud from the hairs on his arm. Rachael met them on the veranda, her welcome melting on her lips as she watched her husband splash water angrily and then grip the rim of the barrel as if to steady his nerves. Ben stayed in place for a long minute, staring at his cloudy reflection. Rachael glanced searchingly at her children. She held a stiffened rod of tightly plaited dry grass and was attempting to make a large fan attached to a pole, the type young boys in pictures waved to cool the air when men in powdered wigs were eating supper. Julian thought Ethan well-suited to that type of job.

Rachael's hair was a mountain of curls and waves that trembled like jelly as Ben walked towards her. He told her the water had stopped and she didn't reply immediately. She was dressed for the coming evening in one of Aunt Nancy's cream blouses and a burgundy-coloured skirt and it was obvious that she was far from interested in hearing unwelcome news.

'How is that possible?' she asked.

Ben dried his hands along mud-crusted trousers and said nothing.

'*How* can it give out, Ben? You once told me that it was a profound and mysterious pool and that our bore would last forever. That the great inland sea the explorers searched for lay beneath our very feet.' It was clear she was mocking him.

'Obviously not,' he said bluntly.

'But—'

'There is no water.' He drew each word out until the very air grew dense, his voice hoarse.

'But—'

'Rachael, for God's sake, listen to what I'm saying!'

'A few bores dried up during the last drought. We read about it in the *Western Herald*,' Julian offered, but no one responded.

Laura climbed the stairs to the veranda carrying a bunch of lavender, with one of her ribbons wrapped around the stems. 'Isn't it possible that it might run again if we get decent rain? That's how the underground water tables fill up, isn't it?'

Julian looked to the man who was meant to lead them, to care for them, to bolster their spirits and waited for him to say that yes, Laura was right, that anything was possible. For the alternative meant disaster and everyone knew it.

'Will the crop survive?' asked Rachael.

'I don't know,' was all Ben said to his wife. 'I don't know.' Then he jerked off his boots and went indoors.

With the departure of his addled father, Julian was forced to remind his mother of more unwelcome news: the bore was also their water supply.

Rachael, Laura and Ethan followed Julian to the water tank near the house. Meg was sitting in the sand at the base, Bony on one side, the fox on the other. All three were scratching in the loose soil, the dog making a hole as good as any of Frank's attempts. Meg was drawing a stick figure with an object in its grasp. Julian guessed it was their father.

Their mother tugged her to standing. 'Get up, Meg. Why can't you behave like the young woman you are?'

'Because maybe I don't want to,' Meg retaliated.

'Don't speak to me like that.' Rachael reached for her daughter and swatted her across the back of the legs with the grass pole.

Meg yelped and ran to Julian. Laura flanked her sister on the other side. Their mother shook her head and threw the pole away.

'Martha Wendell was hanged for killing her stepchildren last year. Hanged by the neck until she was quite dead. The public called her a wicked stepmother, but some days I can quite understand her.' Their mother retrieved the pole and stuck it in the ground as if claiming territory. 'Yes, I understand her very well.'

If Ethan was as startled as Julian, Meg and Laura by their mother's outburst he didn't show it. He merely tapped the water tank and waited, his attention on Julian.

In response, Julian ran his palm against the iron, testing where the coolness met the heat of emptiness. It was half full. 'We could use some of this to water a portion of the vegetables. That would keep some of the plants alive while we try and mend the windmill at the river.'

'What about that old well?' suggested Ethan. 'Does it still work? Can't we drink that water or use it for watering?'

Rachael went pale and Laura gave such an intake of breath it sounded as if someone had physically taken hold of her neck.

Meg walked right up to Ethan. 'Wese can't use that, youse *ijit*. That's where Davey died.'

'That is quite enough.' Their mother took Meg roughly by the arm. Immediately the fox came to Meg's aide, snapping at Rachael, who dropped Meg's arm and moved away. 'That animal should be shot.'

'If youse shoot my fox I'll leave.' Meg trudged around the side of the house, Bony and the fox following.

Ethan looked confused. 'Davey drowned? I thought he must have got sick.' He regarded each of them carefully as if it were their very first morning at breakfast again, when all of them were strangers.

'I thought Mother or Father would have told you, Ethan, or you would have asked.'

Julian was secretly glad their parents hadn't revealed the circumstances of his little brother's death. Glad there was some part of the Dalhuntys that had remained intact and private. At least, until now.

'No one told me,' said Ethan, his voice cracking slightly. 'You all kept it a secret, like I didn't deserve to know.' He moved into the triangle of shade that the corner of the homestead provided.

'It's not that, dear. This is a new start for all of us,' replied their mother. 'Why don't you go and find Ben and make him a good strong cup of tea? Tell him one of your stories from the department store. You know how much he enjoys them.'

Ethan stayed put. 'Did you bring me here to take Davey's place?'

The space between Ethan and their mother grew heavy. Was Rachael about to admit that had been her intention?

'We all deserve to know,' Laura added.

'Well?' said Ethan.

'Oh, Ethan.' She twisted the pole in the ground but could not meet his eye.

Ethan looked at Julian and Laura. 'That's what you two both think, isn't it? That's why neither of you want to be friends.'

Julian studied Ethan. His sallow city complexion was now healthily sun-tanned. He was no longer the spit-and-polish magazine type, but happy to take a crumpled shirt from the laundry pile and eat a grub if Meg dared him. And he was taller; nearly as tall as Julian at six feet. It was as if they had planted a street kid in their unremarkable soil and he had lapped up every last nutrient. He was also no longer afraid to speak up.

'Your coming here had nothing to do with Davey,' answered Rachael eventually, but her reply had come too late.

'I'd like to believe you, Mrs Dalhunty, but considering the circumstances . . .' His features grew anguished. 'I trusted you when you said that I'd be welcome here.'

Ethan strode away.

Rachael took a step, as if she might go after him. Instead she thought better of it and turned back to Julian and Laura. 'You children have been unkind to Ethan from the very beginning. And now look what you've done.'

'Why are you blaming us?' Laura complained. 'It was your idea to bring him here.'

Their mother was clearly flustered. 'I don't understand what's got into Meg. She is so disobedient. She's fourteen now, old enough to know better.'

'Why *did* you do it?' asked Laura flatly, ignoring Rachael's attempts to change the subject. 'Why did you stay away for so long? You deserted us and then you brought him here without asking.'

'All of you have become so argumentative. I don't understand it,' replied their mother.

Julian could tell his sister itched to reply.

'Don't, Laura, there's no point,' he warned.

Laura's annoyance had been building for months. It showed in the way she washed the plates after tea, slopping the water until Rachael complained.

Maybe their mother was too busy keeping the house in order, making knick-knacks and changing her new clothes twice a day to notice, but there was little point attempting to boss them about anymore. Laura was sixteen years of age and Meg was behaving like the boy she clearly wanted to be. They had all done some growing up while she'd been gone. At times Julian suspected he was already an old man, bone-weary, and anxious about what might happen next.

'We'll cart water from the river for the vegetables until we repair the windmill,' Julian said. Overhead the sky was hard and bright. Monotonous perfection. 'Who knows, it might rain.'

Their mother pulled the pole from the dirt examining it for damage. 'And it might not.'

She left Julian and Laura standing there in the heat, sweat trickling down their skin. The land extended out in hazy swirls of rising sediment, the distant timber bowing under drying leaves. They listened to their mother calling out to Ethan. There were footsteps and a door slammed.

'When my hair grows back, I'm going to get a job in Bourke,' announced Laura.

'You're going to leave?' It had never occurred to Julian that Laura was making plans to abandon the family, just as he was.

'One day I'll be getting married. And so will you. We can't all be living here when that happens. If we still own the property by the time that happens. Don't look at me that way. Someone will fancy me. I'll make a good wife.' She retied the scarf about her head.

'But we're Dalhuntys. We can't just marry anyone.'

Laura angled a hip to one side. 'You mean I should marry someone like Father with a scrap of land and an old grand name and be penniless for the rest of my life?'

Julian had no answer to that. Like Ethan on the evening of his arrival, Laura had cut to the core of their lives and found their family wanting.

'Father's doing his best.'

'Then how did we get to where we are?' replied Laura sadly.

Julian pictured his family as a bird with a broken wing, flopping about, jabbing for bits of food, pining for a lifestyle to which it was impossible to return. He was now twenty-two years of age and he no longer saw their remnant acres through his father's storybook lens. He could only see the damage his parents were inflicting on him and his sisters, and he was sorry for the people they had become.

❦ Chapter 23 ❧

The next day, Julian was outside refixing a stirrup iron to the wall when Mr Fraser arrived. He came on a white horse like a medieval knight, accompanied by his son, Ian, who was astride a grey. They wore dark suits cut for the wealthy, their bodies squeezed into creased cloth. They were tall men with big arms and chests, as if they spent their days tossing the trunks of trees for pleasure and the nights sharing a whole roasted sheep before falling asleep in the lignum along the river. As they approached, Julian could see the river's mud still shining on their horse's flanks. Their expressions were stern.

They trotted straight to the house and, on seeing Frank approaching on foot from one of the empty cottages, Mr Fraser whistled to him as he and his son dismounted. 'You. See to these horses. My son's ride is newly broken. Keep a keen eye on the grey.'

There it was. The expectation. The entitlement. Julian hated Fraser.

Frank bowed. 'Yes, sir. Thank you, sir. May I say this is a very fine horse.' He took the reins and led the horses towards the stables.

Julian observed Frank's unexpectedly compliant response with suspicion. No good would come of it, he was sure.

'Julian.' Fraser's voice boomed across the yard fence. His mouth curled up at one end and then flattened out, like a question mark on its side. 'Sorry to disturb on the Lord's Day.'

Julian was taken aback to see the Frasers. Usually it was Ben who ventured forth to beggar help from their neighbour to sell more Dalhunty land. Now there was only the homestead lease remaining. The urge to tell Fraser to get off their property dwindled. What if the man was here to make an offer?

'Father!' hollered Julian, his gaze flickering from the Fraser men to Frank obediently leading the horses to the stables, and then back to their neighbours. Fraser Senior was standing soldier-straight, oblong like a mud brick. His paunch protruded so that his waistcoat stretched open between straining buttons. Ian Fraser was picking his nose and running a finger along the front of his trousers. He was a paler, uglier version of his father. Nothing like his pretty sisters, those new-money girls who thought themselves too grand for Julian's company.

In the distance, Julian saw Frank drop the Fraser horses' reins and the grey promptly trotted off into the scrub. Frank jogged on the spot, as if attempting to chase the horses as they wandered away and gave Julian a thumbs up. Julian concealed his mirth and called for his father a second time, making a point of adjusting one of the stirrup irons on the wall and turning his back on the Frasers.

'Those stirrup irons are a constant reminder of how things used to be here. Pity. It was a fine property in its day,' said Mr Fraser.

'It still is a fine property.' Julian wished his father would hurry up. He knew Ben was in the drawing room reading aloud from Dickens's *Great Expectations*, while his mother inserted wadding into the body of a cockatoo, and a moody Ethan, under instruction, contemplated the piano strings and wooden blocks left scattered across the drawing room floor following Ben's last repair attempt. *Great Expectations* had consumed his father since yesterday's failure of the bore. He had been reading it all night. Out loud.

Julian called for his father again and walked from the veranda towards the gate as Meg sped around the corner of the house. On spotting the Frasers she came to a screeching stop, fully clothed but drenched from head to foot. Sunday. Bath day.

Ben Dalhunty, still holding the Dickens tome, finally emerged from the homestead. Today he was outfitted in a black suit, with a gold embroidered waistcoat. A mark of respect for the defunct bore head perhaps? The effect was rather ruined by three inches of exposed skin at the cuffs and ankle, and the addition of a top hat that had the look of a stretched concertina. Ethan was close behind. Any closer and Julian reckoned they would have been sharing the same shoes. It made sense, considering yesterday's argument. The only person in the family who had been consistently kind to Ethan was their father.

Ian Fraser let out a chuckle. 'Good God.'

Julian was unable to tell if the remark was directed at Meg or his father.

'The Lord is good and the Lord is God, Ian, and I have no problems with you using either word if meant in good taste,' Ben said. 'But if that was not your intent then you must apologise, not only to the Lord but also my daughter who being of the feminine nature and by age, virtuous and pure of heart, is unused to such blasphemy. She may well faint from the shock.'

On cue Meg gave a little wobble and sat on her backside. Then she collapsed onto the ground and began to tremble. The act was impressive enough to keep even Julian entertained until Laura walked around the side of the house. She called out to Meg, and noticing the Frasers, glanced at the visitors and then Julian and finally their father. Meg sat upright and made a spitting noise.

Julian thought Laura quite the picture compared to the rest of them. She wore a wide straw hat with a cream scarf beneath and was still dressed in lilac, having visited Davey's grave earlier. Although her skirt was soaked in places, she was the freshest and cleanest of them all.

Ian tipped his hat in deference to Meg and then Laura. 'I apologise, Mr Dalhunty, if I caused offence.'

Laura adjusted her straw hat and gave the briefest of curtsies.

'I came here today, Dalhunty, to discuss a proposition with you. One with mutual benefits,' began Mr Fraser.

'Yes?' said Ben.

Here it was. The offer to buy them out. Completely. Julian walked to his father's side. He detested the idea of selling to the company Fraser was employed by, however if Ben accepted there would be money for them all. They could start again.

'Perhaps we could go inside and discuss the matter in private,' suggested Mr Fraser.

'I hide nothing from my children.'

'Well then, I'll get to the point. You have a grand name while I manage substantial acres and have just purchased my own run.'

'Yes,' Ben repeated, tucking *Great Expectations* under an arm.

'What if there was to be a union between our two families?' said Mr Fraser.

Julian moved so quickly to see his father's reaction that he almost cricked his neck. He was not marrying one of those Fraser women. He couldn't care less if the Frasers and Dalhuntys never spoke again or if Fraser never wanted to buy another single damn acre. He would starve before he was forced to marry a Fraser.

'Yes . . .?' said their father, stretching out his reply so that it became a question.

'The joining of wealth and name is quite common,' continued Mr Fraser. 'Which is why I would like to propose a match between my son Ian and your eldest daughter, Laura.'

'Laura?' repeated Julian, his voice squeaky.

'It is one thing to marry off daughters. I have arranged suitable matches for them with wealthy families. They couldn't possibly marry anyone with little prospect. But a son is quite another matter. Ian needs more than wealth. He needs more than a passable girl capable of running a country household. The linking of the Dalhunty name with ours would carry substantial benefits. Laura will have made a match beyond expectation and Ian will have married into one of the oldest pastoral names in Australia.'

It was only a small compliment however it made Ben preen as if he was Reginald himself, strutting about the chook pen, surveying his harem.

'Well, Laura, what do you say to Mr Fraser's proposal?' asked their father.

'I . . . I . . . I . . .' was all Laura was able to say.

An awkward quietness descended upon them and Julian watched as Ian's attention drifted from Laura to the treetops. Julian had witnessed more interested men during a drought at the saleyard in Bourke.

At that moment Bony lumbered over and peed on Ian's leg.

'What the? Mongrel dog!' Ian kicked out and Meg leapt forward, ready to defend. Their father grabbed her by both shoulders, holding her tightly until her squirming ceased.

'Laura is most grateful for Ian's offer of marriage. But coming, as this has, quite unexpectedly, she will need some time to deliberate. Which is only proper for a young lady of her delicate background,' their father replied with great stateliness.

'I quite understand. We'll await your answer. Good day to you all.' Mr Fraser, the curling lips unfolding, tipped his hat and then walked towards the stables with his son.

'God damn,' said Meg.

'Yes, quite,' agreed their father. 'Well, Laura, what do you say? Laura?'

Laura had already darted up the veranda steps and was met at the front door by her mother. 'Ian Fraser asked me to marry him,' she said in a high-pitched voice.

The partially stuffed cockatoo dangled at Rachael's side. When she had gathered herself sufficiently, she looked at her husband. 'Ben. Is it true?'

'A truly remarkable day, Rachael,' replied their father.

'An offer of marriage? What of the daughters?'

'Yes. And they are in the process of being married off.'

'Good. No bride needs narky sisters-in-law holding court. Now, we must start planning, Laura. No second-tier nuptials for our eldest girl. I saw just the gown in Sydney. Silk. A high neckline and waistline. And the skirt must be closely fitted with a tulip-shaped top layer. Floral decorations on the bodice and—'

'But, Mother—' said Laura.

'He's the ugliest boy I've ever seen,' commented Meg. 'Laura ain't gonna marry anyone ugly, are youse, Laura?'

'I'm sure your sister does not want to be a Miss Havisham living out her life in a dilapidated house with us.' Their father held *Great Expectations* aloft for emphasis. 'I doubt you'll receive a better offer, Laura.'

'Is that how it's done here?' asked Ethan, incredulous.

'It's how all great families ensure enduring prosperity,' explained their father. 'Marriages have been brokered this way for a thousand years.'

Ethan shook his head. 'But compared to them we have—'

'It is what we *represent* that counts. A golden age. Heritage. Respectability. In any case, such a union will be more than beneficial. Fraser will do his best to support us. A new bore. Yes, he'll assist with that. And in exchange I'll let him run some sheep here. We're saved.'

Ben threw the novel skywards. It landed with a splat of cracked binding and rustling pages.

'Where are our horses?' Fraser was shouting from the stables. 'Where the bloody hell are our horses?'

Ben waved to the father and son. 'Coming, coming.'

'Ben. Wait.' Their mother walked from the house and across the yard. Laura was nowhere to be seen. 'She said no. She says she won't marry him.'

'What? That's ridiculous. It's for the good of the family. Her own good. She'll be wealthy. We'll get a new bore.' He waved his arms frantically, as he spoke. 'Tell her, Rachael.'

'Well, she won't marry him. Foolish child doesn't like the look of the son. And she has it in her head that she'll only marry for love. I wonder where she got that cockamamie idea from.'

❖ Chapter 24 ❖

It was mid-morning, a time when the Dalhuntys were normally out working. Instead Julian sat idle in the kitchen, with his sisters, mother and Ethan, each of them taking turns to play sentry on the veranda as they waited for Ben to come back from the vegetable field. On the shelf, partially concealed by condiments, sat the money jar. Uncle Carter's curled pound notes were tantalisingly within reach. Julian looked away, numbed by tiredness. It had been six days since the bore had ceased pumping. Five days since the Frasers' offer of marriage. Four days of Ben and Rachael begging and cajoling Laura to change her mind. Four days of wedding dress sketches and talk of fine jewellery and a maid to tend to Laura's hair. Of trips to Sydney and fine gowns. Of a life that was due a Dalhunty.

Throughout all of this, though, Laura remained steadfast. It seemed marriage was only an option for her if there was love attached. A scrap of land, a grand name and little money was just fine if the only other choice was a loveless life. And Meg was right, Laura did think Ian ugly. This was the strangest turn of events and it made Julian give thought to the magical Miss Carlisle, who now

165

seemed a figment of his imagination, but one he couldn't quite shake. What if it was the same for him? What if he too discovered there must be love before marriage?

'He's coming.' Ethan slid into a seat.

Rachael had decided to sell the vegetables immediately. Their father's dithering was to be borne no longer.

'We could pack the vegetables in wet bags. That will keep them cool,' suggested Ethan.

'Maybe,' said Julian. Although they had worked tirelessly carting water from the river by dray, a terribly hot stretch of weather had seen the vegetables start to wilt. The produce was not in good order, had not reached maturity, and was likely to end up as chicken or pig feed after being picked over and refused by the savvy house-wives of Bourke.

Ethan scraped his chair away from the table in annoyance. 'If someone else suggested wet bags, you'd be all for it.'

'It's a good idea.' Laura, a sewing needle held mid-air, had nearly completed the large patchwork quilt. The cover was comprised of material taken from men's trousers and ties, calico, and a worn blouse. The skirting was to be squares of kangaroo hide.

Their mother stopped looping homespun wool into a ball and placed it in a sewing basket, shaking her hands in irritation as she freed herself of the fibre. 'I'll thank you, Laura, not to add commentary to a situation that could be made more bearable if you stopped with these foolish notions of love.'

'You're right, of course. As the eldest daughter I should be more concerned about providing for the entire family, rather than trusting that my parents will come to a sensible decision about our future.' Laura sorted through the neatly cut squares of kangaroo hide, avoiding eye contact with anyone at the table.

'I can't believe you would turn down Ian Fraser's offer of marriage, why it's as if you care nothing for your family or yourself.'

Laura selected a square of hide and matched it to the quilt's skirting. 'Let's not discuss Ian's offer again.'

Rachael was yet to fully comprehend Laura's stubborn streak, which was clearly in the Dalhunty blood.

Meg twisted a shirt-button. She was lolling in her chair, legs scissored out, her inquisitive gaze missing nothing. Her hair was cut on the round, as if a basin had been used for guidance, red curls springing up tightly in all directions. 'You've made the right choice, Laura. I'd rather starve than marry that pull-through.'

'At least the river's risen,' said their mother, a little softness replacing newly grown worry lines. 'We can soon expect Captain Ashby with my furniture.'

'Your sister's belongings should go straight to Bourke.' Ben was in the kitchen doorway. He looked haggard, the knees of his trousers threadbare. 'There are quality pieces there, Rachael. You said so yourself. Mahogany and red cedar. Carpets. Oil paintings. The paintings would be extremely saleable. Some wealthy pastoralist will buy them. Why, Mr Fraser might purchase the whole lot.'

Their mother untied the apron she was wearing and tossed it on the table. 'You've sold most of our sheep and now you want to sell my furniture. By the time you are finished we will only have the clothes on our backs left.'

'We still have Laura,' he replied, with just a hint of bitterness.

Laura bowed her head, concentrating on the patchwork.

'Rachael, we need money. We can't live here without drilling a new bore.'

'Your famous ancestors were here long before people started sucking up water from under their feet. Our family needs a decent life. Sell the piano in Bourke. Don't wait for the Captain. That's if you and Ethan can ever put it together again. You never should have purchased it in the first place.' The anger was still strong in her tone but losing its bite.

'But I bought that piano for you,' Ben said gently.

Rachael refused to be swayed.

Their father glanced heavenward. It was as if he was all alone, trying one last time to converse with that higher power that Julian now knew had quit on them years ago.

'Although I'm loath to suggest it we could sell some more acres to Fraser.' Their mother sounded hopeful. 'That's what we always do.'

'If we sell any more land there will be no point staying here,' Ben shouted, moving to grasp the back of a chair worn smooth by previous Dalhunty generations.

'What does it matter? If you only intend to grow vegetables, we hardly need to hang on to the rest of this pauper's block.' Their mother stuck a length of timber in the wood box, snapping the door shut. 'And based on the success of your exciting new venture very soon we'll be in the same situation as last year. We have bills to pay, Ben. And the railways don't freight furniture for free.'

'Exactly. And you'd have us go further into the red so you can have your sister's belongings. Well, I'm not doing it.' Their father's voice rose.

'It is my furniture and it is coming here to this house. If we need money that desperately, sell what's left of the Dalhunty silverware. It's useless to us and that at least will save your womenfolk the bother of cleaning it.' Their mother folded her apron as if to suggest that was the end of the matter.

'Don't you even think of flogging my silver, Rachael. If you'd managed to live within your means while in Sydney instead of borrowing money from Carter we wouldn't be in such a financial mess. Now I have him to repay. And for what? Trinkets and gowns and hats. Bloody scones and ice cream. Oysters and ferry rides. And on top of that then you go and start picking up waifs and strays and expect us all to play happy families.'

The room grew bleak with the harshness of Ben's words. Julian watched with morbid fascination as their father considered each of his family one by one, giving a stuttering comment that was unrecognisable, before saying, 'I'm sorry, Ethan, I didn't mean that.'

Ethan splayed his fingers along the edge of the table. They were short and callused, flattening out gradually as he pressed downwards, growing in width until the tips of his nailbeds were white.

Across a table of empty porcelain cups and cold tea, Julian caught Laura's attention. His sister lay the quilt in her lap. Even Meg was still.

Their mother broke the tenseness in the room. 'He most definitely did not mean that. Your father is overtired and worried. We all are.'

'He's not my father,' said Ethan.

'Come, come. We mustn't get overwrought by misspoken words. Ben, you must deliver the vegetables and the piano to Bourke tomorrow. Julian will go with you.'

Their father plucked at one of the braces holding up his pinstriped trousers and made a show of considering what Rachael believed was already settled.

'Fine,' he concluded. 'I'll leave for Bourke tomorrow. Alone. Ethan, gather up the piano parts and fit them back as best you can.' He looked at his eldest daughter. 'I will send word to Fraser while I'm in town and give him your answer.' Then he left the room. Soon after the front door slammed.

'That's settled then.' Their mother patted Ethan's head. 'Don't look at me that way, Julian. What are we expected to do? Keep starving for the rest of our lives?'

'We ain't never actually *starve* starved. I bet youse 'ave been hungrier than us, haven't youse, Ethan? Ain't much trapping and fishing to be done in the city,' Meg said with authority.

The light in the kitchen was a brittle, hazy blue. Their mother swished the tea towel at the smoke streaming from the oven, adjusted the flue and then concentrated on the stove top, although nothing was cooking. Ethan got up from the table, carefully pushed in his chair and strode from the room.

The front door banged shut a second time and then Rachael left the kitchen. Laura took the cod liver oil from a shelf and went to massage her hair, leaving only Julian and Meg. Meg pulled at the button on her shirt until it popped and rolled across the table onto the floor, coming to rest near the basket of kindling. She searched for the button on all fours, eventually dragging free a crumpled

169

object. It was their mother's fish-scale geranium. Meg placed the embroidery back where she found it and returned to the table.

They sat together in the comfort of the crackling fire. The house was so quiet that the birds on the roof were the only other sounds to be heard. Through the window they could see Ethan placing a bottle on an anthill. He paced backwards through the grass, tossing something in his palm that he then pelted at the target, and missed. He immediately bent over and started scrabbling about in the tufted grass for a fresh missile.

Meg went to Julian, draping an arm about his shoulders. 'Father thought it was strange of Mother to bring Ethan home too. I thought I'd feel good, but I don't. Let's go get Mr Fox and hunt some scrub turkeys. Maybe Ethan could come,' she said.

'Do you want to ask him?'

They watched through the window as Ethan kicked savagely at the base of the anthill.

'Nup,' she said.

⫸ Chapter 25 ⫷

The dray crested the low ridge and came slowly towards the homestead. Julian, repairing a fence in an adjoining paddock, twisted the wire tight and pushed back the brim of his hat. Beneath the melted glass of the sky he watched his father's return from Bourke. Julian had been thinking about what he needed to do with the remainder of his time at Dalhunty Station before his planned escape. The thought of his imminent departure struck more forcefully with every passing hour. He now enjoyed the chores he attended to, appreciated each small exchange with his sisters and was spending the early evenings walking about the tumble-down buildings that once hummed with activity. He was hoarding memories and doing his best to imprint them in his mind.

A little further along the fence some of their former Aboriginal stockmen arrived and began to replace a rotted post. One of the men acknowledged Julian with a brief wave and then set to task digging out the broken post. The request for assistance hadn't been made, however the unspoken agreement between the former stockmen and his father held firm.

When he was a child there had been more Aboriginal stockmen than white stockmen on the station. Most of them lived in huts or humpies and visited their families' seasonal camps at every opportunity. Ben liked those men. He said they knew more about the property than any white man ever could. When the Great Flood came the women and children were already miles away, after having simply gathered their belongings and left. There was something to be said for moveable camps; of not being tethered to a dwelling.

Aboriginal men had advised Julian's great-grandfather not to build the Dalhunty homestead in that location. Big water would come eventually, they had said. It always did. But local knowledge and the remnant watermarks on tree trunks were no match for a man intent on moulding nature to his own design.

The Indigenous people cleared out gradually with the station's demise. Some moved further away to find more work. Others passed of illness. Some families were taken to a mission on the outskirts of Brewarrina, where it was said they were given cod liver oil every morning and forced to wash in sheep dip. Julian didn't know if that was true or not. Everything he knew came from second-hand news-papers, old books and the fragments of conversation. Ben's admission about the lack of Aboriginal domestics and what had happened to Maryanne and her family only highlighted Julian's ignorance. He existed in one of the soapy bubbles Meg had blown as a child.

His parents were not ones for speculation, however Great-grandfather Lance's death by spearing may well have been deserved. During his time on the station, from the 1860s on, Aboriginal women on a nearby property had been accosted and Julian had heard talk of killings. Sheep were speared in retaliation and the troubles heightened. Stockmen, labourers, managers and owners rode out for retribution, convinced of their righteousness – as if the loss of stock were equal to a human life. It was said Great-grandfather Lance went with them, although initially uninvolved and unaffected. There were rumours of a massacre. Julian wasn't sure where the truth lay, but his heart told him the white men had done wrong. Maybe Meg was right. Perhaps the Dalhuntys deserved their downfall.

He rolled up the wire, tucking the pliers in a back pocket, then checked the tautness of the new line, which was subject to breakage by emus. What else was hidden in the soil's memory? Far more than one man could comprehend, he was sure. When Julian looked again, the dray was a good half mile away, then it gradually slowed. His father leant to one side, as if he were searching for something, then kept on leaning until he was no longer visible.

Julian tied the coil of wire to the saddle, as Calamity danced about on her hooves. He waited. The dray was now stationary. The cart received more maintenance than the rest of the property, was greased religiously and when not in use was parked in a shed, however axles broke, spokes still cracked, and wheels fell off when least expected – with or without Frank's interference. Julian placed the pliers in a saddlebag and leapt onto Calamity. There was every likelihood that the weight of transporting the piano to Bourke had caused the cart to fall apart on the way home.

Julian waved to the stockmen and trotted Calamity across the rough ground, hollering hello at his father. There was no response. He felt a twinge of anxiety and clipped the horse's flanks with his heels. Once at the dray he dismounted and walked around to the other side.

Ben was lying face-down on the ground, one arm spread at a right angle. Julian dropped to his side, turned him sky-up and lifted him so that he rested against his chest.

'Father? Dad? Are you all right? What happened?' Julian touched Ben's brow, and propped him against the dray's wheel. There was no sign of injury – or of the man who dwelt within. He fetched a waterbag and trickled the liquid into his father's mouth, which Ben swallowed. 'Good. That's a good sign. Can you stand? Come on, let's try.' He hefted his father, a dead weight. 'I can't do this by myself. Come on.'

With excruciating slowness his father reached for the side of the dray and, very slowly, Julian helped him up into it.

Julian braced him with an arm as they travelled the ribbed ground, every bump and ditch reverberating through his bones. Memories of finding Davey strung upside down in the well coloured each yard that brought them closer to home.

Julian shouted loudly when they arrived at the homestead and the family straggled from various places to meet them – Laura from the chicken coop, their mother from the house. Ethan and Meg paused in the hoeing of the vegetable plot and it was Meg who ran first. She rushed from the tilled ground, keeping pace with the moving cart.

'Is it a snake bite?' Meg panted.

Ethan reached them and jumped up onto the moving dray. 'What the heck happened?'

'I don't know,' said Julian.

They came to a stop at the yard gate.

'Is he hurt? Is your father hurt?' screamed their mother.

Ethan and Julian carried Ben to the veranda, sitting him in a chair.

'He just fell from the dray. I gave him water. He can't speak.'

'Mercy, mercy, mercy. What have you done to yourself, Ben?' Rachael checked Ben's temperature and then removed his shirt. The soiled singlet was sticking out against the white of skin untouched by sun. She examined him for broken bones or bites, and then leant back on her haunches. 'We must make him tea, Laura. Good and strong. And soup. Yes, lots of soup. To warm his blood.'

'All right, Mother,' Laura said, heading straight for the kitchen.

'Where's the nearest doctor?' asked Ethan.

'Bourke,' replied their mother distractedly. 'From the outside there's nothing wrong with him.'

'I'll get the doctor. I'll ride faster than fast,' said Meg.

'No, you will not. None of you will. I won't have him poked and prodded for no good reason. I've had enough of doctors with their black bags and stethoscopes and mournful prognoses. We'll let your father sit here quietly and tend him ourselves.' She searched

174

Ben's pockets and read the credit slip from the general store, showing the paperwork to Julian, who glanced at the pitiful amount received for the vegetables. 'Hardly worth the effort and there's no bill of sale for the piano. Where is it, if it's not been sold?'

She rose stiffly. Julian calmed his mother with assurances that the piano must have been sold, with the money to be deposited into their bank account. They were sure to receive notification very soon.

'Wese should get a doctor,' said Meg.

'No. Your aunt had a fit of the vapours every time the doctor visited. He would stand at her bedside and tut as if she were a wayward child. *Pity she's still reasonably young.* That's what he said. Twice a week. As if she weren't even in the room. As if she were already gone. I'll not subject your father to that.' She clutched her husband's arm as if the very action might revive him.

Ben was a pitiful sight. In his singlet his father was stringy and lean. The muscles in his biceps were firm bulges, like well-grown apples, however the rest of him was as lank as a rag doll, as if all his stuffing had spilled out by the side of the road.

'Julian,' said his mother. 'You're in charge until your father recovers.'

Meg tugged his arm in encouragement, and the burden of expectation caught like a stone in his throat. Only minutes ago he had been storing memories in anticipation of his leaving.

⊰ Chapter 26 ⊱

The following two days passed in a whirl of bed, baths and the putting on and taking off of night clothes. Rachael was convinced that if anything was to raise their father's spirits it would be his love of clothes, and great consideration was given as to what Ben might fancy wearing every day. They began with his favourites hanging in the wardrobe, and when these items drew no interest Laura and Meg rummaged through their ancestors' chests. They dragged out items, some unseen for more than fifty years, holding them high for approval, as moths and other crawlies fell dead to the floor, the stench of camphor almost asphyxiating them.

On the morning of the third day of Ben's illness, the girls paraded numerous garments in front of Ben, with no success. Finally their mother decreed brown twill trousers and a blue, green and white striped shirt with a knotted neck handkerchief of yellow silk would suffice.

Once their father was dressed, the family gathered close to the bed where he lay propped up on frilly-edged pillows. His woolly hair was freshly combed, and his long sideburns were trimmed. A spray of withered lavender nestled on the deep-purple coverlet

176

and the silver-topped cane was propped nearby, as if this single accoutrement would propel him to action. Ben's eyes were open, staring listlessly ahead. The left side of his face sagged against the yellow necktie bunched at his chin.

Ethan fidgeted like a schoolboy. Laura, almost concealed by a bundle of discarded clothes, was nearly white. Julian was unsure whether this was due to the smell of the decaying clothes or the king-like figure laying uselessly before them.

'Youse sure?' Meg balanced on one leg at the end of the bed, a foot perched in the crook of her knee. 'Father's been wearing cricketing whites an awful lot. At least let him have the straw hat. He always wears a hat.'

Rachael's slight bosom rose up and down. 'There is no need for the boater, Meg. He will be in the shade. And stand up straight, girl. What would your father say?' she said sternly.

'Reckon he'd be pleased I was upright, considering the state he's in,' replied Meg, swapping one leg for the other.

'Go and do something constructive, young lady,' said Rachael.

Convinced fresh air and sunlight would help Ben, Rachael ordered Julian and Ethan to carry him outside. They sat him carefully in the squatter's chair on the veranda and under Rachael's direction they crossed Ben's legs at the ankle and wedged a pillow behind his body. Rachael was pleased, convinced her husband was better.

To Julian, there was little change. Rachael took a pannikin from Laura and slowly spooned the mixture of water and sugar into Ben's mouth, massaging his throat until he swallowed. She praised him in an unnatural voice and then sweet-talked a little more of the sugar water down her husband's throat, his gullet ticking softly like a clock running down. Then she mopped the liquid from his chin with the hem of her apron.

Meg came to Julian and looked at him searchingly. He tweaked her nose and tried to invent an explanation that might ease the strain they all felt. She saw his indecision and patted his arm as if he were the one in need of consoling. Then she went to the veranda wall and, finding a space devoid of stirrup irons, slid down the boards until she was sitting on the floor.

Close to the yard fence, the fox was nose-deep in a clump of button grass. Ethan was watching the animal's movements.

'Have you seen anyone sick like this before?' Julian questioned him.

'Why would you be asking me?' Ethan said sharply and walked inside the house.

He was still cranky about Ben's outburst, which, Julian admitted, had been cruel. In the yard the fox padded past Bony. The crafty animal was cunning enough to keep a safe distance as the half-breed dog stretched out the full length of his chain and snapped in annoyance. At the corner of the yard near the drooping orange tree, Frank had set up camp, rigging a piece of hessian from fence to tree for shade and stretching out on the grass. A bundle of netting and a machete – tools for the palm grove – sat next to him. He was waiting to be informed of hospital visiting hours for he thought it appropriate Ben be updated on the quality of the ripening date fruit. He had also recommended the application of leeches to draw out the phlegm accosting his Honoured Brother and had a jar of thick, slimy specimens on hand for when they were required.

'My boy. Death's clammy hand will not take Benjamin yet. He is too irascible to merit entry into the great oasis in the sky. I know. I myself have been refused admittance on a number of occasions. They are quite finicky,' stated Frank.

On the veranda, Rachael held her husband's knee, rocking slowly back and forth, singing a tune that was dampened by worry.

⫷ Chapter 27 ⫸

Early February

Julian lifted the last barrel onto the rear of the dray as Ethan leant nonchalantly against the stable wall, jiggling the buckets he carried. The Natural was perfecting the neutral expression he employed to full effect when he and Julian were alone. He had barely spoken to anyone since the argument in the kitchen when he had been relegated to the status of waif and stray.

The change in Ethan's disposition had taken hold as clearly as the decline that struck his father. Ethan was late to meals, his hearty appetite diminished, and he went about the daily tasks requested of him with an edgy composure and a level of absorption that kept everyone at bay. They were all doing their best to pretend as if nothing were amiss, an impossibility when there were such serious issues in play, issues that made Ethan's discontent easier to ignore than address.

A week had passed and Ben still had not recovered. Whether a fit or some other illness was the cause of his stupor, it was impossible to tell. He spent his days on the veranda barely eating and refusing to speak, except to give a slurred yes or no. It was impossible to tell if his behaviour was due to sickness or stubbornness, although the left side of his face still sagged. But the Dalhuntys carried on as if their lives were unchanged, every hour drudging into the next, the days marked by sameness, persevering with what was expected, while uncertainty stalked them all.

Julian leapt up onto the dray and rotated an empty barrel until it was next to another, readying for the drive to the river to fetch water for the seedling trays and the few straggly vegetables left for their consumption.

'Is there any point to this?' Ethan asked.

'We still need to eat,' replied Julian. This was the first time Ethan had spoken since dinner two days previously, when Rachael had launched into a tirade about the playability of the piano after it had been dismantled and then reassembled with nothing but Ben's sketchy diagrams to work from. That, she concluded, was the reason there was no bill of sale and no letter from the purchaser confirming the deposit of funds into their account. The piano was unsaleable.

'What do you have to say about this, Ethan? You helped put it all back together,' Rachael had asked.

Ethan had tapped a fork on the table, attracting Julian's attention, ignoring the insinuation.

'Pass the salt,' was all he had said.

Julian jumped from the rear of the dray. 'Do you want to drive today? Calamity's easier to control since I've been riding him.'

'Why? I've never been able to budge you out of the seat before,' said Ethan.

'Forget it. Are you ready?'

Ethan slouched back against the knotty wood of the stable wall. 'I didn't think your father was going to come back from Bourke.'

Julian checked the harness on Calamity and the plodder piebald. 'Why wouldn't he?'

'I dunno. He might have decided to take a chance somewhere else.'

'Like you did?' replied Julian testily. He checked the shafts connecting horses to cart.

'Yeah. Look how well that turned out.' Ethan swung the bucket so that it struck the wall with a dull repetitive thud. 'If I'd known none of you wanted me here, I wouldn't have come.'

Julian was so weary of arguments, of the irritation that festered through his family. And yet he was sorry for the comment his father had made in the kitchen. He said as much to Ethan.

Ethan's distrust showed in the directness of his gaze. Over the last months the hungriness in Ethan's eyes seemed to have disappeared, or maybe Julian was immune to it now. He almost pitied him.

'My father never came home. He got run over by a hansom cab. One of the wheels went straight across his neck. Crushed his windpipe.' Ethan stroked the knobby cartilage in his throat. 'Mother put me into apprenticeship soon after and when I came home one night she was gone, along with my brothers and sisters.'

'Why are you telling me this now?' asked Julian.

'Things change but you get to used to it. It's already been a week. He won't come good, you know.'

Before he realised what he was doing, Julian punched Ethan hard on the nose. It was a long time coming and they both knew it. Ethan, half stunned, blood dribbling down his lip, calmly placed the buckets on the ground. Julian readied for the onslaught. He knew Ethan would fight like a gutter kid. They both would. All the long hours spent together, being obliged to sleep in the same room, working side by side from sun-up to dark, meant little when you barely spoke to one another. The closeness forced upon them had only made the relationship worse. Ethan cracked his knuckles and for the first time Julian saw the real Ethan Harris, the person he'd glimpsed at the river all those long months ago. He knew for certain their dislike of each other was mutual.

'Hello, hello.' Rick the Dane appeared out of the scrub, his yellow hair flying. The sight of him caused Bony to bark and the chickens to scatter.

'The boat's in,' Julian commented and lowered his fists. Then he called towards the house, 'Everyone, the boat's in!'

Ethan grimaced. 'Another time,' he said gruffly.

181

Rick was scarcely puffed by the run from the river, though his cheeks glowed through ruddy skin. 'Wool-wrangler, the snag-dodger sends his regards. We're unloading the goods. If you bring the hoof-cart we can lift the furniture onto it.' Rick adjusted the leather strap that angled from shoulder to hip holding a waterbag. He noticed Ethan's bloody nose. 'Are we spear-clashing?'

'Accident,' replied Ethan impatiently.

'Pity.' Rick looked to where Laura walked towards them, the stench of tallow rendered for soap carrying on the breeze. Washing was strewn over the fence and another pile protruded from a basket. She used the arm of her blouse to pat the sweat from her brow and checked the scarf about her hair.

'Freya blesses. And here is your blood. She is no painted jezebel but a daughter of the earth goddess,' said Rick loudly.

With their recent altercation still fresh, Julian kept Ethan at arm's length, ordering him to help Rachael and his sisters pack the dray with the women's fancywork. He and Rick would ride to the river, with the intention of bringing the captain back to visit their father.

Laura flatly refused to go anywhere near the boat. She placed the washing basket on the ground, rubbed her chapped hands and then picked it up again, avoiding Rick, who grinned slavishly.

'The earth goddess likes me,' said Rick admiringly, as Laura left for the house.

'Yeah, right,' said Ethan. 'You're an old man.'

Rick grabbed Ethan by the collar of his shirt. 'Not so old that I can't best you, lad.' He let go of Ethan, and followed Julian to the stables.

Julian and Rick rode abreast towards the *Lady Matilda*. Along the way Julian explained his father's condition, hopeful Rick might have heard of a similar illness. However the Dane was even less knowledgeable than they were. His doctoring skills went little further than cod liver oil and pulling one of his own teeth out with string attached to a thrown hammer.

'Your father. Were he to die with honour he would go straight to Valhalla,' commented Rick.

'He's not a warrior, Rick. And he's not dying. He's not doing anything. He just sits,' Julian called impatiently as they galloped through the timber.

'Ja, ja. Everything is one thing or the other with you, wool-wrangler. Maybe Odin believes your father has fought many spear-clashes. Maybe he is already warrior. And your sister. The little earth goddess. She is of marriageable age?' he asked.

'You can forget about Laura. She's turned down Ian Fraser and he's got land and money.' Julian was still trying to comprehend Laura's decision. After their mother, his sister was the most gentrified of all of them, with her sewing, flower-gathering and struggling herb garden, and dislike for anything that bordered on mucky. The type of life Laura aspired to required money. 'Besides, you're missing one crucial quality as a suitor. She has to be in love with you.'

He expected Rick to reply with one of his usual witty phrases, or at the very least a hearty laugh at this.

'Ah,' said Rick. 'What we all wouldn't do for that heaven star.'

⊰ Chapter 28 ⊱

At the waterway Julian slid from Calamity and sprinted to the river's edge. Captain Ashby was on the platform shouting orders at the crew aboard the *Lady Matilda* while sipping a pannikin of tea. He wore a peak hat of blue and white with gold braiding and a smart dress coat that showed no signs of last year's paunch. Julian skirted a sofa and several paintings that had already been off-loaded onto the deck, and reached the Captain's side.

Ashby greeted him with enthusiasm and commented on the fine pieces of furniture currently being unloaded. Then he resumed watching his men, shouting at them to be careful. The two skinny deckhands, Awang and Joe, passed an armchair to Rick and the Captain chastised the three of them, telling them to use the gangway and not hand the smaller items across the gap between boat and land in case they were dropped.

Julian blurted out the news of his father's accident and subsequent illness and asked the Captain to ride back to the homestead to see him. 'He fell from the dray coming back from Bourke last week and hasn't been himself since.'

'Accident?' The Captain was focused on the steamer's winch,

which was being using to hoist up a large dining table. 'Is he speaking and eating?'

'A little.'

The Captain's attention never drifted from the table, which was now in the air and being swung towards the bank. He drizzled the remains of his tea on the ground and set the pannikin aside.

'Has he his vision and hearing?' Captain Ashby steadied the table as it was lowered, ensuring it landed softly.

'He appears to.'

The Captain undid the leather strapping and checked the table for any scratches. 'Not a mark,' he said satisfied. 'Well then, if his vitals are holding, he's already on the mend. Send him my best wishes and tell him to put a little brandy in water before bed. It will heat the blood and drive out whatever ails him.'

'But Captain Ashby, please . . .' implored Julian.

'Your father is one of my closest friends and under any other circumstances I would already be riding to his door, but when is a riverboat captain's life ever normal? I would have been here sooner were it not for the shearers' strike at the Bowengally shed. After we loaded at Brewarrina we turned like a duck to come here and now we are in a race with this latest river rise. You understand, lad. I know you do.'

Rick unshouldered a rolled carpet, letting it drop at Julian's feet, and returned to the steamer.

'And the furniture? Rick said your men would help load it on the dray.'

'This run doesn't have the push in it of last year. And I'll not be tarrying until I'm safe in Echuca. Although I did want to discuss purchasing that piano back from your father. Tell him that I have little choice but to send a dray to collect it. I was carried away by your father's romantic notion.'

'My father took the piano to Bourke to sell. At least, we assume it was sold.'

The Captain stopped his overseeing of three smaller tables being carried from the steamer, the last of the furniture, and swivelled on his heels. 'What do you mean he took it to Bourke? That you assume it was sold? When?'

'A week ago. I know Father's only paid you half of what's owed, but we never should have purchased it. The bore's gone dry and we need to drill a new one.' It was a pitiful admission. 'We found no bill of sale for the piano when my father returned home and are yet to receive confirmation that funds for it have been deposited into our account. You have no mail for us, do you?'

'No. I don't, lad. That's unexpected. Most unexpected.' The Captain stiffened a little and then ordered Mr Cummins to stoke the boiler. The engineer gave a flippant salute as he secured the winch. Ashby reached for his pocket watch, checked the time and studied the water's current. Branches floated by.

Julian moved to stand directly in front of him. 'Please come and see him.'

'Give my very best to your father.'

He moved to the gangway as Rick and the goat-saving deckhand loaded firewood from the cut pile on the bank.

'But, Captain Ashby, my mother has enough fancywork to pay your freight costs and there will be monies left over. Money that we need,' Julian called after him.

He realised it was useless. The Captain was already on board and the deckhands were running to load the timber. Why was the man in such a rush? As long as the *Lady Matilda* stayed with the front of the flooding there was no immediate risk of danger. What was another five or ten minutes? And was he mistaken or had the captain grown more impatient after learning about the piano?

The men were still stacking wood as the smokestack belched and the paddles started to turn. Rick untied the mooring rope and threw it and himself aboard the towed wool barge before the riverboat pulled from the shore. He pushed a pole against the bank, ensuring the barge didn't beach.

'I will be back to see your little earth goddess.' Rick raised a fist into the air.

The *Lady Matilda* slowly gathered pace. About Julian, his aunt's possessions – tables, chairs, crates, paintings and a rolled carpet – sat in the blaring sun. There was little room for the pieces in the homestead. Where were they to put them? His father was right, his aunt's furniture should have been sold, not railed to Bourke and then floated down the Darling. He stared sullenly at the departing steamer.

The snapping of twigs announced his mother and Meg in the dray. Frank was spurring Henrietta with the crop, steering her one way and then the other in an effort to overtake them.

Rachael called out to the steamer as the cart came to a stop. Lifting a sack from the rear she rushed to the water's edge, as Frank finally manoeuvred past and walked Henrietta to the bank.

'Wait!' she cried out again, holding up the sack. 'Captain Ashby, wait! My handiwork. Please. My fancywork. I have baskets and doilies and fish-scale flowers and—' She dropped the hessian bag on the ground. 'Why is he going, Julian? Why didn't he wait?'

'He probably knows he gave us lice,' said Meg sagely.

'He's worried about how far the fresh will go downriver.' Julian chose not to voice his confusion about the captain's behaviour.

Frank surveyed the furniture from atop Henrietta. 'Mrs Dalhunty, this very fine camel and I, Frank Ukulele Dalhunty, would be honoured to transport your furniture. As you well know, the dray is really not appropriate for precious belongings. They will crack during transportation. And in payment I would require very little. Perhaps that rug that has been dumped on the ground. Admittedly it appears to be of poor quality, however as your Honoured Husband's brother it is only correct that I accept a lesser fee for my—'

'Frank, will you please be quiet,' shouted Rachael.

At that moment Ethan arrived on Goliath and charged towards the deck, a pillowcase swinging from the saddle. His mouth was set firm and straight, as if he too had a hard bit clenched between his teeth. The gelding galloped headlong towards the river with no sign of slowing. Ethan was riding as if possessed.

'Pull up! Pull up, Ethan!' yelled Julian.

Goliath galloped right to the river's edge and without slowing his stride leapt from the sandy bank. The big horse cut through the air and then began to fall. Julian's mother screamed as horse and rider landed with a splash, Ethan instantly unsaddled.

'Blasted horse!' said Julian. 'Why is he even riding him?'

Meg was beside Julian in an instant. 'Will he drown too?'

Ethan came up spluttering and coughing. Julian called to him to swim to safety before the current took hold, but although he was closer to the shore, he made for the *Lady Matilda* and kept right on flailing through the wash, even though the boat gained momentum with every rotation of its wheels. Ethan's head was barely above water.

Frank hooked one leg over the other on Henrietta and pushed tobacco into the bowl of his pipe. 'May the wind always be at his back.'

Julian cupped his mouth and gave a cooee. The shock of the fall must have disorientated Ethan, for he kept on following the boat and barge. Across the river Goliath did a neat circle in the water, scrambled up the bank and trotted into the bush.

Ethan went under the water a second time. Clearly swimming was something The Natural couldn't do. Rachael pleaded with Julian to help him, and annoyance pitted his stomach. What the hell was Ethan doing riding Goliath? Why wasn't he swimming to shore?

Out in the river Ethan's splashing grew more frantic.

'Julian, for pity's sake,' said his mother.

Meg slunk closer. 'You have to save him.'

'Damnation.' Julian reefed off his boots, skidded down the bank and dived into the river. The water was cold. It snaked through his clothes and weighed him down, dragging at his body. He rose to the surface, kicking fiercely at branches threatening to snag him and spat muddy water from his mouth. Shirts floated by. White shirts. Neatly folded shirts that usually sat on the chair at the end of Ethan's bed.

Julian tried to swim as best he could, half-dog and half-crayfish, intent on making his way to the middle of the brown river where the current would take hold and whisk him forwards. After that, he had no idea what to do. If he reached Ethan there was only the barge forging further ahead every minute or dry land to choose from. Land was the only option. Perhaps Ethan could be guided to the riverbank if they broke free of the current and were not drowned in the process. Julian gulped down water. Best not to think about that.

The carcass of a sheep drifted along with him, centipedes and ants riding the woolly raft. Ahead, Julian caught a glimpse of Ethan and, further on, Rick standing at the rear of the wool-loaded barge busy with rope. He tossed a line into the water and shouted. Julian heard Meg scream as the current took hold of his body and he was propelled by the running waters. His arms and legs floundered while old fence posts and a charred stump floated past.

Then something hard and sharp struck Julian in the back of the head and he slipped below the water.

⋘ Part 2 ⋙

The River

⋙ Chapter 29 ⋘

Julian woke to the sound of someone blowing a whistle. Such a blaze of pain filled his head that it took time to separate the throbbing from the rhythmic vibration that rose around him. He opened his eyes to dim light and sifted slowly through the noises and smells. Creaking timber. Heavy footsteps. Woodsmoke. The splash of water. The whistle sounded a second time, short and sharp. Men spoke to each other, their voices rising and falling as if through a dense fog. Julian touched thick wadding wrapped about his skull and with difficulty levered his body upright from the bed towards a square of light. A small window in the cabin revealed a wharf high above upon which crowds gathered. People hurried back and forth. Orders were given. A crane swung a crate labelled WORCESTERSHIRE SAUCE.

A cold sweat broke out across Julian's skin and he coughed. Pain coursed through his head and he lay down again. He swore by everything good and holy not to move one inch until the ache subsided.

He sensed the square of light from the window disappearing and partially opened an eye. Someone was moving about the dark space. He shuddered with heat and pushed away the heaviness covering his body, only to feel the weight secured about him. The woman spoke, telling him to sleep. A coolness rested on his brow. Scents of lemon and lavender layered the air.

He woke later to a brief knock. Daylight striped the room. Julian fixed on the curve of material that moulded the woman's hips and then closed his eyes against the blinding light. He listened as she asked for the door to be closed, explaining that it was important the patient be kept in a cool, dark environment. A man commented on the stifling heat and then requested she leave, her footsteps neat and quick on the timber floor.

'He should be sent home,' said the man.

'And how are we going to do that when he has a gash to the head?'

Julian was afraid that his earlier agony would return if he spoke, so he tried to relax and let his body be lulled by the strangely familiar voices.

'Well, his brains haven't fallen out, so the boy can't be too ill. Five to three he survives. That's pretty good odds, Cap.'

'Are you a complete idiot, Cummins? We don't bet on injured people.'

Julian thought of Noah's Ark. Of pianos and sheep, and vegetables, rotting vegetables falling from the rear of a dray. His father waving. Meg sharpening her knife. And then Ethan, riding like a man possessed towards the Darling. Ignoring the family that had taken him in and jumping Goliath from the riverbank into the water.

Water.

Where was Ethan?

Cummins and Captain Ashby were still talking. They were arguing about him, Cummins protesting that Julian should have been left at the Port-O-Bourke, while the Captain was adamant that he remain onboard.

'Head wounds are messy things, Cummins. A person must lie still and not move. You know this for a fact. Now go and fetch Miss Carlisle back.'

'She shouldn't be here either, what with everything that's going on.'

'There is *nothing* going on,' the Captain snapped.

'Yet,' replied Cummins gloomily.

'After you've brought Miss Carlisle, I want you to go and check on the other boy. Diving a horse into the river. I've never seen such recklessness.'

◄ Chapter 30 ►

Julian woke and looked down to find a woman running a wash-cloth across his stomach in a circular motion. He thought it a dream and tried to prolong the vision, considered the possibilities of where the fantasy might lead . . .

The woman dunked the cloth in a basin on her lap, wrung it out and proceeded to mop his chest. 'I'm Miss Carlisle. I was a passenger on the *Lady Matilda* last year, the day we collected your wool. How are you feeling?'

Julian was not sure how to respond. He hadn't been dreaming. The magical Miss Carlisle was at his side. Her attentiveness was causing myriad sensations. He thought back to the vision at the prow of the steamer, her dress rippling in the breeze, the dark brown of her hair, and then at the young woman before him, the same woman who had been in his thoughts for many months. While her broad forehead and high cheekbones were made less pretty by an angular jaw, she was more than handsome. The wash-cloth swished again across his stomach. He was naked. Julian grabbed her wrist. This was no daydream and he needed her to stop, lest he humiliate himself.

Miss Carlisle's cheeks reddened as she dropped the washcloth unceremoniously into the basin. She got up from the bed and placed the basin on the floor before taking a water jug from a bracketed shelf and pouring the contents into a cup. Returning to Julian's side, she supported his neck and held the vessel as he sipped.

Julian lay back on the narrow bed, feeling the thick bandage about his head. 'Where are we?'

'You're on the *Lady Matilda*, swanning down the Darling like a regular tourist. The Captain's a good man. I hear he saved your parents many years ago,' she said quietly.

'And Ethan?'

'Alive and aboard,' she replied.

This wasn't the way it was meant to be. Ethan was to have stayed, happily, on the property with his parents while Julian sought out a new life. He studied the small room, determined to ignore Miss Carlisle's closeness. Her hands on her hips, the stance accentuating the impossible smallness of her waist. Apart from the wall-bracket, which held the basin and jug, and his clothes, which were hanging from a peg, there was only room for a chair and a small table.

'You talk in your sleep. Meg is your sister? The one with the red curly hair? I remember her. She's feisty. I think she and I would be firm friends,' she said.

'My little sister.' Through the window pelicans lifted from the river, gliding upwards in wide-wing strokes.

The door to the cabin suddenly flew open, and there was Rick the Dane, grinning.

'Ah, the fool-saver lives. Now you will be wondering how this is so. It was I. Rick.' He thumped his chest. 'You will tell your earth goddess sister of this, ja? The women like their heroes.' With that, Rick shoved Ethan, who was holding a pair of shoes, into the room and thrust a tray at him. 'Your new nursemaid. Captain's orders. Make sure he shares the food.'

Miss Carlisle left without a word and Rick closed the door behind her, leaving Ethan and Julian alone. A key turned.

'We're locked in here?' asked Julian.

'Don't complain. Your accommodation is a darn sight better than mine.'

Ethan put the tray and his leather shoes, which were stuffed with paper, carefully on the floor then proceeded to push bread into his mouth and slurp from a pannikin. His concentration was so great that it was a few minutes before he rose to stand at Julian's bedside to offer food and drink. They observed each other guardedly and then Julian mastered a half-sitting position, declined the bread and accepted the tea gratefully. He guzzled some down, and then spat half of it back up. The dark liquid dribbled down his bare chest to pool in his belly button.

Ethan took delight in explaining that the men had taken bets on whether Julian would live or die. The Captain wasn't having any of it, but the Dane and Mr Cummins had exchanged money. He sat in the chair and chewed the bread noisily. He'd known Julian would survive. A bit of a knock on the head never hurt anyone.

Julian used the blanket to mop up the spilt tea. It was probably useless asking Ethan if he knew where on the Darling they were, but he did anyway.

Ethan laughed. 'I've been locked in a room near the boiler. A dark hole if ever there was one. Apparently we're trouble-makers. Well, I am at least. You're damned by association. Anyway we could be heading to France for all I know. Why did you come after me? I would have thought you would have cheered at my going.'

'Meg asked me to.'

'Meg? And have you always done what your baby sister tells you?'

'She was with me that day,' said Julian tiredly.

'What day?' Ethan repositioned the chair so that his legs rested on the bed.

'The day we found Davey. Meg was with me when I pulled him up from the well. She was the one who found him hanging upside down. You don't forget something like that. Ever. She saw you in the water and—'

Ethan tossed the remaining bread on the tray. 'You don't have to tell me about it.'

They had laid Davey on his back and although he was wet, cold and grey his throat made minute clicking noises as if deep within some part of him was trying to get out. Meg set about hammering his small chest with her fists crying over and over, 'Come on, Davey. You can do it. Come on, Davey.' For many nights Julian had dreamt of Meg's desperate pleas.

'I carried him home and his body was so tiny. As light as air. That's when it came to me. He was gone. Meg didn't speak for a whole month.'

He saw it clearly now. Rachael's withdrawal from the entire family, Ben's inability to forgive himself for his part in the accident, and, maybe, Rachael's failure to forgive her husband. Was the wedge now too great between his parents to be repaired?

They sat quietly. The Dalhuntys depended on water. Water for pasture and livestock and paddle-steamers and the blasted growing of vegetables. But it was water that gradually set in motion the family's decline. Too little and too much. Water washed away their sheep. Water took Davey. Water delivered Ethan. Water had changed the direction of their lives. He hated water, yet most nights he prayed for it.

'So, coming after me was because of that. Because of what happened?' Ethan waited, however Julian didn't answer. 'Well, it put the wind up everyone, I imagine, me jumping into the river. Was Goliath all right?'

'He swam to the bank. I'm pretty disappointed at your leaving with Father sick. You're needed at home. I mean, we all are,' he quickly clarified.

'Need met opportunity. I'm not saying sorry, if that's what you expect. Why would I? It's the best for everyone, my going. One less mouth to feed.' He emphasised this. 'I only hope that I can get my old job back at Bon Marche. I know what you're thinking. It's a petty job to you, waiting on others, but there's nothing wrong with being in retail. Plenty of men have made their fortunes in merchandising.'

'You must really like shoes.'

'Who said anything about liking them? To live, you have to be able to put food on the table and a roof over your head. You have to be able to hold your head high when you walk down the street. And it makes a difference to be with people who appreciate you for who you are. I never had much, but I do have some pride. Just not quite as much stubborn pride as you and the rest of your family. So here we are. Locked up together in this tiny room because the Captain doesn't want any trouble.'

Yes, here Julian was, trapped with the boy whom he'd disliked from the very beginning. What a fool he'd been to believe that Ethan could assume his role on the property, while Julian left to live life as he wished. And now here they were: two young men, both of whom wanted to escape. Through the window the river-bank was brazenly red-soiled. Ethan would laugh if he knew the truth.

❧ Chapter 31 ❧

It was late afternoon the following day and Ethan was lying on the floor of Julian's room, ankles crossed, arms behind his head, talking incessantly. It was as if having found himself cabin-bound, his brain was now in overdrive. Julian placed the pillow over his head, trying to drown out the sound of Ethan working his way through reasons for their prolonged captivity. He had managed to convince himself that the Captain and his crew were involved in unlawful activities, as demonstrated by the stacks of crates stored near the boiler room. Pointing out the obvious – that the Captain freighted goods for a living – did little to assuage Ethan, who remained convinced of his theory.

'You did leap into the river on horseback.' Julian's voice was muffled through the pillow. 'Not quite the behaviour to instil confidence in a person, and I've been tarred with the same brush, having jumped in after you.'

'That's right. Julian Dalhunty, the fool-saver. We're both fools, I think.' Ethan sat up, tugged the pillow free from Julian's grip and hurled it across the room. Then he laced his shoes. They were now dry and clean, thanks to the tallow begged from the cook.

Ethan pushed on the toe section with a thumb. Julian guessed the swim in the river had shrunk them. He wasn't sorry for that and wiggled his bare toes, wishing he had not been so quick to remove his boots. Or, for that matter, to dive in after Ethan.

Through the narrow window river life played out in vivid shades of brown and green. Julian sat on the bed, his bandaged skull spared from the timber wall by his rolled shirt, sweat trickling down his stomach. He was currently up to eight pelicans, at least twenty or so cockatoos, three hawks, and a brightly plumed parrot. He'd lost count of the number of ducks.

'You haven't been listening, have you?' Ethan pushed his own bedding – a rolled blanket – against the wall and rested against it. 'Miss Carlisle's probably part of it.'

'Part of what?' Julian was not having anything negative said against her. 'She cared for me.'

'I'm sure she did. Maybe I should be acting poorly as well,' replied Ethan, making spluttering noises as if ill.

The cabin was hot and filled with flies, and they were using a kerosene tin to relieve themselves. It had fallen to Ethan to empty it overboard twice a day, when the door was unlocked for that specific purpose. This task led to a new flurry of complaints from him about the heat, and the dreaded bush and the general un-civilising of men who went inland and were mad enough to remain.

Without warning, Ethan picked up the kerosene tin and began pounding on the door and yelling. The stench from the tin caused them both to gag.

Julian tugged on his shirt and covered his ears, his head pounding with the noise. Through the window a glint of colour caught his attention. There was movement along the riverbank, a formless shape weaving through the timber. He pressed his nose to the narrow pane of glass, doing his best to decipher trees, grasses and kangaroos from the rider. Thirty or so sheep charged out of the timber and down the bank to run parallel with the river. They jumped the exposed redgum roots in runs of twos and threes and then suddenly baulked at the water's edge, their sides heaving in and out with effort. An Aboriginal stockman galloped from the trees, steadied his mount down the steep side and then effortlessly wheeled the animals back up the bank and into the scrub.

'Ja, ja, ja. You feeling better, fool-saver?' Rick filled the door frame. 'You behave yourselves and you can come out. Ja?' He pointed to Ethan. 'If you cause a ruckus I'm to throw you overboard and feed you to the Goddess Hel.'

'If I go under, you're coming too, Julian,' countered Ethan.

Julian's legs were weak as he slowly followed Ethan outdoors. They squeezed through neatly stacked chaff bags and crates containing peaches and sarsaparilla, Worcestershire sauce and condensed milk, to the boat's railings, where they revelled in the evening air. The red disc of the sun shot its last rays through the timber, turning the water a pinkish-grey. Ducks floated laconically behind them as the vessel navigated a narrow bend, the limbs of saplings scraping the hull.

'So much for your theories,' Julian said. 'What was number three on your list of the Captain's treachery? Kidnapping?'

This time Ethan offered no reply. Julian noticed that the wool bales on the barge had been replaced by two cages of hens. He vaguely recalled the bustle of a wharf and the mention of a port. It could only have been Bourke.

The steamer's whistle blew and as the boat slowed at the next twist in the river it sounded again. The approaching bank was well logged of timber. Cut trees spread out in an arc, the river woodlands appearing partially scalped. The *Lady Matilda* moored near a pile of timber and the men hurried to load it, stacking it neatly on deck and carrying the overflow below. Julian and Ethan watched the Captain disembark and stretch his legs, depositing shilling coins in a tin.

'Do you want to keep moving, Cap?' asked Cummins, when Ashby reboarded.

The Captain glanced at the darkening trees that towered on either side of the river. 'The telegraph office at Port-O-Bourke said there was little water in the river at Wilcannia and were doubtful this fresh would make Menindee. But it's a night for bats and owls. I'll not chance steering too close to the bank and sweeping the wheelhouse into the water for an extra hour of travel. We'll stay until first light. But there'll be no slowing for anyone once we're under steam. We'll do what we must and be quick about it.'

'Righto, Cap,' said Cummins.

Ashby may well have walked straight past Julian if Julian had not called out and then made a point of stepping in front of him to block his path.

'Julian! You're on the mend. Good.' His welcome ignored Ethan. 'Come this way.'

The Captain led Julian, with Ethan close behind, up narrow stairs to the upper deck where stencilled lettering above a door spelt SALOON. The room held a gramophone, bookshelves, a table and chairs. Floral curtains decorated the windows on either side and a row of landscapes painted on the backs of cigar-box lids hung above a bracketed shelf displaying a stuffed parrot in a glass display case. The Captain lit the lamp dangling from the ceiling, then turned to briefly survey the riverbank through one of the windows.

'Thank you for saving me, Captain,' said Julian.

'It was the Dane that stitched you up. It is beyond me how a wheat-bag needle and a man's scalp can make a good match, but there was little choice. The task was done before Miss Carlisle boarded.'

They sat at the table where a teapot and pannikins waited. To his pannikin the Captain added a dash of brown liquid from a flask and took a gulp of the scalding brew. Then he poured a generous amount of the same liquid in Julian's tea.

'Rum,' the Captain explained. 'For medicinal purposes. Let us hope your father has recovered from whatever ails him. He is a strong man, so I have no doubt of his fortitude. Now. It is time you two lads shared the reason for your being here. Charging a horse into the river has a touch of wilfulness about it, Ethan. Which seems at odds with what you told me. Ethan said he was taken in by your parents. Is that right, Julian?'

'My mother found him in Sydney and invited him to live with us.' Julian drank the tea, savouring the sweetness of the rum. His first drink.

'Your mother is a matchless lady,' said the Captain with admiration.

'She didn't *find* me. We met in the department store where I worked,' replied Ethan.

'And you jumped into the river because . . .?'

'None of them wanted me there.'

The Captain directed his gaze at Julian. 'I find that surprising.'

Julian could have shared the truth – that his mother hadn't told any of them, not even Ben, about Ethan's arrival – and distressingly it was more than possible that Rachael had intentionally brought Ethan home as a replacement for Davey. Then there was his parents' obvious fondness for Ethan at the expense of their own children. And Legless – how could he explain the hurt that came with his father's decision? However, as he began formulating a reply, he realised how mean-spirited it made him appear.

Fortunately, the Captain came to his aid, highlighting the risk Julian had taken by jumping into the Darling and trying to save Ethan. By the end of the monologue, Julian was a hero and Ethan, a thankless individual who should have known better. It was a tough assessment, one unlikely to endear any man to the Captain, let alone a disgruntled being such as Ethan Harris.

The Captain leant back in his chair and focused on Ethan. 'Rick rescued you, at my say-so. You should be thankful, not only for Julian's part in your deliverance but for the advantage of being taken into the Dalhunty fold.'

Ethan moved his pannikin in tight circles on the table.

Miss Carlisle arrived and greeted each of them in turn. The Captain rose and drew out a vacant seat and she sat at Julian's side. Her hair was tied back with a red ribbon and Julian noticed how white and small her teeth were as she politely greeted everyone and enquired after his health. He tried not to think of his lack of shoes and replied that he was feeling much better, which was true, however his recovery had as much to do with having Miss Carlisle nearby as being released from the stuffy cabin. It was difficult not to be distracted by the young woman. Thoughts of her washing his body brought with it an intimacy that no other man at their table shared.

The Captain and Miss Carlisle launched into an animated discussion regarding the birdlife on the river. There appeared to be a competition of sorts as to who saw a certain type of bird first. As Ethan's sulky bottom lip grew more pronounced, Julian was taken by the way Miss Carlisle threw back her head as she laughed, exposing the whiteness of her throat. Her movements were light and quick as she selected a book from the shelf and located the coloured plate of a particular bird. She was excited to have spotted a dabbling duck on the river only that morning, which the Captain confirmed as a Grey Teal, known for feeding on the water's surface rather than diving for food.

'Do you like birds, Julian?' Miss Carlisle asked, showing him the picture. The bird had mottled brown plumage with white and green flashes on the wings.

'Yes,' he replied with enthusiasm, rising and waiting for her to sit as the Captain had. 'Budgerigars in particular. I've seen them drink the dew in the morning and bathe in wet grass.'

'John Gould, the ornithologist, called them the most animated, cheerful little creatures you could imagine,' said Miss Carlisle. 'I would dearly love to be able to sketch them, however my talents don't extend that far so I must content myself with binoculars and the Captain's expert knowledge.'

'Julian loves birds all right,' stated Ethan in a smug way. 'He traps and kills them, and his mother stuffs them. She has a parrot hanging on a firescreen. And they eat them as well.'

Julian could have cuffed Ethan in the ear. Ethan's comments made his mother sound like a heathen, and he little better. He took another hearty draught of the tea and rum, unsure how to recover from the slight.

'How extraordinary. Your mother is versed in taxidermy? It's an interest I share with her,' Miss Carlisle said, quite unruffled. 'I wish I had known that last year when she travelled to Bourke to catch the Sydney train. She was very gracious and spoke with me at length, although our discussions mainly concerned the latest fashions and her joy at visiting her sister after many years apart.'

Julian had quite forgotten that Miss Carlisle and his mother had been travelling companions. 'My aunt died,' he said bluntly.

'I am sorry. Your mother thought she was only maudlin at her not visiting sooner.'

Julian was sure his mother would not have appreciated the true reason for her trip exposed. He sucked on the news as if it were a lemon, recalling his mother's pained concern for Aunt Nancy when her decision was made to leave the property. How desperate she must have been to get away. To leave her family and spend treasured months among the civilised. And how she must have hoped for Aunt Nancy's life to be extended.

'Mrs Dalhunty is a proficient at making curios,' explained Captain Ashby. 'Flowers and the like being a speciality with her use of fish scales. She has quite a following down south, as does her eldest daughter Laura. I have taken many of her goods on consignment and have never had a problem selling them.'

It was odd that the Captain should be so enthusiastic about Rachael and Laura's needlework when he'd not bothered to wait for their latest batch.

Ethan pushed his chair back from the table and concentrated on the darkening river through the window. The cook bustled into the saloon with steaming plates of stew and a loaf of bread. Cutlery was dispensed, and the business of eating trumped conversation for a time. They dined to the wistful strains of a mouthorgan played by one of the deckhands, until the stillness of the river weaved its way up through the timber hull.

Miss Carlisle rose, placed a record on the gramophone and set the needle down. When 'The Song of Australia' began to play, Julian was ill-equipped for the emotion that rose within him and the memory of that long-ago family trip when Davey was still alive.

'Captain Ashby, am I right in believing we've been through Bourke?' Julian's question broke the spell of the tune and startled everyone at the table.

The Captain's drooping eyelids flickered. 'Indeed. We unloaded the wool in time to meet the Sydney train. I couldn't risk moving you, Julian, not with that injury. Your father will understand.'

'And did you send word to my parents that Ethan and I were all right?'

'Of course,' said the Captain. 'Don't worry so much, lad. You need time to recover and it's already a fair journey back to your property. You will stay with me until you're fully mended, then we can devise the best method of getting you home. If anything were to happen to you, I'd never forgive myself. For that matter, neither would your father.'

Ben's condition weighed on Julian. 'It's my father I'm particularly concerned about. And my mother and sisters, with him indisposed. They will find it difficult to run the property.'

'And what about me?' interrupted Ethan. 'I'd like to return to Sydney.'

'Even if you are convinced that a comfortable existence with the Dalhuntys is not something you're interested in, you should at least have the manners to explain your reasoning to Mr and Mrs Dalhunty rather than running away like a coward,' concluded Captain Ashby.

'I'm no coward.' Ethan bunched his fists together. 'And you can't keep me here against my will.'

'By all means, leave. Strike out into the bush and see how you fair,' challenged the Captain.

'Can you take me to Sydney, at least?'

'Get yourself a forked stick and if you can divine an eastward-flowing river that diverges with the Darling, then, all things are possible,' said the Captain. 'But short of that, this vessel won't run on dry land.'

'Maybe in a few days we could stop at one of the bigger stations? I could beg a horse to get home,' suggested Julian.

'That is an option that sits uneasily with me. First, we're not expected at one of the closer situated properties, which makes the possibility of a miles-long walk very real, and I am too fond of your father to risk his wrath by abandoning you. Second, we are already behind schedule. The Darling depends on unaccountable waters. We can't be certain how long this fresh will last. The very fact we've not seen another steamer since Bourke suggests there's little headwater to depend on. I'll not be inching along a dwindling channel by winch and rope.'

Ashby's knife and fork clattered on the table as he rose and fetched a rolled chart from the bookshelf.

Miss Carlisle moved their plates aside as the starched cloth was unfurled. The primordial Darling River was spread out before them on linen, the cloth spotted with the brown marks of moisture and errant insects. The river was indicated by two lines of varying width, drawn in faded ink and marked with bends, overhanging trees and the squares of homesteads.

The Captain told them that this was his very first river chart. It had previously belonged to William Randell, a paddle-steamer pioneer who recognised the potential of transporting wool along the river after the discovery of gold in '51 saw overland carriers prioritise shorter and more profitable trips to the fields.

Ashby's attention drifted back to the chart and he thumbed at the crosses, stitched in black thread, that noted the numerous snags. There was a sandbar further downstream with the potential of halting their progress if the water dropped. But for now he concentrated on their current position, his finger hovering above the chart.

Julian recognised the name 'Redbank' on the map. It was a well-known coach stop. He recalled a red-soiled riverbank and matched his recollections with their location on the chart. It lay behind them, along with many river miles.

Ashby rolled up the map. 'Here endeth the navigation lesson. We leave at first light.'

With his departure, Miss Carlisle explained to Julian and Ethan that they were heading back to home port – Echuca on the Murray

River. 'If we get that far,' she stated, before addressing Ethan. 'If it's Sydney you wanted you should have caught the Bourke train.'

Ethan pushed in his chair with such force the stacked plates rattled and he stomped from the saloon.

'He's not the most gracious of dinner companions.' Miss Carlisle selected another gramophone record and, once it was playing, moved slowly about the room. 'You were quite moved by "The Song of Australia".'

'It's a tune well-liked by my family, although my father always complains that it is a rather paltry tribute to Australia. He would support it becoming our national anthem, if there were ever to be such a thing, and only if an amendment were made: sheep need to be mentioned.'

Miss Carlisle laughed at this and then returned to the table. She had overheard the story of Ethan coming to Dalhunty Station and remarked that Julian's mother was compassion personified. The interloper was the last person Julian wanted to discuss, however if it wasn't for Ethan's desperation and Meg's insistence, he wouldn't be sitting next to Miss Carlisle. So he told her briefly of Ethan's unexpected arrival, so soon after the loss of Davey. Less easily shared were the resulting fractures within his family, his father's sickness, and the awful reality of what it was to be poor. He kept that a secret.

'You sound upset by your mother's decision. Don't be too hard on her, Julian. It seems to me that in Ethan she was trying to fill the hole in your lives. Come, let's take some air.'

⇜ Chapter 32 ⇝

Outside on deck they stood side by side, clasping the railings. In the darkness, the sounds of birds twittering and creatures plopping in the water were punctuated by the noises of the crew. The men were camping on the bow under the stars, talking in low voices, every sound magnified by the stillness of the river.

'May I ask your first name?' asked Julian, the taste of rum strong on his tongue.

'Odiene.'

'That's a beautiful name.' He kept his gaze on the dark water.

Julian was curious about her life – about her interest in birds, and the reason she travelled alone. 'You know Captain Ashby well. I mean, I saw you select that book in the saloon.'

'I've been travelling with him for the better part of four years. He was a good friend to my father in Echuca. After he died, a steamer ride down the Murray gave me the idea of becoming a river tourist for a while and Captain Ashby agreed to take me aboard. We are a ripe target for the gossips, especially since his wife rarely accompanies him anymore. I'm told they were once inseparable.'

'And you like living on a riverboat? It seems a lonely existence for a young woman with no other female company.'

'I love the river. Although the days can be long and I often itch to stretch my legs, no hour is ever the same. There is nothing quite like watching the wool bales rolling down the embankment to be winched aboard. And no equal to being present when the men arrive from miles inland to take delivery of long-awaited stores. There is a great importance to what Captain Ashby does, and in a small way I'm a part of that.'

'It is a man's world,' stated Julian in admiration.

'Because you think it so? But you are right. In more gentrified circles I am relegated to books or embroidery. Here I'm accepted, welcomed. Why, once the shearers from one of the stations came down to us after cut-out. We sat on the bank and roasted mutton on sticks. That was a grand night.'

When the steamer wasn't running, Odiene explained, she stayed aboard or rented a room in a boarding house and became a landlubber for a time. She'd even once accepted a role as a station governess for ten months when the river was a chain of water holes.

'The river life appeals to me. There are no ties, obligations or expectations to anything or anyone. That sounds quite pitiful, I expect, but not everyone is blessed with land and family.' Odiene's features were barely illuminated by the glow from the saloon's oil lamp.

Julian looked out at the dark river again. 'My life isn't as perfect as you think.'

How much should he share? That they were not grand pastoralists anymore? That, while his ancestors selected huge swathes of land, they had then lost thousands of acres to debt, more in the resumptions, and ever since his parents had been struggling to make a living? Julian dreaded being assessed by this woman. She would be disappointed.

'You are far too humble. Your mother is one of the most gracious women I've had the pleasure of meeting. You have land, and the Captain tells me the new furniture that was delivered is

212

magnificent. I can only imagine the Dalhunty homestead. It must be a mansion.'

'Yes, it's quite something,' replied Julian.

'And what a beautiful evening,' Odiene commented.

It was indeed. They were on a steamer on the Darling surrounded by a vast stretch of country, the sky pricked with stars and a waxing moon. And yet Julian was only concerned with the young, earnest woman next to him, and the knowledge that their time together was limited by his need to return home. He'd finally gained his freedom, yet his responsibility to his family was now calling him even harder.

When it came to a first kiss, he knew there were rituals and waiting – *a lot* of waiting, so his father had advised. Julian thought back on all the necessary steps Ben had instructed him on when it came to courting a woman and tried to sort through each. There was the introduction, the polite drawing-room chit-chat, and then the man would extend an invitation to the theatre or tea or some other ludicrous event that society deemed appropriate. All this was done under the watchful eye of a suitable chaperone, usually a pigeon-breasted woman who ensured decorum was upheld.

But what if the practice of courting was thrown aside? What if a man simply placed himself before a woman, cut out all of society's expectations and dived head first? As if he were plunging into a swiftly flowing river. Who knew when the chance might come to him again?

He crossed the space separating them and gently rested his hand on Odiene's. She did not draw away or give any sign of offence, but kept staring at the river, her profile blurred by the night. He squeezed her fingers and took a step closer. Surely a kiss on the cheek was not so very untoward? He pounced as a cat might and, as he did, she turned unexpectedly so it was not smooth skin beneath his mouth but her lips. Lips pressed against his. Lips that softened. Then the moment was over. And it was he who ended it.

Julian expected Odiene to be affronted, for that was how women were supposed to respond to a stolen kiss. Instead, her gaze was as direct as at their first meeting. Julian searched for words. He was buoyed by his audacity but had no idea what to do or expect next.

'You shouldn't have done that,' she said softly.

Was an apology appropriate? Surely not. The signs were there, the indications his father had deemed all-important in deciphering a woman's interest. Attentiveness in the saloon. Talking and laughing, ensuring her conversation included him. The invitation outside to the deck. The sharing of life stories. And lastly, touch.

'I am older than you. I have no name of merit. No standing in society. Little money, and my reputation is muddied, and those are the least of my flaws. And look at us. In polite society it would be considered quite improper for us to be alone like this.' Odiene walked the short length of the deck to her cabin. 'Goodnight.'

Julian was left with a mighty confusion and a sense of having done well but of also having failed. He tapped the railing of the paddle-steamer and re-ran the scene in his mind, as if he were reading the cartoons in the *Bulletin*. He was not mistaken. He *had* been the first to pull away, not Odiene. The knowledge brought confidence.

Then a strange light appeared.

≪ Chapter 33 ≫

The white light grew brighter. It moved haphazardly through the sparse timber, dipping down and then sideways, then abruptly disappearing. Julian pulled himself up with the aid of the railings, anticipation charging through his body. With a brief glance in the direction of Odiene's cabin, he took the stairs down to the lower deck and walked to the land side of the steamer, carefully navigating his way through the stacked goods to the rear of the vessel. The light returned, fuzzy and disc-shaped, a quarter-size of a full moon and moving just above the horizon beyond the scalped trees.

Julian had seen a similar light only once before, drifting across a back paddock. While out checking a water tank gouged in the ground by a tumbling tommy scoop, Legless had thrown a shoe and bruised her hoof. The light had appeared on the long, dark walk back to the homestead. It kept to the left of him for a good half hour of the journey, and although the hairs stuck up on his arms and the mare snorted and threw back her head, Julian's fear eventually subsided. Sometime later, the unknown light disappeared. By then, he was nearly home.

A week later Davey died.

His father had also spoken of chasing a mysterious light on horseback in his youth, a few months before proposing to Julian's mother. And it was said that Julian's great-grandfather's experiences with a similar light out west had coincided with his decision to settle in the district. Those past sightings and the one currently witnessed troubled Julian. His father believed the linking of the unknown glow and certain milestone events were purely coincidence. Julian wasn't so sure. It was as if some strange force were at play, signalling incidents that were certain to change lives. A tingling sensation ran down his spine as the light grew in size.

'Ah. Abu fanoos returns.'

Julian jolted at Captain Ashby's arrival. 'Who?'

'The man with the lamp, named by those near the Rub' al Khali desert in Saudi Arabia. It is quite some time since I've seen the phenomenon.' The Captain moved to the side of the steamer.

'What is it? Do you know?' The light gradually faded from view, and the bushland once again became a dark fortress. 'It's gone.'

'You're asking me to explain the unexplainable. I've heard tales of the light from lone men come in from the plains. It scares some of them out of their wits. Others take its appearance with the good intention they believe it offers, a guide of sorts. A reminder that even out here, none of us are ever alone. But anything unexplainable takes on a mythic quality, making it difficult to sort fact from fiction. It's said anyone who chases the light and catches it will never return to tell the tale. For me, the most rational description comes from the Aboriginal people. They believe it is the spirits of their elders coming back to look after the country. I hope they send rain, otherwise I'll be forced to find another business. Between the railway and the unreliable water in the Darling, the riverboat trade in this part of the basin is coming to an end.'

The 1895 drought, coming so soon after the Great Flood, had lasted seven years and decimated sheep numbers again, but it had also devastated the river trade. Julian knew that Ashby had been forced to sell two of his three steamers in 1901, and it had undoubtedly taken more than a little doggedness for the

Captain to keep hold of the *Lady Matilda*. How would Captain Ashby react if he were to discover that Grandfather Alfred had been a supporter of the railways?

Alfred had lobbied Sir Henry Parkes and numerous other politicians on the matter before Parkes was elected premier, and Julian's grandfather had been present when the governor of New South Wales declared the railway open at Bourke in 1885. Progress equalled opportunity and substantial rewards, but not everyone benefited.

Money. Julian's grandfather had stored his excess wealth in a strongbox, burying it deep in the bowels of their land, digging up wads of pound notes when the seasons went against him, until the day came when the reserves were gone. Money was like water. Too much or too little of it altered lives forever and the Dalhuntys knew well the slide from boom to bust.

'You must take Ethan back with you when you eventually go home, Julian,' said the Captain. 'It is plain neither of you likes the other, but in deference to your parents, particularly your mother, it is something that must be done.' Beneath them the steamer rocked gently with the river's movement. The sky was dark. It was as if the light had never been there. 'Ethan came to you for a better life and there is still time to save him. All you have to do is look at him, really look at him, to see he is lost.'

'He doesn't want to stay with us.'

'Then you must take the high road. Act the older brother. You've had experience with that.'

A sudden noise attracted their attention; one of pounding hooves and broken branches. The sounds came from along the riverbank. Julian concentrated on a single flare, worried his imagination was playing tricks as the Captain quickly traversed the deck to get a closer view.

Ashby drew air through his teeth. 'We have visitors. Stay in your cabin, Julian. And put out that blasted oil lamp in the saloon. Go!'

Julian scanned the riverbank. The yellow flare had grown to three distinct flames in a short space of time. The deckhands were roused and running, their steps echoing loudly as the Captain issued orders. Julian took a shortcut, feeling his way past the rough wooden crates in the deepening darkness, his injured skull throbbing.

Odiene met him at the top of the stairwell and followed him to the saloon, where he put out the lamp.

'The Captain will take care of everything,' she said calmly. 'He always does.'

With the lamp extinguished they faced each other in the dark. 'You know who these men are?' Julian asked.

'Most likely brigands. Those who are successful attract such types.'

Not a touch of concern showed as she spoke. How many other nights had the paddle-steamer been subjected to the arrival of strangers? He would have asked Odiene more, however she caught him by the arm, leading him around the upper deck to the railings. Directly below he could just make out Rick, Mr Cummins, the cook and the two deckhands. They were crouched next to the jutting paddle-wheel casing, the violent tingling of wind chimes betraying their position. Julian recognised the unmistakable clink of ammunition and the click of a bullet as it was slid into a firing chamber.

'It had to happen,' said Mr Cummins. 'Sooner or later, it had to happen.'

'Ja, ja,' agreed Rick. 'Now I'm in the real Australia and like the tin-headed man I'm ready for spear-clash.'

'Idiot,' replied Cummins. 'And what are you going to do with that wooden spoon, Quaine? Stir them to death?'

'If wese get caught I'm expecting you to be squashed like a cockroach. But we cooks are in high demand,' replied Quaine.

Ethan squatted next to Julian as the riders became visible. 'I reckon they're after the cargo, don't you? I bet the Captain reckoned on something like this happening. I tried to tell you, but you wouldn't listen.'

'Shut up, Ethan.'

Were they being followed? Would these men risk their lives for a few crates of food, some hens and a goat? In the past, sundowners had visited Dalhunty Station, tramps who arrived at dusk pretending they sought work when they only wanted food and shelter and were gone by dawn. His father called them no-good idlers, thieves of a sort. What were these men, then?

Three horsemen stopped in the clearing opposite the steamer. Two of the riders dismounted. One threw his flare into what remained of the pile of cut timber. Another began scavenging for kindling, adding it to the growing flames. The blaze took hold quickly, throwing out sparking embers cascading in red and yellow arcs. The brightening fire lifted the steamer from the night's obscurity and cast the armed strangers into relief. Julian noticed a fourth horse, riderless.

'Captain Ashby, are you aboard?' the man near the fire called out.

'He's bloody aboard,' answered a rider, coaching his horse closer to the steamer.

A figure moved into Julian's view. The tall, spare form of Captain Ashby addressed the strangers. 'What do you want? There's nothing of value here. Basic foodstuffs. That's all.'

'We're here to collect payment for your debts. You owe Mr Fraser and he's tired of waiting,' replied the stranger.

'Is he speaking of the Fraser who owns most of your run?' whispered Ethan fiercely. 'We should hightail it off the boat.'

Julian shushed Ethan to be quiet. Captain Ashby covered more country via the snaking Murray-Darling than most men. Who was to say another Fraser could not be found further south?

The Captain lit a lantern, holding it high. 'And I told Fraser I would pay him.'

'Fourteen months ago,' replied the rider. 'Where's that piano you promised in lieu of payment? Gone. It had the townsfolks' tongues wagging in Bourke when it arrived on that dray with its innards falling out. A good brand, Steinway. Recognisable. Covetable. The rightful owners believed it had fallen into the Darling.'

'A piano. Julian, your piano,' hissed Ethan. 'Ashby stole it.'

Julian felt like a man just woken from sleep.

'A little more time is all I ask. Six months to get back on my feet,' said the Captain. 'How is a man to trade when the water isn't running?'

'That is not Mr Fraser's problem. I'll be asking you to come ashore, Captain, *alone*. Your men are not part of this and if you come quietly and amenably like the gentleman Mr Fraser thought you to be, he'll not be spouting aloud about the other doings you're involved with.'

'You'll not take my *Lady Matilda*?' Captain Ashby's voice quavered for the first time.

'No. Mr Fraser requires a more active repayment from you. An experience that will ensure you won't default again. You're to work off what you owe. He's setting you up as a boundary rider. You should find the job easy. You're known for your navigation of the Darling so it should be no problem to pilot a fence line and see to repairs.'

The men on the bank laughed at this.

'No, no, no.' Rick was quick to reach the Captain's side. 'They are brothers of ravens.' He shouldered a rifle, aiming it square at the rider.

Captain Ashby slowly forced the Dane to lower his weapon. Mr Cummins in turn voiced his opinion. He went to the Captain and the group hunched together for a few moments, talking, Rick's bulk dwarfing the two other men.

'It's best I see Mr Fraser. I'll go with you,' the Captain finally called to the waiting horsemen.

The *Lady Matilda*'s crew were directed by the strangers to pile their weapons on the deck and step away to avoid any skulduggery, and one by one, the crew obeyed. The Captain asked the strangers for a few minutes to pack his belongings and went to his cabin as the riders waited by the fire.

'Well, that's comeuppance,' said Ethan. 'The old sea dog pressed into service. So much for the admirable Captain Ashby. Looks like he sold your father a stolen piano. Perhaps next time you'll listen to me.'

Ignoring him, Julian ran down the stairwell to the lower deck, with Ethan giving chase. 'Sir, I'm Julian Dalhunty of Dalhunty Station. I would like to come with you to see Mr Fraser. The Captain is a good man, he saved my parents many years ago and—'

'We know who you are, boy,' drawled one of the riders, who was squatting by the fire on the bank. 'Not much happens out here folk don't know about. It comes from there being too few people, and not much to fill people's minds. Mr Fraser is treating the Captain favourably. He could have him arrested for this unpaid debt, and I'm sure the police would be more than happy to have a word with him as well regarding certain other matters, but Mr Fraser is fair-minded, and his business isn't with you, even if your sister did refuse his son's offer of marriage. So I'd be appreciative if you could stay aboard like the others and let us attend to this.'

'I *told* you something underhand was going on,' muttered Ethan in Julian's ear.

The Captain returned, a battered Gladstone bag under his arm, a lamp in the other. Odiene was at his side.

'I'm sorry about the piano, Julian. I was swayed by your father's passion at the time and I believed Mr Fraser to be a tolerant man. But,' he said more light-heartedly, 'there is no harm done to Ben. He was unaware of my' – he searched for the right word – '"plans". I am only sorry I'm not in a position to reimburse the money your father paid to date. I used it to keep my business profitable. Wheels of commerce and all that. Your grandfather would have under-stood. Mind you, there is some good to come out of this. Ben is no longer burdened by his debt to me. Your father is a fine man and I value his friendship.'

'You stole someone else's piano! You took our money,' said Julian.

'Not to put too fine a point on it, Julian, however, your father was aware I was delivering it to Bourke. Clearly it belonged to someone else. Yes, yes, he thought I would replace the piano, however his actions weren't exactly top-drawer either.' Captain Ashby passed a dumbfounded Julian the lantern. 'Mr Cummins and Rick are good men. Heed what they say and watch out for Miss Carlisle. You'll do that for me, won't you, Julian?'

'I am perfectly capable of looking after myself,' Odiene spoke up. 'It is you I will worry for, Captain.'

Captain Ashby patted her arm and then pivoted on his heel, surveying the steamer. 'Well then.' He walked down the planks to dry ground.

'I told you. He's a thief,' stated Ethan.

Was this truly the man who had ploughed overland through floodwaters at risk to himself, his crew and steamer during the Great Flood? The man his father considered the most estimable among men? His closest friend? It was too much. That man, it now seemed, wasn't worth a fig of tobacco.

'What do you know of this, Odiene?' he asked as the Captain was led away.

'I know nothing,' came her curt reply.

She moved to the railings, assembling with the deckhands, Rick, Quaine and Mr Cummins, as Captain Ashby was assisted onto the spare horse.

'Wese're doomed. Doomed, I tell you,' moaned the cook.

'You must know something.' Julian pressed her.

'Leave me alone,' was all she said.

The crew watched in horror as Fraser's men removed the penned chickens from the barge and trussed them, flapping and squawking, to the horses. Next, they cut the mooring ropes on both the steamer and the barge. Mr Cummins and Rick's yells of complaint were responded to with an airborne flare. It tumbled through the night sky, spilling streaks of red and yellow, and landed on the empty barge. The Captain cried out as the steamer slowly began to drift, while the flames on the barge flickered and caught.

Mr Cummins walked briskly towards the boiler room and Rick ran towards the wheelhouse, while the two other deckhands frantically worked to cut the rope attaching the steamer to the burning barge.

'You all better pray,' the cook said, lumbering his round frame towards the galley. 'I'm a-packing my belongings and getting off this here boat.'

'You try and leave this vessel, Quaine, and I'll keel-haul you,' shouted Mr Cummins before disappearing into the bowels of the steamer.

'I was j-just saying. Ain't n-no need for v-v-violence,' stuttered the cook.

As the acetylene lamps on the bow were lit, Julian caught the scent of woodsmoke, and then the paddles began to turn as giant trees emerged in the brightness.

'What on earth is Rick doing?' said Ethan. 'We should stay here. You heard what the Captain said, it's too dangerous to navigate the river at night, especially when the water is getting low.'

Julian drew Ethan's attention to the barge, which was being pushed towards them by the current. The flames had quickly spiralled ten feet into the sky, increasing in intensity and spreading the length and breadth of the timber. The barge was now a flaming missile. Julian felt the vibration as the paddles increased in speed, the thrust of the wheels propelling the steamer forwards. He looked ahead to the Darling, reduced to a narrow stretch framed by the ghostly timber, and then back at the inferno.

'We can't stop until the barge burns out and sinks.'

≼ Chapter 34 ≽

After the sinking of the barge in the early hours of the morning, Julian and Ethan went to the wheelhouse to argue the case for their liberation with the steamer's new captain, Rick. Ethan wanted to be dropped at the nearest axe-marked tree that noted the position of a station, and Julian prayed for the steamer to turn around and head back to the Port-O-Bourke, convinced the crew would, with some encouragement, mount Captain Ashby's rescue. Julian would have preferred to never see Ashby again, however he had to try to get their money back.

Rick grasped the wheel with grim determination, studying the waterway from beneath a battered captain's hat, its peak torn from the brim. He opened a hinged Colman's Mustard box hanging on the wall and unfurled the chart to check their route, muttering in Danish as his attention drifted from map to river and back again, ensuring he slowed the vessel at every bend so the boat didn't list and take in water.

'Fool-saver. I've named you well,' he said to Julian. 'You are as river-logged as him.' He nodded at Ethan. 'I am under instructions from the snag-dodger. You are both to stay aboard until this paddle-steamer is either stopped by the mud-riser before us or we reach Echuca. The Captain won't have you dumped to fend for yourselves.' Rick's broad shoulders were raised in irritation as he clung to the wheel – and his new role – with an unexpected fierceness. Loyalty could be a curse.

'And what of Captain Ashby? Are you not going to try and save him?' asked Julian.

'Cargo must be delivered. The crew expects payment. And eventually the insurance company must be told of the barge fire.' Rick's attention never once strayed from the river ahead.

Nothing Julian or Ethan said could convince their new skipper to deviate from their destination further downstream. Rick was intent on fulfilling his duties. He also clearly had no interest in explaining the Captain's activities, legal or not, to them. He was only concerned with getting as far south as possible before the waters became unnavigable.

Julian discovered he was in the unusual position of agreeing with Ethan. They both recognised the difficulties in reaching their ultimate destinations while the determined Dane was at the helm.

'My sister Laura, the little earth goddess, will be disappointed to hear you weren't willing to help us,' said Julian. 'You know how women are. It takes very little to rile them.'

Rick turned at this. 'You think I am the idiot, fool-saver, but I know women. They don't know what they want. They must be told.'

'Boy, do you have a shock coming,' commented Ethan.

'The *Lady Matilda* is my command until the Cap returns,' stated Rick.

'That's convenient,' said Ethan. 'Captain Ashby should be reported for theft and Fraser for trying to remake the law into what suits him.'

'Get out, both of you!' Rick's patience came to a sudden end. 'Or there will be a mighty spear-clash between us three and I will throw you off this boat.'

Back on the upper deck, Julian and Ethan lay spreadeagled, dappled sunlight reaching down through passing tree limbs, the throbbing of the paddle-wheels gently vibrating through their bodies.

'Now I know why Rick doesn't have a woman,' said Julian.

'Too forward you reckon?' replied Ethan.

The two of them chuckled and then looked briefly at each other, unprepared for the shared moment.

'I doubt Rick would be first past the post, but women do like a man to take the lead. Oh, they fret and niggle and go on about propriety, but secretly they like a man to be direct,' said Ethan.

'And you know this how?'

'I've lived in the city,' replied Ethan drowsily, in a tone suggesting there was much happening in the metropolis that Julian could never comprehend. 'Take Laura. She's like your mother with her haughtiness and penchant for feminine pastimes, but she's made to work like a scullery maid. Offer to carry the laundry basket and she's like the rest of them. Grateful.'

'You stay away from Laura.'

'Steady, I'm just saying. Anyway, she barely gave me the time of day.' Ethan spat on a finger working the saliva into the toe of his shoe until whatever spec dulling the shine was gone.

'She's sort of like your sister,' Julian reminded him. There was still the possibility of Ethan heading back to Dalhunty Station. Slight, though it was.

'Now she's my sister. That's rich. Here's Ethan, The Natural. Oh yes, I know what you all call me and I know it's not out of admiration. "Let's ignore him. Kick him up the arse. Treat him like a navvy until he leaves."'

'You haven't worked any harder than the rest of us, except when you embarked on your building crusade,' said Julian.

'What does it matter? There was no paper signed. No binding agreement. I've left and that's the end of it.'

'You're determined to go back to Sydney?'

'Why, Julian.' Ethan looked at him. 'It sounds like you want me to stay.'

How could Julian ever reveal that before the bore's breakdown and his father's illness his plan to leave the property had hinged on precisely that? It was staggering to think he could be his own man and launch out on his own merit. And it was also sobering to realise life offered options and then took them away. Blindingly fast, in his case. He was not being forced to return home, it was simply what must be done. What man would act differently with an ill father, three womenfolk left alone, and money owed them by Captain Ashby? A rational approach was the only chance he had of persuading Ethan to return and so he explained that the train from Bourke was the fastest way to get to Sydney. It was also far safer travelling together. And he was not averse to getting off the steamer at a station stop, but only if they went north not south.

Minutes passed. The scenery was all brown water, a steep-sided bank and trees so close-growing they resembled a brick wall. Finally Ethan spoke.

'The only reason I'm considering going with you is because we have to report what we've seen. The Captain's kidnapping. The piano theft. The burning of the barge.'

Julian thought Ethan a simpleton. 'We can't do that. I'm disgusted by what the Captain has done, but if he is guilty of theft, then he'll be gaoled. How will I ever get the money he owes us for the piano then?'

'You won't see that money in this lifetime. I'm betting if the Captain is indebted to Mr Fraser then he will owe others as well. And what are these "certain other matters" those men alluded to last night?' Ethan tapped the decking with his knuckles. 'There'd be a penny in this. You need to see a solicitor. Considering the Captain's criminal activities, a solicitor would have the right to act on your complaint and make sure the boat was sold to repay the Captain's debts. Your father would expect us to abide by the law.'

Julian had not expected Ethan to be so sharp regarding the situation. 'Well, my father isn't here. Anyway, why are you so keen to bring in the coppers?'

'People should be held accountable when they do something wrong,' said Ethan.

'In most cases.'

'*Most* cases?' said Ethan sharply.

'Forget I said anything.' Regardless of the Captain's trickery, Julian knew Ben would be disinclined to launch anything against Ashby.

Their most pressing problem was knowing if and when to get off the steamer. They couldn't be certain when the boat docked again for wood that there would be a selector or station within walking distance with horses to spare. And while they were aboard they had food, water and shelter. Out there, they'd be on foot. It was a risk. One big enough to consider staying on board for as long as possible.

Mr Cummins walked around the deck and leant on the railing a short distance away.

Julian stood quickly, Ethan slowly, as if he might well get a better perspective of the situation by not rushing. The engineer walked towards them, snapping a twig from a low branch as they travelled underneath it and crushing it between his fingers.

'Captain Ashby has always been a gambler. A man must be if he is to place his livelihood in the vagaries of riverboat life. While I don't condone some of his excesses, neither can I condemn the good Captain for his faults, for each of us gamble at some stage in our lives. Think on your own situation, Ethan. Was it not a gamble for you to leave Sydney for a life unknown with a new family? And you, Julian, perhaps graziers in these parts are the biggest gamblers of all.' Mr Cummins leant in close to Ethan. 'Let's agree you won't speak of what occurred last night and in return I won't hogtie you and leave you on dry ground without shade or water.'

He stayed there for a long minute to emphasise the point. Neither Julian nor Ethan moved.

'Best get back to the boiler. Nice day,' he said eventually, and strolled back the way he came.

'Well, we can forget about Mr Cummins helping us,' said Julian.

'I can understand Cummins and the crew being protective of Ashby and his activities. They're only worried about getting their wages and ensuring the steamer isn't repossessed and sold to repay the Captain's debts. Then they're all out of jobs. But you're going mighty easy on Ashby if you won't report him,' said Ethan with genuine puzzlement.

'I'm betting Captain Ashby has supported all of his crew at some stage. As he did us during the Great Flood. Hasn't anyone ever done anything good for you? Something that makes them stand out from everyone else you've ever met? Someone who you admire?'

'No,' said Ethan adamantly.

'Sure you have. You might not like the place you ended up, but I'm pretty sure my mother falls into that category.'

Ethan looked beyond him, concentrating on the water, where a splash and a series of circular ripples formed. 'All your mother ever talked of was her family, the river and the land. It was all about the property. Holding on to it for the next generation. It's like you all believe without the land there are no Dalhuntys.'

'If I ever did believe that, I'm not so sure I do now,' admitted Julian.

'The whole place is falling down and I don't understand. Any of it. If you're not interested in running it properly why don't you sell and move to a town? Start a business. You can do that, Julian, if your father doesn't recover.' Ethan leant against the railings, his back to the water. 'Can you imagine what it's like for someone like me to leave behind a life scraped together through hard work? Then to see what you have and watch you let it slip through your fingers? Then for me to not be accepted? Your mother promised me a kind, loving family. Involvement in a well-known business away from the constraints of the city. Security. Acceptance. And did I get any of that? So no, I haven't met anyone who's done anything good for me.'

Ethan's words stung Julian. 'I'm sorry we're not wealthy.'

'I should have known better. A wealthy family wouldn't have taken me in,' said Ethan. He turned away from Julian, back towards the river.

≪ Chapter 35 ≫

Late in the afternoon Julian went in search of Odiene. He was reluctant to seek her out after the previous night's awkwardness and assumed she felt the same, for she'd taken breakfast in her room and had not come to the saloon for their midday meal of boiled mutton. It was as if she were avoiding him, which fitted with his father's explanation of womanly behaviour.

Ben had told him to expect a certain cat-and-mouse quality, as well as an abundance of modesty on the female side. The man was required to step up in these circumstances, to persevere until hope ran out. Still, Julian was experiencing a rather unpleasant sensation in his stomach as he searched for her – part excitement and part terror. The latter came from the failure to stick to his father's guidelines, one of which concerned the importance of neither party appearing too keen in the early stages. Well, he rather blew that rule last night.

Eventually Julian located Odiene on the lower deck at the bow of the steamer, partially obscured by a large granite tombstone and shaded by an awning. She was bent over a makeshift table industriously measuring some type of bird specimen and then jotting notes on paper. He hung back, all thoughts of their kiss momentarily pushed aside by his uncertainty over how to approach Odiene's calm response at the arrival of the brigands and Ashby's abrupt leaving.

She cut quickly and deftly down the centre of the bird from the top of the breastbone to the pelvis and then started peeling the skin from the body with her fingers. She wiggled the tail, and, scalpel in hand, carefully cut through the bones before continuing to skin down the back side of the body. Next, she sliced through the knees to separate the legs from the body before attacking the shoulder joint where the wings attached. The feathered skin peeled away from the carcass as neatly as a skinned sheep, the red mass of the bird's muscle and flesh revealed as Odiene manipulated its removal with the gentle plying of fingers. With the bird's neck cut, she lifted the skin to the light and reversed it. It was an owl. Sightless, yet still with its glossy beak, legs and claws.

'I'm sorry to disturb you,' said Julian.

'You are a quiet observer.' She stretched out the wings and displayed the bird skin as if an exhibit. '*Ninox Connivens*. A barking owl, although they are also known by some as the screaming-woman bird, on account of the rare tremulous shriek they utter. Named by a man, I would think.' She glanced at him playfully. 'Pretty, isn't it? Those bright talons. See how the white breast is streaked with brown?' She lay the feathered skin on the table and started scraping the fat from its underside. 'Mr Cummins discovered it dead on the upper deck. I thought I might cut it in half and mount it for bookends. Although the head might prove difficult. Skulls are such fragile things. What do you think of that idea?'

'Maybe.' Julian examined the selection of instruments spread out on the table. They were similar to what his mother used, although her tools were fashioned from kitchen utensils as advised by a pamphlet, while Odiene's different-sized blades, tweezers, hooks, needles, scissors and hammer were clearly bought for purpose. He was pleased the owl had been found already dead. His mother practised on birds they trapped for food, with limited success, which made Rachael's specimens no less distasteful but at least they were not killed for pure decoration.

Odiene cleaned fat and blood from the blade with a cloth and reworked the skin in the opposite direction. 'What of your mother? The Captain mentioned last night she was adept at curios, does that extend to preserving specimens?'

'She only stuffs those animals we can eat and it is a pastime she rarely indulges in now. My father doesn't care for it.'

Odiene's movements were methodical and far more precise than his mother's attempts. She paused to check the underside of the skin, plucking some damaged feathers and setting them aside. 'There is good money to be made from taxidermy. People do love their curiosities, especially those chatting over cups of tea in southern drawing rooms.' She sprinkled powder across the freshly cleaned hide, rubbing it into the skin before applying more of the same. She noticed his interest. 'Borax. First discovered in the dry lake beds of Tibet and imported via the Silk Road to the Arabian Peninsula centuries ago. Your mother would use it.'

'Salt, mainly. She developed her own mixture.' Which was not very successful. There had been more than one rotting specimen tilting precariously on timber perches.

'Ah. One has to be skilled. Sometimes the hides don't dry as well.' Odiene returned the pot of Borax to a leather travelling case that contained phials of different colours. 'These are pigments as well as some herbal medicine – lavender oil and sage.'

Julian selected one of the containers filled with a pale powder.

'Useful for touching up,' Odiene explained. 'Pinking of noses, et cetera, although I usually only work with birds. Normally I would cotton-wrap a wire body, but I have no wire fine enough and no plaster for a mould. I used flour paste once, but the weevils ate their way out, ruining a fine possum. I will have to search for some stuffing rags.'

She washed her hands in the basin, dried them on the apron about her waist and then sat on a deckchair stretching out her legs on a chaff bag, her buttoned boots crossed at the ankles.

'Your father probably considers city folk heathens, with their liking for dead animals and fish-scale ornaments. But such things are fashionable.' She took a sip of water from a glass at her elbow.

Julian knew the time for small talk was over. 'I wanted to make sure you were all right after what happened. The captain's departure was, to say the very least, unexpected.'

'It was and I am. However I have no doubt Captain Ashby will return as soon as he is able. In the meantime we are in safe hands.'

Julian thought her very collected considering the night's events. 'The barge was a loss,' he continued. He replaced the pigment and sat on one of the chaff bags, resting his elbows on his knees.

The shape of Odiene's long, slender legs were visible beneath the drape of her skirt. 'Yes, it was.'

It seemed she was not going to make their conversation easy.

'I wanted to speak with you about Captain Ashby. You were on the steamer last year when the Captain arrived with the piano. Did you know that he originally intended to steal it to repay Mr Fraser's debt?'

'Does it matter?' she asked wearily. 'What business men get up to is of no concern to me. I should change the bandage for you.'

'I can do it.' Julian began to unwind the material, but found that a part of it stuck to his skull.

'Stop. You will cause more injury to yourself.' Rising, she poured a little water from the glass onto the binding, moistening the dressing, then she bent his head forwards and began carefully peeling it from hair and skin.

Odiene's blouse was white and ruffled slightly at the high neck and was sheer enough for the outline of a narrow-strapped chemise to be visible. Julian found he could not stop looking at the strap. He fixated on it. What it was made of. How it would feel.

'He's a mercurial man, our Captain Ashby.' Odiene lifted the dressing and Julian complained with a loud 'ouch' as it came free. 'It will be a few days before the stitches can be removed. It should be rebandaged.'

233

He tentatively touched the wound, feeling the two lumpy stitches in his skull. 'I'll let the air dry it. Odiene, I need to understand why Captain Ashby would do such a thing.'

'Your father is not tainted by what happened. The Captain told you as much.' She bunched the old bandage together.

'What he did was illegal and my father is owed money,' reasoned Julian. 'Do you not want to know the type of man you are travelling with?'

Odiene sat back in the chair, squirming a little to find comfort. 'He is kind, well-read, an excellent conversationalist and quite the naturalist. As a young man he spent time on an iron-hulled clipper sailing between Australia and England. It is highly likely Dalhunty wool was in the hold on one of those voyages.' She paused, as if expecting Julian to speak and then said, 'You do know he classes your father among his closest friends.'

'I find that difficult to believe,' said Julian.

'You're disappointed in Captain Ashby.'

'Aren't you?'

Odiene slowly rolled the dressing into a ball. 'The Captain has been very generous to me. People do what they must to survive.'

'What about the original owners of the piano? Don't they deserve some consideration?'

'It is my understanding those pastoralists own thousands of acres. Clearly they are not short of a shilling. After the Captain sold it to your father, he advised the original owners that it went overboard rounding a river bend. It would have been insured. Augustus is always very particular about such matters.'

Julian would never have expected a young lady to think as Odiene did. 'You are trying to excuse the inexcusable.' His voice rose in reply.

'And your disillusionment with the Captain, while understandable, has made you judgemental. Justice does not always favour those most in need. Consider the difficulties a person must contend with when they run a business. A business they love and cherish, that is both a livelihood and a lifestyle. Now picture losing that business. What else could you do for a living? Do you have any savings to keep you from the streets, from starvation? How will you survive? Some of us have few choices, and they will never fit in with your naïve view of the world.' Odiene dropped the bandage on a bag of chaff.

Who was she speaking about? The Captain or herself? Julian tried not to be distracted by the idealised girl of his imaginings, and yet here he was noting the tiny freckles sprinkling the bridge of her nose. Soft down grew on her upper lip.

'Don't be upset,' he said, reaching for her.

Odiene returned to the work table. 'Don't, Julian.'

'I realise I overstepped last night, however—'

'There was no last night. It was a mistake.'

'A mistake?'

'Yes. I value our friendship. That is all,' she told him.

What to do next? How long did one persevere? Surely something so recently started could not be over so soon. He hoped for some fancy word or compelling idea to come to him, however all he could recall were his father's instructions. Towards the end of Ben's lecture on courting, which had taken place at the chicken coop, an altercation had arisen between Reginald's predecessor four times removed and a pernickety hen. The squabble highlighted the part of Ben's talk that related to ensuring there were no other parties lurking that might sway his intended's affections.

Julian backtracked through his conversation with Odiene, trying to understand her dismissal of what they had shared the previous evening, and also her reaction regarding the Captain's wrongdoings. It was too extreme. Either Odiene was dependent on the Captain for her wellbeing more than he realised or . . .

'Are you and Captain Ashby . . .'

He searched for the right words. What did a person call someone in this situation if they were not married? Or if one were married and the other not?

'Captain Ashby is a fine man.'

Julian accepted that admitting to the relationship was not something a lady was likely to do. But then a single lady should be crafting fancyworks like Laura, spending any free time delving into Mrs Wicken's advice on household management, not living on a riverboat with only men for company. It was no wonder she was the subject of gossip.

'He's a little old for you,' he commented dryly.

'What's age got to do with anything?'

Odiene lifted the owl, smoothing the shiny feathers, and kept her back to Julian as he apologised for bothering her, for taking up her time. He was glad she could not see his disappointment or his anger. He was a fool, just as Rick said.

'Keep the bandage,' he murmured on leaving. 'You'll be able to use it to stuff another unsuspecting creature.'

⇜ Chapter 36 ⇝

In the mid-afternoon the paddles slowed to a stop and the steamer nestled close to a sandy bank. There was no whistle to advise Mr Cummins below deck to ease the pressure in the boiler and no signal to tell those waiting ashore the *Lady Matilda* was mooring. Ethan and Julian kept their counsel as new rope was found to replace the damaged lengths from the wool barge and the vessel was securely moored. They saw no obvious markings on trees to indicate the area as a destination and no trough hollowed into the earth by the passage of rolling bales, only a pile of timber on the bank waiting to feed the hungry boiler suggested life nearby.

Once the steamer was stationary, Rick set off on foot, darting through the scrub, while the winch swung into action ferrying crates from the vessel to dry ground. The men were quiet as they went about their work: Mr Cummins controlling the winch; the deckhands busily moving barrels of beer and crates of rum from the bowels of the vessel and overseeing the landing of the cargo on dry soil. In the midst of this activity, Quaine led the goat on a short lead through the cluttered deck, where he enticed the animal with a dish of grain to jump atop a wooden crate. The cook settled on a three-legged stool, the goat quick to suck on the tail of his voluminous shirt once seated. With a dish placed underneath the goat's udder, the cook busied himself with the milking, taking a slurp from the bucket as his task progressed, talking intermittently to the animal and himself.

'Should've left. What did your mother tell you?' he muttered to himself. 'Son, don't go getting involved with trouble. Once I get to Echuca I ain't never going north again. Gonna get meself a place in town. You can come too, Florence.' He patted the goat. 'We'll cook real food again. Tripe and cow's tongue. Aint nothing like a bit of tongue.' He spied Julian and Ethan staring at him. 'Wot? Ain't you never seen a growned man milk a goat before?'

'Do you know where we are?' asked Julian.

'See no evil, hear no evil.' Quaine went back to the milking.

They sought out Mr Cummins, who was watching the goods suspended overhead and who did not acknowledge them until the crate was safely deposited on the shore. 'You want to know where we are? Supply delivery. Sometimes it's upstream. Sometimes down. This spot is rarely used. It depends on the water level.'

'So there's a station nearby?' Ethan observed Awang and Joe as they stacked crates of vegetables on the bank. 'There must be. There's enough supplies being off-loaded.'

'No, there's not. No town either. And as we've agreed, it's best you stay aboard. Now get out of my sight,' said Mr Cummins.

Julian tugged Ethan away from the engineer. There was surely a station nearby, but why were they being so secretive about it? They went to the upper deck to keep an eye on Cummins.

It took an hour for the rest of the goods to be unloaded and a few minutes after that, Odiene left her cabin dressed in a travelling coat and carrying a carpet bag. Awang and Joe, now free from their duties, lugged a tin trunk, which they deposited with the delivered cargo. Odiene went straight to where Mr Cummins was securing the winch. Their animated discussion was brief as Rick re-emerged from the bush wheezing heavily, and reboarding the steamer, interrupted them. The two men nodded at their female companion and then Odiene walked across the rickety planks towards land. Julian bounded down the stairs and ran across the deck, catching up with her on the makeshift gangway. His embarrassment from their earlier meeting was forgotten.

'Don't you take a step off this steamer, fool-saver,' yelled Rick from the deck.

Odiene adjusted her grip on the carpet bag. 'I will be back directly, Julian.'

'With a travelling coat and packed trunk? Captain Ashby asked me to watch over you.'

'I don't need a guardian. And while I'm away, please don't rile Mr Cummins or Rick. They are good men under orders and while their methods might seem extreme, they have been entrusted with your safety in Captain Ashby's absence.' She squeezed his arm. 'You will stay aboard? For me?'

Julian was confused by her request. And then he realised Odiene was not asking for his sake but rather for the sake of the man she cared for. She let go of his arm and strode purposefully to where Joe waited. Presumably her escort to whomever she was meeting.

Ethan was eager for answers when Julian stepped back onto the steamer. 'Where is she going?'

'I have no idea, but she says she's coming back.' Julian watched as Odiene skirted the crates and barrels and disappeared into the fringe of timber. There was no reason for him to doubt her, none-theless he did.

'Come with me.' Ethan led Julian to the other side of the steamer, and, after ensuring they were alone, shared that he had eavesdropped on a conversation between the engineer and Rick. 'They're worried about a sandbar now the water's dropping. Rick is convinced a straight, fast run at the bar would launch the steamer across the sand. Mr Cummins argued Captain Ashby was only one of a few men who had accomplished the task with success. The crux of the discussion was the decision to leave and head down-river for a few more hours before mooring for the night.'

'And?' Julian's mind was still on Odiene.

'It seems to me if the crew are already starting to disagree with each other and the water level's getting dangerous, now might be a good time to jump ship, especially as Rick wants us locked in one of the cabins again for safekeeping.'

'What?' Julian ran his hand through his hair in annoyance, flinching on touching the stitches. 'That's thanks to you.'

'There's more. Whoever ordered these goods paid Rick by cheque. Captain Ashby only ever accepts cash. The cheque was originally written out to a shearer named Harrington by one of the stations further north. Harrington's name was crossed out and the Captain's was added instead.'

'That's not unusual for out here. A bank will still honour it,' said Julian.

'But the amount was changed as well. Cummins said there's no way they'll be able to cash it, but if the crew chase after payment they'll be stranded here. Seems the Captain's been rorted. Come on. Now's as good a time as any to leave.' Ethan led the way to the lower deck.

'What about Odiene? Did they mention her?'

'No,' replied Ethan.

'I knew she didn't intend to return.' Julian was more disappointed by her deception than he cared to admit.

'And here was I thinking you were getting friendly with her last night in the saloon.' Ethan removed his shoes and, tying the laces together, hung them around his neck. 'Those goods have to be going to a station. We'll slip down into the water and make a run for it.'

Julian took in his bare feet. 'How far am I going to get without boots?'

'I'm guessing a few bindi-eyes never hurt a Dalhunty.' Ethan climbed over the side of the steamer, and dropped into the river with a splash.

Julian knew if he stayed aboard alone, he would be allowed his freedom. It was Ethan Mr Cummins was worried about. Ethan, who was likely to report the Captain to the authorities, given the chance. And how would they ever be repaid for the piano then? Below deck came the familiar sounds of the boiler being stoked. Julian banged his fist on the railing. Ethan kept close to the boat, scuttling through the chest-high water. The paddlewheels started to turn.

'Damnation.' Julian slipped over the side of the vessel, the sandy bottom of the Darling sucking at his feet.

⊰ Chapter 37 ⊱

The wake from the paddle-steamer hit the backs of Julian's legs as he waded from the river and crawled up the steep bank. Ethan scurried like a crab in the shifting sand, beating Julian to the top of the bank where he brushed water from his feet and put his shoes back on. They rested briefly and looked back towards the river. Joe was drawing the last few feet of bow line aboard after having guided Odiene into the scrub. He wound the rope on the deck as the steamer ploughed away, the paddles whipping the surface. They waited a few minutes until the brown and green foliage closed in and the boat was lost to them, and then set off.

Julian took the lead, ignoring Ethan as he swept an arm sideways, as if to say, be my guest. They doubled back, eventually locating the trail leading into the bushland. It was little more than a rough track through gnarled, twisted trees, so tight in places that branches had been cut cleanly from tree trunks to ensure safe travelling. Julian examined the scarred trunks. It was far too narrow a road to be used for the passage of flat-topped wool wagons and numerous bullocks. Nevertheless, the riverboat stop was clearly not a rarely used destination as Mr Cummins had alleged. Wheel tracks were cut deep into the ground. Drays passed through here. Regularly.

Ethan touched one of the knotted, woody plants.

'It's an old trail. Well used,' Julian answered Ethan's question before it was uttered. 'It leads somewhere. The question is, how far will we have to walk?' Through the branches the sky was fading. 'It'll be dark soon. Concentrate on the track and the trees. When daylight falls, you'll be more accustomed to your surroundings and won't wander off in the wrong direction.'

'The lot of them on that riverboat are a bunch of liars and thieves,' said Ethan.

The worst of it was, Ethan was probably right. Everything they had been party to added up to no good, which meant Odiene was probably little better than the men she kept company with. It occurred to Julian that for all his father's pontificating on the birds and the bees, he had been right. Getting to know a person was indeed very important.

'You've known thieves in Sydney, I guess.'

'Sure. And I've seen them in action. Even caught a few of the lowlifes and got them arrested. In the department store a well-dressed lady was just as likely to snatch up some trinket and hide it in her purse as one of the street gangs from The Rocks might thieve a wallet.'

The evening settled in the dense bush faster than Julian anticipated. They kept on walking down the centre of the track, keeping the wheel ruts either side. Little by little, stars dotted the strip of sky above them.

The sound of a horse whinnying made them take cover, half falling over a log before hiding behind it. A man walked by on foot, followed by two wagons, which rattled as they rolled past heading towards the river. The man held a flare, ensuring no axles came to grief in the dark. They waited as the draft horses plodded past.

'Better to be cautious until we know what's what,' said Julian in a low voice. 'We don't know who they are, but we do know they don't pay their bills if that cheque was anything to go by.'

When the carts vanished and there was only the distant creak and the nicker of a horse to mark the traveller's progress, they pushed on along the trail.

After five miles, Ethan begged for rest but Julian paid no attention, planting one foot in front of the other, despite each step hurting his shoeless feet. He knew the wagons would come back this way once loaded, but there was no point stopping in the middle of nowhere and waiting for them. He was distrustful of men moving goods under cover of dark and was more inclined to carry on and see where Odiene might be headed and if there was a camp or homestead nearby. A place where they might find shelter and lay low, undetected.

'Don't say a word about Captain Ashby's wrongdoings when and if we do find anyone who might be able to get us out of this pickle,' said Julian.

'Why? Apart from your admiration for the crooked sea dog.'

'I'm not convinced asking a solicitor to sell the steamer is the best way to get our money back. If the Captain has no business, how will he repay us? Especially if he owes others. Besides, there are people's livelihoods at stake. Like the crew. And what about Odiene? She'll be without a home and protection if Captain Ashby is convicted. That's obviously why she left. To try and find help for him.'

'Well, it does seem that she knows *exactly* where she's going,' stated Ethan.

'Just keep your mouth shut. This isn't the city. We don't tattle-tale on folk without good reason.'

Ethan laughed. 'You really believe there's one law for the country and another for city people like me? Is that what you're saying?'

'You saw what was unloaded from the steamer. What if you're right? If Ashby is involved in something illegal, then there are shady people taking delivery of that cargo, so whoever we find at the end of this road is not going to be impressed if you start talking about going to the pol—'

'Stop right there,' came the sound of a male voice.

Two men emerged ahead of them, blocking their path. The bolt of a rifle made a screeching noise as it slid closed.

Julian immediately tried to greet them as a friend, however Ethan was not so cautious. He ran at one of the men and for his troubles he received a clout across the temple. Julian yielded to the searching of his clothes and the binding of his wrists, while Ethan blasphemed and struggled like a man about to be executed. When they finally gagged him, even Julian was relieved.

'Do we need to do the same to you?' The man smelt of rum.

'No, sir,' replied Julian.

'That's better. There's nothing like a lad showing a bit of respect,' the man replied.

The men marched Julian and Ethan to a clearing where they untied their horses. They mounted up as instructed, each of them doubling behind the men, hanging on as best they could. Then they were riding in single file, swinging back in the direction of the road, the horses picking a path through tightly packed trees.

Julian reckoned on an hour having passed when he first smelt the stink of the gidgee trees, which reminded him of boiled cabbage. Rain was falling somewhere, the wind carrying the scent. Home was where he wanted to be, not swapping the black soil silt of the river country for the red of higher terrain. Sweat dripped into his eyes. The heat rising from the ground met with a dry westerly. He was born to such conditions but existing in a place where moisture was sucked from your skin was far easier to bear on your own land.

The trees gradually gave way to saplings and sparse clumps of saltbush. The curve of the earth spread out before them, vaulted by a sky pressed down with the weight of stars. Instead of feeling relief after the unnerving closeness of their journey through the dense timber the land's immensity now bore down upon him. A man could evaporate out here as easily as the infrequent rainfall that ran across the bare ground.

A speck of light shone close to the horizon, growing in size as they neared. Julian was reminded of Captain Ashby and the man with the lamp, and hoped whoever was showing the way knew the difference between good and evil. The light grew until a campfire became visible. It burned to one side of a timber shack, which stood forlornly in the middle of nowhere. The man doubling Julian let out a cooee and the door to the cabin burst open, a big man filling the frame. He stepped out to greet the riders, demanding what the heck was going on.

Julian was tugged from the saddle, as was Ethan who landed on his backside. The hut had slits for windows, a hangover from the days when white and black men fought. Hessian flapped over missing timber boards. Julian guessed the place was home to a boundary rider more used to unrolling a swag outdoors. Or perhaps it was an abandoned hut, deserted by a once enthusiastic settler. Not that its original purpose made a difference. Their capture was proof something ruthless was in the making.

They were ushered indoors and forced into seats at a table. The hut was bare except for a huge log that had been poked through a hole in the side of the wall and was now burning in the fireplace. A bulky round-headed man swivelled on his heels. One of his eyes was closed shut, the other wide open. The blinkless good eye ranged about the room with startling speed as the man introduced himself as Gentleman Charles Wesley, his English accent suggesting upper-class aspirations. He placed the pistol on the table next to a tatty beaver-skin hat. Julian thought immediately of his father.

'Were did you find them, Alex?' Gentleman Charles asked the taller captor.

'Near our camp.' The man flicked shoulder-length hair as he rested the rifle butt on the floor. 'That one fought and scratched like a she-dog.' He pinched Ethan's ear and Ethan jerked away from him. 'The Dane met Godfrey as planned. The goods should be here by dawn. It'll be slow travelling.'

'Well, it seems a rise in the river *was* on the way. A person can always tell when the bottles start floating down the Darling that something's afoot. There's nothing like the thought of the river flowing to make Bourke's hard drinkers keen for a dram or two,' said Gentleman Charles.

'Did Godfrey arrive with that woman?' asked Alex.

'I'm sorry to say she was too late for Michael. May the Lord keep him. A day earlier and he still might be with us,' replied Gentleman Charles.

'He knew he wouldn't last. Told me himself he'd done his reckoning with the Lord,' said Alex. 'There was time for that at least. He was a good brother.'

'And he'll be missed. Now. To business. What is the story with these two? This one's obviously talkative.' Gentleman Charles gestured to Ethan's gag. He tilted his head sideways, his good eye shining like an all-seeing god as he took in Julian's muddy clothes and bare feet. 'What's your name? Speak,' he commanded. He picked up the pistol and cocked it, holding it against Julian's forehead.

'J-Julian Dalhunty of Dalhunty Station.' Julian knew he stuttered but he persevered. The barrel was still pressed against his skin. He gave a brief account of their journey to date, omitting anything that might elicit suspicion and concluded with, 'And so with the water dropping we decided to try our luck on foot. We thought we might get a lift to a town or at the least be pointed in the right direction.'

Alex roughly inspected the wound on Julian's head, confirming the account of their travels.

Gentleman Charles withdrew the pistol and placed it on the table. 'A Dalhunty, eh? Do you know where you are?' He dabbed at his sweaty brow with a filthy handkerchief. The room was a furnace with every chance of catching alight.

Julian knew he needed an answer that wouldn't raise suspicion. 'Only that station supplies were being delivered here on account of the Darling becoming unpredictable in flow.'

'That's correct. Alex, take Julian to Miss Carlisle, as they're acquainted. She might need some assistance.' Gentleman Charles pushed at the sightless eye with a thumb. 'Julian is to be treated as a guest while he's with us.'

'And this one?' Alex gestured at Ethan.

Julian's mother's prodigy, bound and muzzled, had the demeanour of a man capable of strangulation. And it was not their captors he appeared to be considering strangling.

Gentleman Charles folded his hands over a dense stomach. 'He can stay here. There's nothing like heat for making the most fervent of men docile and pliant. Come morning he might be partial to having the gag removed and a drink of water. If he behaves.'

⊰ Chapter 38 ⊱

With his wrists unbound, Julian was pointed in the direction of a lone tent billowing in the wind. He walked nervously past a group of men clustered about a fire, the soles of his feet burning with each step, as he listened to the accents of those gathered. He caught the deep brogue of the Irish, the lilt of the Scots, a thick-accented Englishman and a sing-song voice similar to Rick the Dane. The men were subdued, their conversation sporadic, and yet in spite of the late hour none of them slept. Or perhaps time had already stretched through the midnight hours, for a waxing moon hung hungry in the sky.

The tent flap was closed but a light burned within, revealing a slight figure. Julian gathered his wits. Captain Ashby had been clear in his request for Julian to safeguard Odiene in his absence. Although he had been rebuffed when reminding her of this on her departure from the steamer, he would give this reason for his being here. Far better to appear the hero than admit he needed assistance.

Julian pushed through the canvas opening. Odiene was leaning over a rough wooden box that was sitting on supports, the type carpenters used to saw timber. He thought about what he should say and how he should say it, but was baffled by the scene before him. The box was a coffin, and Odiene was none too pleased to see him.

'What are you doing here?' She was wearing the taxidermy apron and held a pair of forceps. Inside the coffin wasn't some creature destined for a city drawing room, but the body of a man. 'Did you follow me?' she said accusingly.

Julian edged towards the coffin. Two slush lamps sat on crates on either side, the burning tallow giving off a rancid stench. The corpse was naked from the waist up. There was a hole in the man's abdomen and purple bruising across his forehead.

'What are you doing here?' he asked, as intrigued as he was repulsed.

Odiene returned to the task of stuffing wadding into the body's stomach wound.

'Preparing Michael Flannery to meet his maker, as requested.' She pushed the filling deep into the hole and then cut a length of material from a shirt with a knife. 'Can you lift him into a sitting position?'

Julian stayed quiet long enough for Odiene to press her lips together in annoyance before struggling to raise the man herself. Unwillingly he went to her aide, inwardly recoiling at the warmth of the body. They succeeded in getting him upright and Julian held the body as Odiene wound the bandage around the stomach area, covering the wound and keeping the wadding in place. She tucked the end in and they dressed the body in a clean shirt before laying the corpse back down. Odiene tidied the man's clothing, pulling the shirt out just a little from the waistband, ensuring the trousers were even at the hems, resting his hands one on top of the other, then standing back to admire her craft.

Readying the man for burial had brought up unwelcome memories for Julian, of his mother washing Davey's small body before dressing him in his Sunday best.

'They are burying him at first light,' Odiene explained.

'You didn't answer my question,' replied Julian across the coffin.

'Nor you mine.' She brushed the greying hair of the deceased to one side.

'I'm here on Captain Ashby's orders. He only made one request of me and that was to look after you. And before you start arguing, I'm here now,' said Julian, more forcefully than intended.

'So, you're to rescue me?' Odiene crossed her arms. 'I told you I was coming back.'

He sensed the heat coming from her skin. 'There's no boat to return to, Odiene. It left.' Julian refused to put up with any more lies.

'What do you mean it left? Don't be ridiculous. Mr Cummins would never leave without me. It was all agreed.'

'Really? With your trunk awaiting collection back at the river?'

'I was to be away a day and a night. Two nights at most. Mr Cummins promised he would wait. We already knew the steamer would never make it as far as Echuca. There was not enough push in the river to get to home port.'

'Well, they have a new agenda and it did not include waiting for you.'

Odiene sank onto one of the crates. 'Truly? They've left me stranded here?'

'You really did intend to come back?'

'They promised me they would wait. Are you sure?' she asked.

Julian knelt beside her. 'The steamer was pulling away when I reached the bank. Odiene, what are you doing here with these men?'

He saw the hurt on her face and he knew then that she'd been telling the truth.

Odiene rubbed tiredly at her brow, leaving a smear of blood on her skin. She looked at the coffin. 'I didn't come for Michael Flannery's sake. He fell from his horse and staked himself.' She moved to a basin of water and scrubbed her fingernails with a small brush.

'What was the reason, if it wasn't this?' asked Julian.

'Frankly, the less you know, the better. These men bear my presence because of the services I offer. In return, payment is received and I keep my counsel. Can you keep quiet, Julian? Can Ethan? I assume he is with you?'

'In the hut with the Englishman.' Julian wondered at the services Odiene had mentioned.

'And who followed who this time?'

'You could say it was mutual,' he told her.

'Then you are not the odd fellows you make out to be. But what of Ethan? He won't cause any trouble, will he?'

'I hope not.'

Odiene was growing pale.

'Tell me why you're here. This is no place for a woman.'

'And where *is* my place? Taking in sewing or washing other people's clothes? Because that's the only choice that was left me after my father died.' Odiene suddenly grabbed hold of the coffin's side. Julian steadied her, but she brushed away his assistance and, choosing a cramped space a few feet from the coffin, sat on the ground, her skirt spreading about her.

'I'm sorry, it's been a long day, and night.' She viewed him cautiously. 'Do you know where we are?'

'I have no idea. Odiene, won't you tell me why you're here?'

A full minute passed before she spoke, and when she did it was with hesitancy. 'You saw Mr Wesley. He has one eye that is permanently shut. The other is permanently open. I'm going to try and repair his closed eyelid, so he has two useful eyes, instead of only one. He suffers from a medical condition that causes the eyelid to droop, although I imagine the problem has been exacerbated by frequent rubbing.'

Julian wanted to ask if she had carried out anything like that before. It was an extraordinary undertaking for a woman. And one not without danger with the likes of Charles Wesley as the patient. As he formulated the question so as not to cause offense, Odiene cradled her head in her arms and rested on one of the crates.

He looked at Michael Flannery, lying peacefully in the coffin, and then at the dead man's boots. Odiene was already snoring gently, a tendril of hair fluttering back and forth with each puff. Julian lifted a bruised foot, trying to gauge whether the size would fit. Deciding a too small boot was far better than none at all, he set about freeing the man of his shoes. It was a devil of a business; Mr Flannery and his boots were not easily parted. The planks the coffin rested on moved with every tug, forcing Julian to stop rushing lest Odiene catch him interfering with the body. By the time the boots were on Julian the blanket lining was scrunched up and Michael Flannery was no longer neatly laid out. Julian hastily straightened the man's clothes and flicked the hair back in place, noting how white and dainty Michael's feet were. The coffin lid was leaning against a crate. He lifted the crudely made top, with its cracks and openings, and slid it across the coffin, hiding all evidence of the theft.

❧ Chapter 39 ❧

Julian woke a few hours later. Odiene lay on the ground beside him, her head on his shoulder, an arm across his chest. The length of her body was so warm and close he could feel the gentle thud of her heart. He stroked the hair from her brow, concentrating on her lips. If he repeated the kiss they'd shared on the riverboat he was sure it would drive away the melancholy he'd been seized by these past years – except Odiene had already revealed her feelings about him.

The slush lamps had petered out, pitching the interior of the tent into gloom. Julian doubted the chance to know Odiene better would ever arise. She was as unreadable as the dead man lying in the casket before them. And now they were here, stranded, depending on the goodwill of dishonest men. He thought of Meg and Laura. Mostly Meg. Julian knew a brother ought not to have favourites, yet it was hard not to feel an affinity with his youngest sister. Meg was as tough and as soft as a crusty damper. If she did not live up to their mother's expectations she outshone them in many other ways. Julian hoped she would stay that way, yet he knew that was impossible. Meg was yet to dig herself out of a world that only lived on in their father's memory. One day very soon she would recognise the need for change.

Gradually, first light brightened the tent. The coffin sat above him on wooden supports, the new morning lifting it from the shadows as the camp stirred. During the night the drays had returned from the river. The recognisable sounds of loaded carts drawing to a halt and the curtness of tired men had woken him from heavy sleep. Now the nicker of horses and the gruff team riding with Gentleman Charles declared that the day had started. The tent flap opened and Julian's kidnapper, Alex, entered with another man. The Irishman barely reacted to discovering Julian with his arm about Odiene, pausing only to note his presence. He swung the coffin lid sideways for a last look at his brother and then hammered four nails into the lid.

Odiene bolted upright like a scalded cat, and shook Julian's arm off. Alex gave them a cursory nod before the coffin was lifted and carried outside.

'I'm sorry . . . I didn't mean . . .' Odiene got up and tidied her hair, looking about the tent distractedly.

'Odiene, it's all right,' Julian told her.

The forceps were sitting on a crate. She wrapped them in a scrap of cloth and tucked them into the holdall, spending altogether too much time arranging the contents. Then she drank from a waterbag and washed the sleep from her eyes. 'That was poor of me. Falling asleep next to the deceased. I never do it. Never. Out of respect.'

'Oh. And how many dead people have you . . . ah, tended to?' asked Julian.

Even with the distance between them he felt the warmth of her body. Sensed the same disturbance in her that ran through his veins. He approached her carefully and, reaching for the waterbag, took it from her and drank. Odiene moved around the small interior of the tent, placing the coffin supports between them. Round red spots coloured her cheeks. 'I meant—'

Outside, one of the men started singing. It was a deep, melodious voice that told of lost love in a dangerous land. It was the type of song to make a person stop and listen, not for the sadness of the story being shared but the miraculous voice that made the shabby tent a new and wondrous realm. The singer soared and dropped to depths unmined and then rose again, each time taking the listener beyond the conceivable.

Odiene was looking at Julian. Intently. Strangely. Then she gave a shriek as one side of the tent wall collapsed, followed closely by the second.

'Come on,' said Julian, shielding Odiene. He pushed through the tent opening.

Once outside they discovered the singer to be Gentleman Charles Wesley himself, who was at the rear door of the hut, one arm clenching the lapel of his jacket, the other arm extended in a grand gesture as his voice trembled through the verses. About him the men worked on, rolling swags, drinking tea, packing saddlebags. In the distance two men were digging a hole on a knobby rise.

A man untied a rope from a peg securing the tent, then he took hold of the peg, wiggled it roughly back and forth and drew it free of the ground. He tugged on the canvas, pulling it to one side. The coffin scaffolding, fallen lamps and the carpet bag disappeared within canvas folds. With four moves the tent was folded into a bundle for transportation and the items within scattered.

'What are you doing?' Odiene collected her holdall, checking the contents. 'I'm still to tend to Gentleman Charles.'

'Not here you're not,' the man hissed sourly through a large gap in his front teeth. He stowed the tent on the rear of a dray.

'Julian, that was the agreement. To stay here and operate on his eye,' explained Odiene.

'I'll speak to him,' promised Julian, although with the camp on the move the decision to leave had evidently already been made. Being stranded in the middle of nowhere with no transport or water gave them little choice but to go with the men.

When the song was complete, the men walked quietly to the gravesite on the rise, hats removed, straggling, as if the Grim

Reaper might pull them into the grave as well. Michael Flannery was raised high on shoulders, the casket tilted ominously at one end where two short men did the honours of carrying it. Gentleman Charles was intoning the word of God by speaking aloud the Lord's Prayer in a thunderous tone.

Julian spun slowly, taking in the camp and the dismal hut and the desolate countryside. Bushes, scant trees, few birds, and little water. In all directions. Gentleman Charles's gap-toothed servant was scratching his crotch and guarding their movement. A hymn floated on the wind, the song of praise breaking up as quickly as the grouped men, who were already pushing on hats and ambling away from Michael Flannery. Two men were left to shovel clods on his coffin.

Ethan burst from the hut and headed for the remains of the campfire. Finding a waterbag he guzzled desperately before noticing Julian and Odiene. He took another gulp and then shifted through the embers, picking out a hunk of bread. A bruise showed where Alex's strike had found flesh. 'Thanks for last night. It was hot enough in there to cook a boiler hen.' Ethan broke the damper in half and tossed one piece to Julian, who in turn gave half of his share to Odiene before eating his hungrily.

'What's her story?' Ethan gestured at Odiene who was daintily picking dirt from the bread.

'She's only here because Captain Ashby asked her to do something for Gentleman Charles.' Julian lowered his voice as the returning men grew closer.

Ethan looked distastefully at the bread but kept chewing. 'A favour, is it? For that monstrosity of a man? I'm thinking it'll be a poor ending, Julian, if she's not as friendly with these men as that puffed up One-eyed Englishman suggested last night. What are you here for then?' he asked Odiene. 'Stuffing birds?'

'People, actually,' retaliated Odiene.

The two gravediggers were now walking back to the camp, shovels raised to their shoulders.

'She's to operate on Gentleman Charles,' explained Julian.

257

'What did you say? Operate? On that thug?' Ethan stared at Odiene.

'And who, pray tell, is the thug?'

The three of them turned to see Gentleman Charles waiting for an answer with the expectant air of one used to being attended to, the all-seeing eyeball red in its socket. He drew his pistol, directing it at Ethan as he circled him.

'We don't want to hold you up. If you could give us directions to the nearest town or station, we'll be on our way.' Ethan brushed ash from his hands, ignoring the weapon as the sentence eased from his lips.

'What? Leave now? When we're yet to be properly acquainted? No. You must stay with me, as Miss Carlisle intends to,' declared Gentleman Charles.

Odiene twisted her fingers together. 'Captain Ashby said nothing about moving on from this place. He told me that—'

'Captain Ashby, or should I say, the late arrival of Captain Ashby's steamer, has delayed us enough, Miss Carlisle. The day is already upon us.' Gentleman Charles beckoned to Alex who was standing with the group of returned men. 'Alex, see our friends to one of the drays. Make sure they're comfortable.' He removed his top hat and, brushing the brim, gave a sweeping bow to the woman before him. 'Until our next stop, my dear Miss Carlisle.'

Without warning, Alex shoved Julian, knocking him to the ground. 'What the hell are you doing wearing Michael's boots?' He lifted up one of Julian's legs and pointed out red leather used to mend a hole in the side and then dropped it in disgust.

Men closed in, forming a tight circle. Julian rose unsteadily, feeling the ache of Alex's shoulder in his chest. Outside the ring of gathered men, Ethan jostled the spectators, trying to get a better viewing position.

Alex's face was filled with rage. 'How will Michael rest easy without his boots? How will he be comfortable when he takes the long road to join the others who have gone before him?'

'I meant no offence,' stammered Julian.

'I'm going to give you such a drubbing you'll wish there was a hole next to my brother by the time I'm finished.' Alex undid the leather belt holding a holstered pistol and passed it to one of the gathered men.

'Stop!' ordered Gentleman Charles. He walked into the circle, pushing the men aside. 'It's a sorry state when a man must steal boots. And even sorrier when those boots belong to a dead man, but there'll be no fighting on his burying day. Your mother would grieve anew at the very idea, Alex. We will discuss this another time.'

As Alex took a step towards Julian, a shot was fired. It barely missed them, emitting a puff of dirt from where it hit the ground and leaving the tang of cordite in the air. Julian didn't move.

'*Another time*, Alex,' said Gentleman Charles firmly, holstering his pistol.

'I don't forget. Ever,' Alex threatened, before merging with the grumbling men.

'You've made no friends here, Julian,' said Ethan, when they were left alone with Odiene. 'But I would have done the same if I'd been you.'

Ethan had made few conciliatory gestures to Julian since his arrival at Dalhunty Station and it caught Julian unawares. Over the previous days, The Natural had shown himself to be a smart but also tetchy individual, unafraid of a scrape. If this was his true character, then the question of Ethan's actual personality and background, of which Julian had previously been indifferent to, was now a subject he found intriguing.

About them, eight men lifted saddles onto horses, tightened girth straps and mounted up, rifles and braces of pistols conspicuous. Julian observed their singing captor as he ambled towards his horse, a sleek chestnut mare. Alex was at his side carrying a square, dun-coloured strong box, which was probably a little more than two feet in size and height, the lid painted with a thin black pinstripe design. He placed the box in one of the drays and then brusquely thumbed at Julian for them to get on board as well. Julian glanced down at Flannery's boots, and obeyed.

⋘ Chapter 40 ⋙

The eye operation was to take place in a hut hastily vacated by its owner, a bow-legged individual with a nasal voice and clearly enough reason to understand that Gentleman Charles Wesley would be taking up residence in his home, regardless of whether he was invited or not. The man tipped his hat at Gentleman Charles and his entourage of men and drays and, with a scratch of a greying beard, propped his door open. Hardly a word passed between the two men as one left and the other entered the hut.

Julian roughly totalled the hours travelled and guessed forty miles lay between the previous shack and this new one. The dray horses were in good condition, the men determined and their north-westerly destination reached with only one stop. This was a group used to being on the move. And they knew exactly where they were going.

On arrival, Ethan was drafted to help erect the tent, which was for Odiene's sole use, and unpack the drays while Odiene was soon consumed with trying to locate her trunk. Julian, relegated to obtaining kindling, wandered in a wide circumference about the campsite. The powdery dirt revealed a goanna track, the cloven tread of sheep and the tell-tale half-circle of horseshoes. Based on the angle of the sun, more than twenty horsemen had travelled to the hut from two separate directions, the north-west and the west, the marks imprinted in now hardened rain-dampened soil.

On his return Julian dumped the kindling as ordered and lit the fire, observing one of the men riding out. He guessed he was a messenger sent to advise some other acquaintance of their arrival at the hut. He stoked the fire, listening to the men talk as they worked. One joked their accommodation was unchanged, while another yearned for the evening meal, with riders already despatched to locate some agreeable sheep. Julian decided to search out the owner of the hut, hopeful he might be open to answering some questions. Under the pretence of combing for more firewood if anyone queried his wanderings, Julian moved in the direction of the well.

He found the man sitting next to the timber wall of the water supply, the struts of the windlass offering a miniscule wedge of shade. He had a bottle of rum at one side, a bucket of water on the other. He mixed the two liquids together in a metal drinking cup with the precision and guarded anticipation of an alchemist, adding a little rum and then a splash more water, and then holding it under his nose, his eyes crinkling in pleasure.

'Yes?' The man drew the word out slowly, not once looking up to see who approached.

'Hello, I'm Julian.'

'How nice for you,' he replied. 'Riley Jimm's the name.'

Julian squatted beside the older man, intent on persisting. 'Where are we?'

Riley Jimm gave Julian a look that clearly said, *Why are you disturbing me?* 'Where would you like to be? I've a hankering for Bathurst. There's a sweet young lass down there I met near thirty years ago.' Riley sipped at the rum and water and sighed. 'Nectar.'

'I'm from near Bourke and I'm hoping to get back there,' said Julian.

Riley placed the cup somewhat reluctantly on the ground, grinding it into the sand. 'And what does Gentleman Charles say about your plans?'

'Miss Carlisle has to fix his eye first. You obviously know Mr Wesley,' replied Julian carefully.

'Can a man ever rightly say he truly knows another man?' He shook his head. 'And Gentleman Charles, well, he's the type of man it's probably better not to know. Knowing a man, *really* knowing a man, can get a person into a whole lot of strife. For example, if you knew he'd killed a man down south and was wanted for murder, you'd be worried, but as I never mentioned his troubles, it won't bother you none.' Riley pulled at his knuckles, slowly and methodically. Each made a popping sound. 'Most men have two dogs inside them. A good and a bad. The good dog can be placated with a kind word, but a bad dog once riled is hard to control.'

Julian glanced back in the direction of the hut and then to the land that encircled them, empty and unforgiving. He felt every impulse that he believed a murderer might feel. He wanted to pummel Ethan for leaving the property, and launch a tirade at Odiene for leading them here, but most of all he could not forgive himself for blindly following them both.

'Why are we here?' asked Julian.

'You're a ferreter, aren't you?' stated Riley. 'My father hunted with ferrets. Crafty animals, those. Do you know a ferret's busiest at dawn and dusk? They'll chase down a rabbit quick-smart. They can be slow when they're young'uns. Sleep a good half of their lives. Then one day they wake up and see what's what.' He knocked the side of the rum bottle with his knuckles. 'The most I'll say is Mr Wesley comes through these parts every so often. Sometimes he stays for a while. Other times he rides straight on. It depends if the coppers have got wind of him.' Riley flicked his hat so that it perched on the back of his head. 'Anything else, whippersnapper?'

'Yes. Where are we?' Julian asked.

Riley gave a loud chortle. 'We're west. West of everything. West of women. West of civilisation. West of most people. You're in the margins. The land last settled after the first wave of pastoralists came through.' He gestured vaguely. 'Out there you'll find stations eventually. Plenty of sheep. But not much else.'

'Are you a boundary rider for a property?'

Riley drank the cup dry. 'Not today I ain't.'

≪ Chapter 41 ≫

Odiene was rummaging through her trunk. A pale-blue blouse, a shawl, a billow of white cotton edged in lace, a large medical volume, some toiletries, and the taxidermy kit were all pushed to one side as she reached in and retrieved a reel of linen thread.

'Do you mind?' she asked, on noticing Julian inspecting her belongings.

'You're not listening to me,' he replied curtly. Having seen her undergarments, he turned guiltily and propped his rear end against the dray. 'I said Mr Wesley is wanted for murder.'

Odiene closed the trunk, resting the taxidermy kit, medical volume and cotton reel on the lid. She tested a length of the thread between her teeth and then pulled it taut, murmuring that it would have to do, although her preference was carbolic catgut, a sterile suturing thread that was absorbed by the body. Around them, the men checked the contents of the cargo from the *Lady Matilda* as if they were doing inventory for a store. A number of crates were being carried into the hut along with a barrel of beer.

'I've heard rumours of this accusation. Nothing more.' She packed selected items into the carpet bag, dropping the thread, taxidermy kit and medical volume inside. 'I don't know what else you expect of me, Julian.'

She was as unruffled by Mr Wesley's alleged crime as she had been the morning after Captain Ashby's violent abduction. Far too composed for Julian's liking. Well, he was also capable of self-possession.

'Tell me about Gentleman Charles. I'm sure you asked questions of Captain Ashby before agreeing to this madness.'

'Not really.'

'Odiene?'

She gave an anxious glance towards the camp and, depositing the carpet bag on the rear of the dray, began walking rather absentmindedly straight into the mid-afternoon bite of the sun. Julian caught up with her, circling them back towards the activity and within sight of all.

Julian squeezed her arm. 'Odiene, you must tell me what you know.'

She tugged free of his grasp. 'He runs grog shanties in the outer areas. A different place each month. Captain Ashby has been supplying Gentleman Charles for years. Selling alcohol without a licence is illegal. But out here, does it really matter? The men that work these parts live a barren existence. I can't begrudge them a little entertainment.'

'And the murder charge?'

For all her cool collectedness, Odiene faltered. 'It is said he flogged a man to death in Sydney.'

Julian's body tensed as the futility of their situation struck home. With Wesley on the run, it was doubtful he'd be partial to three unwanted guests, especially if the man was intent on further thieving. The selling of sly grog clearly wasn't all the man was up to, particularly with a team of men gathered together. Something else was planned, and Odiene's presence was a blip in their schemes.

'You said last night you were here to operate on Wesley. Are you trained? I mean there aren't any women doctors, are there?'

'Actually the University of Melbourne Medical School has been accepting women since the 1880s, but I'm not one of them. I'm sorry if the concept upsets the natural order for you, Julian.'

'You know what I mean. He needs a proper doctor. I can't believe I'm even saying that about a murderer.' Julian led them back towards the dray. The gap-toothed tent-packer was watching them from the vicinity of the campfire.

'I'm the closest he'll ever get to one. Gentleman Charles has an abhorrent dislike of authority. His father was a convict, transported to Australia for thieving a pair of opera glasses and tickets outside the Royal Opera House in Covent Garden. Of a stranger theft I have never heard, but there we are. A man is sentenced to the colonies for love of music and his son grows to detest lawmakers and becomes sceptical of any person in a learned position.'

'He is a murderer, Odiene, no matter his past.'

'Don't speak to me like that. I am not an imbecile.'

Julian apologised, although he couldn't help admiring the woman's strong mind.

'I'm not disputing you,' resumed Odiene as if she had never raised her voice. 'His crime is abhorrent, but it is the past that has made him. It has made all of us, whether we like it or not,' she replied.

'Why you?' persisted Julian.

'The last doctor who treated Gentleman Charles left him with a lidless eye. That is why it is permanently open. Nothing can be done with it now. The other . . . well, if I can excise the drooping eyelid skin and stitch it, then I might be able to restore the lid and his sight to working order. Mr Wesley knew of my interest in taxidermy. He knows what my father did for a living. I have knowledge of anatomy and of certain procedures.' Odiene stopped short of further explanation.

'Your father was a doctor?'

Odiene fiddled with the bag at her side. 'He was an undertaker. I was his assistant. You need not say anything, Julian. Working with corpses doesn't instil favourable images. Frankly, there are many nights when those same images keep me awake.'

The idea of Odiene preparing bodies for burial, of plugging and stitching wounds and powdering the countenances of those that would never wake, left Julian slightly annoyed at her father for involving his daughter in such a profession, but he also respected her ability. How did a person live with bereavement every day? For it was not just the bodies of the young and old that required attention, but the deceased's relatives that needed comforting too. He knew that from experience.

'It is a necessary business,' he finally concluded.

Her appreciation was genuine. 'One doesn't rush to the profession. My mother died young. I wanted to be with my father. That's how my involvement began. And now I am here. If I don't try to help Gentleman Charles he will soon be blind. The lidless eye will eventually wither and become useless. It has no protection from the elements, no means of flicking away dirt or dust. So we need to restore the drooping lid on his remaining eye. I'm not a willing participant in this, Julian, and, like you, I doubt my abilities, but I can't knowingly leave a man to go blind.' She lifted the bag.

Julian pictured Ashby and Gentleman Charles discussing their joint ventures in the saloon of the *Lady Matilda*, talking quantities and profits and payment terms, ultimately bartering Odiene Carlisle in return for some shady debt owed. 'I could throttle Ashby. And to think he deceived my father into believing he was a friend.'

'Please, Julian. What is done is done. Agreeing to this allows me to repay the Captain's many kindnesses.'

And after Odiene stitched him up, successful or not, what happened then? Julian felt a net closing down upon them. Riley Jimm hadn't sung Wesley's praises. Gentleman Charles was clearly the type of man who might believe it easier to be rid of them.

Alex was at the door of the hut. He called to Odiene that it was time.

Odiene's fingers plied the handle of the floral bag. 'Will you come with me, for moral support?'

He told her he would remain at her side through the ordeal and they walked stride for stride towards the hut under the watchful gaze of Alex and the tent-packer, who was now guarding the door with a rifle.

Julian left Odiene at the hut, promising to join her shortly, and went in search of Ethan, thumping a fist against his thigh. An idea of sorts was forming. He found Ethan at the end of a dray piled with saddles. Ethan dipped a rag into a quart pot containing a greyish substance smelling of rendered animal fat and soap and applied the grease to the seat of a saddle in a small circular motion.

'Have you finished courting Miss Carlisle yet?' Ethan followed the curve of the seat down across the flaps and concentrated on working the grease into the dry leather.

'I'm not courting her. She and Captain Ashby are . . . well . . .' Unsure of how to finish the sentence Julian wished he had not begun it.

Ethan lifted the saddle and repositioned it. 'You like her. Nothing wrong with that. Have you tried it on with her, then? She might be willing. Especially if she believes in the mighty myth of the Dalhuntys.'

'You can't let it go, can you? Even here,' said Julian.

'It needles me. And no, I can't. I gave up a future for nothing.' Ethan dabbed the cloth in the pot, scooping out more of the mixture and applied it to the leather, leaning in to inspect his efforts. 'Leather keeps on living. If you care for it. That's one of the slogans on the counter at Bon Marche.'

'She's with Captain Ashby,' said Julian.

Ethan set the rag aside and gave a low whistle. 'Are you telling me . . .? Well, that old dog. And Miss Carlisle, eh? Who would have thought? These days there's no telling what a woman will do for security. It hasn't panned out for her though, has it? She's been as ill-used as your father. But, that being the case, we know Captain Ashby isn't a gentleman for all the puff he has about him,

268

which means your Miss Carlisle's cherry is long popped. There's hope for you yet.'

'You shouldn't speak about Odiene that way, it's ungentlemanly and a slight on her character.' Julian decided against asking how Ethan's father had come to substitute cherries for chickens when it came to the education of his boy.

'Up and down the Darling. To and fro. Loading and unloading. Never mind the unaccountable waters that old sea dog moans about. At night when the boiler's gone cold and the water's silky, temptation's mighty powerful.' Ethan returned to greasing the saddle, as if muddying a woman's reputation was of little consequence to him.

Julian was left with visions difficult to erase. Sometimes a person could simply know too much. But he had not come to discuss Odiene. As he briefly explained what he had learnt about Wesley, he picked up a piece of rag and rubbed at a saddle.

Ethan's polishing grew harder. He concentrated on the task, not lifting his head. He had figured as much, he told Julian. Not the murder, but the possibility of the gang being thieves. The strongbox was the clue. 'I'd say we should make a hop for it, except there's nowhere to go to. Is there?'

Julian reached for the pot of grease. 'Odiene's about to operate on Wesley's eye.'

'If that girl gets it wrong, we're in trouble,' said Ethan. 'But either way we need a plan to get out of here. If only I had my father's cutthroat razor. Up under the ribs or in the guts makes for the best results, you know.'

'Really? And you the law-abiding citizen,' mocked Julian. 'Plans are all well and good until you meet the enemy. Remember those pictures on our bedroom wall? Major-General Gordon thought he could hold out against Muhammad Ahmad, but he was eventually outnumbered. Like we are. What we need is a distraction and we'll be getting one soon. This place is a grog shanty apparently so I'm expecting there'll be men coming in from outlying stations,' explained Julian.

269

'There's more people living out here?' Ethan made a show of taking in the mass of land surrounding them. 'Well, I hate grog. It was the demon drink that led to my father's death. A single bottle of rum.' He stopped greasing the saddle as if in thought. 'If this place is a sly-grog shanty then the men will eventually drink themselves into oblivion.'

'Yes, and when the lot of them are passed out, we'll saddle three horses and ride back in the direction the outliers came from. By morning we should be a good distance clear of this place, then we'll head back towards the river.'

'I still owe you a punch in the nose,' grumbled Ethan.

'Well, save it for when we're clear of this place.'

Julian walked towards the hut, mulling over what Ethan had revealed about his father. What type of man knew how to use a cut-throat razor as a weapon? And what kind of person did that make Ethan?

⪻ Chapter 42 ⪼

The tent-packer lay outside the hut with his legs outstretched. He was hatless and the pink of a shiny pate shone through straggly grey hair. The man barely acknowledged Julian, instead lifting a leg at the last moment so that Julian tripped through the doorway into the building. Julian made a lunge for the doorframe, just managing to steady himself. Odiene was flipping through the medical book, her brow already creased, when she looked up to see the disturbance.

'Julian is here to help me,' she immediately said to Alex, who had opened his mouth to protest the newest arrival.

'Do it then. But don't be forgetting, you and I have unfinished business,' Alex cautioned Julian.

Gentleman Charles removed his jacket and waistcoat, revealing a ruffled shirt. He passed the garments to Alex, who brushed them down as if he were a manservant attending to his master's clothes. Alex looked about for a suitable place to put them, and finally folded them over the back of a chair. He then presented Gentleman Charles with a bottle and the big man took a long, throat-gurgling swig before giving an airy wave as if acknowledging an audience. Then, resting the bottle on the edge of the table, he took a comb from his pocket and with expert precision tidied the greasy parting down the middle of his skull. Finally prepared, he stretched out along the table, filling the width and length of the wood, his boots hanging over the end. His stomach resembled the hump of a whale.

Julian moved to the end of the hut where Odiene studied the book. A fire blazed in the room, which was simply furnished, with three chairs and a narrow bed at the opposite end. Riley Jimm could not be accused of hoarding. Shelving displayed chipped plates and pannikins, and bags of flour and sugar. Illustrations from the *Bulletin* were tacked to a wall next to a shuttered window and on the floor was the strongbox Julian had first glimpsed the previous day. The room smelt of warm bodies, stale food and loneliness. He edged around the table towards Odiene. She glanced up distractedly from the medical volume before returning to study the page, her lips moving as she read. Finally she snapped the book shut, sitting it on a chair and then took the taxidermy kit from the carpet bag and selected a needle. Cutting a length of yarn, she moistened the end in her mouth and commenced threading the needle, which took four attempts.

'I think she's blinder than you are, Boss,' said Alex, clearly amused.

'Do you want to end up in a box like your brother?' challenged Gentleman Charles from where he lay flat on his back.

'It's hot in here and I need more light.' Lifting the rum bottle, Odiene took a long, resounding gulp, then she drew the two ends of the thread together and tied a knot.

Alex held a slush lamp close to Gentleman Charles's head. 'He likes the heat. Always has.' In his other hand he held a pistol, which he pointed at Odiene.

'Shoot her if she cuts me,' Wesley said pleasantly.

'Once I start you mustn't move or flinch,' warned Odiene with a nervous glance at Alex, 'and it will be painful. If you keep waving that blasted pistol in my face I *will* cut him.'

The patient took another draft of the rum, the liquid spilling to the floor as he swallowed. 'Keep the pistol ready, Alex, but try not to blight the woman's work and don't you puncture me in the wrong place, my dear Miss Carlisle. I'm no dead man.'

Alex holstered the weapon and gave Odiene more space.

She heated the needle in the fire and moved steadily to the table. Under her instruction, Julian held the patient's head still, pressing firmly against cold skin, confronted close-up with the lidless good eye. Red blood vessels clouded the whiteness, the grey of the pupil an island within a maze. The eye had a life of its own. It may have existed in the body of Gentleman Charles, however it swivelled left and right and up and down like a cornered animal seeking escape. Finally, it stilled and centred on the suspended needle. Julian felt Gentleman Charles's facial muscles tense.

Odiene looked down at the patient in her care and placed a folded cloth over the open eye. Julian offered her a nod of encouragement. The slush lamp in Alex's grip swayed.

With tentative fingers she carefully gathered the drooping flap of eyelid skin in the middle of the closed eye, squeezing until it turned white. She bit her bottom lip and brought the needle close to Gentleman Charles's eye. 'I've decided against cutting the loose skin away. I'm going to stitch the skin of the eyelid together to take the slack out that will allow faster healing.'

Odiene squinted and wiped at the sweat on her brow, then lowered the needle again. She held her the breath, then pierced the eyelid closest to Gentleman Charles's nose, drawing the thread through the tab of skin and raising her arm until the yarn was tight. The patient gripped the sides of the table. Odiene pushed the needle through the skin again, waited and then proceeded, growing surer with every stitch, the thread looping in and out as drops of blood welled at the site of each puncture. Odiene worked methodically, the pink of her tongue protruding from the corner of her mouth, sweat from her brow dripping onto the patient. When completed she tied a knot in the last stitch, cut the thread with scissors, then patted the wound dry. The excess skin was now selvage, as neatly done as any seamstress could produce. Odiene announced the operation was finished and as she removed the folded cloth from the other eye, Wesley's once useless eyelid briefly flickered open and he sat up like a jack-in-the-box.

'Mirror,' he demanded.

Alex produced a travelling case with an attached mirror and magnifying glass.

'You know how to inflict pain, Miss Carlisle.' Gentleman Charles examined the wound. 'But you seem to have done a passable job. I can see out of both eyes now.' He was triumphant as with difficulty he partially opened and closed the stitched eyelid.

'I have sewn the loose skin together. It will feel awkward, having that flap of skin on your lid, and you will have to keep it covered for a time. Make sure it is free of dust.' Odiene dunked the needle in a pot of water sitting next to the fire and then stuck it through the front of her blouse for safekeeping.

'Ashby said you'd be up to the task. Had you attended to me instead of that imbecile down south who removed my entire eyelid I may have two workable eyes. Is there anything you can do with it? Add a bit more skin perhaps? Fashion a new eyelid?' Gentleman Charles checked the result from every possible angle. 'I have glass eyes at my disposal, in case the lidless eye fails me, however I don't want to revert to decoration.'

'As you said, your other eyelid was removed. I've nothing to work with. And I am no magician,' Odiene admitted. 'You must keep the dust out of the wound to ensure it doesn't get infected. And wash the eye out three times a day with boiled salted water.'

Odiene placed a wad of material over the recently operated-upon eye and secured it with a patch. Wesley's good eye swivelled about, watching her every move.

Gentleman Charles heaved his frame from the table and took a long draught from the rum bottle. 'Infection, eh? You must stay with me to ensure there are no problems.'

'But that wasn't part of the bargain,' complained Odiene with dismay.

Her expression grew wary and she looked to Julian for guidance. For once, her nerves had failed her.

Odiene turned her gaze to Gentleman Charles and then Alex, who was unfolding the waistcoat resting across the chair, readying to dress his master.

'But that wasn't part of the bargain,' she repeated more firmly.

Gentleman Charles swatted the air as if swishing away a fly. 'I could have one of my men dump you fifty miles from here, Miss Carlisle. Fifty miles. In those thin boots and that pretty dress, how far would you get? How long would you last in this heat?'

'But there was an agreement. Captain Ashby said—'

'Captain Ashby? I haven't seen the man. Have you seen the good Captain, Alex?'

'No, Boss, I haven't,' replied Alex.

'Come on, Odiene.' Julian waited as she collected her belongings, ignoring Wesley's jibes that he made a pretty nurse. Outside the hut the tent-packer observed them steadily as Julian led Odiene away from the man and the building. She was pale and shaky, fixated with checking the buckle on the carryall and patting at a strand of hair that was plastered to her cheek. She begged to be left alone and cut a path through the men, who were taking chunks of sheep-meat from blood-soaked bags and placing the cuts into pots on the fire. She stopped and vomited, the men staring briefly before returning to their tasks. Then she moved to the dray and the lone trunk holding her few possessions and sank to the ground in the shade.

Had Julian within him the right words he may have gone to her. But what was he to say? How did a man comfort a woman without overstepping the boundaries of friendship? The best he could do was to get her away from this place.

The waiting men ambled across to the hut and Julian found himself gathering with them as they whistled and cooeed as if a miraculous event had occurred.

Gentleman Charles strutted out of the building, dangling a handkerchief. He commenced singing an engaging verse, the crux of which involved being saved from hell's clammy grasp. The men gave a cheer at the end of the song and cheered again when a consolatory glass or two of spirituous liquor was deemed necessary for all as part of his recuperation.

'Quiet. Quiet. In closing, we must address the recent theft of poor Michael Flannery's boots. It is a most severe crime, to be sure.' With evident distaste Gentleman Charles examined Julian, who in turn moved apart from the men. Ethan came to his side.

'But, one must give thought to Julian Dalhunty, who in rescuing one Ethan Harris lost his own boots. It is a brave thing to risk your life for another and it is also a gospel truth no white man in these parts can survive without boots. And none of us here can attest we would not do the same should we be met with such a quandary.'

The assembled men shouted agreement. Someone walked past and punched Julian in the side. He buckled over.

'Stand firm,' muttered Ethan, pulling him upright.

'Still, a dead man's boots are especially revered. Unless they are freely given, the deceased must be honoured.' Gentleman Charles bowed respectfully at Alex. 'All of us have walked and ridden long miles. Who knows how far the journey might take us in the afterlife? Or where. Therefore, taking all I have said into judgement, it is decided that Julian must work off the cost of the boots. That is, unless he can pay for them. Can you, lad?'

'No.'

'Well then, we have a bargain. Honest labour in exchange for a pair of boots.'

The decision was greeted favourably by all except Julian, who could see no angle of escape.

'I've always wanted a lackey,' said Alex, with an air of superiority.

'It's been a long time since they've seen any spit and polish,' Ethan said curtly. 'Why, a pair of boots like that wouldn't be fit to grace the shelves of Bon Marche department store. They're not even worth resoling.'

'Ethan, don't,' said Julian. But it was too late. The tent-packer swung his rifle butt into Ethan's stomach and he dropped to the ground.

'What are you doing?' Julian helped him up from the ground. 'You idiot.'

'Say it like you mean it,' he wheezed, grinning. 'Say it like Meg does.'

Julian dragged him away from the gathered men as Alex proceeded to distribute glugs of rum into pannikins. 'Do you like stirring up trouble? You'll be their punching bag at this rate. If you don't get us all killed first.'

Ethan finally caught his breath. 'I pretty much thought that was on the cards anyway.'

⊰ Chapter 43 ⊱

A dust storm broiled out west, hanging below an egg-yolk sun. It curved downwards, an enflamed line of red cresting as if a massive wave readying to break across an unsuspecting land. It would be nightfall when the worst of the storm reached the shanty. Tomorrow its offering might cover Dalhunty Station. Julian envisaged the property battening down as the wind picked up and the first of the storm was carried towards them to swirl among the out-buildings.

As Frank took shelter with Henrietta in the overseer's hut, his sisters would rush about the homestead, clogging gaps with bags and material, attempting the impossible, while their mother stalked the hallway, raging against the elements. And Ben? He would shout and laugh and roar, exhilarated by nature's fury – but that was before the accident. Outside, fragile sediment would bash against walls and animals. It would drop onto greening plants in seedling trays, cake the empty ditches in the vegetable garden, and sneak through spaces to leave a fine film of red on the vase of fish-scale geraniums. Home. It was so far away.

The rolling grit was gradually consuming the sun, bringing

darkness early. Julian, Ethan and Odiene sat outside the tent, readying to retreat to the safety of the canvas as more and more boundary riders and workers from outlying stations arrived, their horses lathered with sweat from hard riding, their muzzles flecked with foam. The men watered their mounts at the well, avoiding the prostrate body of a drunk Riley Jimm, and then headed into the hut. Their raucous laughter and yells drowned out Ethan's attempts to elicit the gory facts of the surgery. He settled for a brief account, making no comment except for the slightest grimace when the press of flesh and needle were explained.

'You've done some doctoring then?' he said.

'Some, yes.' Odiene made no mention of the dead tended in her father's business. 'How is your head?' she asked Julian.

'Fine.' Apart from a tightening sensation, the injury was all but forgotten. All discomfort was now centred within Michael Flannery's too small boots. He was damned with or without them.

Odiene offered to check his stitches and Julian declined politely. He was already far too aware of the woman by his side to risk her touch. She was accomplished and intelligent and her most recent feat suggested a gumption he presumed few women possessed. How he had held her close for those few scant hours this morning now seemed inexplicable.

Somehow, operations and head wounds had given way to thoughts of pillowy breasts and the single strap of a chemise. A chemise slipping willingly from a fine-boned shoulder. He was wandering, exploring, luxuriating . . .

Julian shook his head. Granted, this was not the first dream about Odiene that went beyond talking and kissing, but it hinted at what his father termed a dreaded moment in a man's life, when daydreams overtook reasonable judgement. Ben warned that was when accidents happened. One day a man was going about his business, the next he was incapable of making decisions.

When Morgana, their second-best hen and third in the pecking order, refused the advances of Reginald's predecessor, Lawrence, the rooster never quite came to terms with the rebuff.

Concerned that with Morgana's rejection the other hens would follow suit, at Ben's decree Lawrence met an untimely demise as a Sunday roast.

Julian berated himself and fell to concentrating on the too-tight boots, as another couple of riders eased out of their saddles and, stretching their backs, walked inside the hut. His daydream had blanked out all other distractions; now he listened with dismay as Ethan revealed their plan to Odiene without consulting him.

'You don't think he won't come after us? Gentleman Charles flatly stated I was to stay and ensure there is no infection. You're a fool for thinking he would let me go,' said Odiene.

'And what does that make you, having agreed to this scheme in the first place?' countered Ethan. 'Besides, this isn't all about you. There is also the small issue of a dead man's shoes.'

The three of them looked at Julian's shabby boots.

'We might be another two hundred miles from home by the time Gentleman Charles releases us. *If* he lets us go.' Julian tasted grit from the incoming storm. He weighed the prospect of staying on with Riley Jimm's image of a bad dog, perpetually hungering for more.

'I don't know. There is food and water here. And Gentleman Charles needs me. Why would he do anything to hurt us?' Odiene formed a steeple with her fingers in thought.

'He might want a wife. And he's probably a better option compared to Captain Ashby,' said Ethan. 'I mean, he hasn't been caught yet.'

Odiene's lips parted, but it was as if she could not quite bring herself to acknowledge what Ethan had said to her. Julian tried again to persuade her of their plan of escape. It was light on detail and depended mostly on drunken men and luck, of which they'd been very much short to date. Finally he was forced to draw his trump card.

'Odiene, if you don't agree to leave with us, then none of us are going.'

'Trust a man to make things difficult,' she said.

It seemed achievable, but for the brittle soil edging towards them. If it had not passed over by the time of their departure it would make their escape tricky.

Ethan waited until Odiene entered the tent and lay down on a pile of hessian bags. 'Lap of the gods stuff, if you ask me, trying to get out of this place.'

Julian believed his father would have the same opinion.

As they sat waiting for dark to fall, the horses were moved to the front of the hut away from the direction of the incoming storm. The drinkers also sought shelter there, choosing the relative cool to the heat of Gentleman Charles's fire. Concern filled Julian. It would be harder to steal the horses when they were so close to the drinkers. He glanced about the camp. The tent-packer was cutting lengths of rope and more than thirty riders were now enjoying Gentleman Charles's hospitality, including the team riding with the Englishman.

Why were there so many men riding with Gentleman Charles? The question became more bothersome the more he thought on it. There was no need for such a number to run a grog shanty. And no matter how fine-voiced a leader Wesley was, the men would expect to be paid for their services.

'What is Gentleman Charles really up to?' said Julian. 'Another robbery? One of the Cobb & Co. coaches? I'd sure like to know what's in that strongbox.'

'His men have to be paid and his guests aren't enjoying themselves for free,' replied Ethan. 'It will be full of money.'

'And if what you say is right about the cheque given to Rick, then Captain Ashby's payment for the goods delivered to Wesley is still in the strongbox too,' said Julian.

'And?' queried Ethan.

Julian got up and paced about, kicking at the film of sand covering the hardened shell beneath. 'Ashby's payment could be used to repay the piano money owed to my father.'

'What?' Ethan squinted at him. 'No, no, no. You can't be considering . . . This isn't you, Julian. You'll regret the very idea of what you're suggesting.'

Julian glanced skywards, seeking answers. What would his father do? Undoubtedly not what he was considering. 'That is Dalhunty money.' He scuffed a line in the sand with the heel of his boot.

'Theoretically,' replied Ethan.

'Maybe that's enough when it comes to righting a wrong.' Julian kneaded his knuckles in his palm.

'Can you even comprehend what might happen if you steal from a thief, particularly a man like Gentleman Charles, who has a gang to lead? And those same men have a vested interest in the contents of that strongbox as well.' Ethan was emphatic. 'Think carefully, Julian. Very carefully. No one can outrun a gang.'

'You don't give a fig about my family. Why would you? All that drivel in the yard a few months back about giving a person hope. Giving my father hope. You're just froth and bubble.'

'That's rich coming from you,' said Ethan. 'I've seen you eyeing the money jar in the kitchen. Figure you'd do a runner, eh? Leave me and your sisters to do your share of the work?'

'Concerned I'd get to the coin first, were you?' shouted Julian.

They charged each other simultaneously, trading punch for punch, blocking and dodging and landing as many hits as misses until they were rolling on the ground.

Odiene emerged from the tent and stepped around their bodies, thumping them with the carpet bag. 'Stop it, you two.'

Alex and the tent-packer came towards them. Alex reached down and took hold of Julian, while the tent-packer grasped Ethan. Julian was forced onto his stomach. Ethan lay a hair's breadth away.

'Stand up the both of you. According to Gentleman Charles's rules of hospitality, the three of you are to stay in the tent tonight. Turn around,' Alex ordered.

The tent-packer held a length of rope, which he bound around Julian's wrists.

'Don't think I'm ungrateful, miss. Now turn around.' Alex bound Odiene as well.

Ethan, however, was not quite ready to quit. His nostrils flared and his fists clenched. Julian feared he might well try to take on all three of them with the rage contorting his body. His eyes sank back into their sockets and he leant forward.

Much to Julian's disbelief, Ethan assumed a boxer's stance and raised his fists. Alex shook his long hair and passed his rifle to the tent-packer. He was readying to fight when Ethan moved sidewards and with a sweeping motion booted Alex in the back of the leg. The impact knocked Alex's legs out from under him and he crumpled to the ground. Ethan directed a sharp kick to his ribs and then raised a boot above Alex's stomach.

The tent-packer aimed the rifle at Ethan. 'Stop it, boy, afore I pepper you with holes for yer feckin' troubles.'

Gentleman Charles's trusted man raised himself from the ground. 'Well, well, well. I've seen that before. Yes I have. It stinks of the Riley Street Gang. So, what's a boy from the slums doing in the north of the state? Trying to catch bigger fish?'

'It wouldn't take much to roll you lot,' snarled Ethan.

Alex's features hardened. 'Oh, you and I are going to continue this tomorrow. It'll make great sport for our guests, having a Frog Hollow tough guy among us.'

Alex spun Ethan around, binding him tightly, and then all three of them were forced inside the tent and pushed to the floor, where their ankles were also tied.

The tent-packer delicately lifted the hem of Odiene's dress, taking time to fondle her shins and calves. Julian shouted at him to stop as Odiene drew her legs towards her chest. The tent-packer tugged them back before coiling the rope around her ankles. He patted her on the leg.

'That's enough, Harold. There's no need to paw our guests.' Alex held open the tent flap as the tent-packer exited. 'Not when they'll be with us for a long time.'

The three of them were left sitting in a half circle. Julian caught Ethan's shifty stare. The boy had little choice. He was about to divulge some well-hidden truths.

'Alex reminds me of Samuel "Jewey" Freeman. Frog Hollow's gang leader,' said Ethan. 'He was a mean one. Robbed people at gunpoint. Spent his free time bashing the boys in the area senseless, most of whom were members of minor gangs. I hated him. Always will.' Ethan concentrated on the flapping tent wall, as if his mind were far away. With the tension from the fight leaving his body, he caved in a little. 'My father was a member. He taught me how to look after myself.'

Julian stared at him in disbelief, until the darkening interior made them shadows. Ethan Harris had been exposed. The Natural was actually a hoodlum from the wrong side of the street.

⋘ Chapter 44 ⋙

Frog Hollow. The Riley Street Gang. The names stuck in Julian's gullet. It was almost impossible to believe his mother had scraped a boy up from the streets – a thief – and invited him into Aunt Nancy's home. She had eaten oysters and ice cream with him and then brought that same thief to Dalhunty Station. Into their home. Into their lives.

A thief to replace little Davey. What had his mother been thinking? He sat for a long time as the anger ran through his veins and he waited for Ethan to speak again, to at least show a little remorse at his deception. But Ethan remained silent.

'We believed you worked at some fancy department store,' Julian said at last. 'That you were a poor boy made good. The truth is you're a thug who wheedled your way into my mother's affections believing she was wealthy.'

'I don't care what you think, Julian. Why should I, when you've always treated me like shit?' he replied. 'No offence, Odiene.'

'Will you share your story?' replied Odiene gently. 'I should like to know. Everyone is entitled to a fair hearing.'

Julian doubted that Ethan would be willing to share much more

285

of his background. It was bound up as tightly as the ropes that held them firm, hidden by a veneer of politeness and the gift of brazenness. However he remained silent as a courtesy to Odiene, and to his mother. One day he would relay the information back to her, the true nature of her prodigy.

'Frog Hollow is in Surry Hills, Sydney,' answered Ethan. 'It's not a good place.' He stumbled over each word as though searching for a better description and failing. 'And the Riley Street Gang is . . .'

'It's what?' coaxed Odiene.

Ethan looked at her as if it were only the two of them present. 'The gang is made up of robbers and murderers. The worst people you can imagine. In the worst place you can imagine. If you weren't with them, you were against them.'

'But you were at the department store, selling shoes,' said Julian. 'Are you saying that was a lie? That you misled my mother by pretending you worked there?'

'No. I don't expect either of you to understand what it's like to be poor. Really poor. My father spent years trying to get us out of Frog Hollow. It was a stinking, dark warren of hovels. Winding alleys filled with mice and mangy pets, thieves, murderers, and prostitutes. A place where people were bashed, women assaulted, and folk died as easily from starvation as the plague.' Ethan gazed out the tent opening to the hut, where rowdy laughter carried across to them. 'My father would leave before dawn in search of work when Jewey didn't need him. "Everything will work out, my lad," he'd say. "It always does."'

'He was optimistic?' said Julian sarcastically, unable to forget he'd shared a room with a thief who was the son of a thief. Fortunately there was little worth stealing at Dalhunty Station.

Ethan looked at Julian. 'He was hopeful. It's important to have hope.'

The tent grew dimmer as the storm neared. The heat settled in.

'Go on,' said Julian.

'My father found a job delivering coal to the gasworks at Millers Point. We were so excited. We talked about leaving Frog Hollow, of Mother taking in laundry, me becoming a paperboy.' He grew animated at the thought of it, his body moving about, leaning in and out. 'Not long after, my father went to the Sunbeam Hotel to tell Jewey he was leaving the gang. He spent ages working out what he was going to say. He practised his speech in the shaving mirror every night.' Ethan drew his knees towards his body as if a child, still within his mother's womb. 'He even took Jewey a present by way of a farewell. A proper bottle of rum bought with his first wages, not the gut-rot booze they drank at the hotel. My mother wrapped it in a piece of brown paper she had been saving for years. It crackled as she folded it around the bottle. Me and my brothers and sisters gathered around the table. My littlest sister, Sally, reaching up on tiptoes, clinging to the edge of the table trying to see. My mum fetched her only hair ribbon and tied it around the bottle's neck. Then she sat Dad down, and scrubbed at the coal dust matting his skin. She kissed him on the cheek, and he ruffled my hair, and we all followed him out the door, watching as he strode down Riley Street, the bottle swinging as he walked. We watched until we couldn't see him anymore. "There goes your father," my mother said.'

Ethan's voice wavered and he cleared his throat.

'Dad never came home. A week later we were told by one of the gang he'd been run over by a hansom cab in Paddington. There was no reason for my father to be in Paddington. It came out eventually. One of the regulars at the Sunbeam Hotel said Jewey didn't take kindly to the bottle of rum. It showed him up in front of his men, my father arriving with that bottle of spirits and them drinking gut-rot. My father having the hide to tell Jewey he was leaving. Explaining he had the opportunity for a better life, as if what Jewey gave him was nothing. The plain truth of it is no one can leave a gang without permission. And permission is rarely given. I didn't know that then. None of us did.'

Julian knew it must have been difficult for Ethan to share his past, but he wasn't entirely convinced by the story. How much was true and how much concocted?

'You still haven't explained how you got the job selling shoes, though. How you went from the slums to neckties and greased hair?'

'Not long after my father died I was apprenticed. Then my oldest sister left to work as a maid. I don't know the in and out of it all. Maybe a favour was owed. Perhaps Jewey took a fancy to my mother or she simply up and left to start again. What I do know is I came home one night and my family were gone. Three days later I left Frog Hollow for good. You know the rest, Julian.'

'Do I?'

'Your mother trusted me,' said Ethan.

'She had no idea what you were hiding.'

'I tried to tell her, but she didn't want to know. She liked me for who I was. And I admired her. And to be fair, your mother wasn't honest about your situation either. She talked of your close-knit family. How I would be accepted by you and your sisters. That I would be welcomed. Loved.' He bit his bottom lip. 'For a lone kid, a shop kid, the thought of being taken in by a wealthy grazing family as an equal was almost too much to comprehend. And Mr Crammer, my employer, talked of the Dalhuntys as if you were royalty. He knew your grandfather, Alfred. Fitted him for new boots. He said he was an absolute gentleman. Anyway, as for me, no one ever wants to hear the truth. Not if it's messy. People want the nice version. Something that makes them feel good and doesn't remind them of their own problems or make them feel uncomfortable.' Ethan shuffled about as if trying to move away but soon gave up and submitted to the ropes binding him.

'He's right. No one wants to know I worked as an undertaker's assistant,' agreed Odiene.

Ethan responded to this piece of information with guarded appreciation, giving her a brief nod.

Julian had a mind to tell Odiene her circumstances were far removed from those of Ethan's, however The Natural had neatly accomplished swaying Odiene's opinion, just like his mother's.

'You still want to steal Gentleman Charles's money?' asked

288

Ethan slowly. 'I wasn't against the idea. I just wanted you to be aware of the consequences.'

Odiene was slack-jawed. 'What? How could you even consider such a thing, Julian?'

Julian would have given anything to be far away. Riding out in the back paddock, skirting saltbush and chasing sheep. 'Wesley owes Captain Ashby, and Captain Ashby owes my family. Anyway, we were only discussing the possibility.'

Julian knew whatever gratitude he may have won from Odiene by assisting her with Gentleman Charles's operation was now dwindling. The worst of it was that her good opinion was important to him, no matter the senselessness of his attraction and regardless of her inappropriate involvement with Captain Ashby.

Odiene was unattainable, and yet having a woman such as her as his haunted and tempted him. What did it mean to place a woman above righting a wrong? Above saving his family? When what might be in the strongbox was impossible to ignore.

⊰ Chapter 45 ⊱

Suddenly dust was swirling into the tent, engulfing them in a choking haze. The canvas juddered and one side of the structure caved in on them, the heavy folds resting across their backs. Through the sacking walls the glimmer of light shining weakly from the shanty was long extinguished, the noise of the drinkers drowned out by the gusting wind. Small mounds of sand were piling up against their bodies, the air so dense it was becoming difficult to breathe.

Twice they had attempted to undo their bindings. In the gritty murkiness Julian tried once more. Twisting awkwardly he moved in a half circle, the crumpled tent wall beating down as he plucked at Odiene's ties, trying his best to undo the knot. Failing, he swivelled again, waiting impatiently as Ethan tried to prise the rope loose from his wrists before his own efforts to release Ethan proved futile.

They slumped together, bowing their heads as outside the wind howled and bashed the tent walls. Occasionally the neigh of unsettled horses carried through the roar of air and the continual spray, until the tempest eased and the wind dropped as swiftly as it had risen.

Next to him Odiene gave a weak cough.

They were sitting closely, their bodies aligned shoulder to hip.

'The Captain talked to me once about the sandstorms in the Sahara,' she began slowly. 'How the hot, dry desert air over North Africa eventually blows towards the Mediterranean, where it becomes humid. Is that what happens here? Does a storm like this begin in the centre of Australia and eventually end in the east as rain? I hope so, for otherwise what is the point of it other than to cause distress?'

'Maybe it does. My father always said East was the promised land.' Julian did not want to discuss the damn dust or continents he'd never visit or his father's fabled Eastern lands. It was all he could do to concentrate with Odiene so close.

Yet concentrate he must, for how were they to escape and reach safety? And what of the strongbox? Was stealing it worth the risk? Especially with Ethan and his knotty upbringing in tow. If he *did* succumb to this chance of recouping the money owed to his family, was he then no better than Ethan? It made him consider if he could ever do what Ethan had done. Remake his life. Alone. Convincingly.

The truth of Ethan's past ruffled Julian deeply. A criminal within their midst. Yet, when the storm was at its most ferocious it wasn't a cunning street kid running with a gang that bothered him, but the thought of Ethan's survival alone in that world. How had the boy found the wherewithal to start anew at such a tender age, when a gang of kids involved in petty crime were probably his closest friends? How had he overcome the terrible loss of his father or the desertion of his entire family, or been able to envisage a future free of crime? Ethan's miserable beginnings were such that his elevation to the shoe department was miraculous. It was testament to his character that he saw other possibilities and seized them.

What then of Julian's own family? Of his mother's deception in making the boy believe she could offer him something better? And what of him and his sisters, so caught up in self-righteous indignation at their mother's absence and their sadness at Davey's death, that a hopeful boy immediately became an unwanted pest? And lastly, most terribly, his father's comment that day in the kitchen. *Picking up waifs and strays.* It would have been like a dagger in Ethan's chest.

An indistinct outline showed itself on the wall of the tent. The shape stalked the perimeter as if searching for the tent's opening and then stooped down and began to dig. They listened as the piled dirt was shifted aside and to the rustle of the canvas wall as someone attempted to lift it.

'They're checking to see if we're still alive. If they stick their head in, I'll boot it back to the shanty,' whispered Ethan, wiggling closer to the prone figure on the opposite side of the wall.

Julian judged the distance from where he sat to the tent wall. Less than two yards. In a couple of strides whoever was outside would be upon them. He bottom-scuttled across until he was opposite Ethan, closer to the flimsy canvas barrier, with the intruder between them and only a foot away through the canvas. They waited, listening to shifting footsteps, then a knife was plunged into the canvas, the blade slicing downwards through the material. This wasn't good. A drunkard with a knife on a dark night. He heard Odiene gasp, and knew what she feared.

A figure pushed through the gap made by the knife. Ethan kicked out and the person moved sideways, far too quickly for a drunkard. The indistinct outline before Julian was immediately recognisable yet he doubted what he was seeing. The person cursed and with the single, drawn out use of the word *shit* he knew immediately who it was.

There was a moment's hesitation, then Meg crawled forward, wrapping her arms about his neck.

'Yes, it's me!' She rubbed her nose against his cheek like a puppy. 'I came to find you. I ain't losing any more brothers.'

⋘ Chapter 46 ⋙

'Youse could have escaped the night those men took the Captain,' Meg said, cutting Julian's ropes. 'I would have jumped off when they fired the barge instead of waiting to see what happened next. That's boys for youse. Can't make youse mind up quick-smart when it counts. I was on the other side of the river,' she explained as she cut Ethan and Odiene free. 'About to make camp and then I heard the men. Why, the noise they made carried clear across the water so I kept pace with them and then I saw the steamer. I heard them yelling for the Captain. And when they set the barge alight I recognised youse and Ethan on deck. That's how I knew youse were still aboard.' Meg sat back on her haunches, placing the knife in the sheath at her waist. 'I've been following youse ever since you rode into the river, Ethan. What was youse thinking? Mother's still fretting.'

'I—' began Ethan.

'No point being uppity out here. People just gotta make the best of things. Anyhows, I went back home with Mother after youse had yourself that conniption, Ethan, and we told Laura and Father what happened. And Father spoke up after all them days of saying nothing. He told us what happened in Bourke. Said a lady who was friends with the piano's real owners recognised it was a Steinway when it was being unloaded. That it was supposed to have gone overboard. The coppers were called to investigate and Father was in a quandary. He wasn't sure what was going on. So he decided to fib. He explained to the coppers he'd purchased the piano from a travelling salesman who'd come down from Queensland. He was so knotted up he simply couldn't tell the truth, that his dearest, bestest friend had lied to him and never repaid the real owners of the piano. He ain't got no idea if the coppers and the owners will put two and two together and know the Captain was involved.'

Meg gave a hiccup that scarcely interrupted her account.

'Then on account of Father not actually owning the piano, he got no money when he tried to sell it. So he went to the bank, 'cause we owe them plenty, and they said time's run out. So then he saw Mr Fraser on the way back from Bourke and sold him the rest of the run. That's what gave Father the fit, all that terribleness, although Mother said it was a stupor. He's got no faith in humanity anymore.'

'What? Father sold the property?' said Julian.

'Every single acre?' asked Ethan.

'Yep. Gone like a lizard down a hole. Mother said wese been living on the never-never a long time. I ain't heard our place called that before but I do knows wese poor. So I got some food and saddled Legless – ain't no horse wants to be called Dalhunty Dame – and started riding after youse.'

The Dalhuntys were ruined. Julian guessed there were no guarantees with anything in life, but knowing the property was no longer theirs took the air from his lungs.

'I can't believe it. And you came by yourself?'

'Well, I'd hardly be asking Laura. She'd have been kneading her backside and complaining a day into the ride and Father's so down-struck I couldn't rely on him to dress 'imself of a morning let alone boil the quart pot. So I left and took the road to Bourke but stopped to sleep, that's how come I missed the *Lady Matilda* at the port. But I did find Goliath along the way. Then I followed the river after that. Takes some riding to catch a riverboat,' she explained matter-of-factly. 'I figured you'd know what to do, Julian. About the station and all.'

Frankly, Julian was unable to think past escaping their current predicament. He was glad they were all pitched in darkness; he wasn't prepared to meet the wide-eyed expectancy of his little sister, in case she saw straight through him. He introduced Meg to Odiene and though Meg went through the courtesies expected, there was no disregarding the shortness in Meg's manner. She made a remark about having seen her swanning about on the river-boat, and not planning on having to rescue her as well.

'I dunno what you did wrong, but all them men, they've drunk themselves to sleep. It seems to me if wese take the horses we need and leave now we'll be a good start ahead of them. It'll be hard going. Youse won't complain none if I let youse come with us, will you Odiene? 'Cause I was only planning on rescuing Julian and Ethan, but youse being a girl, well, those men might get nasty if I leave youse here alone. Reckon I'd feel responsible if anything happened to youse.'

'I won't complain,' Odiene promised.

'Then let's go before wese get caught. I've got two horses. Youse get yourselves a couple, Julian, and I'll meet you at the well.'

They crawled through the gap in the tent and then split up. Julian and Ethan sprinted to the hut and crouched near the horses. Slouched and snoring men were strewn about the front of the hut. The horses were still fractious from the storm. They raised hooves one after another, as if dancing to an unknown tune.

Julian ran his hand along the bare back of an animal, quieten-ing him, and then by feel selected a saddle from the row of riding tack left by the visiting men. He saddled the horse, slipped the bit between sharp teeth and positioned the bridle. He half expected to be caught as the surrounding horses moved back and forth, straining on their leads. One of the men stirred and belched but promptly began to snore again. Holding tight to the reins, he and Ethan led their chosen mounts away.

The pre-dawn light showed itself across a poisoned sky as they met Meg and Odiene near the well. Odiene, already mounted on Legless, was trying to tie the carpet bag to the saddle. Meg was hopping from one foot to the other in anticipation. Julian stumbled over Riley Jimm. He was still collapsed, arms and legs splayed, a little finger linked through the metal cup. Julian rolled him onto his back, hoping the storm had not filled his lungs, then they watered the horses at the trough and filled Meg's waterbags. Time was chasing them.

It struck Julian that there was no clear future before them. The promise of going home, which had remained his intention since Captain Ashby's capture, was now only a stop-gap until a practical alternative for his family was decided upon. 'Meg, are you sure the property has been sold? You didn't misunderstand?'

'Course I'm sure,' she told him.

'And Father. He can obviously speak now. He's better?'

'A bit. He can't walk much and he drools a lot.'

'We don't have time for this,' Ethan reminded them. 'It's not long till daybreak.'

'Meg. The money for the piano. It's in the hut in a strongbox. I'll explain later. But it's *our* money, and I'm not leaving without it.'

Meg scrunched her nose up and then rubbed at it fiercely. 'Seems like you're itching to be bit by a snake, stealing off them people.'

'Trust me,' said Julian.

Meg cocked her head to one side and fingered Goliath's mane. 'If youse reckon it's the right way to go.'

'It's a ludicrous idea. We're risking enough already by you two standing here talking,' said Odiene.

'Ethan, if we do this, I'll be needing your help. You've known men like these,' said Julian.

'I was a kid when I left Frog Hollow.'

'What the shooting star is Frog Hollow?' asked Meg.

'But you remember. Don't you? What they'll expect? How to go about a robbery?' Julian was counting on Ethan. Surely if he was a natural at everything else – well, apart from swimming – and with his experience of stealing, the strongbox should be a doddle.

'A robbery? Youse knows about stuff like that? *S-h-i-t*,' said Meg. Ethan rubbed his palms together in anticipation. 'Yeah, I do.'

⋘ Chapter 47 ⋙

Armed with lengths of timber from the wood gathered earlier, they crept to the rear of the hut and bobbed down beneath the shuttered excuse for a window. It was a tiny opening on the western wall and there was no other way in, except the front door, which was not an option. Julian leant against the timber, the fire within sending a steady heat along his spine. If his father were present he would laugh at their audacity before reminding them of who they were and where they came from, begging them not to choose desperation over reason. But Ben's sense of reason had led his family to poverty and landlessness, and there seemed to be no clean boundary marking out right from wrong. There was only what was owed.

Julian waited for Ethan to formulate a plan. Where before they had barely been able to tolerate each other, now they were collaborating on a shared objective. Ethan had made it clear to Julian that he was no longer accountable to the Dalhuntys and yet here he was caught in a dangerous situation while trying to help them. The willing boy who'd tried to fit in and make friends last year was no longer an interloper, and the subtle change in their relationship was easier to accept than Julian had anticipated, irrespective of Ethan's revelations about his upbringing.

He nudged Ethan, no longer willing to hide his impatience. Surely it was a simple case of breaking in and taking what was theirs. The only issue was the size of the window. He said as much.

'I'll do it,' said Meg.

'You can't send your sister in there. She's only a child,' replied Odiene, from further along the wall.

Meg flared in outrage. 'Are youse gonna do it then?' It was clear that Odiene was not equipped for any sort of important mission in Meg's view.

She moved to squat in front of Julian. She could do it, Meg pleaded. She was small and light. Capable. Noiseless.

But sending his little sister into the shanty was too much of a chance to take and Julian told her so.

'She is the smallest,' Ethan finally agreed. 'I've not been able to come up with anything better.'

Meg fidgeted, scratching the length of the trousers she wore. It was all plain wrong. His sister should have been home, safe on their property, not gadding about the country dressed like a boy. Still, she was here, having tracked them down. More than chance had delivered Meg to them. And it was chance Julian was relying upon now. The night was lifting; already the faintest tint of the new day showed. A difficult decision had to be made.

'All right. Gentleman Charles is in there. He's a big man with a patch over one eye and another that never closes.'

'What? Ever?' Meg's mouth grew round. 'Youse is asking me to steal a man's money when wese don't rightly know if he's asleep or awake?'

'Good point. I'll check first.' Julian placed his fingers on the bottom of the shutter and gave it a tug. Then another. 'It's locked from the inside.'

Ethan borrowed Meg's knife and inserted the blade between the two shutters, running it along the gap between them. When he reached the latch on the inside it was forced up and the shutters partially opened with a squeak. They waited. When no one stirred Julian reached up and pulled the shutters outwards, flat against the hut wall. He slowly raised his head.

The fire was nearly out. Wesley was lying sprawled on the table, his all-seeing eye staring directly at the window. Julian bobbed out of sight, waiting for a reaction, feeling an exhilaration that only heightened his nerves. When there was no sign of the man having seen him, Julian looked through the window again. Their captor was snoring loudly. Alex lay on the floor nearby. Bottles were scattered everywhere. He leant further into the room. The strongbox was sitting next to the wall. Meg would have to step over Alex to reach it.

He bobbed back down, weighing the consequences. The money versus nothing. For that's what the Dalhuntys would end up with if they did not go ahead with the plan or if Meg failed, for who knew if any monies would be left from the sale of their property once the bank was repaid? Dalhunty Station existed on credit, borrowing more each year and repaying what they could after every clip. Now there was no more wool to sell.

The alternative was to take Ethan's advice – tell the police about Captain Ashby, if their investigations had not already led them to him. Then they could speak to a solicitor, which would probably force the sale of the *Lady Matilda* so obligations could be squared. However who knew how many people might be owed money.

Inside, Gentleman Charles's discarded jacket lay on the floor, the waistcoat stretched tight across the hump of his stomach. Ethan leant across to where Meg waited. They needed a key to unlock the strongbox. The man's pockets had to be searched.

Meg edged her way up until she was level with the windowsill. She offered Julian a crooked smile and then he was lifting her. She stuck her legs through the opening and they briefly dangled over the edge of the sill as Julian lowered her inside the hut. He felt her tense on seeing the unlidded eye before shaking off his hold. She stepped over Alex and tiptoed to the table where she waved her hands about and gave a little dance, wiggling her backside.

Julian could have throttled her.

Meg reached for one of Gentleman Charles's pockets, her fingers moving methodically across the waistcoat, snaking into each compartment, smooth and silent. She turned to the window where Julian and Ethan waited, shaking her head.

'The trousers,' mouthed Ethan.

Meg rolled her lips until they almost disappeared and then concentrated once more on the man. She gingerly patted each pocket and shook her head adamantly.

Julian beckoned Meg to leave. He was not prepared to risk her presence inside the hut any longer. She wagged a finger in response and, ignoring his urgent gestures, surveyed the hut's interior until her eyes fell on Gentleman Charles's jacket on the floor. She went to it, thoroughly checking the garment, including the seams before turning once again to the window, empty-handed.

Without waiting for further instruction Meg stepped over Alex and moved to the strongbox itself. She spent a few seconds examining it and then squatted and tried to lift it. On the second attempt she rose unsteadily, bowing under its weight and staggered towards the window, back bent. Her cheeks were puffed with the strain, each step waking ancient timber.

'No, no,' whispered Julian. 'Put it back.'

Meg's features tensed, her steps slowing as she clung to the strongbox. Upon reaching Alex she stepped over his prone body. He flung an arm out in his drunken sleep, causing Meg to lose her balance. Julian flung a leg over the sill but Ethan held him back, stopping him from going to her aid. Meg teetered back and forth until her balance was restored, then she tentatively moved to the window, her cheeks aglow with success.

Ethan reached in and took the box from Meg and Julian grabbed her under the armpits and whipped her to safety. Meg shook her arms and hugged Julian and then spun her lithe body in a series of pirouettes. They all shrank back against the wall of the hut.

'We'll never get it open without a key, will we?' asked Julian, the strongbox at his feet.

301

'They are difficult to break into,' Ethan replied.

Inside the hut the floorboards groaned. Someone was moving around.

'Who's that?' Alex thrust his head out the window. In a flash Ethan picked up a length of timber and struck the Irishman. Alex collapsed, his waist resting on the sill, legs in the hut, arms dangling on the ground outside. Blood dripped from his forehead.

Julian placed a hand over Odiene's mouth, keeping it there until she grew still. Stealing was one thing, clobbering Alex Flannery, well, that was a disaster.

'Now you've done it,' Julian complained to Ethan. 'Let's go. Leave the strongbox. We can't open it anyway. You said so yourself.'

Ethan hefted the box under an arm. 'I said it would be difficult, not necessarily impossible. Besides, *you* wanted it,' he said testily. 'I'm sure I'll be able to open it. We'll take what you think is fair and dump the rest when we get the chance.' He set off at a fast clip, running away from the hut with the strongbox, Meg keeping close to his side.

Julian wrapped an arm around Odiene's waist and hustled her back to the well, as Odiene told him over and over how wrong their actions were. They arrived to find Ethan sitting astride one of the stolen horses, the strong box resting across his thighs.

'No point being all righteous now, Julian,' replied Ethan.

'Damn it, Ethan.' Julian helped Odiene mount up and then threw a leg over his horse, casting a last glance at the hut and the growing outlines of prostrate drinkers in the hardening light. He was all out of choices. Dawn wasn't slowing in its approach. A red line of gloom was already breaking.

They trotted away from the hut, all the while Julian kept a watchful eye on the shanty and the men who were sure to follow. 'You're going the wrong way, Meg. We have to head to the river.'

'Who's doing the rescuing here?' She let Goliath have his head and the gelding answered like a racehorse from a standing start.

⧫ Chapter 48 ⧫

They rode with a torrid sun on their backs. They were heading northwards but keeping the river to the east. Ethan whistled a jaunty tune whenever they slowed and Julian suffered the hackles rising along his spine. Alex's battering and the strongbox were proof of their madness. During a brief stop to stretch their legs, Julian had picked up a stick and hadn't stopped chewing it since. The splint of wood was as mashed as his innards. On his right rode Odiene, her skirt bunched up about her legs. She was tellingly silent. To his left, Meg, refusing to budge from her route, intermittently debated the practicalities of the situation. From her viewpoint there was little point fussing about the decision made at the hut. They needed a safe place to open the strongbox, take what was theirs and then leave it for Gentleman Charles to find.

'We should get rid of it. Just dump it. Untouched,' said Odiene. Ethan rode to his side. 'How about we—'

'Shut up, just shut up.' Julian doubted Ethan fully comprehended the perilous situation he had placed them in. How could he? This was simply another crime by a boy from the slums, where stealing was survival and the risk was always proportionate.

'I don't know why you're so got up about this. It was *your* idea,' persisted Ethan.

Julian was afraid of the Irishman. The stolen boots were a personal issue between him and Alex, but attacking the man? He feared they would all suffer. 'Smacking Alex Flannery in the skull was not my idea'.

'Well, we didn't have much choice. And it's not like they wouldn't have followed us even if we had found the key and only taken what was owed. They're thieves. Anyway, I can open it.'

Julian flicked the reins and rode ahead. He was annoyed at not having considered the ramifications of taking the strongbox more fully. His aim was simply to get hold of the money that was rightfully theirs. And then what? Talk his way out of a fight? Appeal to Gentleman Charles's sense of decency? He was an idiot. And blaming Ethan was not the solution, although it helped distract him and ease his conscience.

The day grew hotter. The sun pricked at their skin, which burned in earnest. They rode through scattered piles of sheep skeletons bleached by the elements, as if the very bones of the country were poking through. Eventually Meg led them into dense timber where they pushed through the low-hanging branches that barely allowed a horse to squeeze through. When the sky dwindled to a bluish streak through the boughs overhead, she raised a hand as if she were a pathfinder of longstanding, and finally said they could rest. It was barely a clearing, yet there was space enough for the horses and a wedge of sand on which to sit.

Ethan dumped the strongbox on the ground and helped Odiene from the saddle, his grip on her waist staying longer than Julian cared for.

Meg inspected the foliage ringing them, before passing the waterbag around. She declared them safe and said that they would hear anyone coming from a mile off.

They collapsed exhausted on the ground. Odiene chose a stump and gathered her skirts about her legs. Her hair, having come loose from the pile atop her head, was messy and tangled and she shook it free, running her fingers through the long strands.

'It's times like these it don't hurt to have a broad arse.' Meg positioned herself against the base of a tree, crossed her ankles and poured water into her upturned hat which she splashed on her face. 'You don't have to sit there all Sphinx-like, Odiene. Dig yourself a little hip-pit and burrow in. You'll rest better.'

Odiene accepted the waterbag Meg offered, took a sip, and then, dampening a handkerchief, cleaned the day's journey from her eyes.

Ethan placed the strongbox in the middle of the clearing and fell to studying the lock. Up close, the pin-stripe decoration was scratched and the metal dented.

Julian tried not to look at it. It was a beacon for trouble. While they were on horseback the act of escape allowed him time to consider their predicament from all angles. The unsatisfactory conclusion was that they were already far past the point of no return. He struggled to remove his boots, pressing at the bloody blisters and cuts that ran from heel to toe on the soles of his feet. 'I need something to break these.'

'Why youse are more messed up than a scalded pig,' said Meg.

Odiene removed the needle from her blouse, which had been there since Gentleman Charles's surgery. 'Here. I have some lavender oil that will help with the healing.' She rose, moved towards Legless and selected a phial from her carpet bag.

Under her instruction Julian took the needle and pierced the blisters, watching yellow fluid ooze from them. He dabbed the lavender on the sore spots and pulled the boots back on with difficulty, the possibility of Wesley and Alex materialising from the trees, readying him for action. He roughly cleaned the needle before returning it to Odiene, who cleaned it again before sticking it in her blouse. Julian wanted to take her aside, to see how she was managing. The morning's ride was long and rough and although she never once complained she was slow to sit on the stump, wincing after hours in the saddle. He almost went to her, however her relationship with Captain Ashby, one that held the trappings of marriage, bound his chest like an iron hoop.

Meg's questioning began almost immediately. Why had they stayed on the *Lady Matilda*? Where was Captain Ashby? Did Julian know the piano was stolen? Who was the man with one eye and what were they doing at his camp?

Julian hobbled about, trying to conceal the tenderness in his feet, the weight of his body filling the boots with gummy liquid. He did his best to answer his sister's questions, finally revealing Odiene's part, having been caught up in the captain's shenanigans.

'And I stole a dead man's boots. Not that they've been of much assistance.'

Meg sat mesmerised while Julian shared the tale. She tilted to one side and then the other, listening in awe, her fists clenching and releasing as if reliving their trials. 'Captain Ashby made you sew that man up?' She assessed Odiene with newfound interest bordering on approval, then her attention diverted again. 'Maybe they're bushrangers, excepting the Captain's on water. Or he was. But he's not like Ned Kelly. Reckon Ned Kelly never betrayed a friend. I mean look at the captain selling us a thieved piano. Youse never can tell what people will do. I saw two men fighting over a hat at the Redbank coach stop. Wasn't much of a hat neither but they clammered each other about the head until they both fell down. Reckon they'd split each other over boots. And that there box of money, well, wese in a stitch. I never guessed youse to steal from a bushranger, Julian. But here wese are and I got nothing excepting my slingshot.'

'We'll be needing more than that,' said Ethan. 'What else have you got in that bag, Odiene?'

'Odds and ends, personal belongings. Why?'

'Could I look at that kit, please?'

Odiene braced herself on the stump and tiredly pushed herself to standing. She trudged back over to Legless and fetched the taxidermy kit out of her carryall.

He thanked her quietly and then inspected the contents. Sorting through the instruments, he settled on a small scalpel and a pair of tweezers, which he broke in half with a solid tug.

'I beg your pardon! My father gave me that set!' Odiene marched towards him, snatched up the kit and placed the taxidermy set back in her bag. 'Break your own belongings, not mine.'

'Sorry.' Ethan tilted the strongbox, steadying it between his shoes, legs splayed as wide as his shoulders, and inserted the implements into the lock, twisting them one way and then moving them up and down.

Meg went to Ethan's side and observed his attempt with fascination. 'I ain't never seen a lot of money. At least not the kind youse need a box for. Where did youse learn to pick a lock?'

'He grew up in the slums, Meg. His father was a thief,' said Julian.

'Holy Henrietta. And I thought youse were well brought up even if youse was an orphan,' replied Meg.

Ethan cast her a sidelong frown and then jiggled the broken tweezers in the lock more forcefully.

'Don't get excited. We're only keeping what belongs to us,' warned Julian.

Ethan gave the lock a final, violent twist and a click sounded. He lifted the lid, clearly pleased with his efforts.

Meg leant over to get a better view. 'God damn.' She dived into the container and held up a glass eye, positioning it next to her own.

Then his sister was pulling out items, holding them high for everyone to see and lining them up on the ground. She stuck a finger in a pot and dotted pinkish powder on her cheeks, sniffed a tub of cream and juggled various shaped eyeglasses and medicinal bottles, naming each aloud as if she were a street vendor publicising wares. Julian could not believe it. He'd been sure a fortune was contained within.

'Throat cure-all.' Meg read the label on a bottle. 'Snake oil, more like.' She placed it with the other objects. 'Why does he have rouge, Julian? Mother has rouge. It belonged to Aunt Nancy.'

Ethan grimaced. 'I'll tell you why, it's because he's a—'

'They were probably his mother's,' suggested Odiene hastily.

Covering the bottom of the box were booklets and clippings from newspapers, as well as a number of gramophone records. Ethan retrieved the collection and deposited all but one booklet of sheet music on the ground, which he opened and deliberated upon.

Julian gently took the sheet music from Ethan's grasp and turned it right side up. An embarrassed expression crossed Ethan's features. Here then was something else The Natural couldn't do well: read.

Odiene flipped through the records. 'Enrico Caruso, Nellie Melba. They're opera singers.'

Meg unwrapped a newspaper-covered package, counting the layers and throwing the packaging aside. A final layer of wrapping revealed a pair of white-and-gold glasses, the eyepieces joined by three bridges. 'They're baby telescopes. For looking at the stars. I can see for miles.' Meg scanned the narrow clearing. 'One of the tubes twists and, why I can see the freckle on your cheek, Ethan, it's got a hair growing out of it.'

'Give me those,' said Ethan.

She scuttled out of his reach.

'Show me.' Odiene examined the glasses with care, turning them around and looking through them. 'They're beautiful. Opera glasses. Made of brass and ivory.'

'What do youse want to see the opera for? I thought it was for listening to,' said Meg.

'The glasses are more for people watching,' Odiene explained. 'I went to the theatre once with my father and during the performance a young woman suffered a fit of the vapours. It was quite an attack. She turned blue and fell from her chair. I never would have witnessed the kerfuffle if it wasn't for my father's glasses.' She passed them back to Meg and began to sort through the newspaper clippings.

The glasses were glued to Meg's eyes. 'Sure wish we owned ourselves a pair.'

Ethan tapped the bottom of the box, flipped it and checked the base. He shook it fiercely and then pushed it aside. 'No money. Now what?'

Julian pinched the bridge of his nose. 'We repack all the contents and then I'll ride back to the edge of the ridge and leave it for Wesley to find.'

'Can wese keep the opera thingees and an eye? This one's blue. I ain't never seen a glass eye before.' Meg bowled it gently across the ground.

'No!' said Julian sharply. He could have scratched the glass cornea of the fake eye with one of Odiene's implements, such was his annoyance at himself. He couldn't even steal properly.

'No need to get all crotchety.' Meg went to the discarded box and started repacking all the items.

'*The Tivoli, 1902. Charles Wesley to perform excerpts from the latest musicals,*' read Odiene. 'These are clippings of his performances. *A melodious voice well suited to the chosen material.* It appears Gentleman Charles was something of a showman, hence the stage makeup. That is, before he took up his current profession. You have yourself a magnificent haul, Julian,' she said sarcastically. 'You've stolen the man's most precious possessions.'

'And if you'd not been so quick to run off and do your lover's bidding we wouldn't be in this mess,' he threw back at her. 'I'm doing my best!'

'Reckon anyone within a cooee would hear you two.' Meg positioned herself in the middle of Julian and Odiene. She waited for Odiene to pass her the newspaper and then, with a sullen glance of reproach at her, replaced the paper in the box before slamming the lid.

'We should probably get some sleep before we make a start again,' suggested Ethan.

Julian was still staring at Odiene, berating himself for losing his temper and wondering how a woman could be so infuriating.

'Good idea,' he said.

≪ Chapter 49 ≫

While the others rested, Julian rode to the edge of the thickly treed ridge, searching for a place to leave the strongbox. There he encountered a group of Aboriginal people, who were walking through the scrubby woodlands. They had formed a single line of men, women and children, fierce and handsome, and carried few possessions – the odd rolled hide, spears and baskets – and wore a mix of traditional dress and white man's clothes. He halted to let them pass undisturbed but they barely reacted to his presence, hardly worrying to look left or right, intent only on destination, although they surely identified him, a foolish white man on his horse.

When they were gone, Julian trotted further out to where the trees eased into open space. A number of sheep skeletons lay scattered about and it was here he dismounted, placing the strongbox on the ground. There was no sign of Gentleman Charles or his men – not even a wisp of dust billowing into the sky to mark their approach. The path they had travelled remained empty as if the land had swallowed every occupant whole. But he knew they were coming. He could feel it in his marrow.

Julian walked about, piling the sheep bones in a grid formation. He lay some intact carcasses lengthways, propping his structure up with skulls and thighbones until the mound reached three feet in height. He positioned the strongbox on the top, sat a skull on the lid and then stepped back to admire the construction. He thought the macabre marker rather suited their predicament. He looked out again at the vacant land and their earlier hoof prints, convinced Wesley would easily find the box and then guided the horse back through the compact timber.

At the camp the others were sleeping. Julian dismounted, tied the horse to a tree limb and stepped over Ethan, who was snoring loudly. Odiene lay on her side, her skirts tucked about her tightly. There was no doubting she was a troublesome woman. Julian suspected it came from too much independence. A woman couldn't enjoy the liberties life aboard the *Lady Matilda* offered without unknowingly forfeiting a part of herself.

Meg was curled on the ground in a hollow she had dug. He touched her gently and she sat upright as if stung by a bee. 'Wot is it? 'Ave they come?'

'Not a sign of them. Meg, what you said last night . . . I need to ask you again. Are you *sure* the property has been sold to Mr Fraser?'

Meg looked about vaguely as if trying to recall where she was. 'Wot? Don't youse believe me?' her tone was waspish.

Julian squatted next to her. 'I guess I didn't want to. How much money did we get for it?'

'I dunno. Don't reckon there's any left over. The bank got it, although I can't see what they need it for. They ain't growing nothing. And Father said wese probably built the bank in Bourke back in them good old days. Mother figured on Mr Fraser offering youse a job but he didn't. Probably on account of Laura sticking her nose up at the son.'

'So it is the end.' Julian got up and walked away from the others. He'd thought that when they stopped moving and there was time to consider Meg's news, he would feel a great burden lift from him. They had been struggling for years, beating themselves up to keep something going that was long past saving. And yet in his mind he could see the cracked paddocks waiting for rain, the child-hood lookout by the river, the way the honey glow of morning light caught the dark green of Frank's swaying palm fronds.

Here he was with the world before him and the freedom he'd wanted for so long so tantalisingly close and he found it was not at all as he'd anticipated. Having land meant something. It gave him something to hold on to. Something to return to.

And now Fraser owned it all.

Meg came to him, sucking hard on her empty wooden pipe, drawing deeply as if the bowl was stuffed with the finest tobacco. 'Ain't nothing wese can do, is there? 'Cause I've been thinking. Maybe wese could get a job on a station. Pretend I'm a boy. No one would know any difference. I could be youse little brother. Wese could go anywhere. Except town. I ain't fit for town living. Reckon I'd be like one of them tadpoles scooped out of the water and left to wiggle until the sun dried me out.' She looked up at him. 'I knows youse been thinking about leaving. I found the timetable for the train in your room. That's why I followed youse when you dove in after Ethan. I wasn't sure if youse'd come back. I figured youse wouldn't leave me behind, but I wasn't gonna let youse go without me.'

Julian placed a hand on the crown of Meg's hat, jiggling it about. There was a downside to being so loved by his sister. 'What about Father and Mother? Where will they go?'

'They're going to move to Bourke. Laura said they might have to clean houses and take in washing but Mama said she weren't anybody's damn washerwoman.'

'My mother was willing to take in washing.' Ethan was lying on his side, his head propped on his arm, and it seemed Odiene was awake too. Julian had not realised they had an audience.

'She didn't mean nothing by it, Ethan,' replied Meg.

Odiene had taken the scissors from the taxidermy kit and had started to hack a good five inches from the dirty hem of her skirt. 'People do what they can to survive.'

'So you've said before. Do you still feel the same way about the great Captain Ashby?' Ethan rolled into a sitting position and stretched. 'I mean, he's a real peach. It beggars belief, a woman like yourself getting entangled with an old man.'

'Youse like the Captain? But youse been staring at Julian ever since wese got here,' said Meg.

'Don't be ridiculous.' Odiene got up and swished her skirt, checking the length. There was a shallow dugout where she'd been lying, a cavity to cushion her hip, just as Meg advised.

Meg shoved the pipe in a trouser pocket. 'I ain't being ridiculous. The only person being ridiculous is a woman making puppy eyes when my brother's got serious matters, real serious matters, to think on. He don't got any time for carrying ons. Once we get out of this fix we'll be heading north, I reckon.'

Meg's insinuation about Odiene heightened every nerve in Julian's body. His little sister was smart, but was she smart enough to understand another woman's mind?

'I overheard what Meg said, about the train ticket. You really were going to leave?' said Ethan.

'Wasn't much need for me once you arrived,' replied Julian stiffly, lapsing back into the irritated state he'd been in at home.

'But you didn't take the money.'

'Neither did you.'

Meg grew skittish with excitement. 'Wese gonna go inland.'

'Really?' Odiene appeared dubious of these plans. She paused as if wanting to say more on the subject, then changed the topic. 'I'm sorry the property was sold. Your family have been there for generations. It's a great loss.' She took the pin from her blouse and stuck it through a piece of felt before returning it to the taxidermy kit.

'Could be worse. At least we've got a name. Dalhunty's a fine name. Reckon a name can set a person up for life, eh, Julian?' said Meg.

'She's right. You put on a bit of dog, dangle that name in front of an employer and you'll be set,' said Ethan, in all seriousness.

313

'Well it certainly had an effect on you,' Julian shot back.

Ethan scowled. 'You try working for wages.'

Working for wages. Was that to be their future? Was he to drag Meg about? Become a sundowner, tramping and scabbing food if a prospective manager or station owner proved unappealing? Did a man with nothing even have the right to be particular about an employer? Especially when there was Meg to consider. And what would happen in a few years when she became more of a woman, a fully grown woman, unable to disguise herself as a boy?

Julian's stomach was all twisted up about so many things. He could haul Meg back to their parents and ride out alone but whether it be a week or a month she would be trailing him, all nobbed up in her boy's trousers and kangaroo jacket, a piece of leather about her waist and that infernal knife tucked away for good measure. Meg didn't belong anywhere except on their land. They both knew it. But there was a mighty gap between knowing the rightness of something and achieving it, and Meg needed to understand their lives could not be intertwined forever.

'Queensland. I've a right hankering to see the Queen's own land,' said Meg.

'Meg,' Julian rumbled, hardening his voice to get her attention. 'We're not going anywhere for a while. You have to be a bit sensible about the future.'

Meg stopped dancing about. 'You're not gonna leave me, are youse? If youse leave me with Mother I'll run. I'll run so fast and so far, ain't nobody ever be able to find me.' She retreated to the edge of the clearing, her small chest lurching, her whole person drawing inwards, closing firmly shut like a river mussel.

Julian hated seeing her so upset. Davey's passing had done this to Meg. Their mother's treatment of her had too. It had made her brave and independent, but also lost. He needed a plan, no matter what it consisted of, as long as it gave his sister something to cling to.

'Maybe we can get the station back,' he said, regretting the lie as soon as it was spoken.

Meg's fine red eyebrows rose, each pointing sharply in the

middle like pyramids. 'And where are youse gonna get the money from?' Her hands went to her hips. 'That's just plain ijit talk.'

'You can't be serious. We'd have no chance. It's been sold,' stated Ethan.

'We? Well, have a look at this, Meg. We're only here because Ethan took a dislike to us and decided to jump in a river. And now he's saying *we*,' said Julian.

'Well, he is our brother,' said Meg.

A silly expression crossed Ethan's face, as if caught partway between embarrassment and delight. His reaction caught Julian unawares, as did Meg's solidarity with Ethan.

'How are wese gonna get the station back?' repeated Meg.

'I don't know,' admitted Julian. 'Let's all think on it.' He helped Odiene astride Legless, holding her ankle firm in the stirrup. He saw no sign of the puppy eyes Meg spoke of, only a strong intelligence.

'If you want something, you should aim for it,' she said.

'At any cost?' he asked.

'There is always a cost,' she replied.

⋘ Chapter 50 ⋙

At the end of the day Meg wheeled Goliath to the east. It was nearly dusk by the time they reached the river. They moved through a grassy understorey toward the steep-sided bank, the horses shuffling and sliding as they reined them in, and walked carefully down the slope. On the opposite side a dry narrow channel, which carved through the bank in wetter times, curved into the scrub. Next to it a large cockatoo was dismantling the branches of a tree, the leafy twigs landing in the trench. At the bottom of the bank Meg sprang from the big stallion and ran into the water. She came up from the depths and lay on her back, sculling about the murky surface like a water insect. The horses, free of their riders, trotted to the river, their reins dragging on the ground, and bowed their heads thirstily.

Julian checked the bank for snakes waiting for unsuspecting rodents who came in the evening to drink, as a platypus slid from a protective tangle of roots into the water. Then he tugged his boots off and limped into the river fully clothed, feeling the slow creep of coolness washing clean the filth of the previous days. He sank under the water, the liquid whirling about his ears and eyes and hair, the grime lifting like melted daub. When he rose, Ethan's shoes were on the sand and he was standing in the Darling washing himself so vigorously one might have thought the boy's own mother watched on.

Julian dunked under the water again and, on rising, watched Odiene in the dying light, wondering what the internal struggle was keeping her from joining them. He lifted a foot and felt the blistering sores as Odiene wandered up and down the sandy bank, and paddled at the edge of the river. When she finally stopped, she unbuttoned her long-sleeved blouse. The material inched from her shoulders, the muscles of her upper back moving slightly as she lay the blouse on the sand. She stepped out of the full skirt to stand in her petticoat, chemise and corset. Little pads of material sat on her hips and these she untied and let fall to the ground. She lingered before pulling the few pins from her hair, which fell long and dark over her shoulders. Her movements were guarded as she edged into the river, her palms skimming the surface. She stopped when she was waist-deep and moved cautiously to where Meg swam. Lowering her hair into the water she swished it back and forth, before finally dropping down to briefly disappear. It was a glimpse of the real woman beneath all the trappings. Julian was mesmerised.

Odiene rose from the water, the material clinging to her body, moulding unknown places. Her form was thin without the bulk of her clothes to round her out. The corset strangled her waist as if it might snap her in two. She was nothing like the Italian paintings in books, with their fleshy proportions.

Overhead, the sky was muted pink and grey. Julian rather thought a trickling stream and moss-green rocks more appropriate for Odiene Carlisle.

'The river narrows about two miles further up. We can cross there.' Meg sprayed water from her mouth. It shot up in a miniature fountain. 'Youse like her, don't youse?' she stated, treading water. 'She's all right. Not exactly like Mother with her bossy ways and not as particular at playing ladies as Laura is. But youse is too young to get hooked up, Julian, and wese have too much to do. Wese need a plan to get the station back and ogling Odiene ain't gonna help us none. Women like her might look to a man to make decisions, but then they'll come out with their own. Now, I'm not saying that's real bad, but it makes life tricky if youse find yourself in a fix and everyone's got a different point of view. Youse know what I mean, Julian. One day a rooster, the next a feather duster.'

Julian tailed Meg as she swam to the bank and scrambled out of the water. She gathered up the horses and waited as Ethan rinsed out his shirt in the river. Odiene was shaking her petticoat and lifting up the material exposing her legs.

'What's the matter with youse?' Meg asked Odiene.

'Leeches.' She picked at her leg.

'Well don't go plucking them, it'll only burrow deeper and make youse sick,' replied Meg in a rush, passing the reins to Ethan.

Julian reached them just as the tip of Meg's blade touched Odiene's leg. 'You better let me. We don't want any more blood-letting than what's required.'

Meg passed him the knife and folded her arms. 'Sure. Youse'll be better at it than me,' she smirked.

Julian ignored Meg's sarcasm and knelt in front of Odiene. 'Lift your petticoat, turn your leg out a little. Good.'

As Odiene inched the material higher he concentrated on holding her calf to steady her and then spaced his fingers either side of the leech, feeling the soft hairs and the warmth of her body. Then he pressed the blade against her skin and slowly prised the leech free. 'Done.' Julian ran his palms over the rest of Odiene's leg and then proceeded above her knee, slowing as he came to her thighs, suddenly aware of the intimacy of his movements.

'What are you doing?' asked Odiene quietly.

'He's checking for leeches. There might be more. Youse don't want them going near your privates,' said Meg.

'Do you need me to have a look?' suggested Ethan.

Odiene reached down, stilling his inspection. Julian mumbled an apology, spat on his fingers and rubbed the moisture into Odiene's leg where the leech had taken hold.

'That's disgusting,' Odiene protested.

'Best cure-all known to the Dalhuntys, though I'm not sure if Julian's spit is up to par with our father's yet. Takes some fermenting, I reckon,' said Meg.

There was little point Julian taking his sister aside and telling her to behave. Meg's limits were bigger than the 64,000-acre paddocks out west.

The riverbank was matted with trees and coarse roots, so they proceeded on foot, leading the horses as the stars burst out overhead. Julian was plum tired out from what his father called cogitating. It was a difficult business worrying about Gentleman Charles, trying to get home and berating his stupidity for ever mentioning the possibility of getting the property back. He assumed the others were also working through the likelihood of retaining the Dalhunty land, for the topic remained unmentioned.

Having bundled her dry skirt and blouse onto the back of Legless like a swag, Odiene walked ahead. Her wet hair hung to the midpoint of her back, her shoulders as fine-boned as his mother's porcelain tea-cups. She mimicked every step Meg took, hopping over protruding tree roots, leaning in when the riverbank grew steep. Her petticoat remained bunched up, propriety swept away by circumstance.

'Here we are,' announced Meg. 'Ain't only up to the horse's belly. Sand all the way. I walked across but wese be fine riding.'

The moon was yet to rise above the timberline and it was difficult to see where the black water and opposite bank met. Julian was keen to keep moving, however crossing a river at night was dangerous. The current was impossible to gauge – deeper channels could be hidden, and who knew what branches and logs might snag the unwary? He glanced over his shoulder as if it were possible to see within a night long settled.

He felt Ethan next to him. It was not the time for any more arguments. 'Will they come after us?' Julian asked him.

'I don't know about Gentleman Charles, he might be happy with the return of his belongings. *If* he finds the strong box. Alex is another matter. I'm no hardened criminal, Julian. I ran with the Forty Thieves. Petty stuff. Picking pockets, that sort of caper, and I was out of it by the time I was apprenticed. But I reckon Alex Flannery would track us to hell if need be.'

The bush was almost as still as the river. The longer Julian concentrated the more he was able to decipher the hum and swish of mosquitoes, the odd cricket, a distant frog. Taken separately, the voice of each grew distinct and amplified other sounds. Branches falling to the ground. Mice scurrying. The swoop of wings overhead. But not the snap of broken boughs or horse-trampled ground. No one trailed them, at least none they could hear. Julian knew it would be better for all if they camped the night here, however spanning the river put them closer to home. To safety.

'Wese should keep going while it's cool,' said Meg. 'Wese can rest tomorrow when wese reach the Jeffersons. They gave me food and water when I told them youse were lost so they're expecting me.'

'And you've only decided to tell me about these Jefferson people now?' replied Julian.

'Youse didn't ask. Anyways, I forgot. Now wese gonna cross or not?'

It was impossible to see anyone clearly. They were all shapeless forms, discernible only by speech. It was decided they would cross nose to tail, with Meg under orders to go first, making sure Goliath didn't race away. Ethan was to follow, then Odiene. Julian would bring up the rear.

They mounted up. Meg clucked her tongue and Goliath stepped easily into the river. Ethan trailed close behind, his shoes strung about his neck. Julian nudged Legless, whom Odiene was still riding, with his stolen gelding and urged her forwards, promising Odiene that the mare would see her safe to the other side.

Odiene gave Julian a testy reply. It had occurred to Julian to ask her if she was comfortable crossing water in darkness, but if she'd said no, what then?

They moved slowly as the river bottom slanted downwards, the water rising gradually to their stirrup irons. Night-birds called in the sweetening air, disrupted only by the swish of horses moving through the water.

Suddenly, Legless became fractious, backing up and bumping into Julian's mount. He gave Legless a slap on the rump and she jolted forwards, water splattering him as he pressed his horse on from behind. Ahead, Ethan called to Meg to slow down. But she was already a third of the way across the Darling.

A hurrying moon tipped the water with light. Julian glanced at the bush they were leaving behind and then focused on Odiene as Legless plodded on. Without warning, the mare moved swiftly to the right, lost her footing and fell into the main channel.

Odiene remained in the saddle, proving that she could ride a bit, at least. Julian yelled at her to get back on course and her lack of response was disconcerting. She made no headway in escaping the current of the main channel and his own mount stumbled on the sandy bed, treading on some sunken object. Julian saw the white glimmer of the opposite bank; he was halfway across the river. He reined his horse in the direction of Odiene and the water rose to his thighs, swiftly inching higher. He called to Odiene as his gelding started swimming.

'Youse are off course!' Meg's voice carried across the water.

Julian slipped from the animal's back and, holding tight to the reins, swam alongside the horse as the gelding struck out against the current. He could barely see Odiene ahead. She was a balloon of white petticoat until the water sucked at the material, gradually drawing it down. He called out to her and was rewarded with a distant reply. He called again and heard only the deep rhythmic breathing of the gelding and the whoosh of water as the animal stretched its head and neck, its legs pumping.

The moon breached the trees and Julian caught sight of Odiene, a few yards to his right. She was still riding Legless, but the old mare was struggling under the burden and losing her fight with the current. Julian struck out, using the flanks of his horse as a springboard to propel him towards her. He shouted at Odiene, grasping wildly for her arm.

'Let go!' she screamed.

Julian wrenched her from the saddle and she went under. He grabbed at bunches of material until he reached the shell of the corset she wore and, with a final yank, brought her up to the air. She thrashed about and he held her tightly as he felt his way along Legless's spine and held on to the mare's tail. The horse regained strength and they were dragged to the shallows.

Odiene pushed Julian away as they crawled up the bank. 'What on earth were you doing? You could have drowned us both!' She coughed and spat up water.

Julian stuck a finger in a waterlogged ear. 'You both would have ended up at the mouth of the Murray.'

She brushed wet hair aside and shook her petticoat as if fury might dry it. 'I was heading for the bank. Not everyone needs saving, Julian.'

'You weren't heading for the bank. The current had you. Next time you're in trouble I'll leave you to it, but I'm not letting you drown my horse as well.'

'Fine!' said Odiene.

'Fine!' replied Julian.

Legless trotted up the bank to where Meg and Ethan waited.

'Youse two have a habit of wanting to tell the whole bush wese out here.' Meg spoke with the tone of schoolteacher.

Odiene tried three times to mount Legless. She clutched at the sodden petticoat, placed her shoe in the stirrup and gave a series of little hops as she attempted to lift herself up with the burden of wet clothes. Finally Ethan offered assistance, which she accepted with a small thanks.

'Feisty, ain't she?' announced Meg with more than a touch of enjoyment. 'But wese got ourselves a bigger problem, Julian.'

'You mean apart from Wesley and the loss of our home and that . . . that *woman*,' he replied angrily.

'Well, yeah,' said Meg. 'Your horse bolted into the scrub.'

⋘ Chapter 51 ⋙

A few hours' sleep at midnight had been their only relief. Now the flies sought them out, biting at exposed flesh, burrowing into heat-crinkled eyes. If they weren't careful they'd end up with sandy blight. Being on the run was an ugly business. Running away and running towards nothing. Ludicrous.

Julian shifted Meg a little to one side, away from his arm, which was numb from her weight. She had fallen asleep after showing him the markings made in the tree trunks with her knife. A trail to lead them to the Jeffersons. People to be counted on, Meg assured them.

A holler came from the direction of a sun-whitened building. White railings were visible through the trees, resembling the frame of an ancient creature. A balcony, Julian presumed, like the second floor of the Bourke Post Office with its fancy wrought iron. He glanced at his stained clothes and twisted in the saddle. Ethan was as grubby as he was, and then there was Odiene in her women's undergarments and Meg in his childhood cast-offs, snoring like a full-grown man. They were hardly fit for society, let alone wealthy pastoralists.

'It's them. The Jeffersons!' Meg declared, sitting up and knocking Julian hard in the jaw.

Goliath's wide girth pushed through the saplings. The house wasn't a house, but the remains of a paddle-steamer sitting among spiky-leafed belah trees and coolabahs. At the bow the redgum-hulled timber was missing, exposing the frame with an opening forming a veranda shaded by kangaroo hides. Two children were running along the upper deck past the wheelhouse. Washing flapped from the railing. They must be in the middle of an old, old sea. The waters that may have once spread like a lake around mountain tops were long gone, leaving behind the great plain where the Darling and other rivers meandered over a flat land. That same flat land had allowed Captain Ashby to leave the river and speed towards Julian's parents during the Great Flood. This paddle-steamer's owner had clearly not been so fortunate with his land navigation.

'Cooee! Mister Jefferson, it's me, Meg Dalhunty!' Meg slipped from Goliath and ran towards the grounded steamer.

A copper sat near the skin-shaded veranda, where there was a table and assorted chairs as well as a hammock. A child straggled in from the bush, joining five other squabbling children and two young women who fought for seats. One of the youngest children screeched for attention, held up skinny arms and was lifted onto the table by a girl close to Laura in age. A racket ensued as slaps and cries rang out, and plates clanged.

A man and woman who were both grey-haired, narrow in build and equally weather-beaten, walked from the steamer to greet them. The folds were so deep across their cheeks that were it not for the woman's dress and the man's globular nose Julian would have found it impossible to tell them apart.

'Indeedy. If it isn't the young adventurer! It's a fine thing when a person accomplishes an important task,' said Mr Jefferson.

'I told youse I'd find them and I did,' said Meg proudly, introducing Julian, Ethan and Odiene as they tethered their horses to stop them wandering.

'An old brother and a new. You're fortunate. Indeedy, you are. Well, you all look worn. Come and sit, we can offer bread, treacle and tea. There's drinking water in the bucket.' Mr Jefferson made no attempt to hide his amusement at Odiene's state of undress, as she rushed to put her blouse on, clutching the river-wet skirt close to her body.

'We appreciate your hospitality,' said Julian as Meg and Odiene sat gratefully in the shade of the hides. Mrs Jefferson poked at the fire, adjusted the pot of steaming water and called loudly to the hoard at the table to mind their manners. The children and young women barely spoke, chomping with their mouths open as they looked from Odiene to Meg.

'Are you a boy?' asked one of the younger children.

'This is young Meg, Betty. Don't be rude.' Although Mrs Jefferson gave Meg's basin haircut and the ratty felt hat close inspection. 'They're bored. When the river's running we make a holiday of it and camp close by. It keeps them entertained. The *Nile*, *Jupiter*, the *Wandering Jew*, they know them all by their whistles. Well, there's no need my telling you, Meg. You'd be seeing them right regular when there's a run. Although it's not like last century when there were more boats than people.'

'I'm terribly sorry for the way I appear. My skirt got wet crossing the river,' Odiene explained to Mrs Jefferson.

The older woman took the skirt from her and spread it across a stump in the sun, then added tea leaves to the pot on the fire and stirred it with a large wooden spoon. 'You'll be needing some salve for that sunburn too. Better to wear your clothes wet than ruin your skin. And you've no hat.' She pushed a finger into the red of Odiene's skin, a white mark appearing when the pressure was removed. 'You'll be pained by this if you're not already.'

Mrs Jefferson took an old tobacco tin from her apron pocket, and, with somewhat of a struggle with its owner, partially removed Odiene's blouse and then pulled at the straps of her chemise until her shoulders were bare. Julian angled away, as Odiene seized the material to prevent it falling further. He could see her trying not to look in the direction of the men, though she needn't have worried about her modesty. Mr Jefferson was too engrossed discussing the decline in the riverboat trade and Ethan behaved as if a woman in a state of undress was a normal occurrence. It wasn't for Julian.

'Never you mind. A cool washer and my goanna fat will see you right,' said Mrs Jefferson.

'You've had a hard time. It must be humbling to have caused such a kerfuffle, Ethan,' said Mr Jefferson.

Ethan looked directly at Meg, who was too busy ladling water into her mouth to bother with his annoyance.

'Is this your steamer?' asked Julian.

'No. It was stranded here nigh on twenty years ago. The captain clearly was out of his depth.' He laughed at his own joke. 'The boiler was gone when I found it. Most of the internals stripped. Like a great fish gutted and thrown aside. Still, it makes a fair home and it's out of the way, which suits the girls.'

Mr Jefferson waited as his wife gave pannikins of tea to Julian and Ethan and then led them to the side of the vessel where a plank of wood straddled two kerosene tins in front of the stationary paddle-wheel. The older man sat on the plank and, pulling out a stick of wood, began to whittle it while Julian and Ethan savoured the sweet black tea.

One of the young women arrived, offering hunks of bread with treacle, the flies settling on the glop. She was short and full-breasted, the dress she wore unhemmed and dragging leaves and twigs. She made a show of turning her neck one way and then the other, all the while displaying a complete set of white teeth as if she were a prize merino readying for her owner's inspection.

'Thank you, Roslyn.' Mr Jefferson was quick to dismiss her.

'You have a large family, Mr Jefferson.' Julian picked a drowning fly from the treacle-covered bread and refrained from shoving the lot in his mouth.

'Indeedy. Too many, although I was not the one to make it so. It's my wife's doing. Lilly is overly romantic, rather a desperate plight for a woman reduced to the constraints of this life. Still, we are never short on workers, although a moment's peace rarely comes before night. Now, you must rest. I'll water your horses and we can talk later.' He tucked the carving away in a pocket and left them to the remains of their meal.

As the extended Jefferson family quietened, Julian and Ethan settled down in the shade of the steamer to sleep. Exhaustion claimed Julian immediately, so it was with a dragging lethargy he awoke some time later to the sound of giggling. He judged it was late afternoon by the listless heat. He sat up and looked across to where Ethan sat with Roslyn and another of Mr Jefferson's daughters. The second girl was willowy and blonde, not at all resembling her sister. She winked at him as she plunged a hand into the guts of a scrawny rabbit and messed about with the entrails, tossing them aside. Roslyn nudged her sister, then whispered to Ethan. He whispered back and Roslyn led him away through the trees. The remaining girl set the rabbit down and washed in a bucket, paying great detail to running the water along her arms. Then she dropped the rabbit in the water and crooked a finger, beckoning Julian.

He shook his head, studied his boots, feeling the stick of leather and flesh. There was no sign of Ethan. Only the girl, who was now playing with the neckline of her dress, and the buzz of flies hovering and settling on the rabbit guts. The girl got down on all fours and began to crawl towards him, her breasts dangling freely in her low-cut dress. Julian dodged her attentions and concentrated on the yellow-and-orange banded paper wasps flying in and out of the top of the wheel casing. He thought of going in search of Ethan, to see what he and Roslyn were doing, until the obvious came to mind.

The girl was still coming towards him on all fours. She moved in an exaggerated manner, rolling and dropping one shoulder and then the other. Her dress was showing the divide between her breasts, exposing the curve of soft flesh. He was mesmerised by the sight and by the thought of what was hidden from view. It was the unseen that made his blood quicken, and the uncertainty of not knowing what might happen next. When she was a scant foot away she ran her palm up the inside of his thigh to his privates. He flinched and she let out a little laugh.

Then she sat on his lap and squeezed her breast. 'Some men like to suckle while I do them. But then you're a grazier's son. They prefer to mount like their rams or horses. Most don't care to do it any other way. Some don't even take the pipe from their lips. Shall I fetch you a pipe? Something to chew on while I work?'

'Leave Julian alone, Marie.' Ethan strode back through the timber.

The girl sat back on her haunches and twisted her hair until it fell across a shoulder. She stroked the bony clavicle at the base of her neck.

'You want me to leave?' she asked.

'That's best, I think,' Julian said hesitantly. Had they been alone Julian doubted an answer would have been required; events would have simply unfolded without the need for a reply. Odiene had not entered his thoughts.

Marie gave Ethan a sour look and then walked back to the bucket and upended it. The rabbit fell out on the ground with the water and she snatched it up along with a knife, before leaving.

'They're not his children.' Ethan sat down on the plank seat. 'His wife rescued them. They were being battered. That's what happens when you sell your wares on the street.'

'They're prostitutes? So did you . . .? With Roslyn?' probed Julian.

'No. It was on condition of her going with us when we leave. She has no qualms with leaving her two bastard children with the Jeffersons,' explained Ethan.

'But you've been with women before?' said Julian. 'I imagine there's a lot to choose from in Sydney.'

'Have you had a Sally on the Side?' asked Ethan.

'A Sally on the Side?' queried Julian.

'Not yet, eh? Well, you're a good farm boy. At least you'll know where to stick it when the time comes.'

'And you?' asked Julian.

'I came close once. There was a girl in the department store. A redhead. I spoke to her every day for a month. Even took her flowers I nicked from a garden. We met in one of the storerooms by accident and when I pressed up against her she didn't move so I figured she was willing.'

'What happened?'

'Guess I thought about all the kids running around Frog Hollow. Guess I thought about myself. Losing my family.' Ethan stretched out his legs. 'I'd say your luck's on the rise. Odiene's depending on you now. Take the advantage and let her know you're interested. Make your intentions clear. Your mother and Laura will be all fuss and bother when she arrives at the property. Now is the time to strike.'

'You make it sound as if I'm mounting an attack.'

'She's a woman. And you *are*,' replied Ethan. 'Gee, that smells good.'

The scent of food drew them to the bow of the steamer. Meg was playing knuckles with four of the children. She held all five sheep bones, threw them up, turned her hand over quickly and caught them.

'Heat woke you, I s'pose. Always does. Only the youngest can sleep through it.' Roslyn and Marie were dropping dirt-crusted potatoes in a pot of boiling water as Mrs Jefferson lifted a cleaver and brought it down expertly in the middle of a plucked scrub turkey. Blood dripped from the bird's neck down the side of the chopping block.

'When we're at the river we can keep our meat cool. Course, weather being what it is, we've been drying and salting what we trap. The crayfish ate the leg off a kangaroo last year. At least, Mr Jefferson thought it a crayfish. We've not seen one in these parts for a time.' She dropped chunks of the meat into a boiler on the fire, the contents bubbling fiercely.

Roslyn placed the skinned rabbit on the block with a sullen slap and it too was cut deftly into small segments, bone and all.

'Is that snake? I'm not eating snake,' mumbled Ethan, as Mrs Jefferson sliced a long black serpent into bite-sized pieces.

'City boy. Meg told me. Perfectly proper to eat, young man. Once the head's off and it's boiled the poison's gone.' Mrs Jefferson scraped the remaining meats up and placed them in the boiler, added water and a knob of creamy grey fat. 'You stir it good and well, Roslyn, and serve up when it's ready. We'll wait until Mr Jefferson and our visitors have eaten.'

The children whinged as Meg left the knuckle-bone game. The smallest child snatched up the bones as Marie gathered all the children together and sat them in a circle, where they started to sing.

Odiene was now dressed in her creased skirt, already flushed from the extra layers. 'I wanted to apologise, Julian. I never gave a thought to Legless having difficulty crossing the river with me on her back. Meg told me the mare's special to you.'

Her regret was offered contritely. Julian wanted to reply that he'd feared for her safety as well during the crossing. For he had, regardless of her stubbornness. However never again was he to admit his deeper concern for her.

'Yes, she is special. Legless was born on our property.'

He thought he saw disappointment flicker across Odiene's face, perhaps at how brief his response to her apology had been, and he considered sharing the story of the wobbly foal.

'Will you let me see to those stitches?' she asked.

Julian allowed Odiene to lead him to a chair. Mrs Jefferson slipped neatly into the role of medical assistant and nipped into the steamer, returning with scissors, blustering about oily hair and cleaning the wound. A swatch of calico was plunged into the pot of boiling potato water, retrieved with a stick and then squeezed out. It landed on Julian's skull with a splat and he yelped as he brushed it aside, the steaming material falling on the ground.

The older woman complained at Julian's fussing, her bosom pressing against his cheek as she tilted his head to examine the injury. 'A man did this you say? Rougher needlework I've not seen.' Mrs Jefferson pressed his skull, commenting on the haphazard sutures and the lack of redness. 'There's no dead or puckered skin. And no need for maggots. Pity, I have some fine specimens saved in case of emergencies.'

Odiene assumed control, her touch sure and calming. The scissors snipped at each stitch and then the sensation of thread being pulled free of skin completed the procedure.

He offered his thanks.

'Don't mind me, the young scarcely have time for the old anymore, but I appreciate your goodwill all the same,' said Mrs Jefferson.

Mr Jefferson emerged from the bowels of the steamer. 'Sit, sit. We'll eat before the children. If we let them go first there'll be none left and I am fond of Mrs Jefferson's hodgepodge.'

They sat at the table as the children sang and squealed and ran about the steamer. Roslyn clanged about inside the boat. A selection of plates and bowls were placed unceremoniously in the centre of the table along with cutlery, which rattled about as if the ship were surging through headwaters. She went to the boiler and spooned the meat into a large bowl and then elbowed her way between Ethan and Meg, the contents sloshing and spilling as she sat it on the table. Mr Jefferson ran a shirtsleeve across the spilt food and licked a finger, as the girl flounced off and returned with a platter of potatoes, which were dumped before them. She snatched one up and then joined the children.

Mr Jefferson served heapfuls of the steaming stew into bowls and plates, each dish formally passed along until everyone was served. Julian stuck a piece of meat with his fork and chewed. It was so long since he'd had a decent meal he wasn't cringing at anything offered. And neither was Odiene, although she barely chewed, preferring to swallow whole.

Mr Jefferson opened a pouch and added a pinch of something dry and black to his meal. 'Ash. It makes all the difference to the meal. Comes from eating too many dampers.'

Meg sprinkled the ash delicately on her plate and ate. 'Actually it's pretty good. Condiment, Ethan?'

Next to her Ethan was sorting through the cuts of meat, apparently unwilling to consume any of the pieces. He peeled and ate a steaming potato, then added the potato skin to a little pile of scrapings growing in the middle of the table.

'We can go for months without seeing a soul but we've been quite the entertainers of late. You're our second lot of visitors since Meg came through here. It's quite livened us all. Even Roslyn and Marie, who are not known for their cheery dispositions, have been more than amiable. And although I was sworn to secrecy, you'll be pleasantly surprised when you eventually get home to your run, Julian.' Mr Jefferson waved his knife about, clearly pleased to be the bearer of good news. 'You have a close friend waiting on your arrival. Indeedy. I must say he was sorry to hear of your troubles and is very keen to see you again. He's an interesting man and was most emphatic he owes you – although in what capacity, he chose not to elaborate. Suffice to say he doesn't strike me as someone who wouldn't fulfil an obligation.'

Julian thanked the heavens. If Captain Ashby was en route to see his father then perhaps their money was not lost after all. 'Captain Ashby must have escaped Fraser's men.'

Immediately they were all a-chatter. Ethan was convinced that the crafty old sea-dog had come to terms with Mr Fraser. Odiene clapped delightedly and set her plate aside as if sustenance was no longer required.

'Captain Ashby?' Mr Jefferson's globular nose flared in confusion.

Meg played with the pieces of meat on her plate. 'I thought youse family knew all the riverboat captains, Mr Jefferson.'

'Indeedy,' he replied. 'I'm not speaking of Captain Ashby. This man's name was Alex Flannery, and he'll be waiting for you all at Dalhunty Station.'

⊰ Chapter 52 ⊱

When Julian woke it was to the sight of white figures painted on reddish rock. They hung above him like a child's mobile, almost within reach, their arms and legs outstretched as if they were bounding across an unknown landscape. It meant something. A story, perhaps. Like the Bible. A form of communication that expressed the knowledge of the land and beliefs. Yet he was only capable of viewing the drawings through a white man's eyes. He shifted his spine on the rocky ledge. Having fallen asleep after midday with the others, sheltered by this history of another time, he was now an explorer entering a distant past, witnessing a place of roaming peoples, stencilled animals and hands immortalised by breath-splattered dyes. Never had he felt more unsure of life.

The ache of their gruelling travel forced Julian from the rocky bed. He hobbled out from beneath the overhang, each step straightening bone and muscle. In the middle of a dry creek bed littered with boulders, he undid the buttons on his moleskin trousers, the sweet relief of making water momentarily clearing his mind. About him, the red of the earth and the dark rocks contrasted sharply with the green of foliage. The Jeffersons were far behind now.

Following the news of Alex's impending arrival at Dalhunty Station their departure had been hasty and, in hindsight, rude after the couple's hospitality. There were promises of further visits to the marooned steamer, although this was unlikely to ever take place. Julian could not see beyond today, let alone into the future.

They'd ridden for part of the night through dull grass-covered slopes and plains, rested, and then spent the morning traversing miles of stunted scrub. The scenery was made familiar by the delicate grey leaf of the mulga and the speckled bark of those Leopardwood not yet succumbed to ring-barking rabbits. They used the mountain in the distance as a bearing, keeping it before them until the red soil met the rocky gorges. Then they had followed the dry creek bed to the rock shelter where they now slept. Julian knew it was foolish to keep pushing on at such a fast pace. They were all wrung out, and even talkative, bossy Meg was lulled to quiet and content to follow his lead. If only Julian knew how to best Alex and his gang. For Gentleman Charles's man was sure to have others with him, despite having presented himself as a lone traveller at the Jeffersons' steamer.

He walked along the rocky bed of the dry creek. Signs of recent rain showed in the water pooled in the rocks and the wet sand in deeper hollows. He cupped the liquid in one depression and drank. At another, where piles of leaves and sticks were massed by a previous deluge the liquid was hot from the heat of the stone. The tangy scent of eucalypts was on the breeze. A huge tree grew among boulders in the middle of the creek and birds darted to the tiny puddles of water, before swiftly dashing up the vertical sandstone cliffs.

Ahead was an Aboriginal woman. She was leaning over with her back towards him, oblivious to his presence as she filled a possum-skin waterbag from one of the small stone reservoirs. She checked the heaviness of the bag and then, sensing an intruder, swung around. She started talking quickly and loudly, taking cautious steps backwards.

'Hello. I don't mean any harm,' called Julian.

Two men emerged from the rocks and trees. They closeted the woman behind them as another female joined the group. The men held hunting sticks and oblong shields, decorated in a colour that reminded Julian of the Reckitt's Blue he'd seen Laura use for laundry. The men were dressed as stockmen with boots and hats, and the women wore housedresses. Julian noticed that the younger woman, the water-gatherer, had a cut to her cheek and a crusty trail down her face had formed where the blood had dripped. Specks of it flecked her dress and Julian watched a damp spot from the waterbag she carried spread like an unfolding flower across her skirts.

'We're only travelling through,' he told them. 'Heading for Dalhunty Station. I thought this was part of Gundabooka Station. My father knows the owner. So all's well.'

The two men blocked his path as completely as the walls of the boulder-strewn gully. They stared at him briefly and then all four of them were leaving, climbing up the rocks, the waterbag swinging.

Julian walked back towards the overhang, picking his way through the stones and flood debris. Meg met him as he stepped from the creek bed. She looked wan in the afternoon light and he saw a little sister who for too long had been too far from home.

'Youse saw them Aboriginals, didn't you? I hope youse didn't scare them off, Julian. They don't mean no harm. More likely they're worried about the womenfolk. One of them was attacked a few days ago. Run down and struck with a whip.'

'How do you know that?' he asked.

'I saw them hours ago. So I waited until everyone was asleep and went and spoke to them.'

'That was plain silly, talking to them alone.' It was just like his sister to go wandering off.

'All this red earth. Makes a person think about the past. Like maybe all the bad times have stained the soil. Youse ever thought about that, Julian? That wese been warring over this land since before Great-grandfather's time, and learnt nothing from all the fighting?'

She knelt in the sand and began to draw inverted horseshoes.

'Six horseshoes. That means six riders. That's how many men came through here two days ago,' she explained. 'The Aboriginals told me.'

'Damn it. You can bet Wesley is with Alex.'

'Maybe the man's eye needs more doctoring or they didn't find the strongbox. Maybe they want their horses back. Or them.' Meg glanced at Julian's boots. Then she drew a cross in the sand. 'This is us. The Aboriginals said we need to head north-east, then cut across to the river. This'—she drew a circle—'is a waterhole. Enough for us and the horses.' She drew a squiggly line. 'This is the river.' Meg looked up at him.

'Is that the waterhole at Byrock?' The railway went through Byrock en route to Brewarrina, and Cobb & Co. still had a changing station there. 'There are people at Byrock.'

'This way's faster.' Meg pinpointed Byrock in the sand. It sat at the centre of a right angle, adding days to their travel. 'Youse go there and we leave Mother and Father and Laura to that Wesley fella and his men for longer. Reckon we should do what the Aboriginals say and head here where there's water.' She placed a thumbprint in the middle of the circle.

'There's no water there,' argued Julian.

'If they said there was water, there's water. That's why wese gotta head back towards the river. Ain't much drinking in between. When we get clear of all this rock and wese on the plains again wese should be able to see the mountain behind us for a bit before Mount Oxley comes into view. It'll be the only feature on the horizon.' Meg rubbed the back of her neck as if she were a woman twice her age. 'There's another thing. Youse going to have to see about Ethan. He didn't want to stay. This all started with him diving into the river. If he wants to go, he should. Once wese reach the river he only has to turn left and follow it to Bourke.'

'You've been calling him our brother and now you want him to leave? We'll need his help. Ethan can fight a bit.'

'They have revolvers and rifles. There'll be no fighting,' Meg chided, as if she were the older of the two. 'Wese have to parley.'

'Besides, Ethan's hellbent on reporting Captain Ashby to the coppers and if he—'

'Maybe Ashby *should* be reported. Youse don't really think wese be able to get the piano money from him now, do youse?'

The sunlight threw a pattern across the rocks in the creek. Julian sat on one of the hard boulders, smoothed by eons of running water, envisaging the meeting with Gentleman Charles. It was one thing to roam the inland west of the Darling, laying low from the law, selling illegal liquor, perhaps planning another robbery, but quite another to venture east. Julian expected the worst. Awful things happened out here. People were corrupt. Martha Wendell slowly killed her stepchildren with spirits of salts. Land owners placed strychnine in flour supplies intended for Aboriginal people. The bushrangers Patrick and James Kenniff, who harassed western Queensland, killed two policemen rather than be caught for theft. If there was to be comeuppance for the events out west then it was on his head.

'I expect I'll have to lead the man to where we dumped the strongbox if he's not found it. Either way I'll have to work off ownership of these boots.' Julian tugged them free, feeling flesh peel from the gluey leather inside. The pain was secondary to what lay ahead. 'If that happens you must stay with the rest of the family. And we'll not be arguing about it. There's no place for you with those men. I'll tie you to the veranda if need be.'

'Reckon I'll be like a yabby, walking miles and miles to find a new waterhole if youse leave me. You know you limp,' accused Meg.

'I'd be disappointed if I didn't.' He splayed his toes on the sand, rubbing them against the coarse grains. Wesley's gang was the least of his worries. 'You do understand, Meg, we have no way of getting the property back from Mr Fraser. It's gone, and we have to let it go.'

Meg approached him, anger building. Julian thought she might combust, like one of the many boilers that blew riverboats apart.

'But youse said we'd buy it back. Youse said youse have a plan.'

'I have no plan and no money.' Julian pulled on his boots. 'It was stupid to even mention the idea.'

'Stupid? Stupid?' she screamed. 'Then why did youse? That's our home! Wese ain't got anything else. Wese ain't got nothing.'

'I lied to keep you from going on about us being together. You're a girl, Meg. Whatever happens, you have to stay with our parents.' He went to her and tried to place an arm about her shoulders.

She pushed him away. 'Leave me alone.'

'There's no way around this mess.' He tried to sound reasonable.

'Liar. You had that timetable hidden in your mattress!' she shouted.

'You shouldn't go poking about in other people's belongings,' he said softly.

'And youse shouldn't lie.'

'What do you want to hear, Meg? That I'm desperate to get the property back? That I've imagined how our lives might be and it could be bloody marvellous. All of us working and living together. The outbuildings restored, and men in them. The paddocks carpeted with grass and sheep. Our wool being carted by lorry down wide Sydney streets with "Dalhunty Station" stencilled on each hooped bale. We've been going downhill for too long. And wishing and hoping is for people with money. So, yes, it's time to leave. Time to realise it's over, and to be realistic about what we're leaving behind. I want more than ghosts and drought and scrabbling for a living and stories of the good old days.'

'Then youse don't have anything to worry about, Julian. It's already gone.' Meg walked a short distance away and plonked down on a rock.

Odiene, accompanied by Ethan, walked down the rocky path from the overhang towards them.

'What's the matter?' she asked. Her skin was patched red and brown from the sun and her nose was peeling. She had wrapped a length of material cut from her skirt around her head and wedged a piece of bark between her forehead and the material, forming an inch of shade.

'Nothing. We should leave,' said Julian. A golden light filtered the afternoon. It was beautiful and yet disconcerting, for it concealed the savagery of men. Those same uncaring men sat behind desks in banks, pretended to be best friends, purchased poor people's land, and waited at his home for revenge. 'Get up, Meg, and stop whimpering. We've got to get home.'

She obeyed with a stern glower and they all walked away from the cool of the creek bed, eventually finding level ground and the horses where they had left them.

Meg scrubbed her face as if she had soap and water. She left Goliath for Julian, choosing to double with Ethan instead.

'Is everything all right, Julian?' Odiene smelt of rendered goanna fat as she looked at him from under the bark brim.

He walked her to her horse, lightly touching the waistband of her skirt, the corset discarded. 'I doubt it ever will be again.'

⋘ Chapter 53 ⋙

It took two long days before they finally reached the Darling River. Kicking the horses down the bank, they fell from their saddles and into the water in a flurry of thirst. Meg lay in the water, flipping from side to side like a johnnycake in the pan, while Odiene and Ethan splashed about as if born to it. Julian plunged beneath the water, repeating the action until the novelty wore thin and he was sprawled with the others in the shade of a gum. Overhead a branch hung low across the river. It could knock the wheelhouse clean off the *Lady Matilda* if struck at speed and Julian found envisaging such an accident quite a satisfying way to spend the time while they rested.

He opened an eye to discover Meg standing over him. She pivoted on her heel.

'Bourke's that way, Ethan.' She pointed downriver, treading on Julian's bare toes, twisting her foot against his for good measure.

Julian swore softly, refusing to give his sister the satisfaction of complaining. He waited for Ethan to react, hopeful he would choose to stay instead of accepting Meg's abrupt invitation to leave. This was his sister's retaliation for his admission regarding the property.

'It's a fair walk,' he said to Ethan.

341

'Ethan's up to it. If he wants.' Meg threw a pebble in the water.

She was practically telling him to go. Julian couldn't understand it. Meg was young and impulsive and yet she must be aware of the danger awaiting them. Was Gentleman Charles supping on Aunt Nancy's tinned turtle soup at the kitchen table? Was the tent-packer ogling Laura? Were his parents trussed like scrub turkeys in the drawing room, awaiting their son's return?

Ethan rolled over on his side and then sprang upwards and looked towards Bourke. The river was listless. The timber gracing the banks devoid of movement. 'How far is it?'

Julian refused to ask Ethan to stay. He had no right. Especially when he'd already placed himself in danger to help them. 'A few days' walk. If you keep with the river you'll be fine, but you'll have no food, unless you can catch it.'

'There won't be any steamers for a while,' said Ethan.

'Nope, but the train runs regular. You should be able to earn the fare in Bourke. Running errands. You've experience,' said Julian.

Ethan surveyed the glassy river. 'Train-hopping. I had mates in Sydney who bragged about seeing the countryside and never paying a cent. It's the best view in the world, I'm told, sitting atop a carriage. Wind in your hair. The houses thinning out until you reach a town's limits, and the bush takes over. Not getting caught is the trick. A person's as likely to be dobbed in by townsfolk as nabbed by the coppers. Mind you, there're two laws, aren't there, Julian? One for city people like me and another for you lot. Would you risk riding illegally?'

'Not in this weather. You'd be fried like an egg within an hour,' replied Julian.

'Youse can come with us if youse want but wese all knows youse don't wanna stay. Youse should go with him, Odiene. We'll only have to traipse right back in a couple of days when youse want to leave and it's a lot, expecting folk to take you to Bourke after the time wese been away.' The foliage on the opposite bank framed Meg's grave expression.

Odiene was stitching a button on her blouse as if it were now the most natural occurrence to be clad only in a chemise in mixed company. The needle pricked her finger and she sucked it carefully. 'I understand, Meg. I certainly wouldn't want to be a burden to anyone.'

Julian had not contemplated Odiene's leaving. All his efforts had been concentrated on everyone surviving the journey home and ensuring his parents' and Laura's wellbeing. And, like Ethan, he could not ask her to stay. Her life was her own and she had given no indication there was more than friendship between them. Yet he found himself brooding over the reasons why Odiene should remain. Her safety, for one. Ethan was no bush survivor. Her prospects, for another. Where would she go? Had she any money saved? Then there was the estimable Captain Augustus Ashby. Julian doubted Odiene could rely on the man ever again. Would she even want to?

'What will you do once you get home?' Ethan asked Julian.

'Whatever is needed to keep the peace,' said Julian casually. 'We'll come to some agreement. If Wesley is there I doubt he'll string me up from the nearest tree.' Hoping was one thing, reality quite another, but he kept his feelings concealed.

'And the property?' asked Odiene.

'It's not ours anymore. There's nothing anyone can do,' replied Julian flatly.

'Is that what you were arguing about at the gorge?' Ethan asked.

'If I was a man I'd get it back.' Meg's expression was still bitter.

Julian wished Ethan had not brought up the subject. His sister's anger was forging itself into a simmering resentment that would be difficult to quell.

'So you and Meg will still head north after you've sorted things with Gentleman Charles,' stated Ethan.

Julian was beyond the point of placating his sister. 'Meg knows that's impossible. She's too young. She'll have to stay with our parents.'

Meg regarded him with a gnarly stare. 'He was planning on leaving anyway. Wanted to up and take the train to Sydney. Don't matter. Wese don't need him. Reckon a person can get on just fine without a brother.'

'Meg, don't be like this,' said Julian.

'Don't speak to me. I ain't got any brothers anymore.'

Odiene returned the needle and thread to the taxidermy kit and put her blouse back on. 'But you didn't leave.'

'No.' Julian replied, although he knew he should have added, *but it wasn't for the want of thinking about it.*

'And what if you can't come to an agreement?' asked Odiene. 'If Gentleman Charles isn't fair? It's doubtful he will be, after what we've witnessed and suffered. The man is dangerous.' She played with the taxidermy kit, opening and shutting it, her anxiety obvious in her abrupt movements.

'Some crooks are all right once you sit down and talk to them, one on one.' Ethan met Julian's gaze.

They both knew he was lying, however the observation stopped Odiene's fidgeting. She sat the taxidermy kit in her lap and waited, as if optimistic of hearing more positive comments about criminals.

'There you go. If a boy from the streets has met honourable men there's hope yet,' answered Julian, pleased to see Odiene set the kit aside and begin re-plaiting her hair.

'I don't rightly believe my dear old pa would be best pleased if I upped and left someone in need. Especially someone who tried to save my life. Eh, fool-saver?' Ethan raised a grin wider than the mouth of the Murray. 'I pay my debts,' he said.

Julian was compelled to shake the hand Ethan had offered. And when Ethan clapped Julian on the shoulder, it seemed natural for Julian to do the same. He was thankful, after all. Meg had not tempted Ethan to head for Bourke. He wanted to be suspicious at this sudden show of goodwill where before there had been little, however Ethan Harris was becoming less of a mystery to him with every day spent together. He was amenable, helpful, brave and willing to take chances for a common cause. Julian now saw The Natural in a very different light.

'Guess you'll be coming along, Odiene,' said Ethan, a renewed vigour to his movements as he helped her to stand.

'Yes.' She dusted off her skirt, avoiding Julian completely.

A short distance away Meg began to sharpen her knife on a flat river stone, the blade making a dull scraping noise as she persisted with the task even as they mounted the horses, readying to set out on the final leg to the station. She only ceased when Ethan asked if she wanted to ride with him. Then she dawdled about, tucking the blade away, before finally accepting his arm as she leapt onto the horse. Not once did she concede defeat, by word or gesture to Julian; the shape of her behind Ethan as defiant as her inability to forgive.

❰ Part 3 ❱

The Homecoming

≪ Chapter 54 ≫

Julian and Ethan crawled on their stomachs through the palm grove of Dalhunty Station, their forearms and legs finding purchase as they moved across the uneven ground. Julian carried a piece of wood with a whittled point on the end, shaped to stick someone at close range. Ethan clasped Meg's knife, obtained after a considerable amount of sweet-talking. Their weapons were no match for firearms, as Meg had constantly reminded them, although her arguing on the best course of action was not the only reason Julian demanded she stay a mile from the homestead with their horses and Odiene. In her current agitated state, his sister was more likely to cause strife than assist them out of it. Meg had been more annoyed than a raided beehive when told she must remain behind. *You're not my brother anymore*, she repeated. *You hear me, Julian? Not. My. Brother.*

Entrusted with Odiene's wellbeing, Meg's disquiet lessened, particularly when Julian added that the very necessary role included the need for her to climb a tree and act as lookout, ensuring she was ready to move should danger threaten. Whether Meg actually followed his instructions was another matter. Her past behaviour made it doubtful, however he had never made such a serious request of her before.

They plotted their way around another of Frank's holes and brushed black-purple meat-ants from their skin. A few inches before them was the nest: a large, oval-shaped mound. The area was cleared of pasture and covered with gravel, pebbles and dead vegetation. Miniature roadways led away from it, the tracks filled with ants swarming from numerous holes, marching back and forth. They took a wide detour.

Not far away, smoke spiralled from the homestead's kitchen chimney. Three fresh sheep hides, the meaty underside showing, were strung on the yard fence. It appeared as if the skins were moving. The ants were undoubtedly making short work of their meal, stripping the wetness and blood with the precision of myriad knives. If Gentleman Charles was here with Alex, he and his men had wasted little time liberating their stock and ensuring their appetites were sated.

'Have you worked out a plan yet? You were filled with gusto earlier,' said Ethan.

Intention was all well and good until presented with reality, which in this case was dangerous men holed up in your family home. Achievement seemed possible before dawn, not so much now. They inched closer to the edge of the palm grove. One hundred yards of open country lay ahead. Then there was the yard fence, a barrier that could be easily hurdled, although it was a risky move in daylight when a hard sprint was still required to reach the kitchen.

'You're the one with the experience.' Julian didn't want to admit he was unable to settle on the best course of action. He had been hoping that Ethan would devise a scheme.

'I ran with a gang, I didn't attack armed men. And I can't say I know the best way to go about this either. Maybe it's better to wait until night.' Ethan slapped at a fly. 'The critters out here are bigger than the rats in Frog Hollow.'

Without warning, Frank's head popped up from under a scattering of palm leaves. 'Where the blazes have you been?' he growled.

'Jeez, Frank. I nearly clobbered you.' Julian lowered the lump of wood.

Frank rested his chin on the edge of the hole, the hinge of his jaw working overtime as he chewed. His cheeks bulged. 'At last. You're here. I require your help.' He waggled a finger at Ethan, his brow as furrowed as a ram. 'And you. By jove, you are very stupid. You came back.'

'I figured that much myself. How many are there?' asked Ethan.

'Six. One with an all-seeing eye. Even at night he's awake.'

'Charles Wesley,' Julian and Ethan said simultaneously. Julian had expected the worst. He had been right to.

'That's him,' Frank confirmed. 'I smelt their wickedness before I saw them. They reeked of sweat and sin. Of soldiers who had no badge of honour but rather a kindred fondness for abuse. I hid Henrietta in the abandoned storehouse and then came back to the homestead, hiding in the gap between the water tank and the house. I watched them ride in. The men prowling about. Checking the outbuildings. Kicking at pieces of tin. Then two of the men knocked on the front door. Your mother answered.'

Frank told them that Mr Wesley had been most polite on arrival two days ago. The man presented himself as a friend of Julian's and appeared to know everything of recent importance. From Julian's attempted rescue of Ethan when he fell in the river, his convalescing on the *Lady Matilda*, through to his decision to leave the paddle-steamer and head home.

Julian heard all this with misgiving. So far Wesley's story was true to the version of events he had shared with the man the first night of their meeting. Then Wesley's cunning stepped in. He contended he had greeted the *Lady Matilda* when ordered supplies were delivered. It was here he first met Julian and Ethan who were aboard. He spoke of Miss Carlisle, and how Captain Ashby's travelling companion had ably assisted Mr Wesley with some medical treatment and that, with all good intention, Wesley tried to help Julian in getting home. However they had become separated when Miss Carlisle fell behind. Concerned for his young friend, he immediately rode to Dalhunty Station to make sure the lad was safe. There had been no need for Wesley and his men to take the convoluted trail to the river Meg insisted upon to cover their tracks.

Frank halted in his recounting of events and then resumed more sombrely. 'Mrs Dalhunty was very appreciative. She invited Mr Wesley and another called Alex to join her, Laura and my Honoured Brother for tea on the veranda. That was when everything fell apart.'

'What do you mean?' asked Julian nervously.

'This Mr Wesley said you stole things from them, Julian. Precious things. And he wants them back. Is this true?'

'No. Yes. Maybe. It's about a pair of boots. Or a strongbox we took, but we left it for them to find.'

'My dear boy, you are a very stupid Dalhunty.' Frank rested a stirrup iron and a whip at the hole's edge and, retrieving a date from his pocket, popped it in his mouth and chewed. With great reluctance he offered each of them a date, before explaining that he had opened the pens in the stables and let the gang's horses escape. Now they were looking for him.

Frank gave another black-toothed grin and Julian caught a whiff of decay. The mad Englishman's surveillance had determined two men were searching for the missing horses. Another two were scouting for him in an ever-widening circle, while Alex and Gentleman Charles spent their time slouched on the veranda or indoors.

They began formulating a plan. Frank was to cause a distraction, with the aim of leading the men on the veranda away from the homestead. Ethan and Julian would then climb through the kitchen window and attempt to get Laura and Julian's parents out.

'This is all very fine until they hit you on head,' rebuked Frank.

Ethan tapped Julian on the shoulder. 'We may need to change our strategy.'

Meg was running from the direction of the bore head straight towards the homestead, her gangly legs pumping like pistons, her

352

arms swinging. She slipped through the yard fence like a river eel, the fox tailing her, and took cover at the chicken coop.

Julian watched, stupefied, as she dashed to the wood pile, then towards the copper, where she dropped to the ground to take shelter. She was little more than one hundred and twenty yards from him and yet Julian could do nothing to stop her for fear of giving their position away. Meg gave a wave in their direction and then turned her concentration to the house. Edging around the copper, she ran again. In a split second she was flattening her body beneath the kitchen window.

Julian dug his knuckles into the ground.

Meg rose slowly to peer carefully through the window as a howling noise rippled through the air. She tapped on the glass pane, just as an excited Bony arrived. The dog yapped and sniffed and leapt all over his mistress as a startled Laura lifted the window.

A brief discussion followed, then Laura shimmied across the window ledge and out of the building. The two girls cowered against the wall as Bony and the fox began to fight, their snarls and barks growing more ferocious.

'She's done it now. That dog will give us away,' said Julian.

Laura began to run towards the palm grove. As Meg sped around one side of the house, the tent-packer appeared from the opposite direction.

'I thought you said all the other men were away from the homestead,' said Julian to Frank.

Laura was at the yard fence and had just gathered her long skirt and climbed the railings when the tent-packer caught sight of her.

'Hey!' shouted Meg. She had backtracked from the side of the homestead and was in full view of Wesley's man.

The tent-packer stopped dead in his tracks. He looked from Laura to Meg and back again, and then he began to run. After Laura.

Frank pushed himself up out of the hole and zigzagged through the palm trees in the direction of the stables.

'Help her, Ethan!' said Julian. 'While I get Meg.'

Ethan needed no encouragement. He raced towards Laura, who was wrangling with her skirt as she climbed the fence, tugging when it snared. She pulled it free and, catching sight of Ethan, ran harder towards him.

Julian passed Ethan and Laura as they met. His sister glanced at him in terror as he kept on running, painfully aware of the limping gait that prevented further speed. He cleared the fence in a single hurdle and collided with the tent-packer, dropping the sharpened stick with the impact. Julian was aware of the dog and fox fighting as the man cracked Julian on the side of the head, causing him to sprawl in the dust.

Seconds later a pistol fired.

Wesley's man walked to where Bony's now-still body lay. He prodded the animal with the toe of his boot.

Woozily, Julian regained his balance in time to see a missile come out of nowhere and strike the tent-packer in the head. The man staggered and yelled, trying to locate the attacker.

Julian caught a glimpse of Meg clutching the slingshot. Then she and the fox vanished behind the homestead.

'Julian,' called Alex Flannery from the corner of the house. His features were swollen and mashed from Ethan's battering. 'Welcome home.'

∝ Chapter 55 ≫

Gentleman Charles was reclining in Benjamin Dalhunty's chair on the veranda, cushioned by the padded headrest, a leg propped up on one of the extended arms. A pale substance leaked from beneath his eye patch and he dabbed at it frequently with a handkerchief, examining the cloth with the scrutiny of a mother monkey searching for fleas. With painstaking thoroughness he inspected Julian, Laura and Ethan. They waited on the veranda like misbehaving children, lined up with their backs towards the stirrup irons, which were glistening in the sun. Charles Wesley was enjoying their discomfort.

'I'm quite partial to this chair.' He tested it for soundness, banging on the arm. 'A man's seat by every definition,'

'I want to see my parents,' Julian demanded.

'In good time.' Gentleman Charles addressed the tent-packer and Alex. 'Where are the others? The cameleer and the boy with the slingshot?'

The tent-packer folded his arms, the pistol resting in the crook of an elbow. The swelling above his eyebrow indicating Meg's marksmanship. 'We're still searching.'

355

Gentleman Charles unhitched his leg from the armrest and straightened. 'You. Julian. Where is the cameleer?'

'What cameleer? There are no camels here,' replied Julian dumbly.

'There is camel dung everywhere, my boy. But no matter. We'll find him,' answered Gentleman Charles with disinterest. 'Ah, look. Miss Carlisle returns!'

Three men rode in. A coiling willy-willy met them, pitching shrivelled leaves and blow-away grass into the air. One of the riders doubled Odiene and the others led Legless, Goliath and the stolen mare. At the gate, the man riding with Odiene dismounted and reached for her, readying to pull her from the horse. She slapped him away, leaping easily to the ground, then straightened her skirts with irritation and studied her surroundings.

Julian recalled Ethan's arrival last year. How the homestead, with its fallen out-buildings, rusted machinery, untidy stack of kerosene tins and partially boarded windows, had left the outsider momentarily bewildered, having expected more pomp and circumstance from Dalhunty Station. Once again they were to be subjected to the same level of scrutiny. Odiene knew of their fall from grace, the loss of the property, but not their dismal circumstances. He was beyond embarrassed.

Odiene shrugged away the bearded handler and with her head high walked across a yard littered with sheep bones and chicken feathers, the imperious attitude rather ruined by her torn and grubby clothing and ragged hemline. She stepped up onto the veranda, acknowledging Julian, Ethan and Laura before presenting herself to the patient.

Gentleman Charles patted the substance running from his wounded eye and then made a peak with his fingers. 'I thought it quite unsporting of you to depart the way you did, Miss Carlisle. I did intend to let you leave, you know.'

'No, I didn't know. In fact, you gave not the slightest indication of that. You and your ruffians should be ashamed of yourselves. It is one thing to provide beverages to isolated people. That's your business and yours alone. However holding innocent people for no reason when an agreement was made for my services only . . . well, that is something else entirely. And then you invade a family home. Quite unforgiveable,' said Odiene tersely.

'How fortunate you have not taken the Hippocratic Oath. I fear your ethical standards would run second to your bluntness.' He reclined a little more in the chair, pleased by his response. 'Will you check my wound?' It was phrased as a request, but was clearly a demand.

Odiene tapped a foot, twice in irritation, the action reminding Julian of Meg. Where was his younger sister? Holed up somewhere with Frank? He prayed they weren't concocting another scheme.

With every second, Odiene's refusal to answer Wesley made the situation more volatile. Gentleman Charles rose from the chair. 'It was you, Miss Carlisle, who agreed to assist me with my difficulty. Granted, it was brokered through Ashby, but a deal is a deal. And you did agree to it. And I remind you all,' he said as he moved towards Julian, 'I did not ask for you two lads to invade my camp. Further, I have stolen nothing from you young people. But *you*, Julian, stole from *me*—'

'And me,' interrupted Alex, from where he leant against a veranda post.

Gentleman Charles waved him to quiet. 'You had the audacity to ruin my tent, and steal my strongbox and horses in the middle of the night.'

'You should have paid Captain Ashby for the goods he delivered to you, instead of sending that sham of a cheque. We were only trying to recover what rightly belongs to my family,' argued Julian.

'But I don't owe the Captain anything. In fact *he* owes *me*.' Gentleman Charles wafted the handkerchief about his body. 'This is quite unbelievable. Your debts are no concern of mine. But stealing from me is another matter. I want my belongings returned to me.'

'I left the strongbox near the big ridge on the western side of the Darling. There are sheep bones everywhere and I piled them up and—'

'We found the box, you half-wit!'

'We took nothing else,' Julian insisted.

'You're lying!' Gentleman Charles shouted. 'I'm talking about my *opera glasses*. Where are they? I want them back!'

Odiene flinched and moved closer to Julian. 'They were the glasses your father stole?' she asked tentatively.

'Ashby has no concern for privacy, I see. *Borrowed*. My father *borrowed* them with every intent of returning them. But what better way to be rid of a manservant who knew more than his master about music than by calling him a thief?'

'So you're saying they are the very same opera glasses?' said Odiene doubtfully.

'My mother carried them with her when she followed my father to New South Wales. She was not of the impoverished classes, Miss Carlisle. Now. Where are they? For I swear on my father's grave I will have them returned to me. I'm not a violent man unless stirred to action, however Alex isn't known for niceties.' Gentleman Charles stopped in front of each of them before reaching Julian. 'Where. Are. They?'

'I don't know.'

It was a poor attempt at ignorance. Julian knew as well as the others the pretty glasses had enamoured Meg. If they weren't in the strongbox there was only one other place they could be.

'Well, until you remember where they are, Alex and Ethan will spend some time reacquainting themselves. There is a score to be settled, I believe. And you, Julian, will bid farewell to your parents. For there is a debt to be squared too for those boots. I swear on my mother's memory I have never met such a difficult lot of young people. Sneaks and thieves, all of you.'

Gentleman Charles resumed his position in the squatter's chair as Alex dragged Ethan from the veranda into the yard.

'Gentleman Charles, please don't do this,' pleaded Odiene, wrapping a supportive arm around Laura's shoulders as she wept.

'Attend to my eye,' he commanded her.

'Yes, yes. But please don't hurt Julian or Ethan. They only came to your camp because of me.'

Her words fell on deaf ears. The tent-packer roughly grabbed Julian and pushed him through the front door of the homestead.

The last Julian saw of Ethan was him being tied to the fence, his arms outstretched as if imploring the Lord.

⊰ Chapter 56 ⊱

Julian was shoved into the dim, narrow hallway and then into the abandoned part of the homestead. The door that separated this part of the house from their normal living quarters closed firmly behind him, the latch rattling. He listened through the wall. Odiene and Laura were whispering close by, then the house grew quiet. A band of sunlight filtered through a ceiling crack onto his shirtsleeve, the same light slanting through spaces in the boarded-up windows. Mice droppings crunched underfoot, and Julian could hear scurrying noises of creatures unused to disturbance. The air was hot and stuffy.

He moved along the hall, feeling the warped boards and the way the floor sloped to the left. Saw the tide mark from the Great Flood, high on the wall. The majority of the soft furnishings had been ruined when the water came. French rugs and upholstery. Paintings and clothing. Family mementoes. Most of Rachael's jewellery had never been found; carried away through an open window, perhaps. On occasion he overheard his mother speaking to Laura about the fine silk gowns lost to the inundation and the salvaged curtains used to make dresses. Of her magnificent pearls, bejewelled hair pieces and the majority of the Dalhunty silverware, all eventually pawned.

The last time – in fact, the only time – Julian had been in this area of the homestead he was just a boy. Davey was yet to be born and Meg was tottering about on chubby legs, dragging a doll along the ground with a piece of string. He had come to find his father, the reason for this lost with time. His searching had led him three doors down, to the only door ajar.

Julian had found Ben sitting on the end of a four-poster bed. There was a cover on it of red and green. Forest green, his father explained, purchased by Alfred after the flood. Not the piecemeal works covering their beds, but a rich, vibrant coverlet made from thick material. A fringed canopy shielded the bed and candles hung from the ceiling, each resting within miniature glass holders. Each holder connected to an arm, also made of glass and each arm descended from the centre, where ribbons of glass cascaded downwards like trickling water.

It was a room fit for a king.

'Eighteen candles,' his father explained when he looked from the floor to his young son gawping at the chandelier. 'Delivered by the caseload. A slaughtered whale to illuminate the long nights. The sailors cut a hole in the poor creature's head and bucketed the spermaceti out. Drained it and dried it and voila, there was light. We are all usable, you see. Beyond the obvious. Even your grandfather. Maybe now he's dead he'll summon rain.'

Julian had been in awe of this new world. A forbidden world. A world just beyond his own. The four-poster bed. The leather-topped desk. The square pigeonholes that once held so many letters. The stacks of paper that toppled to the floor in the breeze.

It was on this day that Ben had nailed closed the windows and secured the latch on this part of the house. It was as if he had known that with the passing of his father the glory days of Dalhunty Station were already slipping away and he could not bear to live among its fading grandeur.

'It shouldn't have come to this,' his father had said.

Outside that very same door, nearly sixteen years later, Julian hesitated. Then he stepped across the threshold.

His father lay propped up on pillows in that very same four-poster bed.

His mother rose upon seeing him, running her palms down her blouse, clasping them together, loosening, clasping them again. 'Julian! You've come home!' She tried her best at a welcome. 'Come,' she entreated. 'Come.'

She was leaner since he had last seen her, at the river the day of Ethan's escape. There was a rangy, wild look to her, not improved by her hair, which was now almost entirely grey. He realised that she was already displaced in the world by the sale of the property. As he was. As they all were. Strangely, he had rather assumed she would have been pleased. The bush did not suit her, probably never had. But now there was nowhere to run to.

'Come say hello to your father.' His mother addressed the prone figure in the bed, 'Ben. Ben? It's Julian. He's come back to us. And Meg, is she with you too, and Ethan? Did you bring Ethan home?' she asked.

Even now it was there, a lilt in her voice for the favoured one. 'Yes, they're all here. As well as Miss Odiene Carlisle, an acquaintance who needed our help. But Wesley hasn't found Meg yet. So you must keep that to yourself,' he told her.

'Good. Good. She's a scratchy child, but smart. What do those men want with you, Julian? Mr Wesley said you stole from him and—'

'The man is a criminal, don't be fooled by him.'

She clenched her hands in worry.

His father's wiry frame rested on patched sheets, his attire almost normal. A buttonless blue Crimean shirt with a wide V-neck and collar showed the angled bones of his chest and stripy blue veins. Curling toenails peeped out from baggy cord trousers. This was how the end came. The unhealthy pallor. The laboured inhalations. A shaking arm that rose trembling. Julian went to him,

362

trying his best to remain composed, aware the line between life and death was now almost invisible.

'Why is Father in here?' he asked brusquely.

'The day those men arrived, he begged me to move him. He said it would be safer.' Rachael's voice quavered.

Julian held tight to his father's hand. Somehow Julian's was now larger, browner, stronger. Ben's grip was loose, the calluses on his palm still there, the skin of a man beaten by his livelihood. Julian wasn't ready for his father to leave him. Wasn't ready for what it would mean: the end of one age and the beginning of another. He patted the scrawny arm and squeezed his father's hand. He felt the pressure returned and saw a glimmer of life in the man before him, as his own eyes welled.

The canopy over the bed was long gone. The chandelier now festooned in cobwebs. The moth- and mice-infested brocade coverlet lay balled against a wall. Even the space once occupied by the desk and swivel chair were empty. A sagging chair in a corner held a frill-necked white shirt, and the toffee-coloured trousers.

'He shouldn't be in here,' Julian said to Rachael. He wanted to add it was morbid, requesting to be moved to this room of all places. The dying room. Blast Meg, even now she was in his head. 'Father?' He leant closer. Ben was thin and one cheek sagged lower than the other, but he was still there. Inside. Julian could see it in his eyes.

'Water,' his father said croakily.

'Yes, dear.' His mother patted his arm. 'He drinks so much. It's not a half hour since I fetched a glass.' She took the cut-glass jug from the washstand and disappeared from the room. Julian listened to her retreating footsteps then heard the knock at the door at the hall's end and its squeaky opening.

''Bout time.' Meg squirreled out from under the bed.

'What the devil?!' Julian exclaimed.

'Come on.' Meg dragged the fox out by the scruff of his neck. The animal sniffed the air and began exploring the room.

'I told you to stay put with Odiene.' Julian wanted to berate her, but he was so pleased Meg was safe he kept quiet.

'I don't listen to youse anymore. I ain't got no brother.' She pulled her chin determinedly to her chest.

'Stop being ridiculous.'

Meg raised an eyebrow and clambered up onto the wide bed, crossing her legs. 'The day would 'ave been gone before youse two boys decided on doing anything.'

Julian frowned at his sister and she looked straight through him, clicking her fingers at the fox until he sat obediently.

'It's better they think I'm poorly. They leave us alone,' replied his father haltingly. His speech was slurred, and a thin line of drool glistened from where it fell from his lips. Their father was as ill as Meg described, but he could speak.

'But you *are* poorly,' said Julian.

Their father struggled up on the bed, moved his head from side to side and moaned. 'Delirium death tremors. That's what the one-eyed cove called them. And if a man's dying then it's best he's in the dying room, readying for the golden sliprails.'

Meg giggled. 'He's right.'

Julian scratched his head. 'So you're not—'

'Dying? Granted I'm not at my best, but neither am I ready to drop from the old perch when least expected like that insufferable Rhode Island Red your mother once purchased in Bourke. Double-combed Hamburgs, they're the ticket, although Reginald seems to have been muddled by our new arrivals. He crows at the most peculiar times. You might bring him to me when all this kerfuffle is over so he and I can have a little chat. Man to man,' his father stated with satisfaction.

'You two are as bad as each other.' Julian walked from the bed to the window, where the gaps between the planks of timber allowed a partial view of the palm trees. He counted slowly, the action doing little to relieve the anger. His father was waiting patiently, watching with admiration as Meg lay some small stones on the bedclothes. Ammunition for her slingshot. Even now with a murderer in their home his father was joking, making light of the ominous situation they were in. Was this impractical man with his liking for clothes and chickens shrewder than all of them?

'Mother doesn't know you're pretending?'

'You know how she is, Julian,' Ben said finally.

'And how did you get in here, Meg?' asked Julian.

'You can tell that person, Father, that I came through the wall Ethan tried boarding up. The Natural ain't good at everything.' She spoke as if she'd known this all along and then grew sombre. 'They killed my dog, Father. Shot him as if he were nothing. People who hurt dogs are no-good, lowlife—'

'That about covers dog-killers,' Ben interrupted in his slow drawl.

'You took the opera glasses, didn't you, Meg?' accused Julian.

Meg placed the stones back in her pocket. 'You stole a dead man's boots. Anyways, how was I to know a man like that would be . . . would be . . .'

'Sentimental?' their father finished.

'Sentimental,' repeated Meg.

'You have to give them back,' Julian told her.

'I lost them.' Meg lifted her head and inspected the room, as if suddenly her environment was of prime importance.

'You're lying.'

'Now, now. If your sister does have these glasses, and she gives them back, will Mr Wesley and his men leave without further incident?'

Julian looked directly at his father. 'I don't know.'

His father nodded. 'My thoughts as well, son. Criminals are an unknown quantity. Your grandfather employed several ticket-of-leave men in 1870. One of them stole supplies from the storehouse on a regular basis and sold the goods for profit to neighbouring stockmen. When he was caught, he blamed the Aboriginal people. I'll not risk my family's safety on supposition. You must buy us some time, Julian, while Meg rides to Fraser.'

'Fraser?' repeated Julian. 'And what good will he do us?'

'Julian knows, Father. Not that it matters much to him,' said Meg.

'I'm sorry, son. The land rightfully should have been yours. It took two generations to make our fortune and one generation to break it.'

'It's not your fault. The Captain deceived you and—'

His father signalled Julian. 'Yes he did. A stolen Steinway is no small issue. I was a marked man by the time I reached Bourke. I was accused, abused and then absolved. The Captain's trickery has been hard to accept, however that is no excuse for my ineptitude.' He patted the bedclothes and Meg scrambled to sit next to him. 'My father liked to read. His father, your great-grandfather, as well. Self-taught, they were. Clever men. Good at acquiring things. Money. Land. People.' He plied the sheet with his fingers. 'But to hang on to those things a person's mind has to be right. Sometimes I'm not sure mine is. It twists about you see, son. Always has. It goes one way, helter-skelter, then another. God save us. There was only me to keep the wolf from the door.'

'Don't say that, Father, it's not your fault,' said Julian. It was one thing to be aware of their father's incompetence, quite another for it to be admitted.

Their father patted Meg's hand. 'I suspect Mr Fraser would be none too pleased to discover the land he has so recently purchased for himself has been invaded by bushrangers. They are bushrangers, aren't they, Julian?'

'They're not good men.' Julian thought of the charges Gentleman Charles had levelled against them. The man had been indignant in the defence of his position, in the way he blamed Julian, Ethan and Odiene for their misdemeanours. The balance of right and wrong was out of kilter. Wesley had cause to be annoyed.

From within the homestead came voices. The screech of the latch at the end of the hallway announced their mother's imminent return.

'I'll ride like the wind.' Meg kissed her father on the cheek and ran to the coverlet balled against the wall. She was through the gap with the fox and tugging the bunched material back into place before Julian could respond.

His mother's footsteps sounded along the hallway.

'Julian, my shotgun is under the bed. Load it for me, will you?'

Julian lifted the double-barrelled gun from beneath the four-poster, took the box of shells next to it and slid the 12-gauge cartridges into the chamber.

'Out here it's more natural for a man to be blown away in a storm, rusted, struck by lightning, white-anted or swept into the Darling by the next flood than be confronted by bushrangers,' said his father. 'Shootings and hangings happen infrequently in the west now, unless self-inflicted. Let us hope we don't change history today.'

They listened to crockery rattling outside. Rachael called for the door be opened. Julian slid the shotgun under the bed, as his father quickly told him that the silverware was hidden in the flour barrel in the pantry.

'Protect your mother and sisters,' his father whispered. 'Don't worry about me.'

When Julian protested Ben grew stern.

'No buts, Julian. Whatever else those men want, start by giving back those boots.' His father reached out his hand and Julian grasped it. 'You're a fourth generation Dalhunty, the last of our name, and you'll do far better than me. You're the best of us, even Ethan knows that.'

A wedge of sadness loosened somewhere inside him, and Julian only just managed to hold back the tears.

'Julian? Are you in there? Will you please open the door?' his mother called impatiently.

'Go on. Don't keep her waiting. You know how she hates tardiness.' His father released his grip. 'Julian, no one is born with a manual on how to raise children or lose them.'

His mother opened the door and bent down to pick up the tray from the floor. 'Was it such an imposition for you to help me?' She entered the room with a rustle of her skirts, carrying water, soup and bread. 'Where are you going now?'

Julian barely slowed to answer. 'To buy us some time,' he replied.

⋘ Chapter 57 ⋙

The tent-packer met Julian at the locked door and escorted him to the main part of the house. There, he found Alex perusing the contents of the drawing-room bookcase, selecting weighty tomes and blowing dust from the covers as he briefly flicked through the pages. Wesley was reclining on the couch, his boots resting on the floral pattern. He was examining one of the grinding stones that formed a part of the collection belonging to Julian's great-grandfather. Julian waited in the doorway, the muzzle of the tent-packer's pistol needling into his lower back. One corner of the room was crowded with Aunt Nancy's small tables and wingback chairs, and gilt-framed paintings were stacked one on top of the other. The tent-packer pushed Julian further into the room and shut the door leaving Julian alone with the two men.

'Crush a man's head, this would.' Gentleman Charles tossed the stone into the air, allowing it to fall to the floor with a thud. Then he interlaced his fingers across his wide girth. 'I wasn't convinced you were of the same family – the Dalhuntys. One of the great empire-makers in the bush. I doubted it, but then a past conversation with Captain Ashby came back to me. A ludicrous yarn of floodwater and a riverboat thrashing through the scrub, and Benjamin Dalhunty and his missus on the homestead roof with a whining baby. Alex tells me there is a tree on the banks of the river with a D carved into the trunk and a wooden platform next to it. I've heard stories of a Dalhunty reciting verse while staring at the Darling.'

'My great-grandfather. Would you mind removing your filthy boots from my mother's furniture,' said Julian firmly.

'My humblest apologies. A man's home is his castle.' Gentleman Charles sat upright and made a show of brushing the armrest, picking at a fraying strand of material. 'The grandeur has faded somewhat.' His statement was matched with a survey of the room. 'And the mahogany table we saw at the river. Are your family partial to supping there at dusk?' he enquired with amusement. 'Have you a menagerie of servants hidden away to cart domed dishes at your leisure?'

Julian wanted to say it was none of his business, however he knew the man was easy to rile, despite the showman's flair. This interview was part exploratory and part diversion from the inevitable. He preferred not to prolong the latter. 'I have not been here to move it. The furniture belonged to my aunt.'

'Ah, yes. The benefits of money in a family. Although this is not quite as I imagined. Had you been wealthy I would have been all airs and graces, politely stated my case, sought compensation for my losses, and left. One doesn't want to upset the aristocracy. But as you are decidedly not monied, I am compelled to seek damages in other ways.' He wiped at the fluid dribbling down his cheek. 'Miss Carlisle has recommended salt washes and bandaging. We shall see how competent she is.'

'Miss Carlisle is not a doctor,' stated Julian.

'Then she shouldn't act like one.' Gentleman Charles folded the handkerchief in half.

'Miss Carlisle was coerced into helping you.' Julian's voice rose.

The man on the couch gave a snort and slapped his thigh. 'I do like you, Julian. And that wonderful haughtiness you possess can only come from having a famous name. What I wouldn't have given for the same. But we are all born to take different paths. Yours, I fear, is going downhill. Mine, however, is on the up.'

Alex stopped surveying the novels. 'Have you got anything with pictures?'

'Where's Ethan?' Julian noticed Alex's nose was crusted with blood; it seemed Ethan had been able to land at least one punch. *Good for you*, he thought.

'Enjoying the sun. It's something newcomers to Australia struggle with. The heat.' Gentleman Charles tapped his head. 'Addles the mind. Makes any man slow to defend himself. Isn't that right, Alex?'

Alex dropped the book he held onto the floor and selected another. 'Here's one.'

Hopping on one foot and then the other, Julian tugged at Michael Flannery's battered leather boots until his ruined feet were freed. He was on the verge of throwing the boots across the room until he remembered where he was. His mother's drawing room. He sat the boots on the floor. 'If you hurt him . . .'

'Shoe peddlers are of no use to us.' Alex tucked a book under his arm and looked from the discarded boots to Julian.

'We're considering going north,' said Gentleman Charles. 'Do you know much about the country in Queensland, Julian? It occurs to me a young man such as yourself, being of Dalhunty blood, would have an inbuilt knowledge of livestock. I would value someone of your experience at my side and if you were agreeable, the debt you owe Alex could be repaid in far more affable circumstances. You may even make some money from the bargain.'

'You want me to help you steal?' replied Julian, affronted.

'One man's property is another's opportunity, and it seems to me, young Julian, you and your family are in need of opportunity.'

'And if I agree to this scheme?'

'When we depart we would do so peacefully, thankful for your hospitality. I'm not one to impose on a family who will soon be grieving for a father, however if you don't come willingly, I fear the situation may deteriorate.'

So there was no choice at all. 'And Odiene?'

'Ah, yes. The lovely Miss Carlisle. We will wait a day or so and see if her ministrations provide me with relief. If so, once the stitches are removed Miss Carlisle will be free from service.' He moved closer to Julian. 'I admire a man of chivalry but I detect more than a passing interest in her welfare.'

'Where is she?'

Gentleman Charles gestured graciously. 'In the kitchen. And Julian . . . my opera glasses, if you please. We won't be leaving until they are returned.'

⋘ Chapter 58 ⋙

Odiene was looking out the window above a slanted board, which had been secured there after Laura's escape. One of Gentleman Charles's men was patrolling the yard. The ruffian strolled casually back and forth, drawing on a pipe and stopping now and then to concentrate on scratching his groin, which he attacked with blatant ferocity. Behind Odiene, on the kitchen table, the contents of the taxidermy kit were arranged neatly on a piece of cloth, each instrument cleaned and polished, a sharpening stone next to one of the blades. Laura was absorbed in the stirring of two large pots on the table. So engrossed that she was unaware of Julian standing in the doorway. Odiene shifted slightly and he saw it was the tent-packer who had captured her attention through the window. She twitched a scalpel against the folds of her skirt.

'I could put enough lye in this soap to eat straight through their skin.' Laura poked at the mixture to ensure the ashes were settled and then skimmed the lye from the top of the pan and added it to a pot of boiled down sheep fat. 'That's if they bathed. By the stench of them, it's once a year. And that Mr Wesley, trying to disguise the odour with lavender water. Lavender water. My father said he considers himself a dandy. Whoever heard of a dandy on the Darling.' She mixed the tallow and lye together and began spooning it into oblong wooden soap moulds, the concoction spilling onto the table from the shaking spoon. 'If those men keep on eating our sheep, I'll have to make candles next. We can't waste the fat. Maybe we can sell the candles in Bourke or barter them for accommodation. Meg has told you, hasn't she, Odiene? About the property being sold. But I'm sure Father will have a plan. He has always been one for ideas.' Then Laura burst into tears. She sat heavily in one of the chairs at the table, tugging the scarf from her hair.

Odiene placed the scalpel with the other instruments and went to her. She started upon noticing Julian at the door. Would she have gone to him if they were alone? Perhaps the fear they felt would draw them closer.

'Look, Julian is here,' she said gaily.

At that moment Alex came slouching along the breezeway, pushing Julian into the kitchen. 'Behave yourselves,' Alex warned as he shut the door between the kitchen and the breezeway connecting the rest of the house, locking it securely.

'Julian?' Laura wrapped her arms about his waist and he held her as she sobbed.

'Come on, sis. Everything will be all right.' Julian looked over Laura's head to Odiene. She was doing her best to remain composed, although the strain of the past days showed. He thought of their brief time together – fewer than seven days. Of their riding side by side and their single kiss. 'Odiene, Wesley told me once the stitches are out he won't be needing your services. All going well. Come, Laura. Cheer up.' He held her at arm's length. 'Meg has gone to find Mr Fraser and Father's not as ill as he would have Wesley believe.'

'Really? You've seen Father? I thought he was very sick. Mother said so.'

He wiped a tear from her cheek with his thumb. 'Nothing's ever as hopeless as it seems. I bet young Fraser cursed black and blue when you refused him.'

'I probably should have said yes. He's not that ugly,' sniffed Laura. 'If we had married, Mr Fraser might have allowed everyone to stay on and manage the property on his behalf. But you wouldn't have stayed, would you, Julian?'

Was he so transparent that everyone knew of his discontent? 'No, I wouldn't have. Managing is not the same as owning. Listen to me, Laura. Gentleman Charles will be leaving very soon. We must simply wait it out. I want you to go to your room and get some sleep so you can look after Father tonight while Mother rests. I'll take over here and cook. Will you do that for me?'

Laura hovered by the table, indecisive, as if not confident in Julian's culinary skills. A fair assessment. Nonetheless her tiredness won out and she recited the food that needed to be prepared. The flour was in the pantry for the four loaves of bread the men would consume. Three joints of mutton were in the meat safe, and potatoes needed to be roasted. And the tea-leaves were to be reused. She had hidden the tea cannister. Laura cleaned up the spilt lye on the table, tucked the damp cloth through the waistband of her apron, and with a final inspection of the kitchen, knocked on the door.

Alex opened it and moved back for her to pass. 'I'll be just outside if you need anything, Julian,' the man said. 'Let me know if he's not up to the task, Miss Carlisle.'

'What is he talking about?' asked Odiene.

'Get out.' Julian slammed the door, barring Alex from the room. 'Nothing. Forget him.'

'You're very good with Laura,' commented Odiene. 'Has Meg truly gone for help?' They kept their voices low, conscious of Alex guarding the door.

'Hopefully, yes, but we can't depend on her success. There is a better, safer way.'

'You're going to leave with Gentleman Charles?' she said softly.

Julian searched for a hint of how she felt about his going. 'Yes, once Meg returns the opera glasses. I don't have any choice, but it means you will all be safe.'

'But when Mr Fraser comes—'

'*If* Fraser comes,' clarified Julian.

'You don't believe he will?'

'I don't trust him. He doesn't think the way we do. He's—'

'Not from an established bush family. That's what you're trying to say. Laura told me all about the Frasers. Just because he worked his way up from employee to landowner does not mean he is immune to the differences between right and wrong. You people with your fine pedigrees and lofty ideals. And why would you even consider going with those dreadful men? Give them something instead. Anything. Laura said you have fine silver and . . . and . . .' She switched furiously at an unsuspecting moth flying through the window.

'I have no delusions of grandeur, but I refuse to give what remains of the Dalhunty silver away. I want my sisters to have a small piece of our history. I'm sorry if you expected more on your arrival here.' He didn't want to hear her politely disagree. They were what they were. 'Maybe my opinion of Fraser is wrong – Captain Ashby certainly gave us all a fine lesson in deception – but I'll not risk my family or you. If Fraser rides in, well and good, if not—'

'You can't go with Gentleman Charles. You might be with them for years.'

'And how do I wrangle myself free of his debt? I have no money. No prospects.' It was a useless situation. 'You must understand I have no choice.'

'You can't go.'

The curve of her mouth suggested there was more she wanted to say. Much more. He took a step forward as a rush of nerves merged with hope. He took another step, and another, until her river-washed hair was within reach. He touched a strand, felt the fine structure of her shoulder, the slight muscle beneath the flesh of her arm. His every move was measured and careful, lest he had misread her. He waited as if the moment might pass, expecting Odiene to swat away his affection, like the moth that lay crumpled on the floor.

'Odiene?' He ran a finger lightly against her neck. The afternoon light left golden tinges across her skin and blouse. 'I only mean to say . . .'

Her finger was on his lips, only briefly, then the heat of her palms burned through his shirt. He pressed his lips to her forehead. He would do nothing else to ruin the moment.

⊰ Chapter 59 ⊱

This time Julian did not draw away as he had that night on the riverboat. He felt the sharp pulse of Odiene's heartbeat against his, the pillow of her tongue, and he drew her towards the pantry, conscious of the men only a short distance away. He was desperate to keep Odiene safe and yet frantic with a powerlessness that overtook sound judgement. The closeness of her body drove Julian on. He pulled the pantry door shut and darkness descended, broken only by a scrap of light from the ceiling. The shelving squeaked with Odiene's weight. Objects rattled and fell. Familiar aromas spilt out, inundating the airless room. Cardamom, fennel and black pepper. His mother's treasured spices.

Julian ran his knuckles down the arc of Odiene's throat, absorbing each ridge of the delicate windpipe, tracing nameless dips and rises like contours on a map. They may well have been on the water, for everything was liquid, the air rippling with a black smoothness, the space listing like a floundering vessel caught midway between land and sea. Julian lifted Odiene's blouse free of the waistband. He thought of Marie, the girl at the grounded riverboat, and the blankness in her eyes and knew his would be filled with hunger. He thought again of what Marie had said and spun Odiene about. He fought with the folds of the skirt, and then the delicate drawers until the white flesh of her bottom was revealed.

'No, Julian.' She freed herself of his grip, turned and unbuttoned his trousers. 'Like this. Like this.'

The shelving shook and Julian feared it would topple.

Distantly there were muted sounds. A voice. Voices. His mother's and Alex's.

'Open the door I want to see my son! Really, the presumption. In my own home. Julian, where are you? I want Odiene to see your father.'

At his mother's voice Julian pressed Odiene to his shoulder and her teeth bit through his shirt. To move would be agony; not to move, calamity. There was only the kitchen and the space they inhabited and nowhere else to go. He released his grasp and Odiene wilted like a flower too long out of water. The strip of light showed beads of perspiration on her skin. Julian buttoned his trousers. 'Promise me you'll stay with my family until I return. Even if you end up in a boarding house in Bourke. You'll be safer.'

The pantry door swung open with a bang. Light flooded the room and Julian's mother took in their dishevelled appearance. Her mouth flapped as she drew a long, disgusted gaze from Julian's sagging trousers and untucked shirt, to Odiene, her blouse undone, her chemise showing. She gathered the edges of the blouse together but made no other attempt to hide her disarray. Instead she reached for a bowl, moving through a mat of flour and the variegated colours of spice and dipped it into a bag of rice.

His mother finally found her tongue.

'You are here in my home, a guest, and you do *this*? And how could you, Julian?'

'Please be quiet, Mother. We don't need Wesley or one of his men in here.'

His mother remained in the doorway. She shifted a little, as if she were battling an unknown internal pressure. 'You will leave my home, Miss Carlisle. Go outside and camp with those

378

heathens. Should they require your services I'm sure you won't disappoint.'

'How dare you speak to Odiene like that.' Julian moved to stand protectively in front of the young woman.

'How dare *you*, Julian. How dare *you*! Just this past hour we were speaking, this woman and I, here in this very kitchen. Oh, she's a fine one striding in here, suggesting broths for your father, offering to visit his sick bed. You've been taken in by her winsome ways. Taken in by a woman of undesirable qualities. Well, young lady, you have given your wares cheaply and there is no reward. We are not the Dalhuntys of old. There is no money here.' Rachael's voice strengthened on this last sentence as she suddenly discovered a benefit to their altered state.

'Mrs Dalhunty.' Odiene's voice was thick with emotion. 'I am not as interested in money, or the lack of it, as you seem to be.'

It was possible Rachael might slap Odiene, such was her rage. Julian maintained his position, blocking his mother's path, separating the two women. He spoke calmly but strongly. 'You have no idea what you're talking about, Mother. And I ask you to stay out of my business.'

'But it is my business. Family business. Women like her don't belong with people like us.' His mother gripped the door jamb, her knuckles matching the colour of the pine timber.

'And would you feel the same about Ethan if I told you your precious boy ran with a street gang in Sydney?' replied Julian.

'He did not.'

'Ask him. He'll tell you straight. Ethan's not ashamed. Why should he be? Not when you lied about our circumstances to him. So let's not talk about who should or should not be accepted into this family.'

Rachael peeled her fingers from the door and then turned on her heel and left the room.

Julian reached for Odiene but she pressed his cheek, warding off further intimacy.

'I knew she wouldn't like me,' she said.

⋘ Chapter 60 ⋙

It was nearing daylight when Julian lifted his head from the kitchen table, rubbed breadcrumbs from his cheek and stretched out his aching neck. The broken spice jars were on the table, a bowl of saved flour was flecked with grime. He reached for the jug of water and drank directly from the spout, the fluid splashing his shirtfront. Birds twittered. A lazy light was edging its way above the horizon. The quietness disturbed more than noise could, as he looked out the boarded window at the copper and spied a lifeless Bony on the ground.

A figure levered itself up from behind the copper. The tent-packer was too busy to notice Julian at the kitchen window. He rested the rifle on the ground and relieved himself, taking enjoyment from the fluctuating spray as he stooped and arched. Then he took hold of the dog and flung the corpse over the yard fence.

A flock of cockatoos rose from the timberline beyond the palm trees and flew towards the house. They perched, screeching, in a nearby tree. The birds may well have been startled by something and it seemed the tent-packer thought the same. Clutching the rifle, he left the homestead yard, climbed the fence and headed out into the paddock. He reached the edge of the palm grove and then abruptly pivoted to the west and then the east and then back towards the homestead. Just what had captured his attention was unclear, however Julian wasn't immune to the man's concern. There was a definite change in the air, as if out in the scrub, where cultivated land met the edges of wildness, the unfamiliar was stirring.

Julian tried the kitchen door, and finding it still bolted returned to the window. If he attempted to kick the plank barring his escape the entire household would be woken by the splintering of timber and the smash of glass. He rummaged in a drawer. The sharpest knives were missing – confiscated. He found a peeling knife, running his thumb across the dull blade. It would have to do. Julian squeezed his arm through the gap between glass and timber. The hammered nails were not flush to the wood. He gave a satisfied *humph* at the shoddy workmanship and lodged the knife blade under a nail head. The steel was not quick to give so he angled an elbow out further, hoping for greater purchase, while out in the paddock Wesley's man slowly patrolled the area.

Julian dug the blade deeper into the timber, flicked his wrist and prised the nail free. Then he set to work on the next.

Another of Wesley's men came into view. Julian recognised the shoulder-length hair and distinct leggy gait. Alex was walking from the direction of the stables, his progress marked by long strides. Alex called cooee and upon seeing the tent-packer let out another, his voice ringing out clear and loud. Then he hunkered down low and scraped at the earth. Fronds and leaves were pitched into the air. Alex had found one of Frank's holes.

Julian saw them then. A line of shapes in the distance, beyond the swaying palms. At first he thought perhaps his mind was playing tricks. It had been known to happen. A play of light across shimmering air. But the figures remained, as if charmed into existence. Distinct. Not moving, just standing. Waiting. Ready. The hairs pricked on Julian's arms. He thought he smelt pipe smoke on the wind.

'Ridiculous. You're being ridiculous,' he told himself.

The tent-packer saw the figures and in acknowledgement started to back away. His retreat was slow, hampered by sticks and palm fronds and broken ground and the frequent twisting of his neck as he checked the path behind him and then swivelled the rifle in the direction of the stationary figures.

And then, the tent-packer was gone. Vanished from view.

Julian stopped trying to prise the nails free and waited for the man to reappear. Some of Frank's holes were deep, too deep for a short man to climb free from, but the tent-packer only needed to yell out to be heard. In the absence of a call for help, Alex remained oblivious to his friend's disappearance. He maintained a steady walk, the rifle slung nonchalantly over a shoulder, a stick in his grasp, which he used as a mountain climber might, as if aiding his balance on unstable trails as he poked the ground for camouflaged holes.

A blur of movement caught Julian's attention, followed by a noise that may or may not have been human, and Henrietta materialised from the scrub. She charged through the palm grove, her body swinging from side to side, neck outstretched, head held high. On her back, Frank cursed and yelled at the top of his lungs as he swung an object and bore down on the tent-packer, who was now climbing from the hole. He struck the man in the side of the skull and he fell back into the bowels of the earth.

Alex released the stick and remained quite still, then he bent low and darted for cover at the base of a palm. He glanced around the trunk and loaded the rifle. Frank was trotting Henrietta towards him, oblivious to the danger.

Julian threw the scalpel aside and pushed at the plank until it cracked. Then he kicked the board free, smashing the glass, before diving out the window. He picked himself up from the hard landing and cupped his mouth.

'Frank! Watch out!'

Alex glanced in Julian's direction as Frank reined in the camel, veering Henrietta away as if flipping a shilling. The camel took neat, fast strides, plaiting her way through palms and holes to safety. Alex's shot was wasted.

Out where land and sky met, the space was empty. Julian scanned the area that only earlier seemed to be filled with people. A wash of streaky light filtered down through the distant timber. He searched for Fraser's men. Searched for what was there no longer. He couldn't understand it. He looked back towards the house. His father's woolly head was angled between glass and wood at the window to the dying room.

'Julian?' he called.

'Everything's all right, Father.'

From within the palm grove another rider galloped. Julian recognised the spearing placement of the hooves, the thrusting motion of strength and the kerosene-tin hatted figure of his sister. Meg never swerved from her path.

'No!' screamed Julian.

Meg rode Goliath straight at Alex, and as the shot echoed across the wakening countryside, Meg barrelled into her attacker, and then fell from the saddle.

⪻ Chapter 61 ⪼

Frank said *hooshta* so faintly it may have been the wind whispering through grass. At the signal, Henrietta sank slowly, her callused knees folding from front to back, thick lips emitting a guttural grunt. Frank slid from the camel and cradled Meg. She was dressed in a concoction of home-made armour. A bundle of hide and cotton and tin. The cuffs of her trousers were wrapped with twine to stop them flapping, her torso thick with padding. Her helmeted head lolled to one side.

When Frank delicately placed her body in Julian's arms, he felt his legs buckle. Meg was still warm. Blood stained the slender hollows of her face. Her rosebud lips were slack. The perfectly formed brows, so often hidden by a wit so sharp it cut at times, rested serenely. Meg was slipping away to the same place as Davey, and all Julian could do was hold her against his chest. His toes clawed for purchase as he crossed the yard towards the homestead. There were too many people assembled there.

'Julian?' The Natural was tied to the fence by his wrists, such a mess of bruises and sunburn he was almost a stranger. 'You bastards!' Ethan screamed, when he saw Meg in Julian's arms.

He strained at the paling fence. 'You shot a girl. *A girl.* Do you hear me, you ugly lump of lard?' He shook the paling fence, screwed his shoulders close to dislocation, bones and muscles bubbling. He pushed at the slats of timber and with an almighty yell, the fence gave way. He ran towards the veranda, his wrists still tied to pieces of timber that spun with velocity like monstrous wheels. Ethan barrelled into Gentleman Charles, striking him with his paddle limbs before Alex was able to restrain him.

A tightening sensation wrenched through Julian's chest. It was as if his life was being funnelled into a distant place. What was he to do if his little sister no longer walked beside him? He saw his movements from above and knew with a clarity how the day would end. He stepped up onto the veranda.

'Leave Ethan alone,' he said forcefully.

Wesley righted his clothes and swept his hair to straighten the parting on his head, as if disconcerted not only by the attack but by the scene playing out before him. 'Untie the lad, Alex. We don't need the homestead demolished by those thrashing planks.'

Alex cut the ropes binding Ethan and the fence palings fell on the veranda.

Ethan kicked at the pieces of timber.

'This wasn't meant to be.' Gentleman Charles pressed at his black eyepatch and spoke directly to his right-hand man. 'You wild Irish, you must always have your pound of flesh. And for what? A pair of boots, Alex. *Boots.*'

'Get Mother,' Julian said, to no one, to everyone, although it was Laura he sought out. She swayed, as if the slightest nudge might topple her.

'Yes. Yes, get Mrs Dalhunty.' Gentleman Charles was slow to respond. He addressed his four remaining men, who were standing about with slack jaws and downcast eyes. Only Alex answered the order and he did so with a gait no longer leggy and confident but stiff and uneven.

Julian pushed away the bile in his throat as Laura vomited over the side of the veranda. It was as if all the blood was draining from

Julian's limbs and pooling into the soil, making liquid of muscle, bone and sinew. He found he was unable to move. Odiene gently led him indoors.

Once they were inside, Alex unwired the door leading into the old portion of the homestead. A shiver centred in Julian's spine. *No.* He was not taking his sister to the dying room. *Never. Never. Never.* The dying room was for old men, gutted by wire or speared in revenge. The buckled floorboards creaked, and jutting nails bit into the wrecked flesh of his soles. The hallway stretched out as if it were the river Stix.

The procession moved along the hallway to the kitchen. Ethan led, trailed by Julian. Laura and Odiene behind. Frank walked slowly behind them, forcing Gentleman Charles to keep a distance.

Meg's limp fingers brushed the wall like the child she was. A thousand happier images crowded in on Julian. There she was pulling a doll by a string, pressing daisies in the drawing room, playing soldiers with Davey. Somehow his little sister had tumbled from childhood too soon.

Laura mumbled a prayer as Ethan cleared the kitchen table in one movement. Flour, spices and their mother's blue-and-white plates clanged and smashed. Julian lay Meg down and straightened her arms and legs, removed the splayed kerosene tin helmet and then the wadding. He sat the helmet on a chair. Gentleman Charles was leaning against the doorframe.

'Get out!' Julian shouted. 'Get out!'

'It was a simple undertaking,' Gentleman Charles bawled back. 'Odiene was to repay a favour owed. Then you arrived. Put your nose into my affairs. Stealing things. Stealing! And now that man of yours' – he pointed at Frank – 'has attacked one of my men. Alex is witness to his heathen crime and he will pay for it.'

Frank gave a low hiss and pulled back the sack coat he wore to reveal a stirrup iron rammed into a leather belt.

Gentleman Charles felt for the reassurance of the pistol at his waist. 'That girl tried to kill Alex.'

Julian pushed the man outside and slammed the kitchen door.

They gathered close to the table as Odiene leant over Meg. She took the scalpel from the taxidermy kit and cut the leather cord lacing the kangaroo coat at the waist and sliced through three layers of men's shirts. The spirited heart of his sister was covered by a thin chemise. Odiene pressed an ear to Meg's chest. Felt her wrist. Called to Laura to boil water.

'Well?' Julian asked. Meg was still warm. Not cold like Davey. Not stiff like Michael Flannery. But there was too much blood. It matted Meg's hair, speckling her like dust. 'Well?' he repeated, louder.

'Her pulse is thready, but she's alive. I'll have to wash the wound and see—'

Ethan held up the splayed tin helmet. There was a hole in the side of it. A bullet hole. Laura gave a gasp and started reciting another prayer. Frank joined her, their voices tumbling together, Laura's soft, interspersed with crying, Frank's loud and resonant.

The door opened and Rachael rushed to Meg, cooing like a dove to a fledgling chick fallen from its nest. She bustled in front of Odiene as if she wasn't there and kissed Meg's brow, then set about parting her hair to find the cause of the blood.

Ethan kept his distance from the table. 'I can't stay here and not do anything.'

'There's nothing to be done,' replied Laura. 'Look how white she is. And the blood. There is so much of it.'

Her mother struck her, hard. 'Don't you dare give up. You must never give up. We must wash her and talk to her and Odiene will help me and we will do what we can. Won't you, Odiene, for the Lord knows you have much to make up for.'

Odiene coolly sorted through the taxidermy instruments as Laura fed the stove with more kindling, the flickering flames matching the red welt on her cheek. Odiene rubbed Laura's back and was rewarded with teary gratefulness, then she lay forceps, the needle in the square of felt, and a roll of thread on the table.

'Your father saw what happened through the window.' Rachael concentrated on working her way through her daughter's hair. 'I told him she was all right. I told him . . .' She sniffed and briefly buried her head in the arm of her blouse leaving wet patches from her tears, then she fetched clean rags and dropped them in the simmering water.

Odiene added drops of lavender oil to the water and held her hands under for as long as she could bear, then picked out a rag with tongs. With the cloth squeezed dry she proceeded to dab at the wound.

'Frank, where are the Frasers?' asked Julian.

'Fraser? Meg went in search of him. She left a message with one of their stockmen.'

'But he's here. You must have seen them. That's what disturbed the cockatoos. At least ten or so men out beyond the dry soaks,' Julian insisted.

Frank tugged at his long nose. He had not seen anything.

Julian bent low, folding himself over as if in doing so he might make sense of things. He uncurled his limbs. If it was not Fraser's men, then who was it? Aboriginal people on walkabout? A wishful illusion. Or the old Dalhuntys, long buried? What did it matter? It was as he suspected. No one was coming to their aid. Even if Meg survived, soon he would be ferried across the river to wander the great expanse of Queensland at Gentleman Charles's pleasure. His family would be left to wither, while their contemptible neighbour stalked Dalhunty land.

'Give me the scalpel, Odiene,' he said.

Odiene, intent on cleaning Meg's wound, lifted the forceps and released the wad of bloody cotton into a basin. She looked at Julian with a dumb expression and then selected the scalpel from the row of implements and drew it slowly behind her back. Her mouth settled into a determined line. 'No. You'll make everything worse – that's if you don't get killed yourself. And Meg wouldn't want this,' she pleaded.

'Meg would say we were ijits for not doing anything,' countered Ethan.

Rachael twisted her wedding band. 'Odiene, give my son the knife.' Her words were as flinty as sparks from a grinding stone.

'Mrs Dalhunty—'

'Give Julian the scalpel,' Rachael repeated.

Odiene placed the blade on the table. 'You are fools to believe you can best them.'

The scalpel was light in his palm. Julian kissed Meg on the cheek and left his sister's side. He wanted to speak to Odiene, to ask her once and for all if she was truly bound to the Captain. To hear her say no. Such an answer would be enough, no matter what occurred next. But how was that to be done in the crowded room? With Ethan and Laura hanging on his every word and Frank back to pacing the crockery-covered floor? He settled for a brief exchange. 'Take good care of Meg.'

'I'll do everything I can,' replied Odiene, although it was as if she too had things to say, for she held his gaze, rather than immediately returning to tending his sister.

'Mother, if the worst happens, go to our solicitor in Bourke. Demand the *Lady Matilda* be sold so you can try to recoup the piano money. It's the only way.' He nodded at Ethan. 'It will give you a start somewhere new,' he told her.

His mother wet her fingers and slicked back his hair, patting it smooth. 'We have nothing left. Only us. Only family. You hear me, Julian? You do what has to be done and then we'll all go and see the solicitor.' She gave a cracked smile, as if part of her was already broken. Julian thought of his father. How desolate he had become during his wife's absence and the change that occurred upon her return. There was something extraordinary about this woman, who had just given her blessing for Julian to do his worst.

'All right, Mother. Frank, stay here with my mother and sisters.'

The old man took up a position at the head of the table, ready to defy any ruffian that entered. Ethan searched the kitchen drawers and was rewarded with a blunt knife. He waited at the door, the bruised pulp of his face signposting a desire for revenge.

'This isn't your fight, Ethan,' said Julian. 'It was my decision to steal the strongbox and, besides, Alex has evened the score with you. This is about Meg and my family. There's no need for you to risk your life for us.'

'You're the only people I have left to fight for,' he replied.

They clasped each other, wrist to elbow. Their mutual understanding of each other only beginning to find depth.

'I'm not sure if we'll ever be friends,' said Julian.

'You'd find it difficult, me being a natural and all.' Ethan tried the door, pushing it open. 'It's not locked.' The sunniness of the day stunned. 'Will you try and negotiate with them?'

Julian took one more look at Meg lying on the table. 'No. We won't be parleying today.'

∝ Chapter 62 ≫

Beyond the breezeway the hallway was long and empty. Julian clasped the scalpel and ran, conscious of his arms and legs flailing in flight. There was a strangeness to his movements, as if he were beyond the life-sustaining elements of fire, water, air and earth. He was vaguely aware of dust and noise, and of Ethan close behind him. Of a torrid beating somewhere deep within his body that spoke of transformation and lines forever crossed. He centred on Alex, who was standing on the veranda, centred on Alex's lank dark hair, and his bitter need for revenge. Centred on what might happen if he did what could never be undone. Then he raised the scalpel and hurled himself out the front door.

A weapon fired, a loud ear-drumming blast. Julian shuddered involuntarily. He expected this and strangely he was not afraid. There was no pain. No shock or recrimination. Only the knowledge of duty failed. He clutched at his chest and gave in to the relief of not having to worry about tomorrow. He was too young to take hold of his father's reins. He waited for his legs to fail him, to sink into oblivion as Meg had done.

Alex was no longer before him. It was another man, the larger one. Wesley dropped like a pebble bouncing across water. Skipped three times. Then fell. In three slight movements, Gentleman Charles crumpled and sprawled on the withered couch grass.

'That about covers thieves and murderers,' Ben slurred, staggering under the burden of the shotgun. Very slowly he slid down the wall, upsetting the nailed stirrup irons, which fell alongside him with jarring *tings*.

Julian observed his father as if through smoggy glass. Then the haze cleared to be replaced with a musty, sulfuric smell. Ethan was calling to him and it was with disbelief that Julian realised he was whole. He ran to his father and, together with Ethan, struggled to lift him up, feeling the pull of gravity in a body past bearing its mass.

'Meg. How's my Meg?' Spittle laced the strung-out question.

'Still alive.' Ethan took the shotgun and propped it against the wall.

'That's something then, isn't it?' said Ben. He had changed his clothes and was wearing the toffee-coloured trousers and the white shirt, the frills about his scraggly neck lizard-like in appearance. 'That's something. Get me my top hat, Ethan, and my stick. I'll be needing both. We've visitors.'

Mr Fraser, Ian and a stockman were at the yard gate, their lathered horses snorting. Henrietta sashayed back and forth enjoying the horses' discomfort. She even went so far as to shimmy close enough to Mr Fraser's mount so the grand chestnut gelding gave a mighty kick, striking the fence.

Alex was leaning over Gentleman Charles' body, righting the eye-patch that had come askew.

'What in the Lord's name?' Mr Fraser dismounted and levelled a pistol at the Irishman. Under his order, Alex joined the remaining three members of Charles Wesley's gang. With sullen looks they threw their guns aside as Fraser took in the scene before him. The men were ready for a fight and they yelled for justice.

'Enough!' Mr Fraser claimed authority. 'Ian, check on that man. How hurt is he?'

His son walked to where Gentleman Charles lay. Ian knelt at Wesley's side and placed a hand a few inches above his mouth, grimacing at the man's shirtfront where a hole marked the trajectory of the gunshot. He shook his head in response and then searched the man's pockets and, removing the pistol hanging at Wesley's waist, held it up as if displaying evidence.

Ethan appeared from the house with the silver-topped walking cane and a black top hat. Frank was with him. The Englishman spent scant seconds appraising the men in the yard. His currant eyes rested on Mr Fraser with dislike, then he went to Ben's aid.

'Splendid.' Ben took the items from Ethan and placing the hat rakishly to one side on his head, leant heavily on the walking cane. 'Your arm, Frank. Give me your arm. I'll not do this unassisted.' With dragging steps, the walking cane clicking, he crossed the veranda.

Mr Fraser directed Ian to guard Alex and his companions. Then he moved to the front of the homestead as Ben staggered towards him. While Fraser waited he set his gaze on Julian and Ethan, his attention drifting to the scalpel on the veranda.

'Afternoon, Ben. You've had some trouble.' Mr Fraser's understated assessment focused on Gentleman Charles, who lay among chicken feathers and the remains of a gnawed mutton leg.

Ben concentrated on descending the steps, leaning on Frank. 'They hurt my youngest. Meg. She's alive, but poorly.'

'And you're ill?' said Mr Fraser, his concern evident.

'Nonsense. I'm good for another thirty years.' He gave a shuddering cough, wobbling with the effort.

Mr Fraser studied the debris of Gentleman Charles's visit with distaste. It was hard to decipher if he really wanted to know the events leading to the deadly outcome. Julian rather suspected he may well have preferred to remain in the dark and so he wasted no time in launching forth into a full account of their misdventure. He knew his speech was garbled and his arms were flailing. Mr Fraser eyed him with increasing doubt.

'Charles Wesley? The singer?' Mr Fraser walked about the body. Wesley's all-seeing eye was staring at the heavens. Fraser hunkered down for closer inspection. 'Aye. It's him all right. Unmistakable.'

'You know him?' Julian grew concerned. Was this another example of the Scotsman's dishonesty? Was he also tangled up with the bushranger? It made sense. How else were Fraser's men able to pinpoint the arrival of the *Lady Matilda* the day they abducted the Captain?

'I saw him perform at the Tivoli in 1904. Charles Wesley has a fine voice – or *had* a fine voice. I read that once he underwent surgery for a drooping eyelid he wasn't considered stage material. And I can see why now. Unless folk are knowingly paying to see a human oddity, audiences prefer their entertainment pretty and Mr Wesley didn't pass muster. I recall he attacked a stagehand who taunted him. Killed the man, I believe. But none of that assists us in the least regarding your predicament,' said Mr Fraser. 'What the heck were you thinking, Ben?'

'He was thinking murder.' Alex shook a fist. He roused the other captured men and once again they shouted for justice. 'That's one man dead and they pushed Harold down a hole. He's out in the paddock knocked out cold. All the boss wanted was his eye tended and his opera glasses returned. And I wanted my brother's boots.'

'Opera glasses and boots?' Mr Fraser made a little circle as he took in the people assembled before him.

'My sister Meg's inside with a bullet wound to the head,' said Julian.

'That girl nearly trampled me and when she didn't, Julian tried to finish the job. And then that old man shot Gentleman Charles. In cold blood. *Cold blood.*' Alex tried to step forwards and was waved back to his place with the point of Ian's pistol.

Ben stooped lower and lower, his thin legs folding like sticks as Frank settled him on the veranda step. Ethan looked worriedly at Julian.

'Wesley's pistol was undrawn. It doesn't appear to me if any attempt was made to fire it,' said Ian almost apologetically to Ben.

Mr Fraser beckoned to Julian, who left the veranda and with leaden legs joined the new owner of their land, all the while his gaze not leaving his father. What had seemed right and just was no longer. Wesley may well have been a murderer, but Julian had wronged the man, and now he was dead.

'This is troubling, lad. I saw your father take that shot. Wesley was unarmed.' Mr Fraser held on to the lapel of his fine cloth jacket as if he were a judge delivering a verdict. He flicked open the lid of a silver pocket watch hanging from his waistcoat, as if marking the exact hour of the murder.

'But he killed a man and held us prisoner out west. Why, they were going to force me to go with them for stealing a pair of boots,' explained Julian.

This last admission stirred more than passing interest from Mr Fraser. The look he gave Julian was one of pity. Julian wanted to rant against Fraser's assumption. He knew what the Scotsman thought, that their most recent dilemma was due to their gradually changed circumstances, one that found them barely scratching a living before being forced to give up their land. Fraser considered it inevitable for the Dalhuntys to eventually resort to thievery.

'You see how this looks. You're landless. You've admitted to stealing. And your father's argument of self-defence does not have merit. Some might say desperation—'

'That man's a bushranger.' Julian was not impressed by Fraser's condescension. 'But I'm guessing you know that. So don't give me a cock-and-bull story about having heard him sing. Good mates, are you? Brokered a deal with him to get your comeuppance on Captain Ashby, I suppose. Took advantage of a hardworking man to increase your pile of coin. Who else are you buying out? What other struggling pastoralist is deserving of your help? By the time you cull us all there'll be no one left to work your precious acres.'

Mr Fraser didn't flinch. 'I don't know Charles Wesley personally, and Captain Ashby has more debts than there are sheep in the west. Lastly, my buying of your land has everything to do with opportunity and, in the case of Dalhunty Station, *your* shoddy administration.' Mr Fraser paused, to let his rebuttal settle in.

Julian may well have been outside the Bourke Town Hall being mocked by its good citizens, such was his humiliation. He digested Fraser's criticism, knowing the man was right. The Dalhuntys were the architects of their own failure, and Julian had seen it coming. Why then had he not tried harder to halt their demise? Simply because his father, Benjamin Dalhunty, was the patriarch. Every decision stopped and started with him, with a kind, quirky, loving man incapable of managing their land, and so what was once glorious had fallen through their fingers. And in response, Julian's answer to the slow decay had been to give up trying to sway his father and to simply run away.

Mr Fraser yelled over his shoulder. 'Ashby? Come here.'

Ethan was with Julian in an instant. 'The bastard,' he muttered. Julian stilled him with an arm.

The third man who had ridden in with the Frasers had stayed with the horses, beyond the yard fence. Julian saw him now as he walked through the gate. He was dressed in stockman's clothes with rotted blucher boots and a torn hat, and his cheek was scabbed and his eyes hollow, but there was no mistaking the proud angle of his shoulders, nor his full white beard.

'Speak up, Ashby,' instructed Fraser. 'Tell the lad the truth or you'll be put out on one of the furthest runs with only wire and pliers for company.'

The sidelong glance Ashby threw Mr Fraser was as slithery as a snake. There was no friendship there.

'Julian,' Captain Ashby began, 'what Mr Fraser says is true. He doesn't know Wesley.'

The statement hung heavy in the air. Julian knew he owed Fraser an apology, however it was hard to give one, to admit to his own shortcomings, particularly as he had never liked the man. Fraser had started his career as a broker trying to win the Dalhunty wool business during Julian's grandfather's time. Now he was a self-made man, rightly gratified by his achievements. That was why

Fraser's presence always chafed. With time, the Frasers would be spoken of in glowing terms and the Dalhuntys would be forgotten.

'How are you, Julian?' Captain Ashby asked.

All thought of past friendship dissipated. Julian recalled his father's fall from the dray on his return from Bourke and the reason behind it. He had sold their land, that was true, but it was his friend's betrayal that had broken Ben Dalhunty's heart. It was all Julian could do to contain his anger.

The Captain noticed his attempt at control and walked directly to where Julian's father sat on the veranda steps. Ben was leaning over to one side. Every time Frank reached across to return him to a vertical position he slanted in the opposite direction, however he straightened in recognition as Ashby knelt down before him.

'I'm sorry, Ben. Like you, I hoped for better years. Every time there was a run in the river I was sure I'd remake my business. Retire with a fortune.' He gave a nervous chuckle. 'I never was like you, able to settle for little. Contented by family. I've always wanted more. Expected more.' He removed his hat and bowed his head. 'I know what I did was unforgiveable.'

Ben lifted his arm and Julian thought his father might place it on Ashby's head, as if in absolution. It would be just like his father to let the felon leave with the undeserved present of forgiveness. However to Julian's astonishment Ben lowered his hand.

'You have done yourself a disservice. No one will ever trust you on the Murray-Darling again.' There was no anger in Ben, only the coldness of fact.

Captain Ashby raised his head, slapped the hat back on and got to his feet. 'You'll be all right. You're Dalhuntys. Why don't you go and dig up some of your father's coin? That will get you out of strife.'

'Leave,' Julian said flatly.

The Captain gave him a brief look, one verging on disinterest, and then went back to the horses. There was nothing more to add – his father had addressed the matter. All of them had realised far too late that Ashby was only a friend to the Dalhuntys for the sake of the business, and in one brief summation Ben had reminded the Captain of all he had lost.

'Ben. You do understand what has happened. A man is dead. There *will* be repercussions,' Mr Fraser stated.

'Y-yes.' Ben thumbed at his chest. 'Me. Blame me.' He tapped the walking cane on the ground until the handle came loose and he was left with the silver lion lying uselessly in his palm. The breakage seemed to cripple him anew, for he blinked and looked to Frank for guidance.

'He has gone in the mind?' queried Mr Fraser.

'Illness. It is just a passing illness.' Julian was processing what Fraser had implied, and Ben's answer. *Blame me*, he'd said. Men like his father were meant to be leaders. The fulcrum from which the bush swung. They were expected to assist in holding the strands of society together. Massage the idiots and nay-sayers to common sense and ensure the land was kept fertile for the next generation. Ben Dalhunty had been unsuccessful in many areas of his life, however no matter his handling of their affairs, Julian was proud of his father's conduct where Ashby was concerned, and he would not have Ben's character tarnished any further.

'I will take the blame for what has happened here,' he said.

Although Ethan cried out denouncing the very idea as ludicrous, he offered no other opposition. They both knew the decision was right.

Mr Fraser appeared relieved that a solution had been reached. He bound Julian's wrists with rope and informed Ethan that Julian was to remain at the homestead under house arrest until the police could fetch him.

Wesley's assembled men, still under Ian's guard, cared little for who accepted the blame for the death of Gentleman Charles, as long as someone hanged. Fraser placed Alex Flannery under citizen's arrest for the injurious shooting of Meg Dalhunty, and bound the lot of them before lashing them to their horses. They were riding directly to Bourke after Fraser spoke to Julian's mother.

⋙ Chapter 63 ⋘

Julian rubbed the welt on his wrist where the rope had been and settled in the chair next to Meg's bed. She was snoring softly, emitting a slight whistling sound. He stared at the ruby of her cheeks, the short, tight curls of damp hair. The sharp tang of tragedy had been replaced with lavender and for now she was a girl in a plain white nightgown. On the table next to the bed sat the vase of fish-scale geraniums from the drawing room and the family photograph taken on their last trip to Bourke. Meg christened the travelling photographer Mr McNasty for he had grown angry at Davey's fidgeting, twice walking from the studio in a fit of what his father called 'artistic temperament'.

He opened the back of the silver frame, removing the picture. There they were: Meg disgruntled in a dress; Laura's nose levelled a touch too high; Davey clutching the slingshot that all too soon would become Meg's. His father was for once sensibly suited, the effect ruined by a baggy cricketer's cap. Next to him the matriarch of the family sat prim and hard-featured, and there was Julian, now unrecognisable, although only a few scant years had passed.

Julian slid the photograph into a pocket and cast a final glance about the room. At the patchwork tacked to the wall, the embroidered runner at the foot of the bed, their grandmother's silver-backed hairbrush. Then he leant under the bed and found the tin of Meg's red-blonde hair. Julian selected a ringlet and tucked it next to the photograph.

His mother entered the room, watching as he replaced the tin where it belonged. She sat a hessian bag on the floor.

'Fraser and the rest of them have gone?' he asked her.

'Yes, including the man who was out in the palm grove,' she replied.

The deal had been struck in the drawing room with only Julian, Rachael and Mr Fraser in attendance. It had been a brittle meeting, with his mother straight-backed and judgemental as Mr Fraser set about explaining the cost of murder. The new owner of Dalhunty Station was unsure what charges might be levelled at Julian, and anticipated Alex Flannery would take to the role of witness with zeal. Even a Dalhunty was not above the law, and Fraser wanted to help them, which neither Julian nor Rachael had expected. Julian worried more about the subsequent ridicule once the scandal reached the papers. The stealing of the strongbox and boots. The sale of Dalhunty Station. The eccentricity of his father. And, lastly, the killing of a murderer. The good name of Dalhunty would be blackened forever by a mixture of fact, innuendo and gossip. Surely Mr Fraser grasped that the rumour-mongering might cost his family the final vestiges of respect. But the value of a venerable surname wasn't why Mr Fraser came to their aid.

Over the decades Ben had sold off the Dalhunty leaseholds, one by one, to Goldsbrough Mort & Co. using Fraser as his middle-man. And with each acquisition, the Scotsman's importance to the company had increased, as had his wealth. Mr Fraser owed his success to Ben Dalhunty and allowing Julian to decide on the best course of action – to stay and front his crime or slip away – had been his way of repaying it.

Rachael rearranged the fish-scale flowers next to Meg's bed, straightening the wire stems. 'Meg woke and asked after the fox. Funny child. No mention of family. Only her pet.'

'You're sure she'll recover?' Julian took in the small figure cocooned in bedclothes.

'Despite the copious blood, the bullet only grazed her skull. She has a lump the size of an egg. She must have knocked herself out when she fell. Miss Carlisle's in agreement.'

Satisfied with the flowers she moved about the room. Sunlight struck her features through the window. There was a gauntness to her frame now, as if the past years had backed up, one upon the other, to catch her unaware. Her wrists were angular, her fingers knobby, and the determined stance he knew so well had shrunk in stature during his time away. The woman who alighted from the riverboat with The Natural in tow was mightily changed.

'You will let Odiene stay with the family, if she chooses,' he said. 'She is capable of contributing to the household in monetary terms.' It concerned him that Odiene might not wish to go to Bourke with the rest of the family. She was a headstrong woman, one used to her independence.

At the hanging patchwork his mother stilled. 'She and I will find it difficult to coexist. Women like that—'

'Need men like me to become so.'

She regarded him closely. 'There is no future in this infatuation, Julian. Not with your leaving.'

'No one knows the future. Not even you,' he replied. 'I'm hoping you'll be cordial to her at least, and you'll keep your promise and not mention my plans to the others.'

'I agree. Your father needs no more distress and I fear there would be a general uprising if a choice were to be made. They would rather go with you than stay with their crochety mother. Will two days lead be enough?'

'It will have to be. Mr Fraser's been lenient.' Julian prayed the police investigations would confirm Wesley's illegal activities, acknowledge the man's invasion of their home and grant Julian mercy.

It was impossible to make the right choice. Wait for the arrival of the police or hide out and pray the charges were eventually dropped. Separate himself from those he loved and save them from further shame or let them be unwilling bystanders to an uncertain end. Stay or leave. Julian was not without fault and it could be construed that a feud existed between him and Charles Wesley, culminating in a revenge attack for Meg's injury. The rule of law was unclear. Prison time was looking more certain. The concern of scandal in comparison with that paled.

He would prise the boards from the western end of the homestead. His family could not be blamed for his escape if the police believed he'd been locked in the abandoned section of the house. He explained this to his mother.

'Where will you go?' she asked.

'Wallangulla. It's a good few days' ride to the northeast. Father talked of the place. It's where they mine opals. You probably know it as Lightning Ridge.' Julian willed Meg to wake, although it was far better he leave without goodbyes. 'Men lose themselves there. Make their fortune there. Maybe I'll come back a rich man.'

'It's a nowhere place,' said his mother sadly.

'It's a safe place,' he replied.

Rachael played with her wedding band. 'I don't like leaving Davey. And I worry about your father. If the change will be too difficult for him. It will be hard for us in Bourke. Small communities, you know how they are. There will be talk. And what will I do with Nancy's furniture? We can't fit it all on the dray.'

'Sell some of it. You need the money.'

She looked at him sharply. 'It means nothing to you, but to me . . .' She pressed at tears with the heel of her palm. 'There will be nothing left of the Dalhuntys except our name.'

Even that was lost to them now. Julian would have to take on a new name at Wallangulla. 'You'll speak to the solicitor about Captain Ashby?'

His mother sat on the edge of Meg's bed, finding the floorboards inordinately interesting.

'Fraser said the Captain swindled him more than once,' Julian said. 'If both families bring their cases to a lawyer, we are assured of compensation.'

This was an awkward point. His mother knew well her husband's fondness for the man who had rescued them so many years earlier and although she had been told of Ben's response on seeing Ashby she was still hesitant.

'We can't be bound forever by an act of kindness. Father's working life is over. You must do this – at least for Meg and Laura's sakes. Besides, Ashby's river trading days are finished.'

'I will do as you say.' She sat the bag on the end of the bed. Inside were his boots, the ones he'd left on the riverbank the morning he'd dived in after Ethan. His mother showed him a pair of thick woollen socks. 'I know none of you bother with socks, it is a city affectation, but God forbid a son of mine walks through life with ruined feet.' She rose and tidied the bedcover, tucking the corners under the mattress and pausing to contemplate her youngest child.

'I thought it might mend the hole Davey left, bringing Ethan here. He was such a nice, helpful lad, and with Davey gone . . . well, there's no need to talk about it. I have not always been the mother you wanted, but then this was not the life I expected when I married your father. What did I know at nineteen years of age? He was a Dalhunty. Everyone knew of the Dalhuntys. My father thought it a brilliant match. It was only after we married I noticed the inconsistencies. The eccentricities.'

'You never loved him then?' asked Julian.

'On the contrary. I loved him too much. Until it broke me. And he broke us.'

❧ Chapter 64 ❧

Father and son sat on the veranda until the sun grew drowsy and threaded its way through scattered cloud. Julian gazed out at the land, etching every tree and shrub and dilapidated building in his mind, trying to capture the angle of the fading light. There were a hundred details requiring attention. The station ledgers and paddock books were to be sorted from yellowing correspondence – the personal to be retained, the rest to be returned to the shelves for the new owner. Trunks of clothes required packing. Furniture selected and discarded. Implements and tools organised. The list grew in length as he scratched at it with a stubby pencil. He would leave it in the kitchen for Ethan to attend to.

'And the chandelier in the main bedroom. I want it.' His father's words ran together like batter. 'We must keep that. It's important for a man to have the familiar about when the time comes.' Ben's rheumy wrists clicked as he toyed with the silver lion. Odiene had insisted he eat scrambled eggs and sip sage tea after the recent drama, and Rachael had spent the afternoon administering spoonfuls of brandy to her husband on the half hour. The food and devotion appeared to have been restorative, although Odiene warned that Ben's muddle-headedness may not improve.

Julian sat the paper aside. 'I saw something this morning. Out near the dry soaks beyond the palm grove. A line of men. But it wasn't Fraser. He arrived later.'

'Fraser. The man's a cunning Scot. If they'd bred more like him they may well have beaten the British at Culloden. It's a sobering thought. The Scots could have gone on to discover Australia. The lot of us condemned to haggis and kilts for eternity. Although a kilt is quite striking. Shows off a man's legs.'

Not once had his father discussed the invasion of their home or Wesley's shooting. It was as if the events had never occurred.

'Father, what I saw this morning, who was it do you think?'

Ben ran a shirt cuff across the lion's mane, polishing it. 'I can't say for certain, son. Maybe we've all been caught up in Meg's delusions. Or perhaps they're not delusions at all.'

'Do *you* think they're delusions?'

'One man's madness is another's brilliance, and your sister is no ordinary girl.' He grabbed Julian's arm. 'This family is as imperilled as ever. Never mind drought, flood or fire. The land will be worthless if Frank keeps on digging holes. What man in his right mind would purchase such a place? Pitted as it is by that mad Englishman seeking treasure long since spent. I told him in so many words. "Frank, there is no buried money." My father spent it all. Spent it after the Great Flood, and the drought and when the resumptions were made law and they seized our southern land. They don't realise. None of them do. Five acres here is lucky to equal half a one in England. Ha. Rubbish.'

'But we have sold the property, Father. You sold it. And you're leaving for Bourke when Meg's well enough.'

Ben peered at Julian as if he didn't know him. His eyes were wide and vacant, ringed by a white film. How old was his father? Not yet fifty. And yet he stumbled and stuttered like an old, old man.

'Another fall from her horse and she'll be a true Dalhunty,' stated Ben. 'Rattled in the brain she is, but still worthy of inclusion in the

Dalhunty Yearbook of . . . of . . . well, you see to that, son. Meg was always the best and the worst of us. Riles her poor mother no end.'

'Ethan will be going with you to Bourke.' Julian did his best not to become side-tracked by Ben's windy reflections.

'Ah yes. The Natural. Hated him at first, didn't you? Arriving unannounced. Damn fine horseman, though. Bourke. I don't mind Bourke. Mrs Plainer makes jelly cakes and jam rolls. Finest jam rolls this side of . . . this side of . . .'

'Dad, you're rambling,' said Julian softly.

'Miss Carlisle. An old bird makes fine broth, but it's the young chook that makes the cock crow, eh, son?' He reached over and tapped Julian's leg. 'Fetch me my straw boater and cricketing whites.'

'Why do you want those? It will be dark soon,' said Julian.

'You'll need them for where you're going. Society loves a young man who plays cricket. Stay clear of the storms, son, when you get there. A man and his dog and near two hundred sheep were struck dead there by lightning near on thirty years ago.' He looked about making sure they were alone. 'Nab some flour and salted meat. Oh, and Voltaire. Don't forget Voltaire. A man's education never ends.'

'How did you know where I was going? Did you overhear us in the drawing room?'

'My father whispered to me,' he said with a seriousness that left no room for comment. 'It's a good idea, son. A very good idea. When you get home, when you've found an opal and made your fortune, we'll muster the sheep.'

⋘ Chapter 65 ⋙

Julian left in the middle of the night on Legless and was across the river and winding through the scrub, covering ten miles or more, before the sun mustered the strength to join him. He would have liked to have sat his family down, explained the temptations and frustrations of a man's life and given them direction on what to do in his absence, but it was no good angling towards a better kind of leaving. He settled for a goodbye reserved for those on the run. A few precious minutes at the kitchen table sharing bread and meat, an excuse of requiring a word with Frank, and then he was at the front door of the homestead for the last time, letting in the fox who padded quietly to Meg's room. It was only when he turned to close the front door that he saw her.

'You're leaving, aren't you?' Odiene leant against the wall. 'You won't let your father be accused of the crime.'

It wasn't a question. She knew him well. Well enough not to condemn or debate, he trusted. There was opportunity to explain his reasoning, to speak of his desires, however he feared worrying her by revealing his concerns. So he said nothing.

'Where are you going?' she asked.

'Nowhere. There's a lot of packing to do. And Mother will be frantic about what furniture she intends to take with her and what has to be sold.' The hallway opened into the darkness of the breezeway where a light shone from the kitchen. Laura was drying plates and stacking them on a shelf. Ethan was walking back and forth, polishing his shoes. He smiled at that. 'How is my father?'

'Sleeping.' Odiene appeared unsettled, as if the bearer of unwelcome news. 'I was unsure whether I should tell you, however your father's condition is indicative of a violent attack of apoplexy. A rupturing of the blood vessel in the brain. It is quite serious.'

'How could you know that?'

If Odiene had been holding a handkerchief Julian was sure she would be wringing it, such was her nervousness. 'Occasionally my father was asked by our local doctor to provide a corpse for morbid anatomy. You must understand he only did it to progress scientific study in the aid of medical research. The people were always without family, usually homeless, and they were buried afterwards, that was my father's condition. A Christian burial. We were not graverobbers,' she added hastily.

'Go on,' said Julian.

'One of those individuals suffered a similar incident to your father. The slackness on one side of his face, the slight impairment to his leg when walking and the slurred speech are all symptoms. Even without today's upset it is difficult to know if he will improve any further. That is my limited understanding,' she concluded softly.

Julian envisaged the two Carlisles, older and younger, overseeing the transport of a coffin from the funeral parlour in the middle of the night, a hawkish doctor in attendance.

'It is a crime, of course, interfering with a dead body, but it was done for the greater good,' she added earnestly. 'I'm sorry. You must think the worst of my father and I.'

Did he? Odiene must have known there was the chance he would be upset by her involvement, yet she was willing to risk his censure to help. Far from being dismayed, Julian was more than thankful for her openness. At least now he knew the malady affecting his father. And he was in no position to judge another. It seemed they were both capable of wrongdoing.

'Sometimes people make questionable decisions for the right reasons,' he said.

'Yes.' Her relief was obvious. 'You're wearing boots.'

'My own, finally.'

She waited, as if expecting him to share more, but he was content to look at her. To have her close. Was it possible that she cared for him as much as he for her? And if so, would she be truly accepting of his decision, which was the only one he could make? Did a woman see life as a man did, as years of unaccountable flows dictated by a higher power and that most elusive of phenomenon, luck? For that was what he was relying on when it came to their future.

Then it settled between them, their coming together, and it felt fresh and promising, like a rise coming down the Darling.

'Do you love Captain Ashby?'

She was like a finely written letter, all curlicues and flourishes. 'No. I was never in a relationship with him. I acted as his companion and hostess as required. He wanted more from me, however I refused his approaches and said I would leave the steamer if he persisted in his attentions. I do believe loneliness eventually made the Captain agreeable to my terms. In the end he was a dear friend, but now, with hindsight, I'm ashamed of my naivety. If the Captain and I had been involved, I believe he still would have sent me to Mr Wesley. It is a disadvantage I have long thought on, that we can't see into another man's soul.'

'Then why did you say—'

She gave a laugh, as if at his foolishness. 'Because everyone knows the Dalhuntys. Even when you sold your last clip the Captain explained you would still marry well, even without the money.'

'What money?'

'The money your grandfather buried before the Great Flood.'

409

Julian laughed. 'Odiene, that money is long gone. Everything you've heard is either untrue or totally exaggerated.'

'And what of your great-grandfather putting down decking and reciting "The Charge of the Light Brigade" by the river? Or Frank? They say he came wandering in from the desert country. That he was in Stuart's exploration party. That he knows the money is buried and that's why he keeps digging holes. Or the fact your father has a liking for fancy dress and talks to chickens, horses and the Lord, some say. Is every story that's ever been told of the Dalhuntys untrue?' she asked.

'Not everything,' he admitted.

'And then there's your name. It is a very fine name. A name is everything.' She took a step nearer. 'Should I come with you? I *could* come with you. I'm used to riding long distances now.'

'I'm not going anywhere.' It was best to stay silent about his plans, and yet it killed Julian that ensuring his father's safety possibly meant losing Odiene. 'You should go to bed. It's been a day.'

She moved along the hallway towards him. 'I won't forget. Anything.' Odiene hugged her arms about her body.

'Neither will I.' There was time for a kiss, but he chose not to. Julian already had enough to take with him, and a kiss would only heighten feelings already too much of a burden to carry. Instead he walked into the night.

He loved his family and Odiene. And he loved this land. It was enough to recognise good fortune, even if the revelation came too late.

⋘ Epilogue ⋙

Mid-August, 1911

Julian stuck the pickaxe through a leather belt at his waist and looked up at daylight. A halo of blue sky beckoned. The beginnings of the horizontal shaft made the fifteen feet already tunnelled above seem easy in comparison. No amount of effort was going to penetrate the opal dirt that he prayed was close by. Which was why his decision to loan Legless to an old miner travelling to Walgett had been made. Wombat (the miner had provided no other name) mined a lease a mile from Julian's and the old fellow owned a windlass and a store of explosives plentiful enough to blow up Bourke.

The loan of a horse for the chance of a piece of black opal was a fair deal. Except in a place where no one used surnames and lives before the opal field were never shared, the exchange hinged on trust. And the truth of the matter was, Julian didn't trust Wombat one bit. They were neighbours on the fringe of nowhere. A place where hundreds of men dug holes in rough ridges, gradually going blind from the shock of the light as they bucketed up shale and clay and soil from the bowels of the earth.

The problem was Julian needed money. Having none at all for months tended to make a person desperate. And parting with Legless was without doubt a desperate act. Legless was his last link to home. The final tangible tie to a life and a family now lost.

Julian poked the wire into a stick of dynamite at the back of the horizontal shaft and rested it on the pile of explosives, then he shimmied up the rope ladder, and, carefully unrolling more of the wire, trailed it across the ground to the detonator box. He blew on icy fingers and walked back to the bark-and-tin humpy. The fire was burning nicely and he rested against the saddle, which had not been part of the deal. A good saddle cost good money and could be sold if Wombat reneged on the agreement.

He settled down to a pannikin of hot water and counted the remaining sticks of dynamite. Wombat maintained the more explosives, the better the result. The problem was one needed to be careful and not blow up the vertical shaft in the process. If that happened then Julian was quite prepared for the police to finally capture him, if it meant a gulp of tea and a bit of mutton was in the offering.

Once warmed by the hot water, he connected the wire to the detonator box and, counting to three, pushed on the handle. Dirt and rocks blew up and out of the hole, throwing him into the air and clean through the back wall of the poorly constructed humpy.

He woke to the sound of a cooking pan and a ladle falling from a rope. Then the humpy slowly crashed to one side. He lay back on the ground as a man-made cloud floated upwards. Wind wafted about him and he closed his eyes. He didn't need to look at the shaft to know it had collapsed under the force of the explosion.

He thought of Gentleman Charles and his offer of roaming Queensland. In hindsight it was a far better alternative, for them both. He laughed at his stupidity. He was an opportunist, like all his family before him. Like Ashby and Fraser. Land. The river. All of them were driven by money. Survival. The SS *Osterley* was now a lifetime ago. Julian considered sitting on the remaining dynamite and lighting the fuse.

People were running through the trees. He could hear the echo of voices and the footsteps of animals treading on leaf-litter. He was so used to isolation that he had become attuned to any noise that invaded his domain. People. Well, that was expected. Fatalities made for good scavenging, although anything of value he had brought with him had long been pilfered. Trying to steal back what had been stolen and then stealing from those who were yet to steal from you was a pastime of sorts out here.

Julian gathered up the leftover dynamite, his few possessions and the saddle, readying to fight to retain them. Then he walked to the shaft. He'd been right. The hole had collapsed. All that beavering away for nothing.

Julian screwed knuckles into his eyeballs, pushing crusted dirt from his sight and tried to shake away the ringing in his ears. There was something terribly wrong with his eyes, for it seemed a woman's striped parasol was bobbing towards him. It was yellow, white and green, with a deep fringe that brought to mind one of his mother's shawls. He plugged his ears and ferreted out a lump of soil from one.

The parasol was on top of a camel and the camel was led by a sack-coated man wearing a cabbage-tree hat, his spiky grey hair sticking up through the crown.

'Julian, is that you? God damn! Youse can't go anywhere without causing a calamity. Now you're blowing up perfectly good earth.'

Two other riders on horseback emerged from the scrub, as well as the camel. One of them was Meg. The other was Ethan.

Julian opened his mouth and then closed it. He feared he was losing his mind. Or perhaps it was already lost, bucketed up with the rest of the earth he had hoed and shovelled and carted and tipped out, only to repeat the process all over again.

Arms encircled his body. He smelt the freshness of spring and he knew it was Meg. He saw she was taller, with red hair tied in a tail like a horse's. She was wearing a blouse with a frilly collar, and the rest, men's clothes that fitted her properly. It was as if overnight his little sister was fully grown. That right winded him, but not more than Ethan, who was changed but unchanged. He came right up and gave Julian a great bear hug as if they were lost friends, then he kissed Meg on the cheek and she squirreled up her nose prettily, as if she wanted what he'd offered. Julian realised she had. Ethan and Meg were together.

'Why's youse look more messed up than a skinned rabbit.' Meg tousled his hair, plucked at the beard he was long used to, and then touched the opera glasses hanging from her neck.

'It's safe now. You're safe. Alex Flannery gave evidence against Wesley. It turns out they'd been robbing banks down in Victoria and Alex knew where some of the money was hidden. So he told the coppers everything to save his neck and saved yours in the process,' explained Ethan.

'H-how did you find me?'

'You leave a track like a wounded bull. If the coppers were really set on finding youse, they would have. Course we knew where to look. Grandfather told Father.' Meg dabbed water from the bag slung across her shoulder on a bit of cloth and cleaned the residue of the explosion from his face.

'But Grandfather's—'

'Dead?' interrupted Meg. "Course he is but don't tell him that.'

Julian was too short on words and too tired to argue. He waited with his arm about Meg's shoulders as Henrietta plodded towards them, the brightly coloured parasol dipping with movement until the camel halted and spat at Julian.

'Honoured Boy, we are here. We are here. Hooshta, hooshta.' Frank clipped the camel on the flank and, with a total disregard for the emotion of the occasion, she folded her legs with infinite slowness, her thick lips clenched, her bones cracking as if an orchestra warming up in the wings.

The parasol was folded and passed to Frank and then Ben stepped to the ground with the aid of a kerosene tin. The silver-topped cane was retrieved from baggage and, dressed in a white suit and pith helmet, he walked snappily towards Julian, swinging the cane as he went.

'Well, my boy. Ready yourself,' he slurred.

'Father! You're all right?'

'Slightly unbalanced, but there's nothing new there.' He clapped Julian on the shoulder. 'Can't say I agree with this opal ferreting expedition of yours. There are easier ways for a man to make a pound, son. Why did you clear out? Another argument with your mother, I suppose.'

Julian stood taller, feeling the firmness of Meg by his side. The months of loneliness and deprivation had eased so quickly that even his father's confusion was welcome. Meg was talking to Ben, willing their father to shush so that she could briefly explain all that had occurred in Julian's absence. Much to everyone's initial disbelief, Laura was walking out with Ian Fraser, while not so surprising was Rachael's constant complaining. Their mother's discontent ranged from the noise of the gutter children in the house next door through to the haughtiness of Mr Webster's wife, the storekeeper's spouse being prone to condescension.

Meg took Julian by the hand and squeezed. 'Odiene's moping about like a woebegone dog in Bourke. W-a-i-t-i-n-g for youse,' she howled with delight.

'She waited?' Julian sought confirmation, wary of believing the unbelievable. Odiene Carlisle. Waiting. For him.

'Aha. Must be love,' said Meg.

'What we all wouldn't do for love,' announced their father.

Frank surveyed Julian's camp, tutting as he poked the few belongings with the short crop he used on Henrietta. 'My dear boy. You have dynamite. Splendid. We'll take some back to Bourke, visit Mr Fraser and—'

'No!' every one of them replied.

Frank was affronted and went straight to Henrietta. 'I have not forgotten about the roof for the cottage. Or the dates. You still owe me.'

'Come on, get your gear, son. We're off,' declared Ben with a flourish of the pith helmet.

Julian ran back to the wrecked humpy, kicked about in the ruins and gathered up a blanket, the saddle and a waterbag. 'Where are we going? Bourke?'

'Bourke? Bourke? No, my boy.' His father lifted the pith helmet and waved it about. 'It's east we are headed. East to fine pastures and flowing waters and fat stock. East to the Promised Land.'

Julian could not believe it. After all the years of hearing about the place he would finally see it.

'God damn. No. Wese not going there,' said Meg firmly.

'We're not?' replied both Julian and his father simultaneously. Julian hefted the saddle from one side to the other.

His father lowered the pith helmet. 'That about covers the Promised Land,' he said sadly.

'No. We ain't going east. Wese got a half share in the *Lady Matilda* with Mr Fraser. Mr Cummins is staying on as engineer, Ethan and I will be deckhands, Mother the cook, Odiene the decoration and Rick will be around as long as it takes him to train you up as the new snag-dodger. It's all been decided. We even get to buy our own goat.'

Frank straightened his crown-less hat and cleared his throat.

'And Frank will be chief purveyor of all items vital to the ongoing welfare of the vessel and crew,' continued Meg, 'including the goat, camel, fox, chickens and whatever else that entails. We still have to work out the finer details.'

'And Henrietta will make camp on the barge. My girl does not like water, but she's willing to make an exception considering the circumstances.' Frank led the wandering camel back to where the kerosene tin waited.

'But the steamer days are coming to an end on the Darling,' argued Julian.

'Which is why, my boy, we are going south to become riverboat gamblers on the mighty Murray,' announced his father.

Julian glanced skywards. 'Lord save us.'

'Amen,' said his father, tapping the pith helmet with the cane.

✺ Author's note ✺

Generally, the Murray-Darling navigation season ran from June to February, depending on river heights, although the Darling season was shorter and less dependable, due to unreliable rainfall. Some three hundred paddle-steamers plied the Murray-Darling River during the main era of river trade, 1864–1914, offering a transport service for delicate and bulky cargo that greatly improved living standards and reduced isolation in remote areas. This invaluable service soon attracted the attention of the New South Wales government, with the river transport of wool from New South Wales to South Australian markets quickly becoming a matter of concern. Ensuring the proceeds from NSW-produced wool remained in the state became a primary objective. With that in mind, a railway from Sydney to Bourke was soon under construction and opened in 1885 with subsidised rail-freight offered to entice wool-producers from the river. Similarly, plans to construct more weirs and locks to maintain river levels and trade on the Darling came to nothing. These reasons among others, coupled with the 1895–1902 drought and the Great War led to the gradual end of the river trade.

The inspirational seed for *The Last Station* stemmed from a chapter in my family's history. In the early 1900s my paternal great-grandmother Sara-Ann Alexander arrived home to our property in north-west New South Wales from her yearly summer sojourn in the Blue Mountains. Accompanying her was a young man, Billy da Silva, whom she had met at Anthony Hordern's department store in Sydney. Sara-Ann took it upon herself, with no prior family consultation, to offer Billy a home and employment. Unlike the fictional Ethan Harris and his fractured upbringing, Billy was of pioneering stock and came from a loving family. He was greeted warmly by the widowed Sara-Ann's sons and when the Great War broke out and my paternal grandfather enlisted, Billy was indispensable in helping to ensure the smooth running of the property during his absence. Billy was a natural at everything, from horse-riding to blade-shearing sheep. The death adder he caught by the tail was kept preserved in methylated spirits in a large glass jar in the station laundry for more than eighty years. Billy was an integral part of the family and business, and it was Billy's life with my ancestors that helped conjure Ethan Harris, although for narrative purposes I decided Ethan would not be so happily accepted into the Dalhunty clan.

There are numerous accounts of the 1890 Great Flood and those erstwhile folks who clung to rooftops and in trees awaiting rescue. An 1890 report counted the losses from the flood on the Barwon and Darling Rivers at 467,550 sheep and nearly 900 horses and cattle. Similarly, the slow demise of pastoral holdings following the land resumptions of the 1880s, and subsequent periods of drought, are well documented. The fictitious Gentleman Charles Wesley is a composite of several bushrangers – rich fodder for a novelist. Wesley's father, the opera-glass aficionado, is drawn from a gentleman's servant transported to Australia in 1840 for relieving another of a pair of opera glasses in London's Drury Lane.

The Jefferson family's home, a grounded steamer, was based on the remains of the P.S. *Wave*. Stranded on land near the NSW town of Bourke following the 1921 flood while traversing flooded paddocks, it became home for the owner and was known locally as 'Noah's Ark'.

Phil Sullivan provided insight and guidance regarding the portrayal of First Nations people in this narrative and I especially thank him for our many conversations and advice. Thank you also to Paula Murry RN for her assistance with the depiction of medical conditions, specifically the stroke suffered by Ben Dalhunty and the condition of ptosis (droopy eyelid) suffered by Charles Wesley. Any errors regarding same are mine.

My usual state library research and field trips were curtailed by the pandemic, then, when travel was possible, floods. I spent many days online trawling through historical articles and academic papers and ordering books on various subjects, the most important of which are included in the below reading list. In the absence of travel I called on my online community for assistance in understanding the landscape of the region where the story is set and received a wonderful response. By the time a travel window opened I already had a solid vision of *The Last Station*'s landscapes and I thank everyone with heartfelt appreciation for the many images sent to me, particularly my cousin Simon Fryer (who also assisted with explosives advice) and Bronwyn Parry. Eventually I spent time in and around the environs of Bourke and Brewarrina, walking in Gundabooka National Park, along the mighty Darling River and visiting the landscapes that my characters traverse in the novel.

Thank you to the Bourke Public Library for filling in my knowledge gaps along with cups of tea, the Back O' Bourke Visitor Information and Exhibition Centre, Brewarrina Visitor Information Centre and those locals who were happy to chat about river life and the area's history.

Producing a novel is very much a team effort, and I have the very good fortune of working with an extraordinary team at Penguin Random House, from publishing through to the publicity, sales and marketing departments. As always, I am indebted to my perceptive publisher Beverly Cousins, who endured the first reading of *The Last Station* on submission and ensured this author's intent matched the outcome. Genevieve Buzo's attention to detail is both thoughtful and insightful and I am forever grateful for her editorial genius. I thank them both for their professionalism in wrangling this story through to the finished product. To Tara Wynne, agent and friend, thank you for your ongoing support. Book eleven. Who would have thought!

Thank you to my friends and family, particularly my mother Marita, whose unending wisdom and love lifts me up when the muse fails, enthusiasm falters and exhaustion conquers. To old and new readers alike and the libraries and bookstores that support my writerly endeavours – thank you, thank you.

During my research for *The Last Station* I found the following works invaluable: *The Two Worlds of Jimmie Barker: The life of an Australian Aboriginal 1900–1972* by Jimmie Barker, as told to Janet Mathews; *The Squatters: An illustrated history of Australia's pastoral pioneers* by Geoffrey Dutton; *River Boat Days on the Murray, Darling, Murrumbidgee* by Peter Phillips; Darling River NSW Maritime Archaeological Survey 2002–3, NSW Heritage Office; *Comfort and Judgement: Nineteenth century advice manuals and the scripting of Australian identity* by Gene Bawden; *The Australian Home: A handbook of domestic economy* (1891) by Mrs H. P. Wicken; *Taxidermy and Zoological Collecting: A complete handbook for the amateur taxidermist, collector, osteologist, museum-builder, sportsman and traveller* (2012 edition, first published 1891) by W. T. Hornaday and W. J. Holland; *Riverboats* by Ian Mudie; *Brewarrina Bric-a-brac: The Brewarrina and district historical society*, compiled by Elaine Thompson; *Flood Country: An environmental history of the Murray-Darling Basin* by G. O'Gorman; *The Darling*, Murray Darling Basin Commission; *The River Trade: Wool and steamers* by Gwenda Painter; *The Relocation of the Market for Australian Wool, 1880–1939* by Simon Ville, Working Paper, Series 2002, Department of Economics, University of Wollongong; *Back of Bourke: A study of the appraisal and settlement of the semi-arid plains of eastern Australia (Volume II)* by R. L. Heathcote.

≪ Reading Group Questions ≫

1. *The Last Station* is a captivating tale of heritage, heartbreak and hope. Which of these themes resonated the strongest with you?
2. The Dalhunty children are born into poverty and must live in the twin shadows of a glorious past and their parents' fractured relationship. How great a part does this environment play in forming the personalities of Julian, Laura and Meg?
3. Ethan's arrival further splinters the Dalhunty family. Why do you think Julian and Meg, in particular, are initially unwilling to accept him into the family? And how does Ethan ultimately manage to earn their respect?
4. Julian Dalhunty is a sensitive, frustrated young man. How strong a part does loyalty play in Julian's decision-making throughout the novel?
5. Meg is funny, fearless and resilient. She represents the best and, in some respects, the worst of the Dalhuntys. Discuss.
6. Rachael is a complicated character. Discuss her attitude to her family and husband, and the reasons for her behaviour.
7. Each of the characters in *The Last Station* has their eccentricities, particularly Ben and Frank. How important is the use of humour in the novel?

8. The Australian landscape is integral to *The Last Station*. How well has the author managed to convey a sense of place in the novel?

9. *The Last Station* offers a glimpse of an old century and a new one. Progress and government intervention, floods and droughts, and the ramifications of the Robertson Land Acts gradually culminate in the end of a romantic age in Australia's pastoral history – the demise of the river-boat trade and the breaking up of huge pastoral runs. Do you feel that the historical threads running through the narrative were handled deftly?

Discover a
new favourite

Visit **penguin.com.au/readmore**